About

Abby Green spent her teens reading Mills & Boon romances. She then spent many years working in the Film and TV industry as an assistant director. One day while standing outside an actor's trailer in the rain, she thought: *there has to be more than this*. So she sent off a partial to Mills & Boon. After many rewrites, they accepted her first book and an author was born. She lives in Dublin, Ireland, and you can find out more here: abby-green.com

The Tycoon's Affair

July 2025
Tempted by Desire

August 2025
Craving his Love

September 2025
Business with Pleasure

January 2026
Stealing his Heart

February 2026
Playing with Power

March 2026
After Hours Passion

The Tycoon's Affair:
Tempted by Desire

ABBY GREEN

MILLS & BOON

All rights reserved including the right of reproduction in whole or in part in any form. This edition is published by arrangement with Harlequin Enterprises ULC.

This is a work of fiction. Names, characters, places, locations and incidents are purely fictional and bear no relationship to any real life individuals, living or dead, or to any actual places, business establishments, locations, events or incidents. Any resemblance is entirely coincidental.

Without limiting the author's and publisher's exclusive rights, any unauthorised use of this publication to train generative artificial intelligence (AI) technologies is expressly prohibited. HarperCollins also exercise their rights under Article 4(3) of the Digital Single Market Directive 2019/790 and expressly reserve this publication from the text and data mining exception.

® and ™ are trademarks owned and used by the trademark owner and/or its licensee. Trademarks marked with ® are registered with the United Kingdom Patent Office and/or the Office for Harmonisation in the Internal Market and in other countries.

First Published in Great Britain 2025
by Mills & Boon, an imprint of HarperCollins*Publishers* Ltd
1 London Bridge Street, London, SE1 9GF

www.harpercollins.co.uk

HarperCollins*Publishers*
Macken House, 39/40 Mayor Street Upper,
Dublin 1, D01 C9W8, Ireland

The Tycoon's Affair: Tempted by Desire © 2025 Harlequin Enterprises ULC.

When Christakos Meets His Match © 2014 Abby Green
Fonseca's Fury © 2015 Abby Green
Awakened by Her Desert Captor © 2016 Abby Green

ISBN: 978-0-263-41747-0

This book contains FSC™ certified paper and other controlled sources to ensure responsible forest management.

For more information visit: www.harpercollins.co.uk/green

Printed and Bound in the UK using 100% Renewable Electricity
at CPI Group (UK) Ltd, Croydon, CR0 4YY

WHEN CHRISTAKOS MEETS HIS MATCH

I'd like to dedicate this book to all the fabulous
Mills & Boon readers and fans who make
my job so much easier, especially on the days
when the task can seem impossible!

PROLOGUE

ALEXIO CHRISTAKOS HAD always known his mother had had affairs all through her marriage to his father. He just hadn't expected to see such a public display of it at her funeral. Her coffin was strewn with lone flowers and there were displays of wet eyes from a handful of men he'd never met before in his life.

His father had stomped away with a glower on his face a short while before. He couldn't exactly claim the moral high ground as he too had had numerous affairs.

It had been a constant war of attrition between them. His father always seeking to make his mother as jealous as he felt. And she…? Alexio had the feeling that nothing would have ever made her truly happy, even though she had lived her life in the lap of luxury, surrounded by people to cater to her every whim.

She'd had a sadness, a deep melancholy about her, and they'd never been emotionally close. A vivid memory assailed him at that moment—a memory he hadn't allowed to surface for a long time. He'd been about nine, and his throat had ached with the effort it had taken not to cry. He'd just witnessed his parents having a bitter row.

His mother had caught him standing behind the door and he'd blurted out, 'Why do you hate each other so much? Why can't you be in love like you're supposed to be?'

She'd looked at him coldly and the lack of emotion in

her eyes had made him shiver. She'd bent down to his level and taken his chin in her hand. 'Love's a fairytale, Alexio, and it doesn't exist. Remember this: I married your father because he could give me what I needed. *That's* what is important. Success. Security. Power. Don't ever concern yourself with emotions. They make you weak. Especially love.'

Alexio would never forget the excoriating feeling of exposure and shame in that moment...

He felt a hand on his shoulder then and looked to his older half-brother, Rafaele, who stood beside him and smiled tightly. They'd always shared the same conflicted relationship with their mother. Rafaele's Italian father had gone to pieces after their mother had walked out on him when he had lost his entire fortune—an unpalatable reminder of their mother's ruthless nature so soon after that disturbing childhood memory of his own.

For years Alexio and his brother had communicated with habitual boyish rough-housing and rivalry, but since Rafaele had left home to make his way when Alexio had been about fourteen their relationship had become less fractious. Even if Alexio had never quite been able to let go of his envy that Rafaele hadn't had to endure the almost suffocating attention he'd received from his father. The heavy weight of expectation. The disappointment when Alexio had been determined to prove himself and not accept his inheritance.

They turned to walk away from the grave, engrossed in their own thoughts. They were of a similar build and height, both a few inches over six feet, drop-dead gorgeous, dark-haired. Alexio's hair was darker, cut close to his skull. Their mother had bequeathed to them both her distinctive green eyes, but Alexio's were lighter—more golden.

When they came to a stop near the cars Alexio decided to rib his brother gently, seeking to assuage the suddenly bleak feeling inside him. He observed his brother's stubbled jaw. 'You couldn't even clean up for the funeral?'

'I got out of bed too late,' Rafaele drawled with a glint in his eye.

Alexio smiled wryly. 'Unbelievable. You've only been in Athens for two days—no wonder you wanted to stay at a hotel and not at my apartment…'

Rafaele was about to respond when Alexio saw his face close up and his eyes narrow on something or someone behind him. He turned to look too and saw a tall, stern-faced stranger staring at them from a few feet away. Something struck him in the gut: recognition. Crazy. But the man's eyes were a distinctive green…and that gut feeling intensified.

The stranger flicked a glance at the grave behind them and then his lip curled. 'Are there any more of us?'

Alexio bristled at his belligerent tone and frowned, '*Us*? What are you talking about?'

The man just looked at Rafaele. 'You don't remember, do you?'

Alexio saw Rafaele go pale. Hoarsely he asked, 'Who are you?'

The man smiled, but it was cold, 'I'm your older brother—*half-brother*. My name is Cesar da Silva. I came today to pay my respects to the woman who gave me life… not that she deserved it.'

He was still talking but a roaring was sounding in Alexio's ears. *Older half-brother? Cesar da Silva*. He'd heard of the man. Who hadn't? He was the owner of a vast global conglomerate encompassing real estate, finance—myriad businesses. Famously private and reclusive.

Something rose up inside Alexio and he issued an abrupt, 'What the *hell*?'

The man looked at him coldly and Alexio could now see the fraternal similarities that had led to that prickle of awareness. Even though da Silva was dark blond in colouring, they could be non-identical triplets.

Da Silva was saying coldly, 'Three brothers by three fathers…and yet she didn't abandon either of *you* to the wolves.'

He stepped forward and Alexio immediately stepped up too, feeling rage building inside him in the face of this shocking revelation. His half-brother topped him only by an inch at most. They stood chest to chest.

Cesar gritted out, 'I didn't come here to fight you, brother. I have no issue with either of you.'

A fierce well of protectiveness that Alexio had felt once before for his mother, before she'd rejected it, rose up within him. 'Only with our dead mother—*if* what you say is true.'

Cesar smiled, but it was bleak, and it threw Alexio off slightly, making the rage diminish.

'Oh, it's true—more's the pity.'

He stepped around him then and Alexio and Rafaele turned to watch him walk to the open grave, where he stood for a few long moments before taking something from his pocket and throwing it into the black space, where it landed with a dull thud.

Eventually he turned and came back. After a long, silent but charged moment, during which he looked at both brothers, he turned and walked swiftly to a waiting car. He got into the back. It drove off smoothly.

Rafaele turned towards Alexio and looked at him. Gobsmacked. Shock reverberated through his body. Adrenalin made him feel keyed up.

'What the…?'

Rafaele just shook his head. 'I don't know…'

Alexio looked back at the empty space where the car had been and something cold settled into his belly. He felt exposed, remembering that time when he'd thought his mother would allow him to protect her. She hadn't. Ever elusive, she was now managing to reach out from beyond the grave and demonstrate with dramatic timing just how a woman couldn't be trusted to tell the truth and reveal her secrets. She would always hold something back. Something that might have the power to shatter your world.

CHAPTER ONE

Five months later...

'*Cara*...do you have to leave so soon?'

The voice oozed sultry sex appeal. Alexio stalled for a second in the act of buttoning up his shirt—not because he was tempted to stay but because, if anything, he felt even more eager to leave.

He schooled his features and turned to face the woman in the bed. She was all honeyed limbs and artfully tumbled glossy brown hair. Huge dark eyes, a pouting mouth and the absence of a sheet were doing little to help Alexio forget why he'd chosen to take her to his hotel suite in Milan after his brother Rafaele's wedding reception last night.

She was stunning. Perfect.

Even so, he felt no resurgence of desire. And Alexio didn't like to acknowledge the fact that the sex had been wholly underwhelming. On the surface it had been fine; but on some deeper level it had left him cold. He switched on the charm he was famed for, though, and smiled.

'Sorry, *bellissima*, I have to fly to Paris this morning for work.'

The woman, whose name he all of a sudden wasn't entirely sure of—Carmela?—leant back and stretched seductively, displaying her perfectly cosmetically enhanced naked breasts to their best advantage, and pouted even more. 'You have to leave *right now*?'

Alexio kept his smile in place and when he'd finished dressing bent down and pressed a light kiss to her mouth, escaping before she could twine her arms around his neck. Claustrophobia was rising within him.

'We had fun, *cara*…I'll call you.'

Now the seductive pout was gone, and the woman's real nature shone through as her eyes turned hard. She knew when she was being blown off and clearly did not like it when the man in question was as sought-after as Alexio Christakos.

She stood up from the bed naked and flounced off to the bathroom, issuing a stream of Italian petulance. Alexio winced slightly but let out a sigh of relief as soon as she'd disappeared behind a slamming door.

He shook his head as he made his way out of the suite and towards the lobby of the plush hotel in the private lift reserved for VIP guests. *Women*. He loved them, but he loved them at a distance. In his bed when it suited him and then out of it for as long as he cared to indulge them—which invariably wasn't for long.

After years of witnessing his mother's cold behaviour towards his father, who had remained in slavish thrall to her beauty and eternal elusiveness, Alexio had developed a very keen sense of self-protection around women. He could handle cold and aloof because he was used to that, and he preferred it.

His father, thwarted by his emotionally unavailable wife, had turned to his son, making him the centre of his world. It had been too much. From an early age Alexio had chafed against the claustrophobia of his father's over-attention. And now when anyone—especially a woman—became even remotely over-emotional, or expected too much, he shut down inside.

Brief encounters were his forté. Witnessing his half-brother's wedding the day before had inevitably brought up questions of his own destiny, but Alexio, at the age of thirty, felt no compelling need to settle down yet.

He did envisage a wife and family at some stage...far in the future. When the time came his wife would be perfect. Beautiful, accommodating. Undemanding of Alexio's emotions. Above all, Alexio would not fall into the same trap as his father: tortured for life because he'd coveted a woman who didn't covet him. He'd been disabused at an early age of the notion that love might be involved.

He thought of his older brother turning up at his mother's funeral and all the accompanying unwelcome emotions he'd felt that day: shock, anger, hurt, betrayal.

Used to blocking out emotions, Alexio had relegated the incident to the back of his mind. He hadn't sought Cesar da Silva out, hadn't mentioned it again to Rafaele—even though he knew Rafaele had invited their half-brother to his wedding. Predictably enough, after that first and last terse meeting, he hadn't turned up.

Emotions were messy, unpredictable. They tripped you up. Look at Rafaele! His life had just been turned upside down by a woman who had kept his son from him for four years. And yet two months after meeting her again he was getting married, looking foolishly in love and blithely forgetting the lessons his own father had taught him about the fickle nature of women.

As far as Alexio was concerned—even if Rafaele appeared to be happily embarking on wedded bliss, and no matter how cute his three-and-a-half-year-old nephew was—his brother had been played for a fool by his new wife. Why *wouldn't* she now want to marry Rafaele Falcone, *wunderkind* of the worldwide automobile industry, with an estimated wealth running into the billions? Especially if she had a son to support?

No, Alexio was steering well clear of similar scenarios and he would never allow himself to be caught as his brother had been. He would never forgive a woman who kept a child from him. Still, a sliver of unease went down his spine. His brother, whom he'd considered to share a similar philosophy, had managed to get caught...

Alexio's mouth firmed and he pushed such rogue notions down deep. He put on a pair of shades as his driver brought the car around to the front entrance and was oblivious to the double-take stares of a group of women as they walked into the hotel.

As soon as the car pulled away Alexio was already focusing on the next thing on his agenda, the introspection his brother's wedding had precipitated along with his recent unsatisfactory bed partner already relegated to the back of his mind.

Sidonie Fitzgerald buckled her seatbelt on the plane and took a deep breath. But she was unable to shift the ball of tension sitting in her belly. For once her habitual fear of flying was being eclipsed by something else, and Sidonie couldn't even really enjoy that fact.

All she could see in her mind's eye was her beloved Tante Josephine's round, eternally childish and worried face and hear her quavering voice: *'Sidonie, what does it mean? Will they take my home from me? All these bills... where did they come from?'*

Sidonie's aunt was fifty-four and had spent a lifetime locked in a world of innocence. She'd been deprived of oxygen as a baby and as a result had been mildly brain-damaged. She'd always functioned at a slightly lesser and slower level than everyone around her, but had managed to get through school and find a job. She still worked in the grocer's shop around the corner from where she'd lived for years, giving her precious independence.

Sidonie pursed her lips. She had loved her self-absorbed and endlessly vain mother, who had passed away only a couple of months before, but how could her mother have done this to her sweet and innocent younger sister?

The never forgotten sting of shame reminded Sidonie all too uncomfortably of *exactly* how her mother could have done such a thing—as if she could ever really forget. Ruthlessly she quashed it.

When Sidonie's father had died a few years before, their comfortable lives had crashed around their ears, leaving them with nothing. Sidonie had been forced to leave her university degree before the start of her final year in order to find work and save money to go back.

Moving to Paris to live with Tante Josephine had been her mother Cecile's only option to avoid becoming homeless or—even worse—having to find *work*. Cecile had not been happy. She'd been used to a life of comfort, relative luxury and security, courtesy of her hard-working husband who had wanted nothing more than to make his wife happy.

It would appear now, though, as if Sidonie's mother's selfish ways had risen to the fore again. She'd encouraged her sister to take out a mortgage on the apartment that had been bought and paid for by her husband because he'd cared for his vulnerable sister-in-law's welfare. Cecile had used this fact as leverage to persuade Tante Josephine to agree to the remortgage. She'd then used that money, and credit cards in both their names, to spend a small fortune. Tante Josephine now found herself liable for the astronomical bills as the remaining living account-holder.

Sidonie had to figure out the best way forward to help her aunt—she had no intention of leaving her to fend for herself. The start of the process had been taking on the burden of the debts into her own name. She hadn't thought twice about doing it—ever since her childhood innocence had been ripped away Sidonie had developed a well-ingrained instinct to cover up for her mother—even now, when she was gone.

Sidonie was facing the prospect of moving to Paris to help her aunt get out of this crisis. She staved off the sense of panic. She was young and healthy. Surely she could get work? Even if it was menial?

In a sick way events had conspired to help her—she'd lost her waitressing job in Dublin just before she'd left for Paris to meet with a solicitor to discuss her aunt's situation. Her restaurant boss had explained miserably that they had gone into liquidation, like so many others. Sidonie was going back to Dublin now—just to tie up loose ends and collect the deposit owed to her on her flat when she moved out.

Her hands clenched into fists at the thought of how her mother had only ever thought about herself, oblivious to the repercussions of her—

'Here is your seat, sir.'

'Thank you.'

Sidonie's thoughts scattered as she heard the exchange above her head, and she looked up and saw a man. She blinked. And blinked again. He was very tall and broad. Slim hips at her eye level. He was taking off an overcoat and folding it up to place it in the overheard locker, revealing a lean, muscular build under a fine silk shirt and jacket. Sidonie was vaguely aware of the way the air hostess was hovering attentively.

The man said in English, with a seductive foreign accent, 'I've got it, thank you.'

The air hostess looked comically deflated and turned away. The man was now taking off his suit jacket, and Sidonie realised she was staring—no better than the gaping air hostess. Quickly she averted her head and looked out of the window, seeing nothing of the pewter-grey Parisian spring skies and the fluorescent-jacket-clad ground staff preparing the plane for take-off.

His image was burned onto her brain. It didn't help when she felt him take the seat beside her and all the air around them seemed to disappear. And it *really* didn't help when his scent teased her nostrils; musky and masculine.

He was quite simply the most gorgeous man she'd ever seen in her life. Dark olive complexion, high cheekbones, strong jaw. Short dark brown hair. Firmly sculpted masculine mouth. He should have been pretty. But Sidonie's impression was not of *pretty*. It was of hard and uncompromising sexuality. *Heat*. The last kind of person she'd have expected to sit in an economy seat beside her.

And then he spoke. 'Excuse me.'

His voice was so deep that she felt it reverberate in the pit of her belly. She swallowed and told herself she was being ridiculous—he couldn't possibly be *that* gorgeous. She turned her head and her heart stopped. His face was inches away. He *was*...that gorgeous. And more. He looked vaguely familiar and she wondered if he was a famous male model. Or a French movie star?

Something funny was happening to Sidonie's brain and body. They didn't seem to be connected any more. She felt a hysterical giggle rise up and had to stifle it. She didn't giggle. What was wrong with her?

One dark brow moved upwards over the most startling pair of green eyes she'd ever seen. Gold and green. Like a lion. She had green eyes too, but they were more blue than green.

'I think you're sitting on my seatbelt?'

It took a few seconds for the words to compute, and when they did Sidonie jumped up as if scalded, hands flapping. 'I'm so sorry... Excuse me... Just let me... It must be here somewhere...'

Sounding irritated, the man said, 'Stay still and I'll get it.'

Sidonie closed her eyes in mortification, her hands gripping the seat-back in front of her, and she hovered, contorted in the small space, as the man coolly retrieved his seatbelt and buckled it.

Sidonie sat down again and attended to her own belt. Feeling breathless, and avoiding looking at him again, she said, 'I'm sorry. I—'

He cut her off. 'It's fine, don't worry about it.'

A flare of something hot lanced Sidonie's belly. Did he *have* to sound so curt? And why was she suddenly so aware of the fact that her hair was scraped up into a messy bun, that she had no make-up on, that she was wearing jeans that were so worn there was a frayed hole at her knee and an equally worn university sweatshirt. And her glasses. If Central Casting had been looking for 'messy grunge student type' she would have been hired on the spot.

She was disgusted at herself for letting a man—albeit a man as gorgeous as this one—make her feel so self-conscious. She forced herself to take a deep breath and looked resolutely forward. Out of the corner of her eye, though, she was aware of big, strong-looking hands opening up a tablet computer. Her belly clenched.

The seconds stretched to minutes and she heard him sigh volubly when the plane still wasn't moving. His arm nearest to her reached up to push something, and she realised it must have been the call button when the stewardess arrived with indecent haste.

'Yes, sir?'

Sidonie heard the irritation in his voice. 'Is there a reason why we're not moving yet?'

She looked over and saw only his strong profile and jaw, and even though she couldn't see it she could imagine the kind of expression he'd be using: imperious. She glanced at the woman and felt sorry for her because she looked so embarrassed.

'I'm not sure, sir. I'll check right away.' She rushed off again.

Sidonie let out a faint snort of derision. Even the stewardess was treating him as if he was some sort of overlord.

He looked at her then. 'I'm sorry... Did you say something?'

Sidonie tried not to be affected by his overwhelming presence. She shrugged minutely. 'I'm sure we're just waiting in line to take our slot on the runway.'

He turned to face her more fully and Sidonie cursed herself. The last thing she needed was his undivided attention on her.

'Oh, really? And what if I have an important meeting to attend in London?'

Something hot flashed into Sidonie's veins and she told herself it was anger at his insufferable arrogance. She crossed her arms in an unconsciously defensive move and said in a low voice, 'Well, in case it's escaped your attention, there are approximately two hundred people on this plane. I'm sure more than one other person has a meeting to make, and I don't see them complaining.'

His eyes flashed and momentarily stopped her breath. They were so unusual and stark against his dark skin. He was like a specimen from some exotic planet.

'There's two hundred and ten, actually, and I don't doubt that there are many others who have important appointments lined up—which makes my question even more relevant.'

Sidonie barely registered the fact that he knew exactly how many were on board and bristled at the way his eyes had done that quick sweep up and down her body, clearly deducing that she *wasn't* on her way to an important meeting.

'For your information,' she said frigidly, 'I have a connecting flight to Dublin from London and I'll be very inconvenienced if we're late. But that's just life, isn't it?'

He leant back a little and looked at her. 'I wondered where your accent was from. It's intriguing.'

Sidonie wasn't sure if that was a compliment or not, so she clamped her mouth shut. Just then someone dressed in uniform with a cap came alongside their seats and coughed slightly to get the man's attention.

Releasing Sidonie from his compelling gaze, the man turned, and the pilot bent down and said discreetly, 'Mr Christakos, sorry about this delay. It's beyond our control, I'm afraid... They've got a backlog of planes waiting to take off. It shouldn't be much longer, but we can get your private jet ready if you'd prefer?'

Sidonie knew her eyes had gone wide as she took in this exchange.

After a few moments the man said, 'No, I'll stay, Pierre. But thank you for thinking of it.'

The captain inclined his head deferentially and left again and Sidonie realised that her mouth was open.ABruptly she shut it and looked out of the window before the man could see. In her line of vision was a similar plane to theirs, standing nearby, with the distinctive Christakos logo emblazoned on the side, along with a quote from a Greek philosopher. All of Alexio Christakos's planes sported quotes.

Alexio Christakos.

Sidonie shook her head minutely, in disbelief. The man next to her—now on his phone, with that deep voice speaking in a language that sounded like Greek—could *not* be the owner of Christakos Freight and Travel. That man was a legend. And he would certainly not be sitting beside her, with his long legs constricted by the confines of economy class seating.

He'd been a case study in their business class at college before she'd had to leave. Astonishingly successful while still disgustingly young, he'd made headlines when he'd cut himself off from his father's inheritance to go his own way, never revealing to anyone his reasons for doing so.

He'd then grafted and worked his way up, starting up an online freight company that had blown all of the competition out of the water, and when he'd sold it after only two years he'd made a fortune. It was that early success that had given him the finances to branch out into air travel, and within the space of five years he'd been competing with and beating the best budget airlines in Europe. He had a reputation for treating customers like people and not like herded cattle, which was a trademark of a lot of Christakos's competition.

He was also one of the most eligible bachelors in Europe, if not the world. Sidonie was not a gossip magazine aficionado, but after they'd studied his entrepreneurial methods in college she'd had to listen to her fellow classmates wax lyrical about the man, drooling over copious pictures of him, for weeks. With a sinking feeling in her chest, she realised why he looked vaguely familiar. Even though she'd not shared in their collective drooling she'd glanced at a couple of pictures, dismissing him as a pretty boy.

Now she knew: pretty he was *not*. He was all male. Virile and potent. She felt like squirming, and she wanted to change seats. She was suddenly acutely uncomfortable and didn't like to analyse why that might be. She wasn't used to someone having such an immediate physical effect on her.

The woman in the seat next to Alexio was starting to fidget. He had to curb the urge to put his hand on her thigh to stop her and curled that hand into a fist. She was clearly a nervy sort from the way she'd reacted when she discovered she was sitting on his seatbelt.

It was intensely irritating to him that he was aware of her at all. That he'd done a minor double-take on hearing her challenge him. He chafed at being in such close confines with another person after years of the luxury of private air travel, but if he wasn't so damned conscientious... *and controlling...* His mouth quirked at the thought of the insult that had been hurled his way more than once.

On the phone, his assistant was informing him of his schedule in London, but Alexio caught sight of a sliver of pale knee peeping out of torn jeans beside him and stifled a snort. Could she be *any* messier? He'd taken in an impression after exchanging those few words—light-coloured hair, a slim body, pale face, glasses. Voluminous sweatshirt that hid any trace of femininity. And a surprisingly husky voice with that intriguing accent.

Alexio did not take notice of women who did not dress like women. He had high standards after being brought up by one of the world's foremost models. His mother had always been impeccably turned out. He frowned. He was thinking of her *again*.

Realising the novel fact that he was not actually taking in a word his assistant was saying, Alexio terminated the conversation abruptly. The woman went still beside him and something tensed inside him. He could be on his way to his private jet right now but he'd refused. Again, not like him. But something had stopped him. Something in his gut.

He glanced over to see that the woman had a capacious grey bag on her lap and was pulling things out of the seat pocket in front of her to put them in haphazardly. Another strike against her. Alexio was a neat freak. She'd pushed her black-framed glasses on her head and his eye was drawn to her hair.

It was actually strawberry blonde. An intriguing colour. It looked to be wavy and unruly if let loose, and he found himself wondering how long it was when it wasn't confined in that high bun, with wisps curling against her neck and face.

Something tightened inside him, down low. Her face, too, was not as unremarkable as he'd first thought. Heart-shaped and pale. He could see a faint smattering of freckles across her small straight nose and it shocked him slightly. It had been so long since he'd been this close to a face without make-up. It felt curiously intimate.

Her hands were small and quick. Deft. Short, practical nails. And just like that Alexio felt a punch of desire bloom in his gut. It was hot and immediate as he imagined how small and pale those hands would look on his body, caressing him, touching him, stroking him. The images were so incendiary that Alexio's breath stopped for a moment.

The girl seemed to have restored her belongings to her bag and now, almost as an afterthought, she took her glasses off her head and put them in too.

She must be aware of his scrutiny—he could see a flood of red stain her cheeks. And that stunned him anew. When was the last time he'd seen a woman blush?

Alexio leant back slightly, noting that her mouth in profile looked full and soft. Kissable.

'Going somewhere?' he asked, slightly perturbed that his voice sounded so rough.

The woman took a breath, making her sweatshirt rise and fall, drawing his eye to the flesh it concealed. He had a sudden hunger to *see* her. And he wondered about her breasts. That desire increased, shocking him slightly with its force. He'd just left a woman in his hotel suite—what was wrong with him?

She looked at him and Alexio's eyes met hers. He sucked in a breath. Without the black-framed glasses they were stunning. Almond-shaped. Aquamarine. Like the sea around the islands in Greece. Sparkling green one second and blue the next. Long dark lashes were a contrast against her pale colouring, and her eyebrows the same strawberry blonde tone as her hair.

She looked resolute, her hands gripping her bag, that soft mouth tight now, eyes avoiding his. 'I'll move seats.'

Alexio frowned. Everything in his body was rejecting the notion with a force he didn't like to acknowledge. 'Why on earth do you want to move?'

This was another novel experience—a woman trying to get away from him!

Alexio settled back further in his seat. The woman opened her mouth again and he saw small, even white teeth. Her two front teeth had a slight gap in the middle. He had the uncanny feeling that he could just sit there and stare at her for hours.

Now she was blushing in earnest.

'Well, you're obviously...you know...' she looked at him now, slightly agonised.

He quirked a brow. 'What am I?'

Her cheeks went an even brighter red and Alexio had to curb the desire to reach out and touch them to see if they felt as hot as they looked.

She huffed now, impatiently. 'Well, you're obviously *you*, and you have things to do, people to talk to. You need space.'

Something cold settled into Alexio's belly and his eyes narrowed. Of course. She'd heard that exchange with the pilot and would have deduced who he was. Still...in his experience once people knew who he was they didn't try to get away—the opposite, in fact.

'I have all the space I need. You don't need to go anywhere. I'll feel insulted if you move.'

Sidonie had to force herself to calm down. What on earth was wrong with her? So what if he was Alexio Christakos, one of the most powerful entrepreneurs of his time? So what if he was more gorgeous than any man she'd ever seen? Since when had she become a walking hormone, anyway? The flight was only an hour. She could handle anything for an hour. Even sitting beside Alexio Christakos.

She forced herself to relax her grip on her bag and said, in as calm a voice as she could muster, 'Fine. I just thought that in light of...who you are...you might appreciate some more space. I mean physically. You're not exactly...' Sidonie stopped and bit her lip, slid her gaze from his uncomfortably.

In an effort to distract him she started to take stuff out of her bag again: a book, papers...

'I'm not exactly what?'

Sidonie could hear the barely suppressed smile in his voice and it made her prickle at being such an object of humour for him.

'You know very well what I mean...' She waved a hand in his general direction. 'You're not exactly designed to fit into economy class, are you?'

She could have sworn she heard a muffled snort but refused to look, thrusting her bag back down under the seat in front. She hated to acknowledge the zinging sensation in her blood, as if she'd been plugged into a mild electric current.

She sat back and crossed her arms, and looked at him to find him regarding her with a small smile playing around his mouth. *Lord.* Almost accusingly she asked, 'Why are you here anyway? Apparently you could be on a private jet rather than waiting here like the rest of us.'

That green gaze was steady, unsettling.

'It's a spot-check. I like to do them from time to time, to make sure things are running smoothly.'

Sidonie breathed out as something clicked in her brain. 'Of course. I read about that.'

He frowned and she clarified reluctantly, feeling hot and self-conscious. 'You were a case study in my business module at college.'

That information didn't appear to be news to him. 'What else did you study at college?'

Embarrassed now, Sidonie admitted, 'Technically I'm still in college… I had to leave before the start of my final year just over a year ago, due to personal events. I'm saving money to try and complete my course… My degree is in Business and French.'

'What happened?'

Sidonie looked at him. On some level she was shocked at his directness, but it was also curiously refreshing. She couldn't seem to remove her gaze from his. The small space they occupied felt strangely intimate, cocoon-like.

'I… Well, my father lost his construction business when the property boom crashed in Ireland. He struggled for a while but it was useless. He only managed to get himself into debt.' Sidonie went cold inside. 'He passed away not long afterwards. Everything was gone—the business, the house… College was paid for up to a point, but then the money ran out. I had to leave and work.'

Sidonie felt uncomfortable under his gaze. It was intense, unsettling.

'And why were you in Paris?'

Sidonie arched a brow. 'What is this? Twenty questions? What were *you* doing in Paris?'

Alexio crossed his arms and Sidonie's belly clenched when she saw how the muscles in his arm bunched under the thin silk of his shirt. She gulped and looked back into that hypnotising gaze.

'I was in Milan yesterday at my brother's wedding, he said. 'Then I flew to Paris this morning to catch this flight, so that I could do my check while en route to London.'

'Are you not concerned about missing your meeting?'

Alexio smiled and the bottom dropped out of Sidonie's belly.

'It's not ideal, but they'll wait for me.'

Of course they would, she thought faintly. Who wouldn't wait for this man?

'So,' he said patiently, 'now will you tell me why *you* were in Paris?'

Sidonie looked at him and unbidden a lump came to her throat for her wayward. selfish mother and her poor Tante Josephine who was so worried. She swallowed it down.

'I was here to meet with a solicitor to deal with my mother's affairs. She passed away in Paris a couple of months ago. She'd been living with my aunt; she's from here originally.' She corrected herself. '*Was* from here, I mean. She moved back after my father died.'

Alexio uncrossed his arms and his expression sobered. 'That's rough—to lose both parents in such a short space of time. I lost my mother too—five months ago.'

Sidonie's chest tightened. A moment of empathy. Union. 'I'm sorry... It's hard, isn't it?'

His mouth twisted. 'I have to admit that we weren't that close—but, yes, it was still a shock.'

That feeling intensified in Sidonie's chest. She revealed huskily, 'I did love my mum, and I know she loved me, but we weren't that close either. She was very... self-absorbed.'

Suddenly the plane lurched into movement and Sidonie's hands went to grab the armrests automatically as she looked out of the window. 'Oh, God, we're moving.'

A dry voice came from her left. 'That's generally what a plane does before it takes off.'

'Very funny,' muttered Sidonie, and their recent conversation was wiped from her mind as she battled with the habitual fear of flying she faced.

'Hey, are you okay? You look terrible.'

'No,' Sidonie got out painfully, knowing she'd probably gone ashen. Her eyes were closed. 'I'm not okay, but I will be if you just leave me alone. Ignore me.'

'You're scared of flying? And you're taking two flights to Dublin? Why didn't you just take a direct flight?' Now he sounded censorious.

'Because,' Sidonie gritted out, 'it worked out cheaper to do it this way, and the direct flights were all full anyway. It was short notice.'

The familiar nausea started to rise and she clamped her mouth shut, feeling cold and clammy. She tried not to think back to the huge breakfast her Tante Josephine had insisted on them both having before they'd left on their respective journeys. It sat heavily in her belly now.

The plane was moving in earnest; this was always the worst part—and the take-off. And the landing. And sometimes in between if there was turbulence.

'Did something happen to make you scared?'

Sidonie wished he would just ignore her, but bit out, 'What? You mean apart from the fact that I'm miles above the earth, surrounded by nothing but a bit of tin and fibreglass or whatever planes are made of?'

'They're actually made mainly of aluminium, although sometimes a composite of metals is used, and in newer technology they're looking at carbon fibre. My brother designs and builds cars, so we're actually looking into new technologies together.'

Sidonie cracked open one eye and cast Alexio a baleful glance. 'Why are you telling me this?'

'Because your fears are irrational. You *do* know that air travel is the safest form of travel in the world?'

Sidonie opened both eyes now and tried to avoid seeing outside the plane. She looked at Alexio. That didn't really help, she had to admit.

She said somewhat churlishly, 'I suppose that the likelihood of the plane going down while its owner is on board is not very high.'

He looked smug. 'See?'

Then he leant closer, making her pulse jump out of control.

'And did you know that of all the seats on the plane these are the safest ones to be in—in the event of a crash?'

Sidonie's eyes widened. 'Really?'

She saw humour dancing in those golden depths and clamped her eyes shut again while something swooped precariously in her belly.

'Very funny.'

Then the plane jerked and Sidonie's hands tightened on the armrests. She heard a deep sigh from beside her and then felt her left hand being taken by a much bigger one. Instantly she was short of breath which she could ill afford to lose.

'What are you doing?' she squeaked, very aware of how tiny her hand felt in his.

'If it's all right with you, I'd prefer it if you abused me rather than my armrests.'

Sidonie opened her eyes again and glanced left. Alexio was looking stern, but with a twitch of a smile playing around his mouth. *Lord, oh, Lord.* She said, a little breathlessly, 'I think somehow that your armrests can withstand my feeble attempts to bend them out of shape.'

'Nevertheless,' Alexio replied easily, 'I won't let it be said that I couldn't offer support to a valued customer in her hour of need.'

CHAPTER TWO

SOMETHING HOT AND shivery went through Sidonie's body. He was flirting with her. She felt as if she was teetering on the edge of a huge canyon, with the exhilaration of the fall reaching out to beckon her into the unknown. He was so utterly gorgeous, and so charming when he turned it on. It was smooth, practised. And she was no match for a man like him.

With her body screaming resistance, Sidonie pulled her hand free from his grip and smiled tightly. 'I'll be fine. But, thanks.'

His eyes flashed for a second, as if he were taken aback or surprised. The regret in Sidonie's body was like a sharp pang.

She clasped her hands in her lap, well out of reach, and turned her head, closing her eyes so that she didn't have to look out of the window. Her battle with fear as the plane took off was being eclipsed by her need not to show it to the man beside her.

More than once she wished that he'd take her hand again. His palm had felt ever so slightly callused. The hands of a working man, not a pampered man.

'You can open your eyes now. The seatbelt sign is about to go off.'

Sidonie took a deep breath and opened her eyes, releasing her hands from their death grip on each other. Alexio was looking at her. She had the impression that he'd been looking at her the whole time. She felt clammy. Hot.

He held out his hand then, and said, 'I believe you already know who I am, but I don't know who you are...'

He wasn't backing off. Butterflies erupted in Sidonie's belly again. She couldn't ignore him. She put her hand in his, unable to help a small smile which was only in part to do with the trauma of take-off being over.

'Sidonie Fitzgerald—pleased to meet you.'

He clasped her hand and once again an electric current seemed to thrum through her blood.

'Sidonie...' he mused. 'It sounds French.'

'It is. My mother chose it. I told you she was French.'

'That's right...you did.'

He was still holding her hand and Sidonie felt as if she was overheating. 'Did they just turn the heating up?'

'You do look hot. Maybe you should take your sweatshirt off.'

He finally released her hand and it tingled. Faintly, Sidonie said, 'I'm sure I'll be fine...' She had no intention of baring herself to this man's far too assessing gaze.

It was then that Sidonie remembered what they'd been talking about. The fact that they'd both lost their mothers recently. That feeling of kinship. Feeling exposed now, she looked away and reached for her book. She held it for a minute and then turned to Alexio again. He had put his head back against the seat, closed his eyes. She felt ridiculously deflated for a moment.

But then she realised she could drink him in unobserved. His profile was patrician. His eyes deep-set, with long dark lashes. His cheekbones would have made a woman weep with envy, but the stark lines of his face took away any pretty edges.

His jaw was firm, even in repose, and she could see the faint stubbling of fresh beard growth. A spasm of lust gripped her between her legs, taking her by surprise. She'd never experienced such raw *desire*. She'd had a couple of boyfriends at college and had had sex, but it had all been a bit...bland. A lot of fuss over nothing. Mildly excruciating. The guys had certainly seemed to enjoy it more than she had.

She could imagine, though, that this man knew exactly what to do...how to make a woman feel exactly as she should. Especially a man with a mouth like his...sensual and wicked. Hard lines but soft contours... Sidonie pressed her legs together to stop the betraying throb between them. She hadn't even known she had a pulse there, but she could feel it now, like a beacon.

'It's rude to stare, you know.'

Sidonie sprang back. Cheeks flaming. One lazy eye had opened and was focused on her, seeing her mortification.

She spluttered, 'How did you know?'

Before she could feel any more embarrassed he bent down and his head of thick dark hair, closely cropped to his skull, came dangerously near to her thighs. Heat bloomed from Sidonie's groin.

Then he straightened up, holding her book in his hand. He took a quick glance at the title before handing it back to her and commenting dryly, '*Techniques for Analysing Successful Business Structures*? That's bound to send you to sleep.'

Sidonie scowled and took the book from him jerkily. 'I'm trying to keep up with my course so that when I go back I won't be too rusty.'

Alexio dipped his head. 'Very commendable.'

Sidonie felt defensive and wasn't even sure why. 'Some of us have to study the subject. We don't have the natural ability or the support to be able to launch a stratospherically successful business first time.'

His mouth tightened and Sidonie knew she'd raised his hackles.

'I didn't have any support—or did your case study not cover that?'

Sidonie flushed and looked down, inspecting a spot of dirt on her jeans. She looked up again. 'I didn't mean it to sound like that... It's common knowledge that you turned your back on your inheritance... However, you can't deny that your background must have given you confidence and an anticipation of success that most mere mortals mightn't feel or experience.'

His face relaxed somewhat and Sidonie felt herself relax too. Weird.

'You're right,' he surprised her by admitting. 'After all, I grew up absorbing my father's business nous whether I want to admit it or not. And I had the best education money could buy... My brother is also a successful entrepreneur, so I learnt from him too.'

Sidonie was itching to ask him why he'd turned his back on his inheritance, but just then the stewardess turned up with a trolley, smiling winsomely at Alexio. Sidonie felt the most bizarre rise of something hot and visceral. Possessiveness. It shocked her so much that she shrank back.

Her sweatshirt felt hot and constricting, even more so now, and Sidonie longed to feel cool. While Alexio was distracted, ordering some coffee from the woman, Sidonie whipped it over her head—only to emerge seconds later to find two pairs of eyes on her. The distinctly cold blue of the stewardess and a green gaze, intent and disturbing.

'What...?' She looked from Alexio to the woman, who now spoke to her in tones even cooler than her arctic gaze.

'Would you like some tea or coffee, madam?'

In fluent French Sidonie replied that she would love some tea. She could sense the small smile playing around Alexio's mouth without even looking. Her skin prickled as she put down her table and accepted the steaming tea. She felt exposed now, in her loose singlet top, even though it was layered over another one.

Before she could reach for her purse Alexio had paid for her drink as well as his. Not a welcome move, according to the pursed lips of the stewardess who moved on with barely disguised huffiness.

Alexio seemed oblivious, though.

'Thank you,' Sidonie said. 'You didn't have to do that.'

He shrugged. 'It's nothing—my pleasure.'

Sidonie shivered a little to think of *his pleasure*.

To get away from such carnal imaginings, she remarked, 'How is it beneficial to do a spot-check on one of your planes if everyone knows who you are?' He quirked a brow at her as he took a sip of coffee and Sidonie blustered a bit. 'Well, you know what I mean. That stewardess will obviously be doing her best to impress.'

'True,' he conceded, and put his cup down.

Sidonie was acutely aware of how dark his hands looked against the cup, how large.

'But I never inform them when I'm coming, and I'm not just interested in the behaviour of my staff—it's everything. I can overhear the passengers' observations too.'

Sidonie frowned. 'But don't you have people who work for you who can do this sort of thing and report back?'

Alexio shrugged minutely. 'I have to go to London today—why not take one of my own commercial flights? If I expect others to do it then I should be able to, too. I am aware of my carbon footprint. I have a responsibility.'

Sidonie could see unimstakable pride in his business on his face. She nodded her head. 'It's smart. Because if anyone ever criticises you you can say that you know first-hand what it's like to fly on your budget flights. And,' she added, warming to her theme, turning more towards

Alexio, 'it gives the customer a sense of kinship with you. You're one of the people.'

He smiled. 'That too. Very good, business student. It's a pity you had to drop out.'

Sidonie glanced away, uncomfortable again under that gaze. It was as if he could see right through her to a place she wasn't even aware of herself. Some secret part she'd not explored yet.

'So your mother was French…and your father?'

Sidonie rolled her eyes and said lightly, 'Back to twenty questions again?'

She sat back and tried not to notice how confined the space was. Their elbows kept touching lightly when they moved. Their thighs would be touching if she shifted hers towards him by about an inch. His legs were so long he had to spread them wide.

Instantly warm again, Sidonie answered before he could comment. 'My father was Irish. My mother went to Dublin many years ago…she met my father and stayed in Dublin and they got married.'

Sidonie slid her gaze from Alexio's, afraid he might see something of her very deep shame revealed. It wasn't exactly the way things had happened, but near enough. He didn't need to know the darker secrets of her parents' relationship and her origins. Or about subsequent shattering events.

She looked at him. 'And you?'

His expression became veiled, piquing her interest.

'My mother was Spanish and my father is Greek. But you probably knew that.'

Sidonie answered, 'I didn't realise your mother was Spanish…'

'I presume your fluent French is from your mother?'

Sidonie nodded and took another sip of tea. She realised

then that if only she wasn't so *aware* of Alexio it would actually be quite nice talking to him.

'She spoke French to me all the time, and my father encouraged it. He knew it would come in handy at some stage.'

'You were close to your father?'

She nodded. 'Why do you ask?'

Alexio reached out and to Sidonie's shock touched her cheek with the backs of his fingers for a fleeting second.

'Because your face softened when you mentioned him.'

Sidonie touched her cheek where he had touched her and felt embarrassed. She ducked her face again, wishing her hair was down so she could hide. 'I loved him. He was a wonderful man.'

'You're lucky to have had that… My father…we don't exactly see eye to eye.'

Sidonie glanced back at him, grateful for the attention to be off her, and laughed slightly. 'Surely he must be one of the proudest fathers in the world?'

Alexio smiled, but it was grim. 'Ah, but my success didn't come through him. I fought for my own piece of the pie and he's never forgiven me for it.'

Just then they were interrupted again, when a different stewardess came along to clear up their rubbish. It gave Alexio a reality check and he balked inwardly.

What on earth was he doing? Blithely spilling his guts to a complete stranger because he was momentarily mesmerised by pale skin, beautiful eyes and a very supple, slim body?

When the stewardess had gone and Alexio was still berating himself he saw Sidonie undo her seatbelt buckle.

She looked at him expectantly before saying, 'I need to go to the bathroom. Please.'

Relieved to have a chance to gather his completely scattered senses, Alexio undid his own seatbelt and stood up. Deliberately he didn't move out into the aisle completely, so that Sidonie had to brush past him. He saw the flash in her eyes, making them sparkle a brilliant blue-green, and felt that punch to his gut again.

As she went past him he saw that she was doing her best not to touch him, but even the most fleeting glance of her hip against his thigh sent shards of desire into his belly. He couldn't help but smell her scent—cool and crisp, with a hint of something floral. That was what she was like—one minute spiky, the next as soft as a fresh rose. And as alluring.

She was taller than he had expected—about five foot seven...

When he'd sat down again, and she'd moved down the aisle to the bathroom, Alexio stuck his head out to watch her, his blood heating through every vein and artery at the way her skinny jeans hugged her slim, shapely legs and cupped her surprisingly lush derriere. To Alexio's consternation he saw more than one other male head dip out to take a look too as she passed.

It felt as if he hadn't taken a proper breath since he'd seen her take off that horrific sweatshirt. He'd happened to look at her for her response when the stewardess had asked if she wanted something, only to find her in the act of taking it off. He'd been unable to look away as Sidonie had fought with the voluminous material, gradually showing tantalising glimpses of pale flesh, slim arms, tiny wrists, delicate shoulders and collarbone.

She'd emerged flushed, and Alexio's libido had been suddenly ravenous. She was wearing a vest top, with a loose singlet over it, so she was showing nothing that wasn't completely respectable. But she might as well have been naked, the effect within Alexio was so violent. He felt like a Victorian man seeing bared arms for the first time; they were almost provocative in their slim, delicately muscled definition.

He'd sat there with a raging erection, trying in vain to concentrate on the conversation and those flashing expressive eyes and not let his gaze drift down to where her small but lush cleavage was revealed under those two tops. The hint of a bright pink bra strap every now and then had enflamed him more than the most expensive lingerie modelled by any of his previous lovers. The memory of his Latin lover of last night was being comprehensively eclipsed.

Alexio wanted to see her—*all of her*—with a hunger that might ordinarily cause him to stop and think. He could already imagine her perfectly formed breasts, made to fit a man's hands like plump fruits. Would her nipples be small and peaked? Or large and succulent? He hadn't been able to resist touching her hot cheek for a second. Her skin was as soft and unblemished as a peach.

This was the kind of desire he'd missed for so long. The kind he'd lamented not feeling last night. Urgent and hot. Utterly compelling. As if he couldn't envisage *not* getting off this plane and taking Sidonie with him so that he could taste her all over. And Alexio had to wonder in that moment if he'd ever really felt like this. Or had it just been a figment of his imagination till now?

The revelation sent him reeling, and he wasn't prepared at all when a soft voice said hesitantly, 'Er…excuse me, Mr Christakos?'

He looked up and there she was, and just like that any semblance of clear-headedness was gone. He was reduced to animal lust again. Her breasts were in his eyeline and he could see the thrust of her nipples against the thin fabric of her two tops, like berries. He had to get up and let her back in, cursing his body, which would not obey his head.

One thing he was sure of as she brushed past him in the small space again and her scent tantalised him: he wanted this Sidonie Fitzgerald with her husky voice with a hunger he'd not known before. And he would have her. Because Alexio Christakos always got what he wanted. Especially women.

Sidonie sat down again and tried to hang on to the control she'd struggled to find in the tiny bathroom space just moments before. She'd splashed cold water on her face, as if that might wake her from the trance she seemed to be in.

Any return of her equilibrium had been short-lived. As soon as she'd got back Alexio Christakos had looked at her—that molten green gaze travelling up from her breasts to her face—and it had been so intense…almost predatory. Her whole body had reacted to it, igniting like a flame. Even the air seemed to be crackling between them now, as if something had been turned up a notch.

He's a playboy, he's a playboy, she repeated like a mantra in her head. *He's programmed to go after anything with a pulse.* But Sidonie grimaced at that. Alexio Christakos, according to her fellow enamoured students, was discerning—only choosing the most stunning models and actresses. The beauties of this era. And Sidonie, with her fair colouring, freckles and wayward hair, did not fall into that category. Not by a long shot. This crazy desire…whatever it was she was feeling…she had to be imagining it.

A wave of mortification rushed up through her body, sending her hot and cold. Was she projecting her own pathetic subconscious fantasies onto this man who had the misfortune to be paired with her for the flight?

She heard him clear his throat beside her and was almost scared to look. She could sense his gaze on her—or could she? With a sick desire to know how badly she'd been deluding herself Sidonie turned her head and met that green gaze head-on. Slamming into it, almost. The breath left her mouth in a little sigh. Her belly swooped and her skin tingled all over. Her nipples drew so tight she could feel them like stinging points, chafing against her lace bra.

'Don't...' he growled softly, intimately. 'Don't call me Mr Christakos again. It makes me feel like an old man. It's Alexio.'

Sidonie could feel the plane dip in altitude. Somehow she found her voice. 'We're landing soon. I won't see you ever again, so it doesn't really matter what I call you.'

'Don't be so sure about that.'

Sidonie blinked. Her heart spasmed in her chest. 'What's that supposed to mean?'

'I'm taking you out to dinner tonight.'

Sidonie had two contradictory reactions. Head and heart/body. Her heart/body leapt and sizzled. Her head said *Danger! Danger!* He was definitely arrogant, and she was loath to let him see that even a small part of her was tempted. A man like this? He would chew her up over dinner and a one-night stand and then cast her out with little or no second thought.

She was a fleeting interest.

Maybe the lack of air and the confines of economy class had gone to his head. Maybe he was bored, jaded, and something about her intrigued him because she was so different from his usual women.

Sidonie crossed her arms and narrowed her eyes. She saw Alexio's jaw clench, as if he was priming himself for a fight, and something deep within her quivered and then went soft and molten. She fought it. They were both oblivious to the stewardess, who had come to check their seatbelts for landing.

'That sounded remarkably like an order and not an invitation. I'm catching a connecting flight to Dublin—or didn't you hear that part earlier?'

Sidonie wasn't sure exactly why she felt so threatened

by his advance, but she did. Even though she knew she was probably right in her suspicions about why a man like Alexio was flirting with her, a very large part of her wanted to leap into his arms and say *yes*.

She would bet that not many women turned him down—if any. But she wouldn't be able to live with herself if she gave in to him for what she had no doubt would amount to one night. She told herself it was because she valued herself too highly, but she knew, treacherously, that she was afraid of how strongly this man affected her. One night would never be enough. She felt it deep in the pit of her belly. And that freaked her out. She was a naturally responsible and cautious person, not given to spontaneous acts like this.

He cast his glance to the very sexy platinum watch on his wrist, and then back to her. 'I'd say you've missed that connecting flight, and as I'm the owner of the airline company the least you can do is allow me to make it up to you. By taking you for dinner.'

Sidonie snorted inelegantly and quashed the swooping sensation in her belly. 'I don't see you offering everyone on this plane dinner to recompense them for missing their connecting flights.'

That formidable jaw clenched again. 'That's probably because I don't *want* to take them for dinner. However, I would like to take *you* for dinner. *Please*.'

Sidonie's chin lifted, but she quivered inwardly at his *please*. 'I'm a terrible dinner companion. I'm a fussy eater and I'm a vegetarian. Vegan, actually.'

That wasn't true, but some devil inside her was working now. Sparking.

Alexio smiled. 'I'm sure you are a scintillating dinner companion, and I know a fabulous vegetarian restaurant—all the eggplant you can eat.'

That humour danced in his eyes again, transporting him from downright gorgeous to downright irresistible.

Sidonie scowled. He didn't believe her for a second. His eyes dropped down her body and then came back up again. A wickedly sexy slow smile tipped up his mouth, telling her better than any words that dinner and conversation were not the only things on his mind. As if she couldn't feel it vibrating between them. This awareness she'd never felt before.

Sidonie glared at him and tried to will down the heat in her body that mocked her with the realisation that dinner wasn't exactly foremost in *her* mind either. Very belatedly she remembered she had taken off her sweatshirt and scrabbled around to find it and pull it back on.

She heard a sound beside her and looked to see Alexio making a face.

'That thing should be burnt.'

Sidonie gasped, affronted. 'It's my favourite.'

'It's a crime to hide your body underneath that shapeless thing.'

Suddenly there was a sharp thudding and crashing sensation and Sidonie's heart stopped. She felt all her blood drain south.

Instantly Alexio had her hands in his and he was saying soothingly, 'We've just landed, that's all.'

Sidonie's heart was still palpitating. Her ears popped. She could see the ground through the window across the aisle and felt the powerful throttle of the plane as it pulled back.

She looked at Alexio, shocked. 'I've never not noticed landing before.' She'd been distracted. By *him*.

Her hands were still in his and she looked down to see them, so much smaller and paler next to his. As she watched he entwined his fingers with hers and between her legs she throbbed. He exerted pressure on her hands and Sidonie looked up, her head feeling heavy, her blood hot.

For a long, taut moment they just looked at one another. Sidonie's breath grew choppy. Alexio pulled one hand free and brought it up to cup her jaw, his thumb moving back and forth as if learning the shape of her cheek.

His eyes were on her mouth now. She wanted him to kiss her so badly. The air sizzled. And then his eyes met hers again and he emitted a guttural sound like a curse. His jaw clenched. He took his hand away. Sidonie had to bite the inside of her lip to stop herself from crying out.

As if she'd been drugged just by that look Sidonie slowly came back to her senses, and mortification gripped her innards when she realised how she must have looked: like some love-starved groupie.

She jerked back. Thank goodness he hadn't kissed her, because she knew that she would have put up no fight whatsoever. And she hated the part of her that felt *bereft* of the experience. She looked away.

'Sidonie.'

The fact that his voice was rough didn't give her any comfort.

'What?' she snapped, reaching for her bag and putting it on her lap so that she could put her stuff back into it.

She found her glasses and stuck them on, even though she only needed them for reading. They felt like the armour she needed. She looked at him and then wished she hadn't. His face was all stark, lean lines. Nostrils flaring. Eyes dangerous.

People around them were starting to stand up, unbuckling seatbelts, reaching for bags.

Sidonie forgot for a moment that he'd even asked her for dinner. She felt ridiculously vulnerable. Exposed.

'I'm sure you have an assistant waiting nearby to fast-track you off the plane and out of the airport.'

Alexio's mouth firmed. She was right. Even now he could see a uniformed official saying, 'Excuse me...' as he fought his way through the crush to get to Alexio.

He grabbed for her hand and Sidonie glanced around

them, but no one was looking. All eager to get on with their journeys.

'Sidonie, I meant what I said. Come for dinner with me tonight.'

She looked at him and still felt that awful sting of rejection because he hadn't actually kissed her. She hated that it made her feel vulnerable. 'I'm going to Dublin. I can't stay in London just on your…whim.'

His eyes flashed. 'It's not a whim. If you stay I'll take care of you—get you home.'

Sidonie pulled her hand free. She shook her head. 'No… I'm sorry, but I can't.'

The uniformed person was at their seats now and he bent down to say something to Alexio, who made a curt reply. He stood up and reached for his jacket and coat. He looked down at Sidonie, whose eyes had been glued to that magnificent torso as he'd stretched up.

'Come with me. At least let me try to help you make your flight.'

Sidonie looked at him and gulped. Now he was distant, unreadable. A shiver went down her spine and she knew in that moment that she would hate to cross him. He would be a formidable enemy.

Stiffly she said, 'You don't have to do this. I can find my own way and wait for another flight if I have to.'

He sighed deeply. 'Just…don't argue, okay? Come with me—please.'

He held out his hand and Sidonie looked from him to it. This was probably the last time she'd ever see him. On some level she realised with a jolt that she felt as if she could trust this man who was all but a total stranger. Even though she was fighting it.

That revelation stunned her. She'd never trusted easily after the cataclysmic events of her childhood. And losing both parents within such a short space of time, together with the recent revelations about her mother's nefarious actions, had made the world feel increasingly fragile around her. As if nothing she knew was solid any more. Yet being in the company of this man had made Sidonie feel more solid than she'd ever felt. Protected. Which was crazy.

Even more crazy, though, was the fact that Sidonie couldn't resist the lure of a few more minutes with this man. Her hand slipped into his almost of its own volition and it was disconcerting how familiar it felt—and yet how deliciously terrifying, as if she were stepping off a ledge.

She was out of her seat and Alexio was leading her towards the back of the plane, guided by the man who had come to fetch him. The back door was open just for them, with the frosty stewardess saying goodbye, sending Sidonie daggers on seeing her hand clasped tightly in Alexio's.

Hating herself for how much she liked the way her hand felt in his, Sidonie followed him down the steps to where another official and a car were waiting. She heard Alexio give her name to the person and instruct him that her luggage should be brought to meet them on the other side. A VIP customs official inspected her Irish passport.

And then they were in a chauffeur-driven car and speeding towards the terminal Sidonie needed to get to for her connecting flight.

CHAPTER THREE

ALEXIO WAS LOOKING at his smartphone but not seeing anything. He was incandescent with rage...and lust. Angry with himself that he'd not taken the opportunity to kiss Sidonie when he'd wanted to. But something had held him back—something that had whispered to him that she wasn't like the women he knew. That the strength of what he was feeling was off the charts.

He prided himself on being a civilised man. With very select tastes. Not a man given to random outbursts or to passionately kissing a woman an hour after meeting her. And yet he'd come within seconds of doing just that.

Yet still...had he let her go? No. He'd all but hauled her off the plane. Sidonie was a tense figure beside him now, her bag on her lap, her hands clasping it.

Unable to help himself, Alexio reached out and touched a finger to her jaw, trailing it over the delicate line. Even that made his body scream with hunger. She tensed even more, but she turned to look at him. Alexio marvelled to himself. One wayward curling strand of hair had come loose and coiled over her shoulder like a burst of silken sunrise. Her cheeks were flushed. No make-up, and those ridiculous black-framed glasses. Her shapeless sweatshirt and those worn jeans. He shouldn't want her. But he did.

He couldn't explain it, but in that moment she was the most beautiful woman he'd ever seen in his life. And suddenly that need was back, even more urgent than before. The realisation hit him: he might never see her again.

Rationality dissolved to be replaced by raw hunger and need. Sidonie obviously saw something on his face, in his eyes, and her own eyes widened, her cheeks getting pinker. Alexio couldn't have stopped himself now if a thousand men had tried to hold him back.

He pulled her into him and slanted his mouth over hers.

That first sweet taste of her soft lips crushed under his made his brain go white with heat. She fell against him, hands pressed to his chest, and Alexio hauled her even closer, his mouth moving over hers, coaxing her to open up to him…

One of his hands moved up her arm to her neck, his thumb angling her chin, cupping her head…and then, after an infinitesimal moment, she opened her mouth on a sigh. He deepened the kiss and all that hunger he'd been holding in exploded in a dizzying rush of desire.

Sidonie was still in shock. Alexio's mouth was on hers, his tongue seeking, thrusting, tasting… She couldn't breathe, couldn't think. And didn't want to. All she knew was that as soon as he'd looked at her so hungrily and then reached for her she'd been ready to throw herself into his arms. The evidence that he did want her was like balm to her ravaged spirit.

There was nothing gentle about his kiss, and she wanted it with every fibre of her being. It was passionate, hotter than anything she'd experienced before. He was tasting and plundering, both hands on her head now, his fingers in her hair, making it loose. Sidonie felt as if she was breaking apart into a million tiny pieces, but it was so delicious…so drugging…that she never wanted it to stop.

A ravenous beast she'd never known before woke inside her and she felt herself matching the passion of Alexio's kiss. Matching it and seeking for more. Now *she* was the one who wanted to taste, nipping at his lower lip with her teeth, feeling the hard resilience of that sensual contour… her tongue automatically soothing where she'd nipped.

She heard a faint sound coming from a long way away. And then Alexio was stopping, pulling back. Sidonie went with him, loath to release him even for a second.

Some sliver of sanity intruded and Sidonie realised that she was clinging to Alexio. And that he'd just been kissing her to distraction in the back of his car. She found the strength to pull herself out of the whirlpool and broke free, breathing harshly. Dazed. Eyes unfocused for a second.

She realised two things at once: the car had come to a halt outside the terminal and it must have been the driver who had made the noise to get their attention.

Alexio's hands were still on her arms, as if she needed support, and his face was still close, those eyes looking heavy-lidded and glittering with all sorts of decadent promises. All she wanted to do was pull him back to her and kiss him again and never stop.

Almost violently she pulled free completely. Her cheeks burned. Her hair was loose and coming down. Quickly she scrabbled with trembling hands to put it back up.

She couldn't look at him. What the hell had just happened? Mutual combustion? And she'd leapt into the fire without a second's hesitation. As much as she'd been a willing participant in what had just happened, it scared Sidonie how quickly she'd lost control.

'We're here,' Alexio said, somewhat redundantly. He was trying to control the clamour of his blood. He felt altered after that kiss. Disorientated.

Sidonie was avoiding his eye, breathing fast. He saw her throat work. She opened her mouth and already he wanted to cover it with his, taste that sweetness again.

There was something so unexpected about her—something that pierced him right through to where he'd never been touched, smashing aside his cynical jaded shell. If he could think for a moment he might even feel suspicious, but right now he was too hot for her to feel anything but carnal hunger.

She glanced at him and all he could see were the swirling blue and green depths of those luminous eyes. She was still wearing those glasses. Then he saw her hand reaching for the door handle, and everything in him rejected the notion that she was going to leave. But before he could stop her she'd looked away, opened the door and was stepping out.

Alexio moved so fast that she was only just straightening up when he reached her side of the car. Her eyes were huge and wary. Someone rushed up with her bag on a trolley and Alexio took it, only just restraining himself from snarling at the completely innocent staff member to leave them alone.

Alexio looked at Sidonie for a long moment, feeling as if he was tipping over a precipice he'd never let himself near before.

'Are you sure I can't change your mind?'

For a second he thought she was about to capitulate, and the blood thundered in his head, but then she bit her lip and shook her head. 'I can't. I need to get back.'

Alexio didn't want to move. 'You have a job?'

She avoided his eye. 'I did… But the restaurant closed down.'

Alexio's body grew tight. 'So there's nothing to rush home for…?' Something very unpalatable occurred to him and he bit out, 'Unless you have a boyfriend?'

Sidonie shook her head quickly and at the same time shot him an insulted look. 'No… I would never do…what we just did…if I had…'

She stopped for a moment, then focused on him again and looked tortured, but it was little comfort to Alexio.

'I just…can't do this. With you.' Her chin lifted. 'I'm not easy, Alexio. I won't just fall into bed with you because you click your fingers and expect me to.'

Alexio wanted to smash aside the trolley, rip off those glasses and grab her, kiss her into submission. Kiss her *again*. Instead he bit out, lying admirably, 'I asked you for dinner, Sidonie, not for sex.'

She blanched and avoided his gaze again, slinging her bag across her body. It did little to douse his desire—the strap coming between her breasts made them stand out, defining their pert shape. *Theos*, what was *wrong* with him? Had he lost all reason in the past hour?

Sidonie took the trolley and said, 'Look…thanks, okay? If I lived in London maybe I'd go out with you, but I don't, and I have to go home.'

She was pulling away, taking the trolley with her case on it, and something like panic gripped Alexio's chest, constricting his breathing. He thrust a hand into his jacket pocket and pulled out a card, handed it to her.

She took it reluctantly and he wanted to push it into her hand, wrap her fingers around it. 'Those are my private numbers. If anything changes…call me.'

After a few torturous seconds she just nodded and said, 'It was nice to meet you…'

And then she pulled the trolley round, disappeared into the departures hall and was swallowed up by a thousand faceless, nameless people.

Alexio did not like this feeling of being out of control. *At all*. It was something he'd fought against his whole life—every time his father had tried to mould him into the son and heir he'd wanted. Every time his father had suffocated him with the weight of his expectations. And most all every time he'd seen his father lose it because he couldn't control his emotions around his cold wife.

And yet this wisp of a woman had managed to slide control out from under his feet without him even noticing.

He cursed volubly.

Twenty minutes later Sidonie was about to scream with frustration. Her body was still sensitive, tingling with an overload of sexual awareness. All she could see in her mind's eye was Alexio Christakos's hard-boned gorgeous face and that mouth-wateringly perfect body, but all she could hear was the airline official saying again, 'Look, miss, I'm sorry. This is the weekend of the England versus Ireland rugby final. There is no way you are going to get a ticket to Dublin today or tomorrow. So unless you want to try swimming the Irish Sea…'

Sidonie felt the press of people behind her, all looking to get home, and felt despair. The official was already dealing with the next person and, despondent, Sidonie turned away. She went back out through the main doors, half expecting to see Alexio still standing there with an imperious look on his face, but he and his car were gone and Sidonie felt absurdly like crying.

Why had she been so hell-bent on denying herself an evening with the most charismatic man she'd ever met? The ghost of her mother whispered to her, reminding Sidonie of her strong instinct to deny anything that was just for herself. She always had to work for it.

She'd vowed long ago not to be grasping like her mother, who had been oblivious to the pain of others around her—especially that of her husband, who had devoted his life to her in spite of the fact that she'd humiliated him publicly. In spite of the fact that he'd always known that Sidonie wasn't even his biological daughter.

And now she had a huge responsibility: Tante Josephine

needed her support. She didn't have the luxury of just thinking about herself. A small voice taunted her. *But you could have had tonight. One night.*

Sidonie felt a lurch as she thought of how for one second she'd almost given in to Alexio and said *yes* when he'd asked if she would change her mind.

The one thing that should have held her back was her aunt—but she had gone on her annual two-week holiday with a local charity group. Sidonie had encouraged her to go, knowing it would take her aunt's mind off things while she sorted herself out in Dublin. For an exhilarating second Sidonie had remembered this and thought it might be possible...but she hadn't seized the moment. Too afraid to throw caution to the wind and trust completely.

And it was too late now anyway. She looked down and saw her hand clenched around his card. Her belly flipped. She had an image of him on his way into London to his important meeting. He would have forgotten about her already. An aberration. She'd missed her chance. Maybe she'd even dreamt him up?

A hollow feeling made her ache inside. She turned around again and faced the door, steeling herself to go back into that throng. She would buy a seat on the next available flight and then she would find somewhere to stay—

'Sidonie.'

Her heart slammed to a stop and the blood rushed from her head to her feet. *It couldn't be.*

Sidonie forgot about the trolley and whirled around. Alexio was standing there, as gorgeous as she remembered. Not a dream. Shock mixed with relief and joy jumped in her belly.

'What are you doing here? You were gone,' she breathed, half afraid she was hallucinating.

Alexio's mouth tightened as if he didn't like admitting it. 'I doubled back...just in case.'

Sidonie made a gesture behind her. 'All the flights are full. A rugby match is on between England and Ireland. I can't get home till the day after tomorrow at the earliest...'

'So you're stuck here at the airport? That's unfortunate.' His eyes were glinting with that dark humour again.

Incredible joy was bubbling up inside Sidonie. He'd come back. *For her.* He hadn't forgotten about her.

She fought back the goofy grin threatening to erupt. 'I was going to rebook my flight and then I was going to find somewhere to stay.'

Alexio put one hand in the pocket of his trousers. His jacket hung open. He was stunning, blinding. Mesmerising.

'I happen to have a very spacious apartment here in London. If you were to agree to accompany me to dinner this evening I'd let you stay. And then I'd make sure you got home at the earliest opportunity.'

Warning bells went off in Sidonie's head again but she ignored them. She was getting a second chance. She'd never thought she'd see this man again, because she would never have had the nerve to call him.

She made a mental decision and took a step into the terrifying and exhilarating unknown.

'I'll accept your offer.'

Something within her leapt to see his eyes flare and his cheeks darken with colour.

She held up a hand. 'On one condition.'

'What?' he bit out, clearly impatient now.

'That you allow *me* to buy dinner...for letting me stay with you.'

Sidonie had a mental image of her bank account and her already close to maxed-out credit card after the flights she'd had to take back and forth to Paris in recent months. She bit her lip.

'Except I hope you like cheap Italian, because that's about the best I can offer.'

Alexio stepped up to her and reached around to get her trolley, taking her small case off it as if it weighed nothing. He took her elbow in his hand and looked down at her, taking her breath away.

'I'll tell you what. We'll eat in—that way we don't have to worry about who's paying.'

'But…' Sidonie spluttered ineffectually as he handed her into the back seat of his car.

He came around and got in the other side and then just looked at her, and it was so stern that she stopped.

'Okay—fine. I get it,' she said a little mutinously, 'but I just don't want you to think that I'm not grateful.'

Alexio issued a terse command in a guttural language and Sidonie saw the car's privacy window slide up silently. Then he was reaching for her and pulling her sweatshirt up and over her head before she had the wits to stop him. When she emerged he had his hands in her hair, taking it out of its confines and making it fall down around her shoulders.

Then he plucked off her glasses—which weren't doing much for her sight anyway.

She slapped at his hands ineffectually. 'What do you think you're doing?'

Sidonie hated that her whole body sizzled at his masterful actions, knowing she should be objecting vociferously.

He took her face in his hands, holding her still. Sidonie's heart skipped and her breath stopped.

'Much better,' Alexio breathed approvingly, just before his head bent and his mouth met hers.

Sidonie groaned deeply, because from the moment she'd pulled away from that first kiss she'd craved this again. In her mind she ordered herself to stop thinking and gave herself up to the dark fantasy of Alexio Christakos, who had just turned her world upside down and inside out.

By the time they pulled up outside a huge, impressive building Sidonie felt completely flustered, aching and undone. Alexio's tie was loose and he looked as feverish as Sidonie felt.

'Come in with me. Wait for me.'

Sidonie's mouth felt swollen. She wasn't sure if her vocal cords worked any more. She just nodded her head. It was as if in the space of the back of that car, in the space of the increasingly passionate kisses they'd shared, some indelible link had been forged between them. She was loath to let him out of her sight.

He held her hand walking in, but Sidonie caught sight of her reflection and balked. She jerked in his grip and he looked down at her and raised a brow.

Sidonie blushed. 'I don't look exactly *corporate*.'

His hot gaze swept her up and down and he said throatily, 'You look perfect.'

But Sidonie knew she was out of place in her chain-store tops, jeans and sneakers the moment the immaculate blonde receptionist sent her a look that could have frozen the Sahara.

When they emerged from the lift there was a veritable entourage of people waiting for Alexio. Someone took his jacket and coat; someone else handed him a folder. Someone else was on the phone. And then someone approached her and said, solicitously, 'Miss Fitzgerald? If you'd like to follow me I can show you where you can wait...'

Sidonie was looking helplessly at Alexio, who glanced at her and then waved her off in the direction of her guide. He was already being spirited away in the opposite direction.

Sidonie was led down plush carpeted hallways. She saw the distinctive Christakos logo on the walls and blanched when she realised that this entire building must be *his*.

The young woman in a pristine trouser suit with her dark hair clipped back showed Sidonie into a palatial office with huge windows looking out over what seemed to be the whole of London. This had to be Alexio's office, with its massive desk near the window.

The woman spoke with an accent that Sidonie guessed must be Greek. 'Can I get you anything, Miss Fitzgerald?'

Sidonie looked at her and felt even more mussed up. 'Er...maybe some tea would be nice?'

'Of course. I'll be right back.' And she left and pulled the heavy door behind her.

Alexio's scent was in the air, faint and tantalising. Exclusive. Masculine. *Sexy*. Sidonie took a deep breath in and walked over to the window to take in the view. It was spectacular, breathtaking.

She could see doors leading out to a terrace and opened them. She went out and was confronted with the real vista—not behind a plane of glass. It was in that moment that she had the full, gut-churning sense of the man she'd met only a few short hours before. He was one of the kings of the world.

'Miss Fitzgerald?'

Sidonie whirled around to see the assistant hovering with a tray. She rushed forward, aghast, and took the tray from the startled woman. 'I can look after it myself. Thank you so much.'

The woman backed away. 'If you need anything else I'm just down the hall. Mr Christakos shouldn't be too long, I heard him say he wanted to keep the meeting short.'

Sidonie's belly somersaulted. Was that because of *her*? She nodded her head and the woman left. Sidonie put down the tray. She didn't want to sit at Alexio's desk so she sat at a small coffee table on the other side of the room. She noticed that her hand was trembling when she poured the tea.

Lord. What was she *doing* here? Sitting in Alexio Christakos's palatial office, waiting for him. He'd picked her up on a *plane*.

Sidonie blushed. She'd engaged him in conversation in

the first place. If she'd buried her head in her book he probably wouldn't have looked twice at her. Sidonie put down her teacup. She knew she could walk out of there right now, get her bag out of his car and melt into the crowds in London and quite possibly never see Alexio again... But, treacherously, she didn't want to.

The novel sensation of putting herself first was uncomfortable. It felt like a coat she'd never worn. Tante Josephine's face popped into her mind...but even Tante Josephine was okay for the moment, on holiday with her friends. There was no reason why Sidonie couldn't be here, doing this.

Sidonie felt a sense of lightness, freedom, and it was heady. Dinner tonight. A place to stay. A chance to get to know this amazing man a little better. She breathed deeply and tried to quell her rapid heartbeat. That was all. And that was all she wanted. No matter what her body might be screaming for. She would emerge from this adventure with her emotions intact.

When Alexio could finally get away from his meeting, which he'd cut ruthlessly and uncharacteristically short, he headed for his office, pulling at his tie impatiently as he did so. *Sidonie*. When he'd ordered his driver to turn around before they'd hit the main motorway into London he'd felt like an abject fool. But the compulsion to go back and see her again had been too great. To find her, persuade her to stay.

And then she'd been standing there, like a lost waif, looking at his card, and the sheer relief that had rushed through him had eclipsed any niggling concerns about his uncharacteristic behaviour.

And now she was here, waiting for him. Alexio gritted his jaw to stop his body reacting. He had to get it together. It had been hard enough to concentrate in the meeting.

When he went into his office he didn't see her and his blood turned to ice.

She'd left.

But then he saw the open terrace doors and his heart started beating again. He went forward and saw her slimly curvaceous form, that plump bottom, as she leant against the railing, taking in the view.

He went right up behind her and put his arms next to hers on the railing.

She started for a moment. 'You scared me.'

Alexio imagined that he felt her heart pick up pace—or was it his? Her lush derriere pressed against him *right there*. And Alexio didn't have a hope in hell of controlling his body.

She was tense in the circle of his arms. 'Your meeting wasn't very long.'

Alexio put out his hand and pulled her long, rippling hair over one shoulder, baring her neck. It was a crime to confine such hair. He bent his head and pressed his mouth to the soft skin just under her ear. Immediately she quivered and her bottom moved against him. His other arm came down and wrapped around her midriff, dragging her in tighter.

Theos. He would take her right here and now if he could.

He drew back slightly, dragging in breath, control. 'I told them I had urgent business to attend to.'

Sidonie turned around in his arms and that was worse—because now Alexio's steel-hard erection was pressed against her soft belly and the hard tips of her breasts were visible through her sleeveless vest tops.

'Alexio…'

Alexio dragged his gaze up and met two pools of aquamarine.

'Hmm?'

'If I stay with you tonight…that doesn't mean I'm going

to sleep with you...' She bit her lip. 'I'm not saying I don't want to, but I'm not like that.' She winced. 'I mean...I won't sleep with you as some sort of payment. I would prefer to stay in a hostel or something.'

Alexio cupped her jaw. She *would* sleep with him. They both knew it.

'I think you've already made your morals clear, and I respect that. Firstly, you are *not* staying in a hostel or anywhere else.' His voice was rough. 'Secondly, I do not expect you to sleep with me to pay me for the room. *If* you sleep with me it will be because you want to. Not for any other reason. We're two consenting adults, Sidonie, not bound by any ties. Free to do as we wish...'

She was breathless now. He could feel her chest moving against him and he wanted to groan.

'Yes...but after tonight we won't see each other again... I don't do one-night stands. We barely know each other.'

Alexio bent his head and feathered a kiss at the corner of one succulent pouting lip. He could feel her yielding against him.

'I already know more about you than I do about my own secretary. And I thought you said you couldn't get a flight for at least a couple of days...so that's two nights... And you know what? You think too much. Tomorrow is a long way away. We have tonight, and that's all that matters right now.'

Alexio's apartment was not as Sidonie had expected. She'd anticipated some kind of penthouse apartment in a sleek building, but his loft-style apartment was in an old converted redbrick building on the Thames, with stunning views.

It had huge windows and exposed brick walls. Sleek and modern furnishings married well with the old shell of the building. Abstract art and compelling black and white photos hung on the walls. The furnishings were unmistakably masculine, but not in an off-putting way. It was comfortable.

Alexio was standing with his arms crossed, watching her. Sidonie blushed and answered his look. She shrugged slightly. 'I'd expected something a bit more…'

'Generic? Without taste?' Alexio put a hand to his chest. 'You wound me…although maybe when you see this your suspicions will be proved right.'

He took her hand and led her to an alcove off the main open-plan living area. It was a dark nook, decorated like an opulent private gentlemen's club, with a pool table and a fully stocked antique bar. A huge mirror behind the bar made the whole space glitter with decadence.

Sidonie smiled. 'Now, this is more like it.'

Alexio let her go and moved to the bar. He disappeared behind the counter to re-emerge holding a chilled bottle of champagne and two glasses.

Sidonie's skin prickled.

He arched a brow. 'Can I tempt you with an aperitif?'

Sidonie saw then how the light was lengthening outside the huge stunning windows and over London. London Bridge was in view—an iconic landmark. She hadn't even noticed that the day had almost flown by.

Vowing to stop thinking so much and just to enjoy, she went and perched herself on one of the velvet-covered stools.

'I'd love one, thank you.'

Alexio expertly popped the cork with only the smallest, most sibilant hiss, and poured them both a glass of the sparkling golden liquid. Sidonie tried not to notice the label, which proclaimed it to be one of the most expensive brands in the world.

Don't think. Enjoy.

He handed her a glass and then came around the counter to stand in front of her. If she widened her legs Alexio could step right between them. Sidonie's pulse leapt.

But he merely clinked his glass to hers and said, 'To us, Sidonie Fitzgerald. Thank you for coming with me today.'

Sidonie couldn't look away from that green gaze. 'Cheers…and thank you for your hospitality.'

They both took a sip and Sidonie blinked at the effervescent bubbles rushing down her throat. She felt buoyed up, heady. Alexio took her hand again and something within her loved the way he did it.

He tugged her gently from the stool. 'Let me give you the tour.'

Carrying their glasses, Alexio brought her through the living area and showed her the sleek kitchen, which again had a lived-in look about it.

'Do you cook?' she asked curiously.

He shrugged minutely. 'I can cook enough for me. I wouldn't put it to the test of a dinner party, though.'

Sidonie teased him to hide her nervousness. 'So what have you lined up for tonight? Beans on toast?'

He looked back at her. 'A chef from one of London's best restaurants. He'll be arriving to serve us in about an hour.'

'Oh…' That shut Sidonie up. For a second she'd almost forgotten who she was with…

Alexio was leading her up some wooden stairs now, with brass railing banisters. There was glass everywhere, all the spaces blending into one another seamlessly as only the best architecture could.

This upper level was like a mezzanine. Alexio was leading her to a room on the left, and Sidonie could see her bag on a huge white-covered bed. A window looked out over the Thames, and the *en suite* bathroom was rustic and yet delightfully modern, with two sinks and an enormous wet-room-style shower. A huge antique bath stood alone.

'It's gorgeous,' she breathed, her hand tightening unconsciously around Alexio's fingers.

He exerted pressure back and she looked at him.

'This is your room, Sidonie. Like I said, I don't expect you to sleep with me...but I won't deny that I want you.'

Just that. Stark. No games. No false seduction. He wanted her. It was devastating in its simplicity.

Feeling shaky, Sidonie just replied, 'Okay...thank you...'

Before they left he showed her how to pull the huge white curtains across the windows that were both walls and door for privacy.

Then he was leading her out along the corridor to another room. This one had to be his. Much larger. Bare but for some choice furniture. An enormous bed, a chair, a wardrobe and a chest of drawers. And again that amazing view.

His *en suite* bathroom was black-tiled, undeniably masculine.

They came back out and Alexio showed her two other guest rooms and an office that looked to be equipped with enough technology to make a space rocket take off.

'London is my next main base after Athens,' he explained. 'I spend most of my time between here and there.'

He led her back down to the bar and Sidonie perched on the stool again. Alexio refilled her glass and then produced a bowl of fresh strawberries from somewhere. Sidonie almost groaned when he dipped one in champagne and handed it to her. The taste of the sweetly tart fruit exploded in her mouth. She wasn't unaware of his intent look at her mouth and she melted inside. She knew that at some point she would have to make things very clear to herself about how far she was prepared to go, because Alexio was waiting for the barest sign of encouragement. And yet she believed him when he said he'd leave it up to her. He wouldn't put pressure on her. He wouldn't have to!

Speaking of inconsequential things as the light outside Alexio's apartment faded into dusk, Sidonie felt herself being more and more seduced. That line she didn't want to cross was blurring and becoming something she wanted to leap over. The sparkling wine did little to help her keep her inhibitions raised.

After a while Alexio glanced at his watch and made a face. 'I don't know about you but I'd like to freshen up—and the chef will be here soon.'

Immediately he said that Sidonie felt sticky after the long day. She nodded. 'I'd love to have a shower…if that's okay.'

Alexio looked at her, and she was shocked and thrilled at the explicitness of it.

'Meet you back down here in twenty minutes?'

'Okay.' Sidonie slid off the stool.

She relished the opportunity to get some space, even for a few minutes. Alexio was so all-encompassing. She still couldn't really believe she was here, with him.

When she let herself into her bedroom she pulled the drapes over the door and windows, marvelling again at the genius design. She went to the main windows overlooking the view and opened one, breathing in the late spring London air.

London Bridge was teeming with traffic, but Sidonie felt deliciously cut off from everything. The real world was fading, being held at bay. With Tante Josephine safe, and away from her own worries, Sidonie could fool herself into thinking she had no responsibilities. She could just…*indulge*.

Realising that she was standing mooning at the view, she galvanised herself into action, unpacked some things and took her shower.

Afterwards, wrapped in a towel, she bit her lip as she looked at her pathetic clothes options. Jeans and more jeans. T-shirts. She had one smart outfit that she'd brought over for the meeting with the solicitor, but that was a black skirt she'd worn for work as a waitress and a black shirt. She'd look as if she was going to a funeral.

Clothes had become a luxury a long time ago, when she'd sold most of her more expensive items to help pay for college while her father had been struggling.

She felt absurdly gauche right then, knowing that Alexio must be used to women who dressed like…*women*. Not impoverished students. Which was what she was. But what she wouldn't give right now for some sleek little black number…

Sighing deeply, Sidonie reached for a pair of dark denims that might be construed as smart and selected a grey T-shirt with a glittery sequin design on the shoulders. She slipped on the slingback heels she'd worn for the meeting and, after inspecting herself in the mirror and balking at her freshly scrubbed pink face, applied some make-up to try and make up for her woefully inappropriate outfit.

She was tempted to put her hair up again, but recalled Alexio taking it down earlier. The thought of those hands and long fingers touching her made her leave it alone. She didn't want to tempt him in any way unless she was competely prepared for his response. But then, she didn't think she'd ever be prepared for the response of a man like Alexio.

Sidonie took a deep breath, as if that might ease the tumult in her breast and in her blood. The ease with which this relative stranger seemed to have sneaked under her skin scared her and exhilarated her in equal measure. It was like being on a rollercoaster ride with no one at the controls.

CHAPTER FOUR

Alexio caught a movement out of the corner of his eye and looked up from where he was pouring some wine into two glasses. His heart stopped in his chest.

Sidonie stood at the bottom of the stairs, her hands clasped together. She was in black figure-hugging denims and pointy shoes. She wore a grey T-shirt with something that sparkled on its shoulders. She hadn't put her hair up—*because she knew he'd just take it down?*—and it tumbled over her shoulders, glowing with an inner fire that flared under certain lights.

Despite the obvious cheapness of her clothes, once again he was struck by her natural beauty, and he wondered how on earth he'd ever dismissed her. The jeans he'd put on felt restrictive, and he gritted his jaw against his newly rampant libido. He had been mourning its dysfunction only twenty-four hours ago. The irony was not lost on him.

He put down the wine bottle and walked over. He saw her cheeks flush as he got nearer. His blood leapt in response. It was as if they were linked. Attuned to exactly the same rhythms. Making love with this woman... Alexio knew instinctively that one night would not be enough, but he pushed that revelation down rather than deal with the skin-prickling awareness of something dangerous that accompanied it.

She looked nervous and gestured to her clothes, clearly

self-conscious, making Alexio feel as if he wanted to reassure her in a way that no other woman of his acquaintance ever needed.

'I didn't come prepared for a fancy dinner. You'll have to excuse me.'

Alexio took her hand. His voice was gruff. 'I want you to be comfortable. I didn't make much effort either.'

He saw her eyes drop to take in his plain white shirt and faded jeans. Bare feet. She looked back up again and her eyes had grown wider, their pupils dilated. Her cheeks were more flushed. *She wanted him.*

She obviously heard movement in the kitchen and said, 'Was I longer than twenty minutes?'

He smiled. 'About forty...but I allowed for that. It seems a safe bet where a woman is concerned.'

He immediately saw the aquamarine fire in her eyes, the way her small chin tipped up, and expected a tart reply. But he wouldn't let her hand go when she tried to pull away. He had to keep touching her. It was like a compulsive need.

'You've known a lot of women, then, to make this empirical study of their time-keeping on a general level?'

Alexio's smile faded. He could see past the bluster to where there was a hint of genuine insecurity. He touched her jaw and saw her mouth firm, as if warding off his effect on her.

'I'm no monk, *glikia mou*. But neither am I half as promiscuous as the press would like to paint me. When I take lovers I'm always up front. I don't offer anything more than mutual satisfaction. I'm not into relationships right now.'

Sidonie looked at him with that incredibly direct gaze that seemed to sear straight through him.

'Okay...' she said, and smiled, showing that gap between her teeth.

Alexio wanted to throw her over his shoulder so that he could take her upstairs right now and to hell with dinner.

She grinned then in earnest, and bent down to do something. Alexio saw her shoes being kicked off on the floor and her height dropped by an inch.

'Well, seeing as you're not making an effort to wear shoes,' she clarified, 'I don't see why I have to go through the pain.'

Before he did something to inadvertently demonstrate how off-centre she made him feel, Alexio tugged her towards the dining area, where a table had been laid for two, complete with lit candles. It was by the window, with a view of London lit up by night beyond the river and the bridge.

The chef's assistant was setting out their starters and Alexio said, 'Thanks, Jonathan. I think we can take it from here. Say thank you to Michel for me.'

The young man exited swiftly.

Alexio had done this many times before—for business meals in his apartment as well as for women—but tonight it felt different. Sidonie was looking at everything with such wide eyes.

'I presumed you were joking earlier about being a vegetarian.'

Alexio lifted the platter's lid to reveal *confit* duck dumplings and saw Sidonie's eyes gleam with anticipation. It had a direct effect on his body, and he wondered if she would have that same hungry look when they made love.

She had the grace to glance at him sheepishly. 'I had you figured for a chest-beating carnivore who would be horrified at the thought of watching me chew a lettuce leaf for half an hour.'

Alexio held Sidonie's chair out for her so she could sit down, and said in a low, throaty voice as she did so, 'I had a vegetarian option lined up just in case...but don't you know by now that nothing you could have said would have put me off?'

He was rewarded by pink cheeks when he took his own

seat opposite her. He raised his glass of white wine and she took hers. *'Yiamas.'*

Sidonie repeated the Greek phrase. They both took a sip of their drinks and Alexio dished out the starter.

'Don't you know by now that nothing you could have said would have put me off?' Alexio's softly delivered words still echoed in Sidonie's head. The steel behind them...

He had just taken their dessert plates into the kitchen and Sidonie was standing on the small terrace which hugged the side of the building, leaning on the railing, with the Thames moving beneath her feet somewhere in the dark.

In all honesty she couldn't have recalled, if asked, what they'd just eaten except to know that it had been exquisite. She'd been too mesmerised by her charismatic dinner companion and how easily the conversation had flowed. Like on the plane, once they'd started they hadn't stopped. Every now and then a tiny jolt of electric shock had run through her at the realisation of where she was and with whom... She'd met him only hours before... She should be back in Dublin, reorganising her life...

She still wanted to cringe when she thought of the way Alexio had looked her up and down when she'd arrived downstairs in her jeans and T-shirt, acutely conscious of how tatty she must look. The fact that he was equally dressed down had been little comfort, because she'd almost melted on the spot at seeing him in the faded hip-hugging jeans and white shirt. He epitomised cool, laid-back elegance.

To give him credit, he hadn't made her feel uncomfortable. Just hot and bothered...

She heard a noise in the kitchen and turned round to see Alexio putting plates in a dishwasher. She shook her head wryly. Who would have believed it?

She walked back in to help. He stood up tall.

'Coffee? An after-dinner liqueur?'

Sidonie put the last plate in the dishwasher and closed the door. She'd made a decision during dinner—a momentous one. It had been helped by the direct way he'd informed her earlier that he wasn't *'into relationships'*. Well, neither was she. Not when she faced such a huge upheaval in her life, and not when she had responsibilities. And certainly not when the man was Alexio Christakos and so far out of her league it wasn't funny.

During dinner Sidonie had recalled the name of a favourite perfume of her mother's: *Ce Soir ou Jamais*. Tonight or never. This evening felt all too ephemeral. She wanted to seize the moment, live it fully. She wanted this man with a hunger she knew was rare. Once in a lifetime.

She turned and put her hands behind her against the counter and looked up. *Was she really going to do this?* Her sex spasmed in response. *Yes.* She wanted one night with this man, just one night of decadent escapism, and then she would walk away knowing what it was like to be truly made love to.

Having no idea how to go about letting a man like Alexio know what she wanted, without declaring baldly that she wanted to have sex with him, Sidonie seized on an idea. 'I'd like a liqueur, please…and did I mention that I'm a mean pool-player?'

Alexio went still and shook his head. 'No, you did not. I believe we touched on many subjects over dinner, including favourite films and music, and you tried to trick me into telling you the secrets of my success, but there was no mention of your pool abilities.'

Sidonie bit back a grin. And a sigh. This man should come with a warning label: *Approach with caution! You are liable to get burnt if you stand too close.* It was too late for her. She would burn for ever in the tormenting hell of regret if she didn't allow herself to indulge in this fantasy.

'Well, I happened to be something of a local champion in college. And I would like to challenge you to a game, Mr Christakos.'

Alexio leant back against the opposite counter and crossed his arms. 'Interesting, Miss Fitzgerald. Tell me... are there terms for this challenge?'

Sidonie crossed her arms too and tried to look mock serious—not as far out of her depth as she felt. 'Of course. My terms are simple: whoever wins gets to decide what we do for the rest of the night.'

Sidonie's heart was beating so hard now she felt light-headed. Alexio looked serious, but his eyes had darkened.

'I take it that if you win your choice will be...?'

Sidonie affected an air of piety. 'To go to bed with a good book, of course.'

His eyes flashed. 'And if I win...and I ask you nicely to come to bed with me...?'

Sidonie shrugged minutely. 'Then I guess I'll have to suffer the consequences.' She straightened up and dropped her arms. 'But you won't win, so maybe I should just leave now...'

She made to walk off and like lightning Alexio grabbed her hand and hauled her into him. Sidonie gasped. His body was hard all over, pressed against hers. Her legs promptly turned to jelly.

'Not so fast.' His voice was low, seductive. 'I believe you challenged me to a game, and in light of the fact that I'm doomed to failure I'd like to raise the stakes a little... For every shot lost, we also lose a piece of clothing.'

Sidonie's blood rushed to her every erogenous zone at the thought of seeing Alexio bared. 'There's no such game,' she said breathlessly as Alexio pulled her in the direction of the bar and games room.

'There is now, sweetheart.'

Alexio let Sidonie go when they got into the darkened

room. After he had poured them both drinks—a liqueur for her and a whisky for him—he took out two cues and handed her one. Sidonie made a big show of chalking it up while Alexio put out the balls.

When they were laid out he flourished an arm. 'Please, ladies first.'

Sidonie moved around the table, deliciously aware of Alexio's eyes on her, and yet still a little terrified. She wasn't sure what demon had made her come up with this idea—as if she thought she could make it look as if her decision *wasn't* fuelled with the desperate need she really felt. As if she played these kinds of games with men all the time.

Eventually she settled on a point to start and positioned herself, drawing back the cue. She was on the opposite side of the room to Alexio and he sat with his hip was hitched against a stool, his legs long, thighs powerful underneath the denim. Distracting her already.

'Take as long as you like,' he said, in a patronising tone which enflamed Sidonie enough for her to scatter the balls masterfully, potting her first one.

She stood up and smiled. 'You were saying…?'

Alexio scowled. 'Beginner's luck.'

Sidonie walked around the table again, aware of the tension in the small room thickening. As she took her next shot she realised too late that her palms were sweaty and the cue slipped slightly, throwing her off and making her lose her aim. She missed.

Alexio tsked and stood up. Sidonie's heart thumped hard. *For every shot lost, we also lose a piece of clothing.* Alexio smiled and it was the smile of the devil.

'I don't mind what goes, but I'd suggest your T-shirt or your trousers.'

Now Sidonie scowled. She'd thought she'd have a little more time. She'd also thought she'd have him almost naked before her, giving her time to get used to it. Then she thought of something and smiled sweetly, executing a nimble move so that she undid her bra, pulled its strap down one arm and then pulled it out neatly from the armhole of her T-shirt. An old boarding school trick.

Alexio's face darkened ominously. 'That's cheating.'

Sidonie grinned. 'Not at all. I took your suggestion on board and ignored it.'

She tossed her bright pink bra onto the seat beside her and saw Alexio's eyes follow the movement and then come back to linger on her braless chest. Her breasts felt tight and heavy, their tips pushing against the cotton of her top. Alexio's cheeks flushed and it had a direct effect on the pulse in her groin.

Slowly he put down his drink and stood up. Sidonie crossed her arms and then quickly thought better of it when Alexio's eyes widened and she realised she was only making things worse.

He took his eyes off her with visible effort. Despite all their play, Sidonie's blood was infused with a heady feminine energy at having this man look at her with such naked desire. But she got distracted when he came close and bent over the pool table right in front of her, and her eye was drawn helplessly to his taut, muscular buttocks.

She couldn't see exactly what he was doing, but he'd hit the ball and nothing was pocketed.

He turned around and said, 'Whoops...' and started undoing his shirt.

Sidonie's mouth went dry at seeing his torso revealed bit by bit. And when he shrugged the shirt off completely she went weak at the knees.

He was stunning. Beautifully muscled. Not an ounce of fat. Broad and powerful. Very masculine whorls of hair dusted his chest, leading down to that tantalising line which disappeared into his jeans. They clung precariously to his hips and Sidonie had to clench her hands to fists to stop herself reaching out to undo that top button. She gulped when she saw the bulge pushing insistently against the denim.

His rough voice cut through the heat in her brain. 'Your turn, I think.'

He turned to walk away and Sidonie felt as if someone had just hit her. His back was as beautiful as his front. Wide and smooth. He turned around at the bar and leant on it nonchalantly, arched a brow.

Sidonie forced herself to move and looked at the table. She couldn't seem to compute what to do any more. She hadn't been boasting—she knew she could play and quite possibly beat Alexio on a good day. But right now...she was useless. Eventually she saw the shot she needed to take. But she couldn't get that torso out of her mind, those muscles rippling under silken flesh. *Hard.*

Predictably, Sidonie missed the shot—because just as she moved so did Alexio. She stood up and glared across at him, feeling hot. 'Now, *that's* cheating.'

He arched a brow, all innocence wrapped up in the devil—*again*. 'I don't know what you're talking about...'

And then his look changed to one so carnal her toes curled.

'Shirt or trousers, Sidonie—unless you've got some very cute way to take off your panties from under your jeans without removing them.'

Of course she didn't. Sidonie huffed. She only had one choice, really. She wasn't about to bare herself completely to the sexiest man she'd ever met. So off came the jeans. She wriggled out of them, deliberately avoiding his gaze, self-conscious in her very plain white panties decorated with flowers.

Alexio watched with a heavy-lidded gaze as Sidonie carefully folded her jeans and put them to the side, near the bright pink splash of her bra. The same pink bra that had been tantalising him all day. The way she folded her jeans made him feel weak inside. There was something curiously vulnerable about it.

Now she looked at him, and her chin was up. *Brave*. She wasn't half as confident as she was letting on. Alexio hid the way that made him feel by focusing on her gently swaying breasts beneath her T-shirt. They were beautifully rounded and pert. Their tips hard. His mouth watered. His erection got harder. He had to shift on the stool.

Her hips were slim, but womanly. Her panties looked positively virginal with their cute flowers. Yet the way she was looking at him now as he caught her gaze again was anything but virginal. *Good*. Because when they came together Alexio knew he wouldn't have the patience to go slowly.

Aware that he couldn't actually stand up without revealing how turned on he was, Alexio said, 'I'm feeling generous. You can have another shot.'

Sidonie looked determined this time. 'That's the last piece of clothing I'll be removing.'

She picked up the cue and moved around the table again, clad only in her T-shirt and panties. The soft white cotton hugged her bottom, revealed in all its lushness now.

Alexio had to admit that his jaded palate was well and truly *un*jaded now. He'd never been so turned on in his life. He'd never been brought so close to the edge without even touching a woman before.

And then Sidonie stopped right in front of him, her back to him. He saw a sliver of pale skin, the gentle curve of her lower back just over the band of her panties. He saw the two dimples of Venus above her buttocks and nearly groaned out loud.

When she bent over the table and widened her legs to get a better aim the tiny thread holding his control together snapped completely. With a feral sound Alexio wrapped an arm around her bare midriff and deftly scooped Sidonie back against him, ignoring her soft squeal of surprise. He took the cue out of her hands, throwing it to one side.

She was breathing heavily. 'That's not fair. That's blatantly against the rules. Obstruction.'

'Damn the rules,' Alexio growled, turning Sidonie around to face him. Her eyes were dark blue now, the pupils huge.

'You win. I forfeit the game,' he said.

Sidonie couldn't hide the crestfallen expression on her face as she obviously considered for a second that she had been hoist by her own petard. Alexio wanted to howl in triumph, but he played it out.

'So I guess this means you're going to bed with a book then?'

Sidonie looked sheepish. 'I don't have one with me apart from my textbook.'

Alexio made a face. 'Too bad…maybe I can change your mind?'

'How are you going to do that?'

Sidonie's breath was getting choppier. Her breasts under their thin cotton covering were teasing his bare skin now, making him harder.

'Like this…'

Alexio picked her up and sat her on the edge of the pool table, then came to stand between her spread legs. He cupped her face and her jaw in his hands and did what he'd been aching to do all evening: he covered her mouth with his and sank into dark, sweet, urgent oblivion.

Sidonie clutched Alexio's wide shoulders, her fingers digging into smooth hot skin. The question had been asked and answered. He knew she wanted this.

He felt so good between her legs—so big. Instinctively her bare thighs tightened around him, and the friction of her skin against the tough denim was exquisite. Their tongues met and duelled fiercely, stroking, sucking. Between Sidonie's legs she spasmed and squirmed, seeking more contact with Alexio.

She was barely aware of one of his big hands leaving her face and going to the bottom of her T-shirt, tugging it up, urging her to lift her arms so he could lift it off completely, breaking the contact between their mouths to do so.

She opened her eyes and felt dizzy. Her T-shirt was a blur of grey behind Alexio, hanging precariously on the stool. Now she only wore her panties.

He looked down between their bodies and his hot gaze rested on her bared breasts. Sidonie had been naked in front of a man before…but it had never felt like this. As if she was on fire from the inside out. Her breasts literally throbbed for his touch. Aching…

He cupped them, making her flesh tingle. His thumbs rubbed back and forth across her tight, sensitised nipples and Sidonie dragged in a painful breath. Her heart was beating so loudly she thought it had to be audible.

'You're beautiful…'

Sidonie shook her head, about to deny his compliment, but he took the words out of her mouth as he pushed her back slightly and bent to take one straining peak into his mouth, sucking hard. Sidonie gasped. One hand went to his head, fingers tangling in short silky hair, the other moved behind her, balancing.

It was as if a wire of need was linked directly to the pulse between her legs, tightening the tension inside her, making her arch her back towards him. She felt desperate, wanton. When he moved to her other breast his hand cupped her intimately between her legs, and Sidonie moaned as he pressed against her where every nerve seemed to be screaming out for release.

One of Alexio's fingers slipped behind her underwear

and stroked her where she ached most. Sidonie's breath stopped completely. His mouth was on her breast and that wicked finger was circling, exploring...

She was approaching her peak... She could sense it... The rhythmic pulsations of her body were gathering force—and then Alexio abruptly pulled back and stood up. Sidonie had to put her hands on his hips to stay upright. Everything had turned molten inside her.

'Not here...' he said roughly, his breath uneven.

'Wh—?'

But Sidonie's question was halted as she was scooped up into Alexio's arms and he strode through the apartment to the stairs. Her arms had gone around his neck automatically and the friction of his chest against her deeply sensitised breasts was almost excruciating.

She looked at his face and his jaw was tight. He glanced down at her and that sexy mouth tipped up at one corner. Butterflies danced with the lava in her belly.

He said, 'I refuse to take you on a pool table for the first time. I've been fantasising all day about laying you out and tasting every inch of you, and for that we need a bed.'

The heat inside Sidonie shot to boiling point at the thought of him *fantasising* about this, and at the thought of being spreadeagled, naked, for this man to explore. And that this would be their *first* time, not their only time.

'Oh...' was all she could manage as Alexio shouldered his way into his room, which was dark apart from one low light in the corner and the glittering lights of the city outside.

When he got to the bed he laid Sidonie down and stood back. She was breathless. Her body was still hovering on the edge of fulfilment and she ached for completion. But she sensed that Alexio wasn't about to allow either of them a quick release.

As if reading her mind, he said throatily, 'I want you so

much that I'm tempted to take you now, hard and fast... I want to...'

She'd never experienced hard and fast. She'd experienced mundane and underwhelming. Feeling unaccountably shy, although she was all but naked and panting for the man, Sidonie said in a small voice, 'I don't mind...'

Alexio shook his head and looked grim, his hands going to his jeans, where Sidonie's eyes dropped to watch with mounting fascination.

'No, you don't get off that easily—not after that little sideshow back there.'

Sidonie couldn't drag her gaze back up. She could only watch, helpless, as Alexio opened his buttons and then pushed his jeans down, taking his underwear with them. Her eyes widened and she went even hotter, if that was possible. He was...*magnificent*. And *big*.

A shiver of trepidation ran through her and finally she managed to look at him.

He almost grimaced at her wide eyes. 'Another reason why this won't be hard and fast... I need to make sure you're ready... I don't want to hurt you.'

His concern made Sidonie's chest constrict, and even through the heat haze engulfing her she was aware of a little voice: *danger...danger...*

But then Alexio was bending over her, his big hands making quick work of her underwear, tugging it off her hips and down her legs.

He stood back and looked at her again. Sidonie wanted to turn away and hide herself. Instantly self-conscious. Was he measuring her up against his last lover? Finding her wanting? A disappointment? Did the fact that she wasn't shaved everywhere turn him off?

She brought her arm over her breasts and turned her head, unable to watch him looking at her so intently. And then the bed dipped and his long, powerful body was beside her, legs touching hers, his erection between them, his arms coming around her.

'Don't feel shy...' His hand tipped her chin towards him so she had to meet his gaze. 'You're beautiful...and I want you more than I've ever wanted anyone.'

Sidonie looked into those gorgeous exotic eyes and searched for some hint of insincerity. She couldn't see it. She could see something, though—something unguarded for a moment, as if he was surprised by what he'd said. She was afraid of the tug of emotion in the pit of her being.

Suddenly Sidonie was aware of thinking too much again, and she put her hand up to touch his jaw, reached up to kiss him. All she knew was that she wanted him too—more than anything she'd ever experienced.

When he drew her into his body so that they were touching length to length a wave of intense desire washed through her, brushing aside any doubts and questions. She wanted Alexio to slide into her right then, couldn't bear the thought of the drawn-out torture he'd promised to inflict, and as if reading her mind—*again*—he stopped and pulled back for a moment.

His voice was guttural. 'I don't think I can wait—as much as I want to...'

Sidonie moved so that his leg slid between hers. She could feel how wet she was, ready for him, and she moved against his thigh. His eyes flared.

'I don't want you to wait... I need you too.'

It was a primal, urgent request. Alexio reached behind him to a small cabinet by the bed and took something out. Sidonie realised what it was when he ripped open the foil packet and stroked the condom onto his thick length.

Pressing her down, Alexio came over her, pushing her legs apart. He reached between them and touched her with his fingers, stroking her, entering her. She bent her knees on either side of him and had to bite the inside of her cheek to stop herself from begging him to stop…to go on.

And then he took his hand away and he was guiding the thickness of his erection to her soft folds, pushing in gently, stretching her. Pushing deeper. He was awe-inspiring as he loomed over her. Shoulders broad and powerful, chest sheened with sweat. He pushed her knees further apart, baring her to him completely. Demanding she open up to him.

Something was happening inside Sidonie—some awakening. She'd had sex before, but this felt different. Infinitely different. Slowly, inch by torturous inch, Alexio slid into her, giving her time to adapt and take him, his eyes never leaving hers. She saw sweat break out on his brow, felt the tension in his big body.

'*Moro mou*…you're so tight…'

Instinctively Sidonie tilted her hips, forcing Alexio to thrust deeper, and the movement made her gasp. He filled her now completely.

'Are you okay?' he asked.

Sidonie was speechless. But she nodded. She *was* okay. More than okay. She felt whole, joined to him like this. She moved her hips again experimentally and Alexio drew out a little. Her body clasped at him as he went, already relishing the moment when he would slide back in again, seeking for that delicious friction.

With slow, deliberate thrusts Alexio moved in and out, and the storm grew again inside Sidonie, increasing in its strength and power. With every move of Alexio's body within hers something tightened inside her. He thrust a little harder and Sidonie welcomed it, feeling it burn but not noticing because she ached for it too much.

The tempo changed, became more desperate. Sidonie was aware of small sounds coming from her mouth—moans and laboured breathing, incoherent words. Alexio's body moved faster within hers now, gathering pace. He came closer, hands cupping her face, tangling in her hair, as his mouth met hers and his body thrust powerfully over and over again.

His tongue stabbed deep and she stroked him fiercely, teeth nipping, holding him to her with a desperation as they raced together, hearts thumping in unison.

Sidonie's arms were around his neck, her breasts pressed flat against his chest. She wrapped her legs around his hips. The crescendo was building, leaving her no control over anything. She was part of something huge, magical. Their mouths clung, their kisses became more desperate, biting, and then, just when she thought her body would break in two with the building tension, it broke apart into a million tiny pieces on a wave of orgasmic pleasure, robbing Sidonie of every rational thought. She was flung high into a place she'd never dreamed existed.

Alexio's powerful body thrust one more time and he broke free of their kiss and shouted out as his release swept him up too, seconds behind her.

Sidonie realised she was trembling in the aftermath and was horrified. She tried to pull away from Alexio but he only dragged her closer, wrapping his arms around her until the tremors ceased. She felt more than a little overwhelmed. Alexio pulled his head back and looked at her. She was almost afraid to look at him—afraid he might see something she wasn't ready to expose yet.

'Sidonie…?'

Reluctantly she looked at him and his eyes were molten, still. It had an instant effect on her body. Already. She felt ashamed. How could she want him again so soon?

He was frowning now, pulling away from her, and she tried not to be acutely aware of her nakedness, of feeling vulnerable.

He rested on one elbow. 'Did I hurt you? You weren't innocent?'

Sidonie came up on one elbow too. She shook her head, her hair falling forward. Alexio brushed it back and something about that small gesture heartened her. 'No,' she admitted huskily. 'I've been with a couple of guys. In college. But…it was never like that…I didn't…'

She stopped and went puce, looked down at the sheet. Predictably Alexio tipped her chin up again, not letting her escape.

'You didn't…what? Come like that?'

Sidonie shook her head, mortified to be talking about this when she imagined that his usual post-coital repartee must be far more sophisticated. Still, she was stuck now.

'No,' she got out. 'I mean, I've…*come*…before, but not during sex. Not with a guy.'

Alexio's voice seemed to drop an octave and it sent shivers of sensation right to her core. 'You mean you've experienced it when you've…?'

'Done it to myself. Yes…'

Sidonie glared at him now, beyond embarrassed, and not remotely mollified by the way his eyes had darkened suspiciously. 'Can we stop talking about this now?'

Sidonie reached for the sheet, trying to tuck it around her, but Alexio swatted her hands away and pulled her into him, making her gasp when tender flesh came into contact with his fast reviving arousal.

'I'm glad you told me,' he said gruffly. 'And those guys were idiots.'

The embarrassment drained away, leaving Sidonie feeling the effects of their lovemaking again. Her body was sensitive all over, but sated in a way that was truly wicked.

With awe-inspiring strength Alexio scooped her up and took her into the bathroom with its black-tiled shower. He put her down, keeping an arm around her, and leaned in to turn on the powerful spray. Then he walked her into the shower, following right behind her.

It was pure bliss to have steaming water pounding her skin and then Alexio's big hands, soapy, running all over her body. Over her breasts and belly, down between her legs, across her buttocks. His touch wasn't overtly sexual, but she could see his erection and her body hummed with satisfaction, ready to flare fully back to life if only she wasn't feeling equally ready to crawl into a small space and sleep.

She could only sag against the wall and look at him, so huge and dark in the hot mist, like some kind of pagan warrior. She was boneless, and as if he could sense the lethargy rolling through her body he turned off the spray and wrapped her in a towel, rubbing her brusquely before scooping up her long hair and wrapping it up turban-style.

Then he picked her up again and Sidonie protested weakly. 'I *can* walk, you know.' But even as she said the words she doubted that she could walk right now.

Alexio pulled back the covers and laid her gently on the bed. Sidonie's eyes were already closing and she fought to keep them open, aware of the towel on her head.

'My hair will be frizzy...' she protested sleepily.

Alexio pulled a cover over her, still naked and damp from the shower himself. Sidonie was very aware of that.

'Shh, it'll be fine. You need to rest now. I'll be back in a minute.' He pressed his mouth to her forehead.

Sidonie cracked her eyes open enough to see Alexio drag on his jeans, leaving them tantalisingly open, before he walked out of the room. And then it was too much to fight. She slid into sweet oblivion.

CHAPTER FIVE

WHEN ALEXIO POURED whisky into the glass his hand was shaking. He'd had to get away from Sidonie and he cursed himself for thinking it would be a good idea to take her into the shower. Washing her supple body, seeing her delicate skin marked after their making love and knowing he couldn't touch her again so soon, had been a torture he wouldn't inflict on an enemy.

He'd barely been able to walk away from her in bed, even though her eyes had been closing.

Sex. It had been sex. Alexio knew all about sex. He'd been having it and excelling at it pretty much since he'd been seduced by the sister of a friend of his older brother at the age of fifteen.

But what he'd just experienced up there in his bedroom, with someone he'd met mere hours before, had not been any kind of sex he knew. It had blown his mind. And yet they'd done nothing kinky... Apart from that little striptease downstairs it had been perfectly straightforward. Sidonie obviously wasn't experienced.

Alexio's brain struggled to grapple with this anomaly. Was it that? That she was a little gauche? Was his palate so jaded that the sheer novelty of an inexperienced lover turned him on?

But he knew in his gut it was more than that. Deeper. And he hated to admit it. Alexio threw the whisky down his throat as if it could burn away the hunger that was already building again, which had abated only for mere seconds after his orgasm. He prided himself on his stamina, but this was ridiculous.

When he went back into his room Sidonie had shifted to lie on her front. The sheet clung precariously to her bottom, barely hiding its voluptuous swell, and those dimples were making his mouth water. Her hair had come out of the towel, which had been flung aside haphazardly, and the damp strawberry golden tresses were spread out around her head like glowing halo.

Alexio curled his hands into fists. No way could he go near her on that bed and not rouse her and make love to her again. Silently he turned and took his aching body to his office, where he tried to distract himself with some work.

After staring at the computer screen for a while and seeing nothing but the memory of Sidonie's face as he'd slid into her tight body for the first time, he sat back and rubbed his hands over his face. This was crazy. He was useless. He needed Sidonie again. *Now.*

When he padded back into the bedroom she had moved again and now lay on her back, the sheet pulled up, just about covering her breasts. She moved minutely, as if sensing him. He came close to the bed and saw those dark lashes flutter on pale cheeks scored with pink. Her mouth moved and he wanted to cover it with his. His gaze was riveted to its lush lines and he wondered again how he'd dismissed her at first glance.

'Hey...'

Her husky voice startled him. Her eyes were open, slumberous. Shy. Something punched him in the gut. He had the bizarre feeling that everything in his life up till now had been a bit of a blur and he quashed it ruthlessly. This was no different from anything he'd done before. It was a little more intense, maybe...good chemistry. That was it.

'Hey, yourself…mind if I join you?'

Sidonie shook her head and Alexio undid his jeans, taking them off. When he got into bed he couldn't *not* reach for Sidonie and she came willingly, her arms sliding around him like missing pieces of a jigsaw fitting together. Their mouths found each other and before Alexio could articulate another word he was giving up any attempt to rationalise what was happening because the urge not to think and just to *act* was stronger than anything he could resist.

'I want you to come to Greece with me.'

Sidonie was in paradise. A paradise where she felt at peace and sated and in a state of bliss she'd only ever read about. And that gorgeous voice…

'Sid…wake up.'

Sid. No one had ever called her that before. She liked it. A mouth brushed hers and Sidonie instinctively followed it, seeking more. The by now familiar spurt of desire and awareness was rousing her. *Arousing* her.

She opened her eyes to see Alexio's hard-boned stunning face and bare torso. She was aware of light flooding the big sparse room. Daylight. She blinked. Alexio hovered over her on one arm. His jaw was dark with stubble and she recalled feeling the delicious abrasion on her skin, her thighs. Her belly swooped alarmingly. A jumble of X-rated images tumbled through her mind and she had to breathe to try and not let them overwhelm her.

She remembered him waking her last night…making love to her again. Showing her that the first time, as spectacular as it had been, had only been a precursor. She'd never known it could be like that—so intensely, violently pleasurable. So altering. She felt different.

Alexio was looking at her, waiting for her to say something. Her voice felt rusty, hoarse from crying out over and over again. 'What did you say?'

His hand was on her bare belly under the sheet now and it quivered. Instantly Sidonie's body came to life, nerves tingling, skin tightening. As if well aware of his effect on her, Alexio moved his hand up with exquisite slowness until he cupped her breast, trapping her nipple between his fingers, tightening it gently, enough to pinch.

Sidonie sucked in a breath, wide awake now.

'I said,' he repeated, 'I want you to come to Greece with me. I have a place on Santorini. I've decided to take a few days' break…'

Sidonie automatically went to shake her head but Alexio's hand left her breast and swept up to cup her chin.

Softly he said, 'We've been here before, Sid…you know what happens if you say no to me.'

Sid. The way he said it made her feel as if she were drowning—as if she'd known this man for aeons when it had been a mere twenty-four hours. All she could see were those amazing golden-green eyes, hypnotising her. Drugging her.

'You said yourself you don't have a job to go back to…so why not extend your trip for a few days? Come with me… and I'll show you paradise.'

He bent his head to kiss Sidonie and she felt like letting out a short, shocked laugh. He'd already unwittingly shown her paradise. But then his mouth was on hers and she couldn't think. She struggled to try and focus. She knew that her aunt was safe and secure for a couple of weeks. All that responsibility hovered in the wings, but it didn't have to be dealt with right at this moment—could she stretch one night into a few days? She wanted to, with a fierceness that surprised her.

As Alexio moved over her body, sinking his hips between her thighs, his erection hard and ready, Sidonie was melting, weakening. She wasn't ready to walk away yet…

she wanted more of this man. More of this fantasy. More of this wicked self-indulgence.

She wrapped her arms around his neck and opened her legs to him and then, when he stopped kissing her for a few seconds, just before he joined their bodies, Sidonie looked up at him and said huskily, 'Okay…I'll come with you.'

Alexio Christakos was a magician. A sexy, devilish magician. Just over twenty-four hours after meeting him he had magicked her to an island in another country. Where everything was painted blue and white, where the sun sparkled overhead, and where the glittering sea stretched as far as the eye could see. There was nothing but the hazy shapes of more islands in the distance to break the horizon line.

Her hand was wrapped tightly in his as he showed her around his stupendously gorgeous villa near Oia, on the north-west coast of Santorini. Sidonie could feel the faint burn of secret muscles after the long hours of intense lovemaking the previous night. If she stopped to think about it all for a second she might explode…so she bit her lip and tried not to gape as he showed her into the master suite, which led directly out to a terrace featuring an infinity pool.

He glanced back at her, saying, 'I know you didn't exactly come prepared…there are some clothes here for your use.'

Sidonie watched as he let her hand go to open double doors which led into a walk-in closet. His clothes were hung up and laid out on the left hand side and the right hand side was bursting with a glorious kaleidoscope of colours and textures.

A funny pain lanced her chest. Of *course* he had a wardrobe stocked with women's clothes. This had to be a frequent pitstop for him with his lovers/mistresses. He was a generous man. She was sure many of the garments must still be unworn.

To buy time, and hide her reaction, Sidonie reached out and fingered a piece of silk which felt as delicate as air in her hands.

This whole experience was transitory and all this was doing was driving the point home. She had to *not* think about things like how attentive he'd been on the flight to Athens on his private jet—distracting her from her fear of flying with drugging kisses. Or the revelation on the helicopter flight to the island that instead of feeling her fear increasing she'd felt exhilarated.

Sidonie forced herself to smile and said with bright joviality, 'Well, at least I won't have to worry about washing my knickers out in the sink. I'm sure your housekeeper would be horrified.'

She looked at him and her smile slipped a little as she saw something hard in his eyes—something she hadn't seen before. But before she could dwell on it he'd stabbed his fingers deep in her hair and tipped her face up to his, distracting her with a mind-altering kiss.

When he finally pulled away they were breathing harshly and Sidonie's body trembled all over. She still wasn't used to this unprecedented physical reaction—as if she were some kind of a puppet and he could control her responses at will. It made her feel intensely vulnerable.

'Get changed and let's go for a swim.'

Sidonie burned at the thought of seeing Alexio's seminaked body just for her private pleasure.

She managed a rough-sounding, 'Okay.'

And when he gently turned her around and pushed her in the direction of that wall of clothes again Sidonie tried in vain to stem the flood of emotions that made her hands shake as she searched for the relevant garments.

Sidonie wrapped her legs around Alexio's waist and her arms around his neck. His back was broad, strong and smooth between her legs and against her chest. They were both wet and salty after swimming in the sea at the bottom of a precipitous set of stone steps leading directly down from the villa. His arms were looped under her thighs as he carried her piggyback-style back up.

The sun was hot on Sidonie's back and Alexio grumbled good-naturedly, 'I'm not a mule, you know.'

She grinned and pressed a kiss to Alexio's neck, feeling his arms tighten under her legs. 'I know. You're much, much better-looking than a mule, and far more comfortable.'

She rested her head on his shoulder for a moment, squinting her eyes at the glittering endless azure blue of the sea. Three days had passed since they'd arrived at his villa. Three days of sun, sea and… She blushed at the thought of all the mind-blowing sex.

They'd only left the villa once. Yesterday evening Alexio had taken her out on a small boat into the Caldera where he'd surprised her with a light supper complete with wine. They'd had prime position for watching the famous Santorini sunset and Sidonie had never seen anything so stunning or special.

She'd felt absurdly emotional at the beauty of everything…at the experience that this man was unwittingly giving her when her life was about to change so dramatically. She was storing up every moment—morsels she would take out at a later date and comfort herself with.

An all but invisible housekeeper at the villa left out food at strategic times, so she and Alexio had done little but eat and sleep and make love. Sidonie felt sated on a level she'd never known before. Sated…but curiously unfulfilled too.

Conversation with Alexio never went beyond the superficial. It felt almost as if the level of closeness and intimacy she'd experienced when they'd first met had been closed off.

But then what had she expected? This was transient.

Alexio didn't do relationships, and neither was she in any position to cleave herself to a man.

Sidonie had realised that the only way she could get through this and remain in any way protected was to try and fool Alexio into believing that this wasn't half as special for her as it really was. So she was doing her best to project an air of vague nonchalance. Every time her mouth wanted to drop open in awe, or she wanted to squeal with excitement, she reined it in.

Because if she let her guard slip for a second Sidonie was terrified he would read the depth of her emotions—and as she wasn't even prepared to inspect them herself she certainly wasn't ready for his laser-like gaze to see them.

'I want to take you out tonight.'

Sidonie murmured something indistinct. Her cheek rested on Alexio's chest and one of her legs was thrown over his thighs. He could feel his body stir against her and despite the sated languor of his body he could have groaned. When would it end? This ever-present hunger?

His fingers trailed up and down Sidonie's spine. After carrying her up the steps from the sea earlier he'd walked her straight underneath the outdoor shower on his terrace, near the glittering infinity pool. The cool spray had done little to stem hisdesire. Within seconds Sidonie had been in his arms, her body pressed against his, and they'd inevitably ended up in bed.

Alexio forced his mind from the memory because it made him uncomfortable. 'Did you hear me, Sid? I want to take you out tonight...'

Sidonie eventually lifted her head and looked at Alexio with slumberous eyes and deliciously tousled hair. 'You might have to give me a piggyback again.'

Alexio tipped her chin up, averting her hungry gaze

from his mouth to his eyes. 'No. You're not going to tempt me again. We'll pretend we're civilised if it kills us.'

Sidonie shifted slightly so that she was moving on top of Alexio. His blood started to sizzle all over again. She spread her thighs either side of him and her breasts touched his chest, the hard nipples scraping against his chest hair, making him thicken with need.

He could see something in her eyes—something innately feminine and full of wicked mystery. She wriggled her bottom so that his erection pressed against her body, where she was already damp, ready for him again. And just like that Alexio had to give up any pretence that he could be civilised.

He took her hips in his hands, pushing her back so that he could thrust up and into her. Sidonie gasped at the intrusion and then sighed voluptuously as her body began to move against him, the delicious dance of desire starting all over again.

'Witch…' Alexio muttered as their movements became more urgent and they gave themselves up to the inexorable ride into ecstasy.

Alexio was waiting for Sidonie to emerge from the villa after her shower late that evening. The sun had set a while ago. They'd watched it from a lounger by the pool, both languid after their intense lovemaking. The spectacular sky was now fading into a faint orange and pink hue and the famous lights of Santorini's west coast were coming on.

Alexio was oblivious to it, though. He was feeling more and more off-balance. Exposed. And, even worse, vulnerable. The last time he'd felt like this had been in front of his mother as a child, when she'd coldly infected him with her cynicism. From then till now it had formed a part of his protective armour. It had become a second skin, and everything in his life had merely compounded his world view.

As soon as he'd turned his back on his inheritance so publicly his coterie of so-called friends and hangers-on had left him—apart from one or two people and his brother. Then, as soon as he'd shown signs of making a fortune, they'd come back in their droves.

Nothing much had surprised him after that telling experiment in human nature—as if he hadn't had enough lessons from his parents. *Until Sidonie.* She surprised him. She was like a whirling dervish, smashing everything in her path and taking him with her. He'd had no intention of taking a few days' holiday until he'd woken up beside her in London the morning after that night and felt the insistent throb of hunger in his blood and his body.

No way could he have let her go.

He'd known one night wouldn't be enough, but he'd felt then as if a month wouldn't be long enough to sate himself with her. Feeling slightly panicked, Alexio had decided that the best thing to do would be to take her away, so that he could indulge this desire day and night and let it burn out.

However, this was the third night, and he felt as if a lifetime wouldn't be enough to sate himself with Sidonie. He'd done his best to hold her at a distance, deliberately curbing the way she made him want to relax and speak whatever was on his mind. But it was hard. And getting harder.

When she'd leapt onto his back earlier, to be carried up the steps, Alexio's chest had swelled with an emotion that had made him shake. No woman he knew was so impulsive, so tactile, so effortlessly affectionate.

Yet despite her easy affection she wasn't suffocating him with emotion—far from it. She was holding back—exuding an air of nonchalance.

Something dark inside him had raised its ugly head. *Suspicion.* He remembered showing her the closet full of clothes on that first day. He'd expected shock, awe, gushing gratitude. Even his most cynical lovers never failed to put on an act when he presented them with gifts. But Sidonie, whom he would never have put in their category, had been completely blasé, and since then he hadn't been able to push down a niggle of disquiet.

One minute she was like an open book, her expressions as unguarded as a child's and equally disarming. The next she was as mysterious as the Sphinx, exhibiting an age-old feminine mystique that made him wonder if he was being completely naïve.

Alexio didn't like the reminder that from the moment he'd met Sidonie on that plane he'd been acting out of character. He *never* encouraged a woman to stay overnight in his apartment, even if they'd had dinner there. And he certainly never took off at a moment's notice, throwing his normally rigid schedule out of the window.

The growing doubt had prompted Alexio to put in a call to his most trusted employee and personal friend—his solicitor—just a short while before. He was one of the few who had stuck by Alexio's side through his lean times. Pushing down a feeling of guilt, he had instructed him to engage someone to do a background check into Sidonie.

His friend had chuckled. 'I thought you only did this when you wanted to take over another company or find an adversary's weak points? Now you're including your lovers?'

He'd answered far more curtly than he'd intended. 'Just do it, Demetrius. I don't expect a discussion about it.'

Despite the guilt he'd felt at taking such action, when Alexio had put the phone down he'd felt some semblance of equilibrium return. Sidonie hadn't scrambled his head so badly that he wasn't still aware of protecting himself. He *was* in control.

That control was about to be shot to pieces, though, as he heard a sound and turned around. Sidonie had emerged onto the terrace and for a long second Alexio literally lost his breath. All he could feel was his heart pounding as it struggled without oxygen.

The dress was a burnt orange colour and silk. Looped over one shoulder, and strapless on the other side, It had a big hole cut out over one hip, showing off the naked indentation of Sidonie's waist. A hint of one breast was visible just above the top of the dress as it swooped over her chest, hugging the delicious curve. The silk fell to her knees, but one leg peeped out of a thigh-high slit.

She was wearing nothing that he hadn't already seen on other lovers. He'd seen far less. But Alexio had to battle the very strong urge to tell her to go back and change, like an over-protective father. Or a mindlessly jealous lover, imagining the effect she'd have on other men. That thought alone made him stop and take in a breath. His chest swelled painfully.

'Is it okay?'

Sidonie was frowning, plucking at the dress. She looked at Alexio and this was one of those moments when she looked endearingly exposed, reminding him of the woman he'd met on the plane—all at once spiky and yet vulnerable.

'Come here,' he husked.

Sidonie moved towards him and Alexio had to bite back a groan of need. One long, slender leg was displayed in all its provocative glory as she walked towards him, her dainty feet encased in gold peeptoe heels.

She stopped before him and looked up. Her hair lay loose and long around her shoulders, glinting like golden fire in the dusky light. Her skin had already taken on a golden glow from the sun, despite the copious amounts of factor fifty he'd insisted she keep putting on—much to her disgust. Her freckles had exploded and magnified across her nose and cheeks. And her shoulders.

When Alexio finally felt able to touch her without tipping her over his shoulder and taking her back inside, he slid a hand around the back of her neck. That silky fall of hair against his hand made his body throb.

'You look...stunning.'

The vulnerability he'd seen dissipated and Sidonie smiled. 'Thank you...so do you.'

Alexio was used to compliments and they always felt empty. Except when she said it. He took his hand away, because he knew if he did something like kiss her now he'd never stop. Instead he took her hand and led her out of the villa to a nearby hidden garage which housed a sports car—one of his brother's new models.

It was a convertible, and Sidonie whistled in appreciation as she got in. Alexio held the door open for her, trying his best not to look at her exposed leg. Dammit, maybe he *should* get her to change?

Gritting his jaw, and wondering why on earth he'd thought taking her out would be a good idea, he got in the other side and soon they were driving along the coast, towards the bustling night-life of Fira.

As Alexio's car swept them along the coast of the island, and the sky became darker over the expanse of the sea, the lights of the houses and dwellings and the approaching town of Fira made everything look like a fairytale. Alexio was driving relatively slowly on the narrow roads and the cool evening air was delicious on Sidonie's sun-heated skin.

She shivered when she thought about how gorgeous Alexio had looked on the terrace against the setting sun, dressed in a dark suit with a dark shirt. The more time she spent with him, the more gorgeous he seemed to get. She felt weak inside when she thought of how protective he was, too, making sure she wore a high-factor cream in the sun.

'But I want to get *some* colour!' Sidonie had protested earlier.

Alexio had held her down easily on the lounger and proceeded to slather her with cream, saying sternly, 'You are *not* damaging your skin.'

Then she'd got so distracted by where his hands were going that she hadn't had the strength to fight him...

'Are you cold?'

Sidonie blushed in the darkening light and shook her head. 'No, I'm fine. I like the freshness.'

Alexio looked back to the road. 'I should have made you bring a jacket. It still gets cool at night this time of year.'

Sidonie smiled. 'You can't help yourself, can you?'

'Can't help what?'

'Being protective. I bet you were like that with your mother.'

Alexio made a noise then. It sounded like something between a snort and a cough and Sidonie looked at him. After a minute he glanced at her and she could see that his jaw was tense. The air was definitely cooler now.

'Believe me...' his tone was icy '...my mother did not need a protector. Anything but.'

Sidonie frowned, 'Why do you say that? What was she like?'

Alexio's jaw got even tighter. Sidonie could see it reflected in the lights of the dashboard.

'She was self-contained. Aloof. And she didn't need anyone.'

Sidonie held in a gasp at his stark words. 'Everyone needs someone—even if they don't want to admit it. You make her sound lonely.'

Eventually Alexio responded, just as the town of Fira came into view. 'Maybe she was... But I don't really want to discuss my mother when we have far more exciting things to talk about—like where I'm going to take you clubbing.'

Sidonie felt the door slam in her face with his terse delivery. His personal life was obviously a no-go area. She thought of the darkness in her own past, and how she'd hate for Alexio to know about it, and figured maybe it was for the best that he wasn't inviting this kind of intimacy.

She turned and faced the front and saw the stunning cavalcade of lights in the town as it seemed to drop precipitously to the gaping black of the sea. Momentarily distracted, Sidonie breathed, 'This is beautiful.'

Alexio was parking the car outside an upmarket-looking hotel and a young man was rushing out. 'We have to walk from here; the streets are pedestrianised,' Alexio explained as he got out.

He threw the keys to the young man, who was all but drooling at the sight of the stunning car, then came around to Sidonie's door and opened it for her, giving her his hand to help her out. Sidonie felt shaky and insecure at the thought of being seen in public with Alexio.

He kept her hand in his and said a few words in Greek to the man, whose face went pale. Then they walked away.

'What did you say to him?' Sidonie asked curiously.

Alexio smiled. 'I told him that if I came back to find one mark on the car I'd break his legs.'

'Oh...' Sidonie held in a giggle when she thought of the man paling so dramatically. 'Well, that makes things clear for him.' Her fingers tightened around his hand and she looked up. 'You wouldn't, though, would you? Break his legs?'

Alexio stopped and looked down, horrified, 'Of course not—what do you take me for? I just told him he'd be paying me out of his wages for the rest of his life.'

Sidonie tucked her other arm around Alexio's and said with mock relief, 'Okay—that's so much better than broken legs.'

Alexio looked down. He could see the smile playing around Sidonie's mouth, and that tantalising glimpse of long and slender leg. He could feel her breast against his arm and had to grit his jaw. It still felt tight after her questions about his mother... *'You make her sound lonely.'*

The truth was that Alexio had always had the impression that his mother *had* been lonely, and he didn't like the way Sidonie's innocent comments had brought him back to a time when it had been all too apparent that he couldn't protect his mother simply because she would not allow it. Not even when she needed it.

He forced his train of thought away from that unwelcome memory. They were approaching a narrow street with a glittering array of jewellery shops and Sidonie had stopped, enthralled, outside the first one.

She sighed deeply and sent a quick rueful glance to Alexio. 'I have to admit to a deeply unattractive trait: a love for glittery objects. My father used to say I was like a magpie, obsessed with shiny things. I used to collect the most random objects and put them in a box in my room and then take them out to look at them.'

Sidonie looked at the display again and Alexio couldn't stop the prickle of something across the back of his neck. The sensation of exposure was strong, along with something like disappointment. A feeling of inevitability. This was what he was used to. Women cajoling, seeking something. And even though Sidonie wasn't going about it in a way he was used to wasn't it the same thing? She was hinting that she loved jewellery and that she expected him to spoil her with some.

She looked up at him then and must have seen something in his expression. She frowned. 'What is it?'

Quickly he schooled his features. 'Nothing.' His voice was tight. 'The club is just down here.'

CHAPTER SIX

SIDONIE FELT AS if she'd done something wrong. The look on Alexio's face just now had been almost...*disgusted.* She felt stupid for blurting out that she'd always loved glittery things. It was a trait that she'd inherited from her mother and Sidonie didn't like to be reminded of that. Especially when she knew deep down that it wasn't like her mother's love for real jewels. When she'd found her childhood jewellery box during the clearing of the house after her father had died she could almost have laughed, because it was full of ten-cent pieces, buttons and tin foil. Hardly a treasure trove.

Sidonie tried to push down the sense of disquiet and followed Alexio into a very mysterious-looking doorway with no name on it. A man in a black suit with an earpiece let them in with a deferential nod to Alexio.

Determined to put his reaction out of her mind, Sidonie tightened her hand reflexively in Alexio's and he looked down at her. She was relieved to see that the tightness in his expression was gone and that the lazy, sexy insouciance was back.

Another entrance was just ahead, with billowing white curtains wafting in the breeze. A stunning glamazon of a woman stepped out, dressed in a tiny black dress which showcased her astounding body.

Sidonie nearly tripped over her heels and Alexio steadied her, looking down. 'Okay?'

Sidonie nodded, still struck dumb by the dark-haired Greek beauty who was now greeting Alexio *very warmly* with kisses on each cheek—far too close to his mouth for Sidonie's liking. She felt something rise within her—something hot and acrid. *Jealousy.*

The woman turned her gaze on Sidonie and dismissed her with a cool glance before turning back to Alexio. She pouted ruby-red lips and proceeded to talk to Alexio in Greek, which Sidonie of course couldn't follow.

Alexio replied in English, though, saying, 'I've been too busy to come back. This is Sidonie—Sidonie, this is Elettra.'

Sidonie smiled, but the other women barely smiled back at all. It was like the air hostess all over again. Far from making Sidonie feel triumphant that she had the man everyone wanted, it only made her feel insecure. Was Alexio even now looking at this woman and wishing he was availing himself of her charms instead of gauche, inexperienced Sidonie's?

But then the sight of the interior of the club took every thought out of Sidonie's head. It was a massive, cavernous, breathtaking space. Dark and dimly lit with what seemed to be a thousand lanterns. A huge bar took up one entire wall. There was a dance floor with glowing boxes of neon lights in the old Studio 54 style. There were booths and private tables dotted around the place, and then there was a whole other level down below which was already heaving with people.

Beautiful people were everywhere. Funky music throbbed from the sound system. It was achingly hip and exclusive.

Elettra was leading them to a booth, her hips swaying sinuously in her teeny-tiny dress. When they got there Sidonie could see that they had a bird's eye view of the entire place, and almost immediately after Elettra left—with clear reluctance—an equally stunning-looking waitress was there to take their orders. She was dressed in tiny shorts and a white shirt with very low-cut buttons. She had a pinafore-style apron that did little to detract from the sexiness of the outfit—if anything it fetishised it slightly.

Sidonie felt seriously out of her depth.

After Alexio had given an order he leant back and looked at her. She knew she must look like some wide-eyed hick.

'Well? What do you think?'

Sidonie sat back, overwhelmed, and gave a little laugh. 'I think that we're not in Kansas any more, Toto.'

Alexio frowned and Sidonie explained with a wave of her hand. 'When Dorothy ends up in Oz...' She shook her head. 'This is out of this world. I've never seen anything like it. I'm used to grimy college student bars.'

The waitress came back with small plates of finger food and a bottle of champagne. Sidonie groaned softly. She hadn't realised she was hungry and she stole a glance at Alexio, who was watching her with amusement.

'My appetite is just one big joke to you, isn't it?'

He shrugged and prepared some pitta bread and tzatziki, handing it to her. She ate it with relish and took a sip of the sparkling wine.

Joking, she said, 'I could get used to this, you know.'

She missed Alexio's enigmatic look as she plucked an olive from a bowl. When she did look at him he was lounging back, regarding her with an expression that had her blood heating up. It was *that* look. The one that made him look hungry and made her feel hungry. But not for food.

'I want to dance with you.'

Sidonie swallowed what she was eating. The mere thought of dancing with this man made any appetite she did have flee. A slow, sexy hip-hop song was playing, its beat sending tremors of sexual awareness through Sidonie's body.

'Okay...'

Moving out of the booth seat, Alexio stood and held out his hand. He looked so young in that moment, and so breathtakingly gorgeous, that Sidonie had to relegate it like a snapshot to the back of her mind because it was too much to deal with.

His hand in hers, Alexio led her to the dance floor, which was filling up with similarly minded couples. He drew her into his arms, close to his body, and it was the most natural thing to loop her hands and arms around his neck.

His hands were possessive on her, sexual. One hand rested over her buttocks. The other slid under the gaping hole at the side of her dress to splay across her naked back. *Lord.* How was she expected to stay standing when he touched her like that? As Sidonie looked into his eyes the infectious beat of the music throbbed through every vein and made her tingle. She realised, not for the first time, how far under her skin he'd sneaked.

There was something so...so up-front and unashamed about him. He was too confident to play games. Too assured. She knew exactly where she stood. And even though that brought misgivings about how cool she was with that—which was a lot less cool than she pretended—she couldn't blame him for her growing confusing emotions. Her attachment.

The fact that she trusted him was huge. She'd never trusted anyone, really...not since those awful days when her mother had exposed a very ugly side of reality and herself. Sidonie suspected now that her highly developed reticence had influenced her experiences with her first two brief relationships. No wonder they'd been unsatisfactory; she hadn't let either of them get too close.

But Alexio... Alexio had smashed through a wall she'd been barely aware of building around herself and now all that remained was rubble. And her exposed beating heart.

It hit her then, as she looked up into those golden compelling eyes...she was falling for him. And it was too late to stop herself.

Her arms tightened around Alexio's neck in automatic rejection of her thought, as if she could ward it off if she squashed it right away. But Alexio couldn't read the stricken nature of her revelation. He saw only those wide aquamarine eyes and felt Sidonie's arms tighten around him and he pulled her even closer.

Her breasts pressed against him, her hips welded to his, and his arousal was urgent and insistent. Damn her. He *never* lost it like this.

Wanting to punish her for something he wasn't even sure of, Alexio cupped the back of her head and, as the throbbing beat of the music changed and got faster, bent his head and took her mouth in a bruising passionate kiss.

As if something was holding her back, Sidonie didn't respond for a moment. Incensed by this, Alexio used every skill in his arsenal to make her respond—and when she did his blood ignited.

After long, drugging moments, Alexio struggled to drag himself away from Sidonie's mouth. He felt dazed. The music was faster now. People were dancing around him. They were the only ones standing still. She was slow to open her eyes. They looked slumberous, filled with hidden depths. Filled with...emotion. Instantly Alexio waited for that cold feeling to infect him, but it didn't.

Before he could feel any more disjointed he all but dragged Sidonie off the dance floor and back to the booth. The food had been cleared away. They sat down and Alexio took a swig of champagne. But it was no good. He couldn't feel civilised sitting next to Sidonie with that provocative dress testing his control every time she moved.

He took her hand and she looked at him. Her mouth was swollen. Her eyes were huge, pupils dilated.

'Let's get out of here...'

She opened her mouth, paling slightly, as if she saw something in his expression that frightened her slightly. He felt feral.

'But we only just got here.'

Alexio forced himself to calm down and tried not to think about the fact that when he usually came to a club with a woman it was a very different experience. He was usually a lot more in control.

Tightly he said, 'If you don't want to go we can stay...'

'Why do you want to go?' she asked, surprising him. Most women would have pouted or sidled up to him, trying to distract him, cajole him.

'Because,' he offered with brutal honesty, 'I'm afraid if we don't leave that I'll get arrested for making love to you in front of an audience, and the last time I checked this wasn't a sex club.'

'Oh...' Sidonie said, in a small voice barely audible above the music. She took a swift sip of her drink and then looked at him. She was all at once shy and confident—again that intriguing mix. 'In that case maybe we should go...'

Relief and anticipation swept through Alexio as he grabbed for her hand and led her out of the booth—this time back to the VIP exit.

The return journey to Alexio's villa in the car was torturous. Sidonie was acutely aware of the thick sexual tension that enveloped them. Alexio had looked so...*primal* back at the club. She hadn't had a chance of pretending everything was normal after that dance and after his bald declaration. She'd wanted them to be alone as badly as he had.

Alexio looked at her now and lifted his arm for her to come close to his side. Sidonie didn't hesitate. She slid her arms around his hard-muscled torso and rested her head on his chest. Alexio's hand found the hole in the side of her dress and sneaked underneath, climbing up until he could cup her breast, his fingers pinching a nipple.

Sidonie's breath grew choppy. Between her legs she was embarrassingly wet.

By the time they reached the garage and he stopped the car Sidonie had to peel herself off Alexio.

He growled softly, 'Where do you think you're going?'

Sidonie stopped and looked at him. He had that look again, and it sent tremors of excitement into her blood. 'Inside?' she said hopefully, already imagining the huge bed.

Alexio shook his head and as he did so moved his seat back. 'No time. I can't wait. Take off your knickers.'

Sidonie's eyes went very big when she saw Alexio's hands go to his belt. He started undoing it. They were going to do it here. Right now. Heat washed up through Sidonie and her hands shook with need as she did as she was bid, sliding her panties off and down her legs.

When they hit the floor of the car Alexio reached for her and brought her over to straddle his lap. Sidonie's heart was out of control as Alexio dragged her dress down to bare one creamy white breast, its nipple already hard and pouting flagrantly for his mouth and tongue.

She groaned out loud when he surrounded it in sucking heat and clasped his head. Her hips were already grinding gently against his lap and the hard bulge she could feel there, still constrained by his trousers. Feeling frustration build, Sidonie reached down, lifting up slightly, and almost wept with relief when she could feel Alexio's naked arousal pushing against her where she ached.

When he thrust up and into her their mingled breaths were harsh in the quiet of the small space. Sidonie could feel the steering wheel digging into her back, the gearshift against her knee, but she didn't care. Her body rose and fell against Alexio's. They were both so turned on and ready that their mutual completion shattered around them in minutes. Sidonie could only sag against him afterwards, her mind a blissful blank of nothingness.

As dawn broke over the eastern side of the island and bathed the western edges in a pink glow Sidonie lay awake, with her cheek resting on Alexio's chest. Despite their frantic coupling in the car as soon as they'd got back, their hunger for one another hadn't been dented.

She knew he was awake too because she could feel the tension in his body. The master bedroom of the villa, despite its vast airiness, felt like a cocoon around them. Sidonie never wanted to leave this place, or this man. For a second she resented the inevitable intrusion of reality and *responsibility*—and then felt immediately guilty when she thought of Tante Josephine. Of course she couldn't expect her aunt to deal with the debts incurred by her mother.

Sighing deeply, Sidonie snuggled closer to Alexio, hating how a shiver went down her spine, as if someone had just walked over her grave.

'What's wrong?'

Sidonie shook her head against him and whispered, 'Nothing.' *Everything*, she didn't say.

A question she'd wanted to ask him for days rose up within her and, longing for a diversion from her own thoughts, she lifted her head and rested her chin on her hand against his chest.

He looked at her and she almost smiled at the wariness of him. As if she were some kind of unexploded device.

'Can I ask you something?'

A small smile played around that gorgeous sexy mouth. 'Do I have a choice?'

'Not really,' Sidonie said cheerfully, and then, 'Why did you turn your back on your inheritance to make your own way?'

She'd asked him the question that first evening in his

apartment but he'd deflected it easily. Now his face became inscrutable, and Sidonie prepared herself for another brush-off, but to her surprise his chest rose and fell in a deep sigh. As if he was giving in.

He said carefully, 'You *do* know that if I tell you I'll have to kill you?'

Sidonie nodded with mock seriousness. 'I know. However, I feel like I've packed a lot into my twenty-three years, so I'm prepared to go if I have to.'

Alexio took some of her hair between his fingers and caressed it, saying, 'Such a pity…but if you're positive…?'

Mock resolute, Sidonie said, 'I'm positive.'

Joking aside, Alexio lifted one shoulder and said, 'It's really not that exciting.'

'I'm intrigued. It's not many people who would turn their back on an Onassis-sized inheritance.'

Alexio grimaced. 'The size of the inheritance was vastly exaggerated…'

Sidonie stayed quiet.

With clear reluctance Alexio told her, 'I am my father's only son. Even though my half-brother grew up with us, my father used to taunt him every day that he would not receive a cent from him. I always resented my father's lack of generosity and the way he wielded his power over everyone else. But I saw how it forged in my brother a will to succeed and prosper on his own. I envied him because he wasn't constrained like I was. Bound to my father's expectations. My father used to pit us against each other all the time, me and my brother.'

Alexio grimaced.

'Obviously this didn't do our relationship much good, and by the time my brother left home it's safe to say we hated each other's guts. My father just assumed I would be joining him in his empire. He never listened to me long enough to know that I had no interest in his shipping business. I rebelled against that expectation. The business wasn't even his—not rightfully. He was the second son and his brother had died at a young age, leaving him in line to take over. His own father hadn't wanted it for him, but my father grabbed it with both hands and ousted my grandfather as soon as he could.'

Sidonie's eyes grew wide. 'But that's so…'

'Ruthless?' Alexio interjected with a grim smile.

Sidonie nodded.

'That's my father's way. To grab at things. Take them. He wanted me to inherit and join him—but not as an equal, as someone he could control.' He sighed. 'In the meantime I saw Rafaele, my brother, single-handedly resurrecting his own family name and business out of the ashes. All those years of rivalry were still in my blood—if he could do it so could I.'

Sidonie spoke softly. 'So when your father expected you to follow in his footsteps you said no?'

Alexio looked into Sidonie's clear eyes and felt in that moment as if he could just spill all the secrets in his guts and keep spilling. It was dangerous. Too dangerous. He stifled the impulse with effort.

'I said no. And walked away. He disinherited me and now here I am.'

'Probably more successful than he is…'

Alexio was surprised that she'd surmised that but it was true. What he didn't tell her, though, was how his success hadn't given him any measure of satisfaction where his father was concerned. It had never been about besting his father. It had been about distancing himself from a man who had made him fear *he* had the same lack of emotional control in his own make-up. Fear that he might be similarly greedy and never experience the thrill of making it on his own as his brother had. Fear that he'd never get away from that sterile house full of tension and hatred. *Violence*.

He felt cold inside all of a sudden.

Just then Alexio's mobile phone beeped on the nearby bedside cabinet. He reached for it and saw the text message icon winking. He opened it and saw it was from his solicitor.

I have information about your Miss Fitzgerald. Call when you get a chance. D.

Instantly something cold slithered into Alexio's gut.

'What is it?' Sidonie asked with obvious concern.

Alexio put the phone back, face down, and looked at her. 'Nothing important.'

Guilt warred with something much deeper inside him. Superstitiously he wanted to pretend he hadn't just seen that text and that there wasn't something dark lurking in the wings.

He came up and hovered over her, feeling that familiar heady rush of desire when he looked at her body, breasts bared and tempting. Her mouth was enticing him ever downwards, where he wouldn't have to think about anything…for a little longer.

'What did you just say?' Alexio asked faintly.

He was stunned. The sun was high outside his villa's office. His body was still humming in the aftermath of seriously pleasurable lovemaking and he couldn't really compute this information.

His solicitor repeated himself. 'Her mother went to jail for two years.'

Alexio went cold all over. 'Jail? Why?'

Demetrius sighed. 'I really wish I didn't have to tell you this. Her mother was prosecuted for stalking and blackmailing her married lover. She'd been doing it for years, in ever increasing amounts. It would appear that her husband, Miss

Fitzgerald's father, wasn't making enough to keep her in the style to which she wanted to be accustomed. Even though it also appears he did his best to try and keep both his wife and daughter in comfort and relative luxury.'

Alexio struggled against the shock. This information was not pleasant, but it hardly condemned Sidonie.

His friend continued, 'When her mother was released they moved to another part of the country to avoid the scandal and Miss Fitzgerald's father's business started to boom. Sidonie went to one of the best local schools, had a pony…the works. Her mother was a regular on the social scene…designer clothes and jewellery. They managed to keep her past a secret for the most part. When the property market collapsed so did her father's business and they lost everything.'

Alexio was feeling increasingly uncomfortable. 'Demetrius, is that it? I think I've heard enough.'

'Well, not quite. I think you should hear the rest. After Mr Fitzgerald died his wife went back to Paris to move in with her younger sister.'

'Demetrius—'

The man butted in. 'Alexio, I did some more digging via some colleagues in Paris and you need to hear this… Sidonie's mother persuaded her sister to take out a mortgage on a flat her husband had bought and paid for years before. She also maxed out credit cards in her sister's name. She died leaving the woman in so much debt that she'll never recover.'

Alexio felt angry now and gritted out, 'What does this have to do with Sidonie?'

'You met her when she was on her way home from Paris?'

'Yes,' Alexio agreed curtly, regretting having ever involved his friend like this.

'She'd just signed an agreement to accept responsibility for all those debts on her aunt's behalf. Now, let me ask you this—has she given any hint at all that she's a woman with a huge financial burden on her shoulders? If not,' his friend went on heavily, 'you have to ask yourself why she's acting as if nothing is wrong.'

When Sidonie woke again she was alone in the bed and for some reason her belly went into a ball of tension. Something was wrong. She could feel it.

She lifted her head and looked around. No sign of Alexio. Maybe he'd gone for a swim? He was a powerful swimmer and liked the sea as opposed to the pool.

Muscles protesting pleasurably as she sat up, Sidonie got out of bed and went to the bathroom, tying her hair up so that it wouldn't get wet in the shower.

When she came out again she rubbed her body dry with a towel and looked at the vast array of clothes hanging in the walk-in wardrobe. Something bitter struck her again to think of his other women, but Sidonie shoved it down. She didn't have the right to feel jealous, possessive.

She found some shorts and a green halterneck top and stuck them on and then went to find Alexio, still with that odd feeling of foreboding in her belly. Before she could leave the bedroom, though, she heard the sound of her phone ringing. She kept it on mainly in case Tante Josephine was looking for her, and when she located it at the bottom of her bag she saw that it *was* her aunt.

Expecting nothing more than her aunt wanting to chat, Sidonie sat on the edge of the bed and answered warmly in French. Her smile faded in an instant, though, when all she could hear were racking sobs from the other end of the phone.

Instantly Sidonie stood up. 'Tante Josephine, what is it? Please try to stop crying…'

Eventually her aunt was able to calm down enough to

start talking, after Sidonie had encouraged her to breathe slowly. Her aunt was prone to panic attacks and Sidonie didn't want one to happen before she could find out what was wrong.

Through fits and starts it transpired that someone on her *vacances* had heard about Tante Josephine's financial woes and put the fear of God into her by telling her all sorts of horror stories about repossessions and jail sentences for not paying debts. No wonder her aunt was hysterical.

But no matter what Sidonie said it didn't seem to have any effect. Her aunt was working herself up into another bout of hysterics. Desperate, Sidonie racked her brains for what she could say that might calm her down. Tante Josephine didn't understand nuances, and Sidonie knew that if she tried to placate her with reassurances that the debts were now in *her* name it would have no effect. Her aunt still believed the debts were hers.

Her aunt only understood *right now*—and right now, she was panicking. Sidonie knew that in her aunt's mind the threat was as real as if *gendarmes* had just turned up to arrest her.

Tante Josephine needed to hear something concrete, even if it was a white lie. 'Okay, look, Jojo—are you listening to me? I need you to listen because I'm going to tell you why you don't have to worry about a thing.'

To Sidonie's relief her aunt stopped crying abruptly at the use of the nickname that had come about when, as a toddler, Sidonie hadn't been able to pronounce Josephine. She hiccuped softly. Sidonie's heart ached for this poor, sweet and innocent woman who did not deserve this stress.

'Jojo, everything is going to be fine...I promise you.'

Unbeknownst to Sidonie, who stood facing away from the view and the open terrace doors, a tall dark shape had approached and stopped.

'But Sidonie...*how*?'

Sidonie could hear the hysteria approaching again and cursed the distance between them. 'I'm not going to let you go through this alone, Jojo, do you hear me? Didn't I promise to do everything in my power to get us out of this mess?'

Her aunt sniffled and Sidonie pressed on, seizing the advantage, knowing how fragile her aunt was mentally.

'You don't have to worry about a thing because I've...'

Sidonie faltered. She'd been about to say she had everything in hand, but she knew that would sound vague to her aunt, so she mentally crossed her fingers, squeezed her eyes shut and said, 'I've met someone, Jojo...and he's really, really rich. One of the richest men in the world. And you won't believe how we met—it was on a plane, and he *owned* the plane.'

Immediately her aunt, who was always enthralled by stories like this, perked up. 'Really, Sidonie? Truly? Is he your boyfriend?'

Sidonie opened her eyes. 'Yes, he is. He's crazy about me. And I've told him all about you and he's promised to take care of everything.'

As much as Sidonie hated using Alexio like this, she knew it would resonate with her aunt, who was simplistically old-fashioned. After her father had bought the apartment for Tante Josephine she'd believed all men had the power to sweep in and make magic happen.

Her aunt's voice quavered, but this time it sounded like relief. 'Oh, Sidonie...I'm so happy... I was so worried—and then when Marcel told me those things and—'

Sidonie cut her off before she could work herself up again and behind her the tall, dark shadow melted away, unnoticed.

'Jojo, don't talk about this to anyone again—and if Marcel says anything just know that you have nothing to worry about.'

Sidonie felt awful, lying like this, but she knew that her

physical presence would reassure her aunt when she got back to Paris. She could then tell her that something had happened with the *'boyfriend'*. The idea was laughable. Alexio was no boyfriend.

'Oh, Sidonie…is he handsome?'

Sidonie felt ashamed, but she was relieved to hear her aunt's natural effervescence return—she loved stories about people meeting and falling in love. Sidonie tried to gloss over the details about Alexio as much as possible, and before her aunt terminated the conversation she made sure to have a chat with one of the supervisors, to warn them that she was particularly vulnerable at the moment. She castigated herself for not thinking of doing it before the holiday.

When she put her phone down she felt drained, but at least happier that Tante Josephine should be okay until the end of her holiday. The supervisor had promised to keep a close watch over her.

Sidonie turned round and her eyes widened when she saw the tall figure of Alexio, standing with his back to her at the railing of the terrace outside. He was dressed in faded jeans and a T-shirt. That feeling of foreboding was back but Sidonie tried to shake it off. And also the sudden fear that he might have heard some of her conversation.

She padded out on bare feet and went to stand beside Alexio at the railing. He didn't look at her. Sidonie forced her voice to be bright. 'Hey, you…I was wondering where you'd got to.'

Alexio was trying to hold in the cold rage that had filled his belly when he'd overheard her poisonous words: *'He's crazy about me…he'll take care of things…'*

Here was the very unpalatable proof that his solicitor had been right to make Alexio question why Sidonie hadn't told him about this before.

Forcing his voice to sound neutral, he asked, 'Who were you on the phone to just now?'

He couldn't look at her. His hands tightened on the railings.

Sidonie was evasive. 'Er...just my aunt. She's away at the moment, on holiday...'

Alexio felt a hard weight settle into his belly. Everything from the moment he'd met her unspooled like a bad film in his mind. All the little moments when she'd appeared shy, naïve, mocked him now.

So this was how she was going to do it: she was going to bide her time, wait to catch him in a weak moment and then launch into her sob story, seducing money out of him. And maybe even more. Maybe he'd be so weak by then he'd offer to buy her a place, set up her and her aunt completely? He felt dizzy at the thought.

He thought of how weak he'd felt in the aftermath of their lovemaking—how he'd blithely allowed himself to spill his guts, how he'd almost spilled *more*, telling her everything. How close he'd come to making a complete fool of himself.

Thank goodness he'd had the sense to investigate her. When he thought of how guilty he'd felt to have instigated such a thing, the conversation he'd heard just now taunted him. Where had his cynical shell gone?

Sidonie touched his arm. 'What is it, Alexio? You're scaring me.'

Alexio jerked his arm from her as if burnt and stepped back, finally looking at her. He saw her go pale and welcomed it. He couldn't hide his disgust and despised the way his body reacted to seeing her in short shorts and that sexy halterneck top.

'You really think I'm that stupid?' he sneered.

Sidonie looked at him and blinked. He could see something like fear flash in her eyes.

'What did you hear?'

Alexio felt murderous now, because her guilt was obvious.

'Enough,' he spat out. 'Enough to know that you and your aunt think that you can use *me* to clear your debts.'

Sidonie just stood there, looking a little shell-shocked. No doubt because she'd been found out.

She said faintly, 'You speak French.'

'Of course I speak French—along with two or three other European languages.'

He was dismissive.

Sidonie's eyes seemed to clear and she reached out with a hand that Alexio stepped back from. 'You don't understand. I didn't mean a word of it. I was just saying what I could to reassure her—she was upset.'

Alexio could have laughed at her earnest expression, which was a travesty now that he knew everything was twisted and black and nothing had been real. He felt betrayed, and that made him even more incandescent with rage. He *never* let women get close enough to do this to him.

'You expect me to believe a single word from the daughter of a criminal? You obviously learnt well from her—but not well enough. If you had had the decency to *tell* me about this—come to me and merely asked me for help—I might have given it. Instead you insisted on this elaborate charade. Maybe you got off on the drama?'

CHAPTER SEVEN

FOR AN AWFUL second Sidonie thought she might faint. She couldn't actually believe that Alexio had just said those words...*daughter of a criminal.*

She went icy cold, despite the heat, and forced words out through numb lips. 'What do you mean, the daughter of a criminal?'

His voice flat, he admitted, 'I know all about your mother, Sidonie. I know that she blackmailed her married lover and went to jail.'

The words fell like shattered glass all over her. The old shame rose up to grip her vocal cords so she couldn't speak, much in the same way as had happened when she'd been eight years old in the schoolyard and her classmates had surrounded her, jeering, *'Your mother's going to jail...your mother's going to jail...'*

Sidonie could not believe she was hearing this. It had to be a nightmare. Perhaps any minute now she'd wake up to Alexio saying, *Sid...wake up. I want you.*

She blinked. But nothing changed. Alexio was still standing there. A stranger. Cold and remote. Condemnatory. She felt dazed, confused.

Somehow she managed to get out, 'How on earth do you know about that?' Something else struck her. 'And how do you know about my aunt's debts?'

Alexio crossed his arms and now he looked completely forbidding. 'I had you investigated.'

This information made Sidonie literally reel. She had to put her hands behind her on the railing just to hold onto something or she was afraid she'd fall down.

'You had me *investigated*?' she whispered incredulously, looking at him, at this complete stranger.

Alexio lifted one shoulder minutely and didn't look remotely ashamed or sheepish. 'I can't be too careful... Someone, a complete stranger, comes into my life... I got suspicious.'

'My God,' Sidonie breathed, horrified. 'Who *are* you?'

She felt sick. And then angry. It was a huge surge of emotion, rising up within her. She stood up straight, let go of the railing. She was shaking.

'And how *dare* you pry into my private life? What my mother did has got absolutely nothing to do with you.'

Sidonie had lived with that shame all her life but had finally come to terms with what her mother had done—not least because she understood a little of why she'd acted the way she had. Something that she could never explain to this cold stranger. She hadn't even let her guard down enough with him to tell him of her deep private secrets. He'd gone looking for them.

Sidonie was aware of parts of herself breaking off inside, shattering. She knew she had to hold it together.

Alexio spoke again, his voice as cutting as a knife. 'But it wasn't just that, was it? She put your aunt into severe debt, to fund her own expensive tastes.'

Shame heaped on top of shame. Sidonie felt horribly exposed. From somewhere deep inside, and far too late, she reached for and pulled up an icy shield.

'That is none of your concern.' Because she'd never intended to tell him about it. It was part of the real world, which *wasn't* part of this fantasy world.

Alexio's mouth twisted. 'But it would have been, wouldn't it? You were waiting for the right moment, when enough intimacy had been established, and then you were going to make your move. I just wonder if you were going to ask only for enough to cover the debts or more...based on how many nights we'd spent together? Based on how duped you thought I was by then?'

'Theos.' He was lashing out now, making Sidonie flinch. He narrowed wild-looking eyes on her.

'You were good. I'll give you that. But there were a few signs... The way you were so blasé with the clothes, as if you had expected nothing less. That little wistful moment outside the jewellery shop... Were you hoping to wake up and find a diamond bracelet winking at you on the pillow?'

Sidonie desperately tried not to let the awful insidious insecurity take hold, telling her that despite everything she *was* her mother's daughter. Had something about the sheer level of Alexio's wealth called to her? More than the man himself? Suddenly she doubted herself. She had to take deep breaths to avoid throwing up right there on the terrace.

The sheer depth and evidence of Alexio's cynicism was astounding, shocking. The lengths he'd gone to because he hadn't really trusted her... Because he'd *suspected* something.

The things he'd found out... The fact that she had so fatally misread this man. *How* had she not seen an inkling of this? Only those most fleeting moments when a look would cross his face...hardly enough to make her wonder.

Nevertheless, a small, tender part of Sidonie not lashed by this terrible revelation was making her say, 'You have it all wrong. I was only telling my aunt something to reassure her. She was hysterical. I didn't mean it. You were never meant to hear that and I had no intention of asking you for money.'

To Sidonie's own ears it sounded flat. Didn't sound convincing. She couldn't seem to drum up the necessary passion to convince him. She was too stunned, too shocked... too wounded.

Predictably, Alexio didn't believe her. His eyes were a dead, emotionless void.

'I do not wish to discuss this any further. We're done here. I am going back to Athens within the hour. If you come with me I will ensure you get a flight home.'

Sidonie felt devoid of all feeling except one: she hated this man. And she couldn't believe how gullible she'd been—how naïve not to have assumed that a man as powerful as him would, of course, be suspicious and cynical by nature.

She said flatly, 'I would prefer to swim home.'

Alexio shrugged minutely, as if he couldn't care less. 'As you wish. There's a boat leaving for Piraeus this evening. My housekeeper's husband will take you to the port.'

Sidonie welcomed that. Because right now she hated herself for automatically thinking about what it would be like to get on a plane again without this man distracting her from her fear with his charming sexy smile. With that wicked mouth.

He turned away and then turned back abruptly, his eyes dark. Something in his voice was a bit wild, but Sidonie was too traumatised to notice it.

'Tell me...was it on the plane, when you knew who I was? Did you decide then to try and hook me by making me believe you were different from every other woman I've ever met?'

Sidonie just looked at him. Words of defence were stuck in her throat. She had no defence—not when this man had proved that he had suspected her of something long before he'd even had a reason to. And he still had no reason to. She had trusted him, blindly, right from the start, never suspecting for a moment how dark he was inside. How he could so easily condemn her.

She never wanted to see him again because he had just proved that she would never be free of the past. He had broken her heart into a million pieces and she'd never forgive herself for that weakness. Or him.

His condemnation would be her defence, so she said, 'Yes. On the plane. As soon as I knew who you were.'

Alexio looked at her for a taut moment and then he turned and strode away, leaving her standing there. As soon as he was out of sight Sidonie blindly made her way into the *en suite* bathroom of the bedroom where they'd made love too many times to count and was violently ill.

Afterwards, when Alexio's helicopter had left and she'd changed into her own clothes and packed her bag, Sidonie sat on a lounger outside with the glorious view unnoticed in front of her. She was still numb. Devoid of any substantial feeling. She knew it was the protection of shock.

One thing impinged, though: disgust at herself for having indulged in this fantasy. She'd wanted one night and had then grabbed for more... Had she on some level hoped that Alexio would want her for longer? Deeper? Had she ignored her own usually healthy self-protective cautious nature because she'd been blinded by opulence? The thought made her feel sick again.

Bitterly she surmised that she should have listened to him more closely when he'd told her his reasons for turning his back on his inheritance. He was driven and ruthless—had dashed his own father's expectations and dreams to fuel his own desires.

She'd believed his reasons were justified when she'd heard them at first—she'd heard the way his voice had constricted when he'd talked about his father, as if even now he felt the unbearable yoke of expectation. She'd admired him.

But now she saw him for what he really was: an amoral, ambitious, greedy man who would step over his nearest and dearest to get ahead. She hadn't stood a chance. He might have heard her damning conversation with her aunt, but he'd already investigated her at that stage and had clearly believed her worthy of judgement because of her mother's criminal record.

Those two years of her mother's incarceration were etched like an invisible tatoo into Sidonie's skin. A stain of shame that would never be gone, but which had faded over time…until now.

Sidonie's well-ingrained sense of responsibility rose up. She should never have indulged herself like this. She had her aunt to worry about now, and clearing the debts.

She heard a car pull up somewhere nearby. It would be the housekeeper's husband. She stood up and tried not to let the emotion brewing within her break free. She couldn't let it. She was afraid of its awesome power. Of how much it would tell her about a hurt that shouldn't be so deep—not after just a few days with a man she hadn't even known.

A man appeared, old and bent, with a weathered face and black eyes. His dour expression gave Sidonie some sense of relief. If he'd been kind she might have broken apart altogether. He took her bag and at the same time handed her a white envelope with nothing written on it.

Sidonie opened it and saw a cheque with her name on it inside. It was for an amount of money that took her breath away. Enough to halve her aunt's debts at least. The signature at the bottom was bold and arrogant. Reeking of condemnation and disgust.

Fire filled Sidonie's belly. She stalked straight back into the villa and went to Alexio's office.

She took the cheque out of the envelope and ripped it

up into tiny pieces. Then she put them back in the envelope and wrote on the outside.

It was never about the money.

And then she left.

Four months later...

Alexio looked down at the craggy dark island below him with its distinctive white and blue roofs. The helipad on his own villa loomed into view and tension made his gut hard. Alexio grimaced as his solicitor's words came back to him. *'You're heading for burnout, man. I've never seen you like this before.'*

Alexio couldn't remember being like this before either—not even in the days when he'd been struggling and working night and day to make a success of his business. But for the last four months he'd barely stopped to breathe. On automatic pilot.

His fortune had doubled. His acquisitions had extended to North America, making him the first European budget airline to secure such a lucrative contract. Now he was global, having taken half the time people had predicted.

But Alexio felt as if an essential fire inside him had been doused. He rejected the thought immediately. Nothing was different. He was still the same—held the same values and ambitions.

As the small aircraft circled lower and lower he fought *her* memory. This was precisely why he'd avoided coming back here before now. During daylight hours he had to make a concerted effort not to think of her; that was where work came in. But in the nights she haunted him. Stopped him from sleeping. Made his body ache so badly that he had to ease it like a horny teenager.

He wouldn't mind if he could alleviate his frustration with another woman, but he could barely look at a woman these days without feeling a measure of disgust. And a disturbingly flatlining libido.

He told himself it was because he'd come so close to being burnt. A vivid memory came into his mind as the glittering sun-kissed sea below the villa came into view—Sidonie launching herself onto his back as they'd walked up the steps from the sea, kissing his neck, joking, laughing. And all the time plotting to feather her nest.

Alexio felt sick, and he almost told the pilot to keep going...but they were landing now and Alexio refused to let a memory override his intellect.

He'd finally agreed to go somewhere for a few days' R&R after he and his brother had almost come to blows for the first time in years. Alexio had been closing a deal with Rafaele to create a joint company which would invest in research for future technologies in cars and aircraft. They'd been in Rafaele's *palazzo* outside Milan, where he was spending the summer with his family.

Alexio had been keen to keep working one day and Rafaele had looked at him incredulously. 'Are you crazy? We've been working all day—Sam is making dinner tonight and Milo's back from summer school in Milan. I haven't seen him since this morning. I have a family now, Alexio... things are different.'

Alexio had felt a completely irrational anger erupt at his brother's very valid reasons not to keep working. Since he'd arrived he'd found the domestic idyll of Rafaele's family almost too much to bear. The openly loving looks between him and his wife. His precocious and gorgeous nephew, who bathed everyone in his sunny charming nature. The way he was doted on by both Sam and Rafaele. The way Rafaele's relationship with his own father had clearly undergone a transformation for the better.

It had brought Alexio back to that dark place when he'd believed such things existed, only to find out that they didn't. It had brought back the resentment that he'd felt because he'd witnessed something ugly in his own family that Rafaele had never had to witness simply because he'd been free to get on with his own life, leaving Alexio behind in a toxic atmosphere.

He'd been caught in the grip of that darkness, emotions swirling in his gut, and he'd sneered, 'You're losing your touch, Rafaele, ever since you let that woman get to you—'

His brother had stepped right up to him, chest to chest, and Alexio had felt the heat of his anger.

Rafaele had blistered at him, 'Do not ever call Sam *that woman* again. Whatever is going on with you, Alexio, sort it out.'

Sam had come into the study then, smiling widely, oblivious to the tension at first. And then her grey eyes had grown wide and concerned as she'd immediately looked to her husband. Something in that look, something that had seemed so naked and *dangerous* to Alexio, had made him push past his brother.

He'd found the wherewithal to stop and say tightly, 'I'm sorry, Sam. I have to leave. Something's come up…' and then he'd left the *palazzo* as if hounds were at his heels. Running from that picture of domestic bliss which he wanted to believe was a sham…but which he knew deep down wasn't.

He'd avoided the repeated phone calls from his brother since then.

He was here now, so he'd get it together if it killed him. And maybe tonight he'd go to that nightclub and his libido *wouldn't* flatline in the presence of other women. Maybe it would surge back to life and he would finally be able to erase *her* image from his mind once and for all, claw back some sense of equilibrium.

* * *

Sidonie gave a groan of satisfaction as she slid into the steaming water of the cracked and discoloured bath. Tante Josephine had squirted in enough bubbles to hide Sidonie's body from view completely, but she didn't need it to be hidden to know what she'd see without the bubbles: a small bump protruding over the waterline, as it had started to do over the last week.

It seemed to be getting bigger by the day now as she became more noticeably pregnant.

Her boss at the café had pulled her aside earlier and said bluntly, 'I have five children. You're pregnant, aren't you?'

Sidonie had blanched, too shocked to deny it, and nodded her head.

Her boss had sighed. 'Okay, you can stay for a couple of months, but as soon as you start to get big you're gone—this is not work for a pregnant woman.'

Sidonie had gasped, but he'd walked away. She'd realised the irony of her boss being a chauvinistic Greek man but hadn't felt like laughing.

She bit her lip now with worry. So far she and Tante Josephine were doing okay. When Sidonie had got back to Paris and moved in with her aunt she'd gone to see a financial advisor who had helped them consolidate their debts to a monthly total. Now all Sidonie had to do was earn enough to make that payment. Every month. For a long, long time into the future.

They were just about managing, with Tante Josephine's job and Sidonie's two and sometimes three jobs. But now that a baby was in the mix...

Sidonie bit down on her lip hard and put her hand over the small swell. Since the moment she'd seen the first pregnancy test turn positive, and then the next and the next—five tests in all—she'd forged an indelible bond with the clump of cells growing inside her. She'd never consciously thought about having a baby—it was something she'd put off into the distant future, not really wanting to consider the huge responsibility, especially after her own damaging experiences—but crazily, in spite of everything, somehow it felt *right*. And Sidonie couldn't explain why, when she had every reason to feel the opposite.

Sometimes, though, panic gripped her so hard she had to stop and breathe. She fought it. She would get through this somehow.

It didn't help that Tante Josephine kept asking Sidonie, 'But where is your boyfriend? The one you told me about? Won't he want to take care of you? I thought he was going to make everything okay?'

Sidonie would take her aunt's face in her hands and say firmly, but lovingly, 'We don't need him, Jojo, we have each other. We're a team and we're invincible. I won't let anything happen to us, okay?'

Her aunt would sigh and then quickly get distracted by something—usually talk of the baby. She'd already decided that if it was a boy it would be called Sebastian and if it was a girl Belle, after a favourite cartoon character.

As Sidonie lay in the bath now, after a punishing day of work, she felt helpless tears spring into her eyes. Immediately she cut off the emotion ruthlessly, as she'd been doing for four months. Anger rose and she welcomed it. She cultivated it. It was the only thing that kept her sane, kept her going. And now the baby.

She would never contact *him* and she had to stop thinking about *him*. For a man who had accused her of being a gold-digger on the basis of conducting an investigation into her private life and overhearing an admittedly unfortunate conversation, news of a baby would consign her to the hell of his condemnation for good—and she would not give him the satisfaction.

Her anger rose, swift and bright, washing away those

dangerous tender feelings that hovered on the periphery and had no place after what he'd done to her.

Alexio returned to the villa feeling more disgruntled than ever. After sleeping for almost eight hours on a lounger on the terrace he'd gone to the club.

Elettra, encouraged by the fact that he was alone, had twined herself around him like a clinging vine, making him feel nothing but claustrophobia.

In a fit of darkness he'd taken the same booth as last time and had been bombarded with images and memories: Sidonie's dress, the way the silk had clung and moved with her body. How it had felt to dance close to her, sliding his hand under her dress to touch her naked back. The insistent throb of the music, with the same beat as the desire rushing through his blood. The way she'd looked at him, hungry and innocent.

Innocent.

Except she'd never been innocent. She'd been scheming the whole time, just reeling him in, waiting for an opportunity to secure her future, debt-free.

Bile had risen up inside Alexio after all these months, just as it had that awful day. Immediately he'd had to get out of there.

And now here he was, looking over the inky blackness of the sea. Thoroughly disgusted with himself, Alexio felt the lure of work—even though he meant to be avoiding it. But he knew he wouldn't sleep, and especially not in that bed. It had been a terrible idea to come here. He should have gone to the farthest corner of the world and he vowed to do so the next day. He'd wanted to check out the potential of setting up in South East Asia anyway...

When he went into the office and sat down heavily on the chair he saw an unexpected white envelope sitting squarely on the blotter. Saw the writing in a feminine scrawl.

It was never about the money.

Feeling something in his belly swoop and his skin prickle, Alexio picked up the envelope. As he did so something fluttered out. The torn pieces of the cheque he'd left for Sidonie in a fit of tumultuous anger and disgust. If she wanted the money so badly then he'd give her some. But now he felt dizzy. Disorientated. He opened the envelope and more and more pieces fell out. Nothing else.

It was never about the money.

He hadn't even checked to see if or when she'd cashed it. He'd just assumed that she had. He hadn't wanted to know. But she hadn't. She'd left that day and taken a torturous eleven-hour ferry to Piraeus. His last contact from her had been via a message relayed to him by one of his Greek assistants whom he'd instructed to meet her at the port with a plane ticket for a flight to Dublin.

She'd not taken the ticket and had said succinctly, *'Tell Alexio Christakos he can go to hell.'*

The message had been relayed with great trepidation by the employee after Alexio had instructed him to tell him her words *exactly*.

Alexio had put it down to anger that he'd thwarted her plans. He'd felt vindicated. But now he felt sick. Why hadn't she just taken the cheque?

Holding the jagged remains made a conflicting mix of things rush through him. Not least of which was the poisonous suspicion that this was a desperate ruse to pique his interest—make him go after her to find out *why*. So that ultimately she might get even more money.

Even now Alexio could feel anticipation spiking in his blood just at the thought of seeing her again, but...*damn her*...had she counted on this?

He felt something underneath him then, and shifted slightly to find that he was sitting on Sidonie's tatty university sweatshirt. She must have left it behind that day. Her pale face and wide, stricken eyes came back to him—the way she'd flatly agreed with him that, *yes*, she'd set out to seduce him on the plane. Something about that felt off now. His gut twisted...

She had protested her innocence. But he'd been so incensed he'd been unable to feel anything but the bitter sting of betrayal and anger at his own weakness for her.

Emotion, hot and impossible to push down, made his chest go tight. Without even thinking about what he was doing he brought the sweatshirt up to his nose and breathed deeply. Her scent, still faint but there, hit him like a steam train, that intriguing mix between floral and something spiky.

Galvanised by something that felt like a combination of panic and desperation, Alexio stood up and went into the bedroom. He hadn't opened the closet doors yet but now he did. All of the clothes were still hanging there. The clothes that he had ordered to be delivered for Sidonie before they'd arrived. She'd taken nothing. Not even the dress she'd worn to the club that night.

He could hear her voice as if she was there right now: *'Well, at least I won't have to worry about washing my knickers out in the sink. I'm sure your housekeeper would be horrified.'* This time Alexio heard and recognised the over-brightness of her voice and his sense of discomfort grew.

'You'll have to do it again. It's not good enough.'

Sidonie fought down the urge to scream and smiled as if her boss *wasn't* a sadistic control freak. There was nothing wrong with the way she'd made this bed in the five-star hotel where she worked for minimum wage three days a week.

'No problem.'

'And please hurry—the guest is due to arrive within the hour.'

Sidonie sighed deeply and stripped the bed in order to make it again. She ached all over and she longed for a hot bath like the one she'd had the other night. She hadn't had the time since then, because she'd taken on a full-time waitressing job in a Moroccan restaurant near the apartment six evenings a week. Her boss there had no qualms about hiring a pregnant woman, unlike the boss of the café where she worked the other two days a week when she wasn't at the hotel.

Finally her shift was over and she stretched out her back, instinctively putting a hand over her small bump, feeling the prickle of guilt. She knew she shouldn't be working so hard but she had no choice. A small voice taunted her. *You could contact him.* But she slammed her locker door shut in the staff changing room.

No way. Not going there. The thought of crawling to Alexio for help was anathema. She never wanted to see his cold, judgmental face again.

But when she emerged from the staff entrance at the side of the hotel and walked to the top of the lane his was the first face she saw. Shock held her immobile. He was leaning nonchalantly against the bonnet of a gleaming sports car, with his hands in his trouser pockets and his legs crossed at the ankles. Then he saw her and tensed, straightened up.

She blinked, but he didn't disappear. He was looking right at her with those golden-green eyes. For an awful treacherous second emotion rose in a dizzying sweep inside Sidonie. Her blood grew hot in her veins and her breath shortened. Her nipples tingled. All the signs of a woman in the throes of a lust that had lain dormant.

The oppressive, muggy August air seemed to seize the oxygen going into her lungs. For a second she felt so light-headed she thought she'd faint and she sucked in breath. It couldn't be him, she told herself, in spite of his not disappearing. It was a mirage. An apparition from her imagination torturing her.

In a bid to convince herself of that Sidonie turned and started to walk down the street. She heard a curse behind her and then her arm was taken in a strong grip. A familiar grip. Immediately Sidonie reacted violently to the effect it had on her body and soul and whirled around, ripping herself free.

She looked up and felt dizzy again. It was Alexio. In the flesh. That gorgeous flesh. He had no right to look so gorgeous. She frowned. Even if he did look leaner than when she'd last seen him and even if there were lines around his mouth and face. Lines she recognised, because she saw them in her own mirror every day. But he was still gorgeous, and she was still aware of the woman who had just walked past and done a double-take.

Anger flared and she seized it like a drowning person might seize a buoy.

'What do you want?' she spat out, her belly jumping with panic and a mix of other things she didn't want to investigate.

Sidonie vaguely noticed his open-necked light blue shirt and dark trousers and became very belatedly aware of her own woeful state of dress. Skinny jeans which she had to wear with the button open, flip-flops and a loose sleeveless smock shirt. Panic gripped her and then she reassured herself. He wouldn't notice the bump.

The fact that he hadn't come looking for her sooner stung her more than she liked to admit. She was pathetic.

That hatred burned bright within her, giving her strength. 'Well? What do you want? As far as I recall I didn't take anything on my way out of the villa.'

'No,' Alexio said heavily, 'it's what you left behind.'

Sidonie went blank for a moment, and then she saw that cheque in her mind's eye and felt fury all over again. Suddenly it made sense and she said out loud, 'You went back to the villa and discovered I hadn't cashed your precious cheque?'

'Yes,' he admitted.

Sidonie didn't like the way that made the fury diminish slightly. She'd assumed that he'd known all along that she hadn't taken his money and that it had made no difference. But all this time he'd thought she'd cashed in. Still, that didn't change anything.

'And this...'

Sidonie looked to see him holding out her university sweatshirt and was immediately bombarded with memories of meeting him on that plane, feeling like a hick.

She took it from him and said cuttingly, 'You came all this way to deliver my sweatshirt?'

A muscle in his jaw popped and Sidonie felt increasingly vulnerable.

She looked at her watch, and then at him, and injected her voice with false sweetness. 'Look, I'd love to stay and chat, but I have work to get to—so if you don't mind...'

She turned to walk away but he caught her arm again and Sidonie's blood leapt. She stopped and turned around and said in a low voice, 'Let me go, Christakos. We have nothing to say to each other.'

Except for the fact that he's the father of the baby growing in your belly.

Sidonie ignored her conscience. She needed to get away from him before her composure slipped.

Alexio battled to control the lust that had almost felled him the second he'd laid eyes on Sidonie again. His libido was back with a vengeance. He felt the fragility of Sidonie's arm under his hand. She'd lost weight—weight she could ill afford to lose. Her face was more angular... giving it a haunting beauty. Her eyes looked huge and there were shadows underneath. She was exhausted. He recognised it well.

He frowned. 'Aren't you just leaving work?'

She tried to pull her arm out of his grip but he had an almost visceral fear that if he let her go he'd never see her again. That glorious light golden hair was duller than he remembered, and scooped up into a bun much as it had been when they'd first met. Her neck looked long and vulnerable.

'I have two jobs—daytime and evening. Now, if you don't mind, I don't want to be late.'

'I'll give you a lift,' Alexio said impulsively.

He was still trying to get his head around seeing her again. His conscience pricked hard. She hadn't taken the money and she was working two jobs. To pay off the debts. Debts that weren't even hers. Because she had never wanted the money from him in the first place. The ramifications of this, if it were true, made Alexio reel.

This time Sidonie wrenched her arm free. She glared at Alexio and her eyes spat blue and green sparks at him. 'No, thank you. I do not want a lift or anything else from you. Now, please, go back to where you came from and leave me be.'

She turned and hurried away, her bag slung over her body. She looked very young. Alexio was grim. No way was he going to walk away until he knew what she was up to. The fact that he was clearly the last person she wanted to see only made him more determined.

As Alexio battled not to go and grab her again, and watched her disappear down the steps of a nearby metro station, he took out his mobile phone and made a terse call.

CHAPTER EIGHT

THAT NIGHT WHEN Sidonie left the Moroccan restaurant she felt so weary she could have cried. It wasn't helped by the state of agitation she'd been in all day after seeing Alexio. She'd kept expecting him to pop up out of nowhere again and she couldn't forget how he'd looked so drawn. Intense. He hadn't looked like the carefree playboy she remembered.

Still... She firmed her mouth. She'd done the right thing by sending him away. He had no right to come barging into her life again just because he wanted to solve the riddle of the mysterious uncashed cheque.

She would never forgive him for delving into her private life, seeking out her most painful memory and then throwing it in her face as an accusation. He hadn't been remotely interested in listening to her protest her innocence because he'd been all too ready to believe she was just as guilty as her mother. Although Sidonie winced slightly when she thought of the misfortune of him hearing that phone call when he had.

As Sidonie approached Tante Josephine's apartment she saw a familiar low-slung vehicle parked outside. Clearly out of place in this run-down area of Paris.

Her heart thumped erratically. The car was empty. Sidonie looked up and could see the first-floor apartment's lights blazing. Tante Josephine was usually in bed by now. Sidonie had a horrific image of her beloved Jojo being confronted by a tall, dark, intimidating Alexio and stumbled in her haste to get in.

When she almost fell in the front door she saw an idyllic scene of domesticity. Her Tante Josephine was perched on the edge of a chair, holding a cup of tea, and Alexio was seated opposite her on the couch, drinking a cup of coffee.

Tante Josephine put down her cup and stood up, her small matronly bosom quivering with obvious excitement. Her cheeks were bright pink. Sidonie could have rolled her eyes in disgust. The Alexio charm offensive had struck again.

Her aunt took her hands as she came in and Sidonie shot an accusing look at Alexio, whose face was unreadable. But something in his eyes made her heart jump. It was dark. Hard. As it had been on that day.

'Oh, Sidonie, your friend called by earlier. I told him he could wait here for you and we've been having the most pleasant chat.'

Alexio stood up then and made the small apartment laughably smaller. He looked pointedly at her belly and said, in perfect accentless French, 'I believe congratulations are in order?'

Sidonie went cold. *No.* Her aunt couldn't have... But she was notoriously indiscreet—especially with strangers...

Sidonie looked at her with horrified eyes but Tante Josephine, having the nous to suspect that something had just gone very wrong, fluttered nervously and said, 'Well, it's past my bedtime. I'll leave you young people to catch up.'

And then she was gone, leaving Sidonie facing her nemesis. The air was thick with tension.

Sidonie lifted her chin and waited. It didn't take long.

'You're pregnant?'

She tried not to be intimidated by the murderous look on Alexio's face. She'd never allowed herself the indulgence of daydreaming about this scenario, but for a man who didn't even want *a relationship*, this was pretty close to what she might have imagined.

'Yes,' she confirmed starkly, reluctantly. 'I'm pregnant.'

Alexio went pale under his olive skin. His voice sounded rough. 'Whose is it?'

Sidonie gaped at him. She'd also never envisaged that he would doubt the baby was his. She started to speak but a flash of anger rendered her speechless again. Incensed, she stalked over to him and planted her hands on her hips, looked up into that remote hard-boned face.

'Well,' she said, her voice dripping with sarcasm, 'I *did* have a threesome shortly after you cast me out of your life like a piece of unwanted luggage, so it could be Tom, Dick or Harry's baby. But we won't know until it's born and we can see who she or *he* looks like.' She was breathing hard.

Alexio just looked at her.

Growing even more incensed, Sidonie stabbed at his chest with her finger and tried to ignore how hard it felt.

'It's yours, you arrogant jerk,' she hissed, mindful of Tante Josephine. 'Cold-bloodedly seducing another billionaire hasn't exactly been high on my priority list lately.'

Alexio looked down into that furious face and felt numb. He welcomed it. His solicitor had failed to mention the very poignant fact that Sidonie's aunt had mild mental health issues.

And now...now *the baby. His* baby. Ever since Tante Josephine had excitedly informed him that Sidonie was expecting a baby, Alexio had felt as if he'd swallowed nails.

At first he'd told himself it couldn't possibly be his: they'd used protection every time. He'd been fanatical about it. Except for when they'd come home from the club and made love in the car, unable even to walk the few steps into the villa. That night was almost sixteen weeks ago now. Sixteen weeks of living in a blur. And now suddenly everything was in focus again.

Disgust at the memory of his lack of control that night had curdled his insides as Sidonie's aunt had chattered on, blithely unaware of the bomb she'd dropped. And then Sidonie had come in, looking panicked. Guilty.

The knowledge that she was telling the truth sank into him like a stone, casting huge ripples outward. He wanted to walk out through the door and keep walking. The sum of all his fears was manifesting itself right now in this room. He wasn't anywhere near ready to contemplate bringing a child into the world. Not after the childhood he'd endured.

A child had perhaps existed in his future life—far in the distant future—along with his perfect blonde wife. He had vowed long ago to make sure that no child of his would see the ugly reality of marriage, because any union *he* would have would be a union of respect and affection—not one punctuated by cold silences, bitter rows, possessive jealousy and violence.

'Well?' Sidonie demanded, hands on hips. 'Aren't you going to say something?'

Alexio's gaze narrowed on her and he realised he wanted to say plenty—but most of it involved his mouth being on Sidonie's. And then his gaze travelled down and he saw the small proud bump evident under her light jacket and the black clingy top she wore. Something within him seemed to break apart. Crumble.

Her hand went there automatically, as if to protect the child, and Alexio felt incensed at that. He thought of the recent revelation of the existence of his oldest half-brother and how his mother had kept him a dirty secret. After abandoning him. Would Sidonie have kept this child from him?

Finally he found his voice, and it was accusing. 'Why didn't you come to me?'

* * *

Sidonie let out a small mirthless laugh and backed away a step. Standing this close to Alexio was hazardous to her mental health and to her libido, which had decided to come out of its ice-like state.

She'd been dreadfully sick for the first trimester of her pregnancy but thankfully that had stopped and she was finally beginning to feel human again. She did not welcome this resurgence of a desire she had no control over.

Alexio was looking increasingly explosive as the news sank in and Sidonie felt a twinge of conscience. She recalled her own shock at finding out about the pregnancy, four weeks after she'd come back to Paris and with no sign of her period.

She crossed her arms tightly. 'You really think I would come to you with this news after you accused me of being a gold-digger? After you judged and tried me—after you had me *investigated* like a common criminal?'

Alexio flushed. 'Why did you agree with me, then, and let me believe that you set out to seduce me?'

Sidonie's arms tightened. 'I told you the truth, but you weren't interested in listening. Would you have believed me if I'd insisted on protesting my innocence?'

Remembering the excoriating feeling of betrayal was acute. Sidonie's emotions were rising and she knew she was too tired to hide them. She stood back and gestured to the door.

'I'd like you to leave now, please. I have to be up early.'

Alexio's eyes widened; his nostrils flared. He looked huge and intimidating, and Sidonie hated the impulse she had to run into his arms and beg him to hold her. She gritted her jaw and avoided his eyes.

Silkily he said, 'You expect me to just walk away?'

Sidonie nodded. 'Yes, please. We have nothing to discuss. You found me, I'm pregnant—end of story. You have nothing else to do here. Please go.'

Alexio's voice was tight with anger. 'We have plenty to discuss if I am your child's father. And you still haven't told me why you didn't take the money.'

Sidonie rounded on him again, eyes blazing, two spots of pink in each cheek. 'I didn't take your damn money, Christakos, because I wasn't interested in your money. I wasn't then and I'm not now.'

Emotion was getting the better of Sidonie, rising, making her shake.

'I will never forgive you for going behind my back and prying into my life. You had no right to judge me on the basis of something my mother did years ago. She paid that due, *I* paid that due, and so did my father. I want nothing to do with you and I wish I'd never laid eyes on you.'

She turned and went to the door, opened it.

Without looking at Alexio she said, 'I have to be up in five hours. Get out or I'll call the police and tell them you're harassing me.'

Alexio made some sort of sound—half anger, half frustration. To Sidonie's everlasting relief, though, he came to the door. She didn't look at him.

He said, with deadly precision, 'This isn't over, Sidonie. We need to talk.'

'Get out, Alexio.' Sidonie's voice had an edge of pleading to it that she hated. But finally he left.

For three days Sidonie had refused to talk to Alexio. She stonewalled him if he was waiting for her to come out of the hotel. She walked in the opposite direction if he was there when she emerged from the café. And at night she was tight-lipped if he offered her a lift for the short distance to the apartment after finishing her shift in the Moroccan restaurant.

Alexio seethed with frustration. He was getting her message loud and clear. She wanted nothing to do with him. She preferred working herself into a lather doing menial jobs rather than turn to him for help. But Alexio had had enough. He'd already set things in motion. Sidonie was pregnant with his child and that changed everything. As he'd watched her for the past three days the knowledge had sunk in more and more.

He needed to talk to her, though. And even though she looked half dead with exhaustion Alexio's body burned for her. Even now, from his car, where he was parked outside the restaurant, he let his gaze rake her up and down, taking in the black skirt, sheer tights and black top. The apron that barely disguised the growing swell of her belly. *His baby*.

In the past few days he'd had time for the news of the baby to sink in, and much to his surprise he'd found himself *not* feeling as trapped as he might have expected. Instead he felt a fledgling sense of excitement, wonder.

He thought of his nephew Milo and wondered if he'd have a son too—precocious and cute like him. Or a daughter, like Sidonie, with golden hair? When he imagined that he felt a tightening sensation in his chest so strong he had to take deep breaths to ease it.

She was serving a big table of men now, and she plucked the pen out from where she'd stuck it into the bun on the top of her head. She looked tired and harassed. Pale.

Alexio saw one of the men put a fleshy hand on her arm and a red mist came over his vision. Before he'd even realised what he was doing he was out of the car and pushing open the door of the small tatty restaurant.

'Sir,' Sidonie gritted out, 'please take your hand off me.'

'Don't tell me what to do. You're serving *me*.'

Sidonie felt a frisson of fear cutting through her hazy exhaustion, but even that didn't give her enough adrenalin to pull free. Just then a blast of warm evening air hit Sidonie's back and she looked around automatically to see Alexio, bearing down on her, his face tight with anger, his eyes fixed on where the man still held her.

Her heart thumped unevenly. For three days he'd dogged her heels and she'd ignored him. She'd seen his car outside and had hated to admit to herself that a part of her liked knowing he was there. She'd told herself stoutly that she hoped he was bored to tears and that she'd irritate him so much that he'd leave and never come back.

Alexio was right behind her now, and treacherously she wanted to lean back, to sink against him. That kept her rigid, fighting the waves of weariness which seemed to be gathering force.

His voice came low and threatening over her head.

'Let her go.'

The heavyset man was drunk and belligerent. He tightened his grip on Sidonie's arm, making her gasp out loud. Alexio reached around her and prised the man's fingers off her arm. He drew her back against him, his other hand going around her midriff, where her belly was round.

It was his touch that did it. It burned like a physical brand. It was too much. Alexio was turning her around now, looking down at her, asking something, but she couldn't hear it because a white noise was making her head fuzzy.

As if standing apart from herself, observing, Sidonie saw herself looking utterly fragile and helpless, with Alexio's hands huge on her arms, and she felt a moment of disgust at herself before everything went black.

Sidonie was in a dark, peaceful place with a soft regular *beep-beep* sound coming from somewhere nearby. Slowly, though, as her consciousness returned so did her memory, and she remembered looking up into Alexio's face and seeing him frown.

Alexio.

The baby.

Tante Josephine.

Sidonie's eyes opened and she winced at the bright light and the stark whiteness of the room. She went to move her arm and something pulled. She looked down to see a tube coming out of the back of her hand.

Her head felt slightly woolly. She noticed a movement out of the corner of her eye—something big—and then Alexio loomed into her vision. Tall and dark. His shirt open at the neck, looking crumpled. Stubble on his jaw.

The faint *beep-beep* sound got faster.

Automatically Sidonie's free hand went to her midriff, where she felt the comforting swell of her baby. Even so, she looked at Alexio. 'The baby?'

He looked grim. 'The baby is fine.'

'Tante Josephine?'

'Is fine too. She's been here all night. I sent her home a while ago.'

'All night?'

'You collapsed in the restaurant. I brought you straight to A and E in my car. You've been on a drip since you arrived and unconscious for nearly eight hours.'

'Am I okay?'

Some of the obvious tension left Alexio's jaw. 'The doctor said you're suffering from a mixture of exhaustion and stress and are generally run down.'

'Oh.'

Alexio started to look grim again, making flutters erupt in Sidonie's belly.

'You've run yourself completely into the ground…'

Something dangerous welled up inside her at his obvious censure and she looked away, terrified of the way her throat was starting to hurt and of the emotion which wouldn't go down.

In a voice that was far too high and tight she said, 'Thank you for bringing me here. You can go now.'

Alexio merely walked around the bed until he was in her eyeline again and folded his arms. Succinctly he said, 'No way.'

Just then the door opened and Sidonie turned her head to see a doctor and a nurse come in.

The doctor declared in French, 'You're awake! You gave us a bit of a scare, young lady...'

While he and the nurse did some tests and elaborated on what Alexio had told her Sidonie was busy trying to block out his presence in the room.

The doctor was soon sitting on the side of the bed and saying, 'You're due for your twenty-week scan in a few weeks, but after what's happened I'd like to do a scan now, just so we can double-check everything is okay.'

He must have seen something on her face because he said quickly, 'I've no reason not to believe everything is fine, but we'd like to be sure.'

Within a few minutes Sidonie was being wheeled in her bed to another part of the hospital. Alexio was by her side. She felt panicky. She was about to have a scan with Alexio looking on. She'd never envisaged *this* happening.

After they were wheeled into the room it all happened very fast. Sidonie's belly was bared and they were smoothing cold gel over it. She felt acutely self-conscious all of a sudden—which was crazy considering Alexio had seen more of her naked body than she probably had herself.

When the doctor put the ultrasound device over her belly a rapid sound filled the room. The baby's heartbeat. Immediately Sidonie's focus went to the screen, which was showing a fuzzy grey image. Her heart thumped as emotion climbed upwards again—but this time it was a different kind of emotion.

After a few minutes the doctor smiled and said, 'Everything looks absolutely normal. You have a fine, healthy baby, Sidonie—a little small, but developing well.'

Then he looked at her and at Alexio.

'Would you like to know the sex?' he asked. 'It's quite clear at the moment.'

Sidonie looked at Alexio, mortified that the doctor had assumed they were together. Even if Alexio *was* the father.

Alexio looked inscrutable and then said, 'It's up to you.'

Sidonie wrenched her gaze away from his with more effort than she liked and looked at the doctor again. She said hesitantly, 'I…I think so.' And then more firmly, as a sense of excitement took hold, 'Yes. I'd like to know.'

The doctor beamed at them. 'I'm very pleased to tell you you're having a baby girl.'

Sidonie felt something joyous erupt in her chest and heard a slightly choked sound coming from beside her. She looked up to see Alexio's eyes fixed on the screen, and there was an expression on his face that she'd never seen before. A kind of wonder.

Her belly swooped. She'd never allowed herself to imagine this kind of scenario. She'd expected to have the baby and then see how she felt about informing him, making sure she did it in such a way that he knew she wasn't telling him in order to get his money.

The thought of being likened to her grasping mother again had made her feel sick. But now that had all been taken out of her hands and she had the very uncomfortable sensation that Alexio was about to get a lot more prominent in her life.

Especially when the doctor wiped the gel off her belly, rearranged her clothes and said, 'We'll keep you in for one more night to help you get your strength back, and then I've been assured that your partner here will be getting you the best care and attention until you're back on your feet.'

Sidonie's head swivelled from Alexio's determined expression to the doctor's equally stern-looking face. *Her partner.* The words sent more flutters into her belly. After three days of being followed, she knew the likelihood of shaking Alexio off when she was feeling weak and vulnerable was extremely unlikely.

She looked at Alexio and said, 'I don't have much choice, do I?'

'No,' he agreed equably.

And that was that.

A week later

'You've done *what*?' Sidonie's mind was hot with rage and she felt her heart-rate zooming skyward, the flutters increasing in her belly. She even put a hand there unconsciously, barely noticing how Alexio's eyes dropped to take in the movement. She was too incensed.

Alexio faced her across the expanse of the beautiful first-floor apartment living room, overlooking the Jardin du Luxembourg. He was dressed in a steel-grey shirt and black trousers and Sidonie didn't like the way she was so *aware* of his physicality. The way she became even more aware of it each day as she grew stronger.

Alexio's voice was low, deep, 'I should have known Tante Josephine couldn't keep it quiet. I asked her not to say anything until you'd had a few more days' rest. But I didn't want her to be worried with you out of work.'

Sidonie struggled to take this in—along with the reminder that Alexio and Tante Josephine seemed to have forged a mutual admiration society.

Sidonie had been in this apartment, which Alexio was renting, for almost a week now. A week of Alexio being cool and solicitous. The consummate host. Paying for a nurse to come every day to check on Sidonie. Taking her outside to the Jardin du Luxembourg across the road to get some air. He was seemingly unperturbed by her continued campaign of obdurate silence, which was more due to her wish to avoid this reckoning and his probing gaze than to anything else. Her searing anger had been proving hard to hang onto, as if merely being in his presence on a daily basis was wearing away at it.

Except now it was back, and Sidonie welcomed it.

Her aunt had just left, to be taken home by Alexio's driver, but before she'd gone she'd spilled her secret.

Sidonie had marched straight into Alexio's office without knocking and declared, 'We need to talk.'

He'd looked up from his papers and sat back, arching a brow. '*Now* you're ready to talk?'

Before she'd had time to regret her impetuous action Sidonie had turned on her heel and walked into the vast living room, not liking how intimate the office space had felt. She had also been very aware that his assistant, who was there every day, had left. Until now she'd been a master at staying out of Alexio's way in the spacious apartment.

Sidonie crossed her arms over her chest and almost winced at how sensitive her breasts were. They had grown bigger. That awareness made her voice curt.

'Answer my question.'

Alexio looked as immovable as a rock, tall and intimidating. At that very moment Sidonie had a vivid memory of lying naked beneath him, spreading her legs wide to accommodate his body, feeling the bold thrust of his arousal against her slick body. Her legs wobbled alarmingly but she held firm.

Thankfully Alexio spoke before Sidonie's wayward memory could take over completely.

'I have paid off all of the debts and ensured that your aunt's mortgage has been paid in full.'

The sheer ease with which he'd been able to magic their debts away made her feel disorientated.

'How dare you?'

Sidonie was trembling. But she was afraid it was more to do with his proximity than her anger.

Alexio's eyes narrowed on her. 'I dare because you are carrying my child and we are now family. Tante Josephine is as much my responsibility as you are—and the baby.'

Sidonie's arms grew so tight she could feel her nails digging into her skin. She spoke from a deep well of hurt and rejection at this attempt to muscle into their lives. 'We are not your responsibility. I never came to you. I want nothing from you. As soon as I'm feeling better I will go and find work again and pay you back what we owe.'

Alexio's mouth went into a bitter line. 'I think you've more than proved your point, Sid. You'd prefer to put our child's health in jeopardy in order to save your pride.'

A lurch of hurt emotion rose up, strangling Sidonie for a moment. Then his words *our child* and *Sid* impacted.

When she'd gathered herself she said with quiet ferocity, 'Do not call me that. My name is Sidonie. And the last thing I want to do is put *my* child in danger. I will keep working because, in case you've forgotten, you called me a hustler and I would prefer to work than to be accused of being that again.'

To her horror, Sidonie's voice had cracked on the last words and she turned now, facing blindly away from Alexio, breathing harshly, emotion getting the better of her.

She heard him move behind her and said rawly, 'Don't come near me.'

He stopped. Tears stung at Sidonie's eyes; her throat ached. She hated him. And she repeated this to herself as she struggled to regain her equilibrium.

His voice came from behind her, tight. 'Sidonie, we need to talk about this... I recognise that I was too hasty that day. I didn't give you a chance to explain.'

Sidonie let out a half-choked laugh at that understatement and said bitterly, 'No, you'd obviously made up your mind and couldn't wait to see the back of me.'

She heard him sigh. The shadows outside were lengthening into dusk. His voice was gruffer now. 'The chef has left some food for us. Let's eat and then we can talk…okay?'

Like a coward, she felt herself wanting to make up some excuse, say that she was too tired, but in truth she felt fine. She turned round, arms still crossed, and faced him. His eyes were intense and her skin prickled. She couldn't keep putting off the conversation.

'Okay, fine.'

Within minutes Alexio was serving them both a light chicken casserole in the dining room off the kitchen area. They ate in silence, but tension was mounting inside Sidonie as she tried to avoid looking at Alexio's large hands and remembering how they'd felt on her skin.

Sitting here eating like this was bringing back memories of that first night in London. The sheer fizzing exhilaration of anticipation. And as if her body was some dumb appendage—an assortment of limbs that wasn't attached to her brain—that same fizzing anticipation was rushing through her right now. Gathering force.

She was uncomfortably aware of every erogenous zone. Her breasts felt tender, sensitive. Swollen. She couldn't stop imagining Alexio's mouth lowering towards one thrusting, naked peak…

With a spurt of agitation, Sidonie let her knife drop with a clatter to the plate. Alexio looked up, that gaze narrowed on her flushed face.

Sidonie stood up, feeling feverish. 'I've had enough. Food.' *God.* She couldn't even articulate a sentence.

Alexio looked as cool as a cucumber while Sidonie felt a bead of sweat trickle between her breasts.

He wiped his mouth with his napkin and said, 'Coffee?'

Sidonie seized on the chance to escape that incisive gaze

and nodded her head. 'Some herbal tea, maybe…the housekeeper brought some today.'

Alexio got up and left the room. Cursing herself for this very unwelcome resurgence of desire, Sidonie went back into the drawing room to stand at the window. Praying for control. Praying that the butterflies in her belly would cease.

She put her hand on her belly and was half frowning at how strong the sensation was when she suddenly realised something. She gasped out loud.

A voice came from behind her, concerned. 'What is it?'

Sidonie whirled around, alight with her discovery for a moment, forgetting everything else. 'For a few days I've been feeling butterflies, but I thought it was—'

She stopped dead, because she'd been about to blurt out *just your effect on me*.

She blushed and said, 'It's the baby. I can feel the baby moving…'

Alexio was holding out a cup towards her and she grabbed it before she could see the effect of her words on his face.

She had a sudden image of one of his hands splayed across her belly and said quickly, 'It's not strong enough yet for anyone else to feel…'

Sidonie took the cup and moved away, taking a sip to hide her burning face.

Alexio gritted his jaw at how Sidonie moved so skittishly away from him, that golden hair looking so much shinier and thicker now, down and shielding her face from him. In the space of only a few days of rest and being well fed she was already looking so much better. The hollows of her cheeks were filling out.

He felt as if he was going to snap soon with the tension building inside him. With every second that passed he wanted to turn into a feral animal and strip Sidonie bare and take her, sating himself and drowning out the recriminatory voices in his head.

But he couldn't. She was pregnant. And she hated his guts.

She looked incredibly young now, in leggings and a loose T-shirt. Of course she'd refused his offers to get her some clothes, so her Tante Josephine had brought her some.

When he could finally move his gaze up from those slim shapely legs and over her belly, hidden under the loose material, to her face, she was looking at him with that aquamarine gaze, something determined in their depths.

'Why did you have me investigated?'

Alexio put down his coffee cup onto a nearby table. Sidonie had her hands wrapped tightly around her own mug.

He looked into her eyes. He owed her this.

'Because what happened between us made me nervous. Because I'd never taken a woman to Santorini before. Because for my whole life I've been cynical and when I was with you I forgot to be. And it freaked me out enough to think that by investigating you I'd still be in control.'

CHAPTER NINE

SIDONIE BLINKED. SHE tried to take his words in. Her belly felt as if it was dropping from a height, and she felt unsteady. 'I'm…you hadn't taken a woman there before?'

He shook his head, eyes intent on her reaction.

She couldn't even hide it. She thought of something. 'But…the clothes…I assumed they had belonged to other women…' Sidonie felt very gauche now.

Alexio frowned and then emitted a disgusted, '*Theos*. You think I would do that? Buy a wardrobe full of clothes and just hope that they would fit a stream of women?'

Sidonie glared back at him, stung with embarrassment. 'Well, how would I know? I thought that was some lovers' bolthole.'

Alexio ran a hand through his hair and said, half to himself, 'No wonder you sounded funny…and yet you didn't say anything.'

Now Sidonie was squirming. 'I didn't want to look stupid…or naïve. If you'd had lovers who were used to that kind of thing…'

The clothes had been bought for her alone. The knowledge made her reel. They hadn't been cast-offs. Sidonie felt increasingly as if she wanted to claim fatigue and run away. But Alexio had a familiar stern look on his face now.

Sidonie went and sat down on a nearby couch, placing

her cup on a table. She clasped her hands on her lap to stop them trembling.

Alexio walked away and stood at the window with his back to her for a long moment, as if he too had to gather himself. When he turned around he looked bleak.

'My solicitor had rung me with what he'd learned about your past that day... I told him it had nothing to do with you. But then he told me about the fact that you'd taken on your aunt's debts, and that put a question in my head as to why you hadn't mentioned this—why you were acting as if you didn't have this huge thing hanging over you.'

Sidonie replied, with a trace of bitterness, 'Because I was escaping from it. I never had any intention of telling you about it. What did it have to do with anything? I knew we were only going to be together for a few days...it was only meant to be one night.'

That last came out almost accusingly as Sidonie recalled how persuasive he'd been and how easily she'd capitulated.

'I knew my aunt was okay—she was on holiday with a group she travels with every year...'

Alexio's voice was hard. 'My solicitor put the seed of suspicion in my head. I refused to believe the worst, though. I told him that. I was angry with myself for even asking him to investigate you.' He sighed heavily. 'I went looking for you. I was going to confess what I'd done and ask you about it...and that's when I overheard part of your conversation.'

Sidonie felt as if the wind had been knocked out of her for a moment at hearing this. When she could speak she admitted, 'I can appreciate how damning that conversation must have been to hear, but my aunt was in hysterics. Someone had fed her with horror stories of being repossessed and worse. I knew she wouldn't feel placated with any reassurances that I'd be there to take her burden. You've met her—you can see for yourself what she's like. I knew she'd only understand something emphatic like someone else saving us. She wouldn't have believed that I could get jobs and pay off the debts over time unless I was physically there to reassure her.'

Sidonie cringed when she thought of how she'd told her aunt *He's crazy about me* and looked down.

'I panicked and said the first thing I thought of.'

She looked up and Alexio's face was unreadable. Sidonie hated the suspicion that he still didn't fully believe her. But then he came and sat down on a chair near the couch and looked at her.

'Will you tell me what happened with your mother?'

Sidonie was about to blurt out that it was none of his business and then she felt those delicate flutters in her abdomen again. *Their daughter.* He had a right to the full story.

She sighed deeply. She'd never told anyone about this before. Feeling it might be easier to talk without Alexio's cool gaze on her, Sidonie stood up and went to the window, arms hugging her midriff.

'She was born in the suburbs. She and my aunt had an extremely impoverished upbringing. Their father ran out on my grandmother, leaving her to raise two daughters on her own—one with special needs My grandmother had drink problems…mental health issues…depression. Neglect was a feature of their lives. She died when my mother was about seventeen. She had to look after Tante Josephine full-time then…which she resented. She was young and bright. Beautiful. She craved opportunities beyond the grim reality of the suburbs.'

Sidonie turned round.

'My mother never told me much, but Tante Josephine's told me enough for me to know that it was pretty tough. When my mother was twenty she won a local beauty competition. Part of the prize was a trip to Dublin for the next round. She went and never came back, leaving my aunt to fend for herself on social protection in their mother's flat.

That's why my father bought her the apartment when he could. He always felt sorry for her—for how my mother had treated her...'

Shame rose up within Sidonie but she forced it down and kept looking at Alexio, determined not to allow her mother's shame to be *her* shame.

'My father was the married man my mother had the affair with—*not* the man she ended up marrying. He owned the language school where she'd signed up to do an English course with the prize money from the competition. When he found out she was pregnant he dumped her. She never forgave him for it. My stepfather met my mother around the same time. He was crazy about her and stepped in and offered to marry her.'

Sidonie's chin lifted imperceptibly.

'She was avaricious and selfish. No one knows that better than me and my aunt. And my stepfather, who stood by her despite the public humiliation she put him through. She put us all through hell when she ended up being prosecuted, and yet my stepfather never once let me feel anything less than his own child. She was put in jail for two years when I was eight years old. I had to endure taunts at school every day, because we couldn't afford to move until she was released from prison.'

Sidonie's voice shook with passion.

'I spent my whole life dreading someone finding out about her past. That's why I don't talk about it. But I am *not* her, and you had no right to assume I was like her—no matter what evidence you thought you had...'

She recalled one of the things he'd hurled at her. 'Not even the fact that I told you I liked jewellery. I'm a woman, Alexio. A lot of women like glittery shiny things. It doesn't mean we're all inveterate gold-diggers.'

Alexio stood up too, and immediately a flare of awareness made Sidonie take a step back. His eyes flashed at her movement and something tightened between them.

His mouth was a grim line. 'I'm sorry that I didn't give you the chance to tell me this, for misjudging you and for leaving you to go through what you have for the past few months. You should never have had to deal with this on your own...'

The lines of his face grew stark and his voice roughened.

'But I'm not sorry you're pregnant. I want this baby too.'

He came closer and everything in Sidonie tightened with anticipation. She tried to ignore it.

Heavily, Alexio continued, 'I should tell you why I jumped to such conclusions. My mother was the most cynical person I've ever known. She taught me not to trust at an early age, and the world and my peers have only confirmed her lesson. I'm used to lovers as cynical as I have become. You were so different from anyone I've ever met before...'

His words resounded in Sidonie's head, shocking her. She felt weakened by this mutual confessional. The hard knot of tension and pain inside her felt as if it was dissolving, treacherously.

Alexio went on. 'My parents' marriage was not happy. It was sterile, loveless. I told you why I decided to break with my father...but there's more to it than that. Once he beat my mother. I rushed in to stop him, to protect her, but she put me out of the room and went back in and closed the door, shutting me out.'

Alexio's mouth twisted.

'She didn't want or need my protection—not even then... And that's why I wanted nothing more to do with my father.'

Sidonie's heart clenched. She felt increasingly vulnerable and was aware that only inches separated them now. When had they even moved that close?

Alexio's hand closed around one upper arm, warm against her bare skin, setting off a chain reaction.

'I'm sorry, Sidonie. Truly.'

Something moved between them. Something fragile and yet something very earthy too.

But Sidonie was reeling. It was too much. She pulled her arm free and said weakly, 'I'm tired now. I should go to bed.'

Alexio just looked at her in the soft glow of the lamps. 'Yes.'

Sidonie knew she should move, but for a second she couldn't seem to. All she could see was that mouth, and all she could think about was how she wanted to feel it on hers right now. She had to get out of there before she did something stupid. Exposed herself.

Backing away, eyes huge, as if she was afraid he might pounce on her, Sidonie left the room and shut herself inside her bedroom. Her heart was beating as rapidly as if she'd just run a mile. Alexio's words swirled in her head and every cell in her body was protesting at being out of his proximity.

Trying her best to ignore the insistent throbbing of her blood and pulse, Sidonie washed herself and put on her nightshirt, got into bed. But as soon as she lay down she knew sleep was an impossibility.

She clenched her hands into fists. It was as if his words had unlocked something tight and painful inside her and replaced it with pure desire. She needed Alexio with an almost physical pain. Hunger for him made her grit her jaw. Hormones were flooding her body, stronger than anything she'd felt before.

Almost without thinking, operating on some very base level, Sidonie got out of bed and opened the door of her bedroom. She went back into the drawing room and saw Alexio standing at the window, looking like a remote figure. For a second she hesitated, but then he turned round… and she was no more capable of going back than she was of ceasing breathing.

Rawly, she blurted out, 'I need you to make love to me.'

Alexio thought he was dreaming. He saw Sidonie silhouetted in the light of a nearby lamp. Her flimsy nightshirt clearly showed the shape of her body and the fact that she wore no underwear. His blood boiled, blanking his brain of everything he'd been thinking about. Lust surged, making him so hard it hurt.

Her breasts looked bigger, he could see the swell of her belly, and something deeply primal within him exulted fiercely. *His* seed in her belly. After their conversation he'd been feeling ridiculously exposed, but that was incinerated by the heat he felt right now.

Fearing she might disappear, Alexio instructed her throatily, 'Come here.'

Sidonie moved with endearing jerkiness, and then she was in his arms and Alexio's mouth was on hers. Her body was pressing into him so hard it felt as if he'd be branded with her shape for ever and he was devouring her…and wondering dimly how he'd survived for as long as he had without this.

Sidonie groaned deep in her throat as sheer wanton pleasure burned up inside her at the feel of Alexio's arms around her again, his mouth on hers, his tongue stroking hers.

She barely noticed him lifting her up into his arms, feeling weightless as she wrapped her arms around his neck and sank deeper and deeper into the kiss. They only broke apart so that Alexio could lay Sidonie down on his bed, and she looked up at him as he pulled off his shirt, revealing the hard-muscled perfection of his torso. He looked leaner, harder than she remembered, and everything feminine within her sighed voluptuously.

He took off his trousers and underwear and he was unashamedly naked and aroused. The dusky light from outside bathed him in a golden glow.

'I need to see you.' His voice was hoarse.

Sidonie's body was on fire. She couldn't remember feeling so desperate, so sensitised. Her breasts were literally throbbing, aching with need. And between her legs she felt damp and hot.

She sat up slightly and pulled her nightshirt off, but her hands were awkward.

Alexio said roughly, 'I'll do it.'

He reached down and pulled it up and then all the way off. She was naked but she couldn't drum up any embarrassment. She needed him too badly.

She could see Alexio's jaw tighten as his eyes devoured her. And then his gaze moved down to the swell of her belly. She lay back on the bed, her breathing tortured. Alexio moved between her legs, forcing them apart slightly, and then came down, resting over her on his hands. Sidonie put her hands on his arms and he bent his head again, kissing her deeply, intimately. His tongue stabbed deep, sliding along hers, making her moan with need.

When his mouth moved across her jaw and down further Sidonie's nipples tightened unbearably. Torturously slowly he came closer and closer to that distended hard tip, and when he drew it into his mouth and suckled she cried out. It hadn't been like this before. This intense.

His hand was cupping her other breast, kneading it gently, fingers pinching that peak. Sidonie's hands were in his hair, clasping him to her with a death grip. When his mouth left her breast and his head moved down Sidonie let out a gasp of disappointment which quickly turned to something else when he pressed a kiss to her belly. For a second her desire was eclipsed by something much more profound and dangerously tender.

Before she could dwell on it Alexio was moving lower, spreading her legs wide, his breath feathering across the incredibly sensitised nerves between her legs. She had to put her fist to her mouth to stop from crying out again when his mouth covered her. His tongue swirled and suckled with merciless and expert precision until she couldn't hold it back and a flood of ecstasy rushed through her in unstoppable waves.

The intensity of her orgasm left Sidonie trembling all over and she had a moment of *déjà vu*, remembering her first time with Alexio and how intense it had been. He loomed over her now, broad and awe-inspiring, and she wanted him deep inside her with a ferocious urgency that made her feel desperate.

Sidonie hooked her legs around his thighs, drawing him closer.

He emitted a guttural, 'I don't want to hurt you…the baby…'

'You won't,' she assured him breathlessly.

With a low groan, Alexio pressed closer, and then she felt the thick head of his erection sliding into her. So big.

Sidonie let out a sound of frustration, needing more, drawing him even closer, and then with one powerful thrust he sheathed himself deep within her tight, slick body. Tears of emotion sprang into Sidonie's eyes and she closed them fiercely in case Alexio might see the betraying glitter.

He was moving now—slowly, ruthlessly, in and out. The ride was slow and intense. Tension tightened inside Sidonie, making her moan and plead incoherently for Alexio to never stop.

When her climax approached Sidonie's eyes flew open. She could only see Alexio's green gaze boring into her. He held her suspended on the crest of the wave until he thrust one last time and her whole body convulsed with pleasure around his.

* * *

At some point, in the silvery glow of the moon, Sidonie woke up to feel Alexio behind her, pressing kisses to the back of her neck, making her shiver with renewed arousal. He bent over her, scooping her back against him, coming behind her, a hand reaching to find her breast and cup it, making her moan with sleepy and delicious desire.

He said softly beside her ear, 'Come up on your knees.'

Sidonie was wide awake now, and practically panting with need. Just like that—within seconds. She did as he asked and came up on her knees, her legs spread. Her upper body was on the bed, her elbows bent. Alexio stretched over her back and she could feel his steel-hard erection move against her. He took her arms and stretched them over her head. Her hands automatically gripped the pillow.

And then his thighs were behind hers, his legs moving hers even further apart. Like this, she felt unbelievably exposed and wanton. And yet never more aroused. He drew his hand down her spine, fingers tracing her bones, and then his hands spread around her hips, drawing her back and into him.

She turned her cheek to the bed. Her hands tightened to white knuckles when she felt one hand move between them to explore how ready she was. She could have wept when she felt the tremor run through his body on feeling the evidence of her desire.

Taking his hand away, he replaced it with his potent erection, and as he thrust deep and started the relentless slide of his body in and out of hers again Sidonie felt as if she was losing it completely. All that control she'd held on to for four months, the hatred... It was being washed away and leaving her vulnerable, defenceless. Raw.

Alexio's body moved with awesome power, wresting away Sidonie's ability to think rationally. When he bent close over her back and drew her hair aside, so that he could press a kiss to her exposed skin and cup her breast, she couldn't hold on any more and shattered to pieces for a third time.

When Alexio woke in the early dawn light he kept his eyes closed for a minute, relishing the hum of satisfaction in his body. Slowly, though, the satisfaction faded as memories took over.

Alexio opened his eyes and realised he was alone in his bed. If not for the crumpled sheets and that hum in his body he might have imagined that he'd had another night of dreams so vivid he woke up aching and aroused.

But sleeping with Sidonie had been no dream. It had surpassed any mere dream. She was more than he remembered—even more responsive.

Why had she left him? Suddenly irritated at the empty bed, Alexio threw back the covers and jumped out. He pulled on a pair of discarded jeans nearby, left them open, and prowled through the apartment to Sidonie's room. The door was shut. He opened it softly and went in. His heart clenched. She was in her nightshirt, lying on her side, with her legs pulled up. Long golden copper hair was spread out around her head. Lashes were long and dark against her flushed cheeks. Her breaths were deep and even.

He stood transfixed for a long moment and realised with a creeping sense of fatality that everything he'd ever known or believed in had spectacularly blown up in his face.

Yet even now he could hear his mother's cold voice in his head, mocking him: *'It's all an act, Alexio...she's fooling you even now, making you want her. Making you believe that she'd do anything but take your money when she has your baby in her belly, the best insurance a woman can get...'*

Alexio blocked out the voice with an effort. He couldn't believe he'd told Sidonie *everything* last night. The darkest, dirtiest secret of his father's violence. He'd never even told Rafaele about that. He'd never forget his mother's beautiful face, bruised and battered. But she hadn't cried out. She hadn't let him help. She'd put him from the room and closed the door and contained the incident. Always so cold, so frigid.

He could feel the remnants of the same rigidity that he'd learned from her in him, and also the desire to let it loosen. He thought of everything Sidonie had told him last night. He believed her. He *wanted* to believe her. But some deep part of him was clinging to the tentacles of the past like a drowning man clinging to a buoy.

One thing was for sure: there was no way she could not agree to the fact that Alexio was going to be an integral part of her life from now on—and his daughter's.

When Sidonie woke the following morning her whole body felt deliciously lethargic and sated. And then her eyes opened and horror coursed through her. *Alexio.* She'd begged him to make love to her last night like some kind of lust-crazed wanton.

She cringed. But then she recalled their conversation and that sensation of something giving way inside her, melting. In the cold light of day, and after what had happened last night, Sidonie couldn't keep pretending to herself that she hated Alexio. Far from it.

She'd fallen for him on Santorini—if not as early as that first night in London. *Who was she kidding?* she castigated herself. She'd probably fallen for him on that plane, before they'd even kissed. And, yes, she'd hated him for the way he'd treated her, but she'd really never stopped falling for him.

And after what he'd told her about his mother and his father... It didn't excuse him, but it made her weak heart want to empathise with how a man had become so cynical at such a young age and never had any experience to counteract that.

No wonder he'd checked himself and doubted what was going on between them if he'd never allowed a woman that close before…

Feeling dangerously dreamy all of a sudden, Sidonie got out of bed and took a shower, all at once eager to see Alexio and cursing herself for having left his bed because she'd felt so raw and exposed.

Since he'd come back into her life he'd done nothing but support her, and had taken the news of her pregnancy on board with admirable equanimity. And what had she done? Thrown everything back in his face…scared in case he got close enough to see how deep her feelings ran for him. Scared in case he'd see how flimsy that hatred was because she knew she still loved him and hated her own weakness.

He'd paid off the debts to ease her aunt's mind and to take the burden of pressure off *her*. And even though that still made Sidonie feel uncomfortable she knew that he'd undoubtedly done it out of concern for her health and the baby's.

Those debts were a drop in the ocean for him, But she was still concerned enough to make a case for paying him back. The thought of just letting him pay off debts her mother had been responsible for made Sidonie feel faintly ill.

But after last night—surely something had shifted between them? Maybe something of what they'd had before hadn't been irretrievably lost…?

Sidonie's heart beat fast at that. Maybe the lines of communication could be a little more open now. Surely he would respect her desire to pay him back?

When Sidonie went in search of Alexio and found him reading a newspaper at the breakfast table she had a smile on her face. It soon faded, though, when he looked at her with a cool expression, his face unreadable.

'Good morning.'

'Morning...' she said faintly, wondering if this clean-shaven epitome of elegance in a dark suit and shirt was the same man who had driven her to the brink of her endurance three times last night. Now she didn't feel so bad about leaving his bed. The sense of rawness and vulnerability was back with a vengeance.

The housekeeper who worked for a few hours every day, preparing meals and cleaning the apartment, bustled in with breakfast for Sidonie and she sat down silently. The doctor had recommended a diet full of nutrients to help her get back on her feet but she couldn't stomach anything now. She felt a little sick.

'Okay?' Alexio's question was cool.

Sidonie nodded and avoided his eye, picking at the food. It was as if nothing had happened.

He finished his coffee and put his paper down. 'We should talk...' he said.

Sidonie gave up pretending to try and eat and pushed her plate away slightly. She looked at him and wished she could block out the images from the previous night. The way he'd looked so intense... And she wished she could block out her feelings too, but it seemed as if now she'd admitted how she felt to herself she'd opened a dam.

'Talk about what?'

Alexio looked serious. 'About us...where we go from here.'

Something went cold inside Sidonie. She'd imagined a conversation like this, but not with Alexio sounding as if he was about to discuss profits and losses. Foolishly she'd imagined something altogether more passionate.

In her silence, he clarified, 'We can't go on in this state

of limbo... You're feeling better. I have to get back to work. We need to figure out the logistics.'

Limbo. Was that what he thought last night had been about? While Sidonie had been realising how much she loved him?

She slid out of her chair and stood up. Alexio stood too, instantly dwarfing her. She moved back.

'I don't think I'm quite getting your meaning.'

His hands curled around the back of his chair. 'What I'm talking about is where we'll live—how we will proceed. I'll have to buy a new house, of course. The apartment isn't suitable for a baby... Or maybe you want to be here? Near to your aunt?'

Sidonie's mouth had fallen open at the way he'd laid everything out so starkly. There was no emotion involved. She recovered her wits and felt anger rising at his cool arrogance.

'This baby is not *logistics*—it's a baby. Our daughter.'

Those words pricked her heart. She put her hands on her belly, the by now nearly constant fluttering comforting her.

'I don't expect *us* to *proceed* anywhere. I do expect *me* to go on with *my* life, though.'

Alexio looked every inch the powerful tycoon in that moment. 'This isn't up to you, Sidonie. You *will* allow me to provide for you and the baby.'

Sidonie cursed herself for ever having cast him in the role of benign benefactor. Emotions bubbled over. Enough for the both of them.

'Her name is Belle. Not *the baby*. And I stupidly thought that after last night something had changed...that—' She stopped and cursed herself silently. She'd said too much.

Alexio looked disgusted. 'Our daughter is *not* going to be called Belle—what kind of a name is that?'

Sidonie replied faintly, 'It's Tante Josephine's favourite name.'

She felt dazed at how naïve she'd been. *Again*. Nothing had changed.

That green gaze narrowed on her. 'You thought *what* had changed?'

Sidonie shook her head, feeling sick at how she'd almost given herself away. Disgusted with herself for allowing some confessional conversation and some hot sex to melt away her feelings of anger. She'd only ever been a transitory visitor through Alexio's bed. And now he was stuck with her.

'Nothing. I'm not doing this, Alexio—committing to some sterile arrangement just for your benefit.'

'We desire each other. Last night proved that beyond a doubt.'

Sidonie felt as exposed as if he'd just stripped her naked. A few hours ago he had.

Lifting her chin, she said tautly, 'That was hormones.'

Alexio looked comically confused for a moment. 'Hormones?'

Sidonie nodded, desperate to convince him that he had it wrong. 'It's in my pregnancy book—you can read about it. It's very common for pregnant women to feel more…' Sidonie faltered. In spite of her best efforts she blushed fiercely. 'More…amorous. It's because of all the extra blood.'

The confusion left Alexio's face and now he looked livid. A muscle throbbed in his temple. 'Hormones…? *Extra blood*? That was chemistry—pure and simple.' He was almost roaring now. 'Are you trying to tell me that any man would have done to satisfy your urges last night?'

Sidonie's face burned, but valiantly she affected as much insouciance as she could and with a small shrug reiterated, 'I'm just telling you what's in my pregnancy book.'

Alexio's face was rigid with rejection, and even she felt the sting of her conscience.

'You wanted me as much as I wanted you. There might have been extra hormones involved, but it was inevitable.'

Sidonie cursed silently. So much for hoping to convince Alexio that any man would have done. *As if.* Even now she wanted him, in spite of his being so arrogant that she wanted to hit him.

Sidonie clenched her hands into fists and glared at him for making her love him. For making her want him. For humiliating her.

'Nothing has changed, Alexio. We're exactly where we were when you arrived in Paris. The only difference now is that I owe *you* money instead of a bank.'

Alexio looked livid again. 'Stop saying that. You owe me nothing. I want to try and make this work, Sidonie.'

Sidonie felt bitter. '*This* is not a car, Alexio. And I can tell you that it's not working. Desire or no desire. That's not enough. I won't allow you to put me and our daughter up like some kind of discarded mistress and her child. I am not a sponger. I will work to pay my way for me and my child, like millions of other women around the world.'

Alexio's mouth was a tight line of displeasure. 'Millions of other women around the world haven't had the sense to fall pregnant by a billionaire.'

Sidonie gasped and went pale as his unspoken words throbbed silently between them: *So stop pretending that you don't want my support.*

Alexio immediately put out a hand. 'Sid...wait. I didn't mean it like—'

Sidonie cut him off with ice in her voice, even as her heart was breaking all over again. 'I've already told you *not* to call me that. My name is Sidonie. And you've said quite enough. You still don't trust me, do you?'

She saw the flare of guilt in his eyes and something inside her withered and died. She couldn't say another word.

She shook her head and backed away, and then turned and walked out of the room.

Alexio watched her go and then tunnelled his hands through his hair. He closed his eyes and repeated every curse he'd ever heard under the sun. Watching the way she'd gone pale just now... Something inside him had curdled and now he felt the acrid taste of panic. That hadn't gone at all the way he'd expected it to.

As if one moment of this relationship with this woman had *ever* gone the way he'd expected it to...

From the moment she'd appeared at breakfast with that shy smile Alexio had felt the dam of emotion inside him threatening to burst free. But he wasn't ready yet. It was too much.

When he came out of the dining room he saw Sidonie putting on her coat and lifting her bag. The panic escalated, making him feel constricted, rudderless. As if he were freefalling from a great height.

'Where are you going?'

Sidonie avoided his eye. 'I said I'd go over to Tante Josephine's this morning.'

She looked at him then, but there was no expression on her face or in her eyes. She was pale. The swell of her belly was visible under her top. Alexio had a sudden urge to beg Sidonie not to go, but something held him back. The memory of his mother's cold face when he'd blurted out, *Why can't you love each other?* Those tentacles were dragging him back, stronger than he could resist.

He assured himself he was overreacting. Sidonie would be back this afternoon and they would talk again. When he'd regained some sense of being in control. He was still shaking with rage at the insinuation that she would have slept with any willing red-blooded man last night because she'd just been horny.

'My car and driver are outside if you want to use them.'

Sidonie said a quiet, 'Okay.' And then she opened the door and left. Alexio had the awful sensation that even while he was so intent on retaining control he was losing it anyway.

Alexio spent the morning and early afternoon on the phone to his offices in London and Athens. But he couldn't get his poisonous words to Sidonie out of his head: *Millions of other women around the world haven't had the sense to fall pregnant by a billionaire.* Or how stricken she had looked after he'd said them. She'd looked that stricken on Santorini.

A cold fist seemed to be squeezing his heart.

His solicitor Demetrius rang and asked him, 'When are you going to stop playing nursemaid and come back to work?'

A volcanic rage erupted deep inside Alexio as he recalled how this man, *his friend,* had unwittingly fed Alexio's deeply cynical suspicions four months ago, and he slammed the phone down before he could say or do something he might regret. Like fire him. Alexio had no one to blame but himself.

He looked at the phone belligerently. The fact was that he had no desire for work. He had desire only for one thing and he was very much afraid that he had just let that one thing slip out of his grasp.

He picked up the phone again and dialled. After a few seconds a recording of Sidonie's voice sounded in his ear: *'I'm sorry I can't take your call. Leave me a message and I'll get back to you.*

Short, economical. Up-front. Alexio felt sick, and the back of his neck prickled. He didn't leave a message. He made another call and asked Tante Josephine if Sidonie had left her yet.

Tante Josephine answered him and the panic rose high enough in his throat to strangle him.

He forced himself to sound calm. 'When did she leave?'

She told him and Alexio did rapid calculations in his head. Somehow he managed to get out something vaguely coherent and then he put down the phone and stood up. And then he sat down again abruptly. Alexio didn't know what to do, and he was filled with a sense that for the first time in his largely charmed life he couldn't predict the outcome with his usual arrogance.

An image of his brother Rafaele came into his mind's eye, and he recalled how turbulent his emotions had been at seeing his brother embrace love and a family. Alexio realised now that he'd been poisonously jealous of his brother. Jealous of what he'd reached out for when everything in his life should have told him it wasn't possible.

Something was swelling inside Alexio's chest now—something bigger than the past. And with it came the fear that had held him back that morning. But for the first time Alexio didn't fight it. And then he felt another very fledgling feeling take hold: *hope*. Did he dare to think that he too could reach out and take hold of something he'd once believed in? Even if there might be nothing on the other side?

With a grim sense of resolve, and knowing that he just didn't have a choice any more, Alexio made the first of a series of calls and then instructed his driver to have the car ready.

CHAPTER TEN

SIDONIE SAT IN her seat, legs tucked up beneath her, and looked out of the small oval window of the plane. A faint heat haze shimmered off the tarmac outside. She felt bad about leaving her aunt behind, even if she *had* assured Sidonie she was fine. She was going to Dublin to enquire about getting back onto the college programme for her final year.

But then she felt the flutters in her belly and panic gripped her. How could she be thinking of going back to college when she was due to have her baby before Christmas? Tears pricked her eyes. She cursed her impetuousness. She hadn't really thought this through at all. She'd just wanted to get far away from Paris and Alexio's ongoing mistrust before he reduced her to rubble.

She couldn't believe she'd left herself wide open to his cynicism again.

She heard the sound of the air hostess saying, 'Your seat, sir.'

Sidonie's heart stopped for a moment and she looked around. An incredible sense of disappointment lanced her when she saw a small, very rotund man, sweating profusely, taking off his jacket before he sat down. She looked away, cursing herself again. What had she been hoping for? For history to repeat itself and Alexio to turn up when she wasn't even on one of his planes?

Sidonie choked back the tears and told herself that she was the biggest idiot on earth for letting her defences down so spectacularly. She bundled up her sweatshirt and put it under her head against the window, hoping to block everything out—including the take-off and landing and disturbing images of a cynical expression that softened only in passion.

'I'm sorry, sir, I'm afraid we've made a mistake with your seat. I'll have to move you.'

Sidonie woke up and blinked, surprised to see that they were in the air and she'd missed the take-off. Then she recalled why she was so tired and scowled at the memory. The air hostess was helping the man beside her out of his seat and apologising profusely while he complained vociferously.

Sidonie didn't mind. His elbow had been digging into her, and if no one else sat down she could—

'Is this seat taken?'

Sidonie stopped dead in the act of laying out her sweatshirt on the seat beside her as a pillow. She went hot and then cold. She looked up.

Alexio. In a dark suit and shirt. Looking dishevelled and a little wild.

In a daze, half wondering if she might be hallucinating, she said, 'Well, I was hoping that it would stay empty.'

Alexio grimaced. 'I'm sorry, it would appear that all the seats are taken. This is the only one left.'

Sidonie lifted up her sweatshirt and held it to her like protection. She tried to ignore the jump in her pulse at the way Alexio slipped off his jacket and sat down, infusing the small space with his scent and magnetism. The sense of *déjà vu* was heady.

Her eyes narrowed on him. She was wide awake now.

'How did you know where I was?' And then she answered herself. 'Tante Josephine.'

Alexio's mouth quirked but the smile didn't reach his eyes and for the first time Sidonie saw something in their depths she'd never seen before: nervousness. It made her pulse leap even more.

'Yes.'

Sidonie shook her head and tried to stave off the emotional pain of seeing him again—especially here. 'What do you want, Alexio?'

He shrugged minutely and looked tortured, and then he said, 'You…and our daughter.'

Sidonie fought back the tears and bit her lip before saying, 'I know you do. You feel a duty, a sense of responsibility…but it's not enough. I won't be that woman who takes from you just because you're the father of my child. And you don't trust me…'

Alexio's eyes burned fiercely now. He angled his body towards Sidonie, cocooning her from the rest of the plane. He took her hand and she could feel his trembling slightly. It stopped her from pulling back.

'I do trust you, Sid…*Sidonie*…'

Sidonie's heart clenched at the way he'd corrected himself.

His grip on her hand tightened. 'I *do*. I should never have said what I said earlier. It was stupid and I'm an ass. I didn't mean it for a second. It was a reflex. I was still clinging on to the last tiny piece of my cynical soul because I was too scared to let my past go… I was nine when my mother told me not to believe in love, that it was a fairytale. I watched her and my father annihilate each other all my life… I thought that was normal. I always chose women who were emotionally aloof…who demanded nothing. Because I had nothing to give. And then I met you, and for the first time I wanted more.'

His mouth twisted with self-recrimination.

'And yet at the first opportunity I chose to mistrust you, and then I turned my back on you…telling myself that I'd been a fool to expect anything more.'

Feeling shaky and light-headed, Sidonie said, 'That phone call was very bad luck…'

Alexio's mouth was still tight. 'But I gave you no chance to defend yourself—and why would you want to after I'd had you investigated like a common criminal?'

Sidonie wanted to touch his jaw but she held back. This moment felt very fragile. 'I can't escape the fact that my mother *was* a criminal. That's pretty damning, even if you hadn't overheard me talking to Tante Josephine. That's partly why I agreed with you when you asked if I'd set out to seduce you once I knew who you were… I felt it was hopeless…'

'The last four months have felt pretty hopeless.' Alexio's voice was bleak.

Sidonie said quietly, 'You were the first person I'd trusted in a really long time—if ever—and you hurt me…'

Contrition made Alexio's face look old all of a sudden. He went grey. 'I know. And I don't expect you to forgive me… But I wanted to tell you something.'

Sidonie looked at him and her belly hollowed out. 'What?'

His hand tightened on hers. His voice was so rough and his accent so strong that she almost couldn't make out what he was saying.

'I've fallen in love with you.'

His words dropped between them. Sidonie struggled to believe she hadn't dreamt them up.

He smiled, and it was almost sad. 'I think I fell for you on that plane…' His smile faded. 'If you give me a chance I'll spend the rest of my life making it up to you…'

Sidonie shrank back, pulling her hand free. She shook

her head, everything within her trying to dampen down the incredibly sweet swelling of joy. The fall would be too great if—

'You can't mean it…you're just saying that.'

Alexio looked fierce and affronted. 'I've never, ever said that to another woman and I never intend to.'

Sidonie felt a mix of tears and laughter vying for supremacy. But still she couldn't afford to believe. Visions of her stepfather's sad face came back to haunt her. Sad because he'd loved his wife his whole life when she hadn't loved him. Even though he'd sacrificed so much to be there for her. Alexio was saying this…but he couldn't love her as much as she loved him.

'You don't…don't mean it,' she got out, too scared to hope for even a second.

Alexio reached for her and put his hands on the bottom of her top, pulling it up to reveal her belly. Sidonie squeaked with shock, but before she could stop him Alexio was putting his big hands on her, spanning the small compact swell, and he was bending down, his mouth close to her bump, saying with a none too steady voice, 'Belle…I'm doing my best, here, to convince your mother that I love her and trust her and want to spend the rest of my life with her…and you…but it's not going so well. I don't think she believes me.'

Sidonie felt a very definite kick then—the first proper kick apart from the flutters. In shock, her eyes wide, she watched as Alexio came back up, his hands still on her belly.

There was a look of wonder on his face. 'I felt that…'

And then the look cleared, to be replaced with one of determination.

'Belle is clearly on my side. It's two against one.'

Sidonie couldn't prevent the tears from clogging her throat and flooding her eyes. She was overwhelmed by

Alexio's hands on her belly, the baby kicking for the first time...him saying he loved her.

But she ignored all that for a moment and choked out, 'I thought you said we couldn't call her Belle...'

Alexio smiled, and this time it looked slightly less nervous. 'It's growing on me—and Tante Josephine will never forgive me if we call her something else. But next time it's my choice.'

'Next time?' Sidonie choked out through even more tears.

Alexio was just a blur now, and his hands left her belly to come up and cup her face, thumbs wiping at her tears.

'Next time...if you'll have me,' he said gently, 'And the next time and the next time...'

And then his mouth was on hers and Sidonie was shaking too much to do anything but submit and allow herself the first sliver of belief that this was real and that Alexio meant what he was saying.

When he pulled back Sidonie's mouth tingled. His hands were still on her jaw, cupping her face. She looked into his eyes, searching, and all she could see there was pure... *emotion*. For the first time. No shadows. No cynicism.

She took a deep shaky breath. 'Alexio...'

'Yes...?'

'I love you too...even though you really hurt me. I fell for you when we first met and I never stopped. I'm still falling. Every time I look at you. I told myself I hated you...but I couldn't.'

Alexio's hands tightened around her and his gaze grew suspiciously bright. 'You love me?'

Sidonie wanted to take a snapshot of this moment. Alexio Christakos, multi-billionaire and playboy. Arrogance and confidence personified. Eyes shining with tears, doubting her word.

She reached up to touch his face, feeling the spiky

prickle of his stubble. He was a different man from the one who had so coolly laid out his plan that morning. He'd been hiding all this emotion. Suppressing it.

'Of course I love you. I love you so much that I'm terrified I love you more than you love me.'

Alexio just looked at her for a long moment and shook his head, smiling a little ruefully. 'Not possible, I'm afraid. You're getting the full force of years and years of repressed loving and then some more...'

He reached into his pocket for something, and pulled out a small black box. Sidonie looked down at it and back up.

Alexio looked nervous again. 'Sid... *Sidonie*...'

'No...' she said urgently, and then, more shyly, 'I like it when you call me that... I just... I was angry...'

She could see the pain in his eyes at that and she touched his jaw. Alexio dragged his gaze away and opened the box. Sidonie looked down and gasped when she saw a stunning heart-shaped diamond ring glittering up at her. Alexio took the ring out of the box. He took her left hand in his and looked at her so deeply that he took her breath away and made fresh tears well.

Looking endearingly unlike himself, palpably nervous, he asked, 'Will you marry me, Sidonie Fitzgerald?'

The tears overflowed and fell. Sidonie couldn't speak. She was too overcome.

Suddenly Alexio disappeared again, down towards her bump, and she heard him say, 'Belle, I've just asked—'

Alexio yelped when Sidonie grabbed his hair and pulled him back up.

'Yes!' She looked at him. 'Yes...' she said again, framing his face with her hands. 'I'll marry you, Alexio.'

Alexio kissed the palm of her hand and then took it in his again, to slide the ring onto her finger. 'I had a jeweller meet me at the plane and I picked that one out because it reminded me of your pure heart...but I can change it...'

Sidonie shook her head, looking at the ring glinting at her. 'No..' She felt more tears coming after what he'd just said. 'I love it…and it's really glittery.'

Alexio pulled her in close. 'I'll give you glittery things for the rest of our lives…'

Sidonie stiffened and pulled back, making Alexio frown.

'No… I don't want anything from you, Alexio… I mean it. I know you say you trust me, but I don't want you to ever doubt that I want nothing from you except you. I won't marry you until I can sign something that says I'm not after you for your money.'

Alexio sighed. 'Sid, don't be ridiculous.'

Sidonie pulled away and dragged her top down over her bump. She shook her head again and crossed her arms. 'No marriage unless you agree.'

Sidonie saw Alexio's eyes slide down to her bump and she put a hand over it.

'And no more cutesy manipulation of our daughter before she's even born.'

Alexio rolled his eyes heavenward and then threw up his hands. 'Okay—fine.'

His eyes glinted with determination then and he reached for her, pulling her into him so tightly that she didn't know where she ended and he began. Sidonie slid her arms around his waist and snuggled against him. They rested like that for a long moment, the calm after the storm.

'Sid?'

'Hmm?'

'Are you going to sleep?'

Sidonie nodded her head against Alexio's chest and said sleepily, happily, 'It's those hormones again. I have a feeling you're going to be keeping me up late, so I should really nap now. And also pregnant women shouldn't be subjected to too much excitement—it takes it out of us.'

She felt Alexio tense slightly and heard his affronted,

'What happened last night was more than hormones and you know it. Luckily we have the rest of our lives for me to prove it to you...'

The rest of our lives...

Sidonie smiled and moved closer to Alexio, deeper into his embrace, and he moved slightly so that he could put a possessive hand over her belly, setting off a chain reaction of desire.

'Okay,' she admitted sheepishly, lifting her head to look at him. 'Maybe it wasn't just pregnancy hormones...'

Alexio cupped her jaw with his hand and looked down at her. 'Excuse my French in front of Belle,' he said with a wicked smile, 'but damn right it wasn't.'

Two days later, Dublin

'Now I just want to make absolutely sure I haven't missed any loopholes or sneaky amendments. This was all drawn up very quickly because my fiancé has arranged our marriage for two weeks' time in Paris.'

Sidonie ignored the snort of insult from the man pacing the solicitor's office. She smiled sweetly at Mr Keane, who looked as if he was having trouble holding back nervous hysterics. No doubt he hadn't expected to see one of the world's foremost self-made billionaires in his office, never mind in this position.

Sidonie went on. 'Is it absolutely clear that if we divorce—'

'There will never be a divorce,' came the fierce pronouncement.

Sidonie rolled her eyes at the solicitor and then looked at her fiancé.

'Well, of course *now* we don't think there'll be a divorce, but you never know what will happen in life and I want to make sure that if and when such a time comes I walk away with not a cent of your fortune.'

Sidonie felt absolutely sure that there would be no divorce either, but it wasn't a bad thing to keep an alpha male like Alexio on his toes.

Alexio was bristling. He stalked over and put his hands down on the desk to glare at Sidonie. The intensity of that glare was diminished somewhat by the way he looked at her mouth so hungrily.

'There will not be a divorce while there is breath in my body.'

Sidonie stretched up and pressed a kiss to Alexio's cheek, causing his expression to turn positively nuclear. 'Well, we have to get married first, of course. Don't get all excited.'

She turned and smiled again at the very flushed-looking solicitor. 'So, in the event of a divorce any children will be provided for, and custody arrangements have been outlined, but I will get nothing—is that right?'

The solicitor ran a pudgy finger underneath his collar, his gaze flicking uneasily to the man who all but towered over his pregnant fiancée. Having had a lot of experience with pregnant women, thanks to his own healthy brood of seven children, he figured the lesser of two evils right now was Alexio Christakos, even if he *was* paying his bill and practically had steam coming out of his ears.

'Yes, that's exactly it, Miss Fitzgerald.'

'And ninety per cent of the money that Mr Christakos is insisting on giving me as an allowance has been designated to the various charities I mentioned?'

The solicitor quickly scanned the pages again and said, 'Yes, I believe so.'

'Great!'

Sidonie reached over and took the pen and signed her name with a flourish. Then she smiled sweetly at Alexio and handed the pen to him. He signed on the line with much unintelligible muttering under his breath.

Two weeks later a radiant and glowing Sidonie walked down the aisle of the biggest *mairie* in Paris on the arm of her matron of honour—her aunt, who grinned from ear to ear and was resplendent in a lavender suit. It had been bought by Alexio, who had grumbled that at least he could lavish gifts on *someone*.

Alexio hadn't had to turn and see Sidonie arrive. He'd already been waiting impatiently for her to appear.

He was still unprepared, though, when she did. His breath caught and he couldn't stop the tears clogging his throat and making his eyes shine. He'd been holding his emotions back all his life and now they overflowed. And he loved it. He'd even been oblivious to his brother Rafaele's smug *welcome to the club* look.

Sidonie's hair was half up, half down, held in place with a plain diamond art deco clip. She wore no other jewellery apart from her engagement ring. Her dress was strapless and had an empire line under her bust to accommodate her growing bump. The off-white material fell in loose, unstructured folds to the floor. Her skin glowed, and as she came closer, her eyes fixed on his, his heart almost stopped at the sheer strength of his love all over again.

He held out his hand to her and she put hers in his and smiled at him. At that moment Alexio felt all the pieces of his life slide into place, and he drew the love of his life forward by his side and hoped that they could get to the kiss as fast as possible.

Outside the office of the *mairie* afterwards, Cesar da Silva thrust his hands into his pockets. It had been a mistake to come. He didn't know what had got into him, but that morning he'd seen the invitation to Alexio's wedding on his desk and something had compelled him to make the journey to Paris from Spain.

He'd arrived late and stood at the back of the civil office. Alexio and his wife had had their backs to him as the ceremony was conducted, but he'd seen his other half-brother, Rafaele, near the front, holding a small boy high in his arms, with a dark-haired woman beside him, her arm around his waist. His wife.

He'd been invited to their wedding too, just months before, but the rage within him had still been too fierce for him even to contemplate it. The rage he'd felt at finally coming face to face with his half-brothers at his mother's funeral. The rage he'd felt at the evidence that she'd loved them above him. That she hadn't abandoned *them*.

But he knew it wasn't their fault. Whatever the stain had been on Cesar's personality that had led their mother to leave him behind had nothing to do with them. Maybe, he surmised cynically, they were just more lovable.

God knew, he'd felt dark for so long he was constantly surprised that people didn't run in terror when they looked into his eyes and saw nothing light. But they didn't run. And especially not women. It seemed the darker he felt, the stronger the draw to his lovers. More than one had been under the erroneous impression that they could *heal* Cesar of the darkness in his soul.

He wasn't surprised at women's eagerness to put up with his less than sunny nature; after all he was one of the richest men in the world. His mother had taught him that lesson very early on. After cutting Cesar from her life like a useless appendage she'd gone on to feather her nest in fine style—first with an Italian count and then, after he'd lost everything, a Greek tycoon.

He could see Rafaele putting his son down now—an adorable-looking little boy. *His nephew.* Cesar felt it like a punch to his gut. He'd been about the same age when his mother had left him with his grandparents and everything had gone dark and cold. To see that small boy now, swinging between his parents' hands, was almost too much to bear.

And then his youngest half-brother Alexio emerged from the *mairie*'s office with his new wife. His *pregnant* wife. More new life unfolding.

The pain in Cesar's chest increased. They were beaming. Eyes only on each other. Besotted. Cesar could feel his blackness spreading out…infecting the people around him like a virus. He caught one or two double-takes. People were wary around him. Women were fascinated, lustful. Covetous.

It gave him no measure of satisfaction to be as blessed as his brothers in his physical appearance. It compounded his cynicism. His looks merely sweetened the prospect for avaricious lovers, and they had proved to him from an early age that women were shallow. If he had nothing they'd still want him, but they wouldn't have to put on the elaborate pretence of not being interested in his fortune. Sometimes he almost felt sorry for them, watching them contort themselves into what they thought he wanted them to be.

Alexio was lifting his new wife into his arms now. Hearing her squeal of happiness, and seeing her throw her bouquet high in the air behind her so the women could catch it, made something break apart inside Cesar. He had to get away. He shouldn't have come. He would taint this happiness with his presence.

But just as he turned someone caught his arm, and he looked back to see Rafaele, with his son in his arms. The small boy was looking at Cesar curiously and he could see that he'd inherited his grandmother's eyes. *His* eyes. He felt weak.

As if Rafaele could see and understand the wild need to escape in Cesar's chest, he said, 'Whatever you might think our lives were like with our mother…they *weren't*. I'll tell Alexio you came. Maybe we'll see you again…?'

Cesar was slightly stunned at Rafaele's words. And at the way he'd seen his need to get out of there. That he wasn't pushing for more.

His chest feeling tight, Cesar nodded and bit out, 'Give him my best wishes.'

And then he turned and walked away quickly from that happy scene, before his wondering about what Rafaele had meant about their mother could tear him open completely and expose the dried husk of his soul to the light.

* * * * *

FONSECA'S FURY

This is for Helen Kane—thanks for going to Dubai and letting me rent out your house and possibly the most idyllic office space in Dublin. And I do forgive you for leaving me behind in Kathmandu (on my birthday!) while you went off and romanced your own Mills & Boon hero! x

CHAPTER ONE

SERENA DEPIERO SAT in the plush ante-room and looked at the name on the opposite wall, spelled out in matt chrome lettering, and reeled.

Roseca Industries and Philanthropic Foundation.

Renewed horror spread through her. It had only been on the plane to Rio de Janeiro, when she'd been reading the extra information on the charity given to her by her boss, that she'd become aware that it was part of a much bigger organisation. An organisation run and set up by Luca Fonseca. The name Roseca was apparently an amalgamation of his father and mother's surnames. And Serena wasn't operating on a pay grade level high enough to require her to be aware of this knowledge before now.

Except here she was, outside the CEO's office, waiting to be called in to see the one man on the planet who had every reason to hate her guts. Why hadn't he sacked her months ago, as soon as she'd started working for him? Surely he must have known? An insidious suspicion took root: perhaps he'd orchestrated this all along, to lull her into a false sense of security before letting her crash spectacularly to the ground.

That would be breathtakingly cruel, and yet this man

owed her nothing but his disdain. She owed *him*. Serena knew that there was a good chance her career in fundraising was about to be over before it had even taken off. And at that thought she felt a spurt of panic mixed with determination. Surely enough time had passed now? Surely, even if this *was* some elaborate revenge cooked up by Luca Fonseca as soon as he'd known she was working for him, she could try to convince him how sorry she was?

But before she could wrap her head around it any further a door opened to her right and a sleek dark-haired woman dressed in a grey suit emerged.

'Senhor Fonseca will see you now, Miss DePiero.'

Serena's hands clenched tightly around her handbag. She felt like blurting out, *But I don't want to see him!*

But she couldn't. As much as she couldn't just flee. The car that had met her at the airport to deliver her here still had her luggage in its boot.

As she stood up reluctantly a memory assailed her with such force it almost knocked her sideways: Luca Fonseca in a bloodstained shirt, with a black eye and a split lip. Dark stubble shadowing his swollen jaw. He'd been behind the bars of a jail cell, leaning against a wall, brooding and dangerous. But then he'd looked up and narrowed that intensely dark blue gaze on her, and an expression of icy loathing had come over his face.

He'd straightened and moved to the bars, wrapping his fingers around them almost as if he was imagining they were her neck. Serena had stopped dead at the battered sight of him. He'd spat out, *'Damn you, Serena DePiero, I wish I'd never laid eyes on you.'*

'Miss DePiero? Senhor Fonseca is waiting.'

The clipped and accented voice shattered Serena's

memory and she forced her feet to move, taking her past the unsmiling woman and into the palatial office beyond.

She hated that her heart was thumping so hard when she heard the door snick softly shut behind her. For the first few seconds she saw no one, because the entire back wall of the office was a massive window and it framed the most amazingly panoramic view of a city Serena had ever seen.

The Atlantic glinted dark blue in the distance, and inland from that were the two most iconic shapes of Rio de Janeiro: the Sugar Loaf and Christ the Redeemer high on Corcovado. In between were countless other tall buildings, right up to the coast. To say that the view was breathtaking was an understatement.

And then suddenly it was eclipsed by the man who moved into her line of vision. Luca Fonseca. For a second past and present merged and Serena was back in that nightclub, seeing him for the first time.

He'd stood so tall and broad against the backdrop of that dark and opulent place. Still. She'd never seen anyone so still, yet with such a commanding presence. People had skirted around him. Men suspicious, envious. Women lustful.

In a dark suit and open-necked shirt he'd been dressed much the same as other men, but he'd stood out from them all by dint of that sheer preternatural stillness and the incredible forcefield of charismatic magnetism that had drawn her to him before she could stop herself.

Serena blinked. The dark and decadent club faded. She couldn't breathe. The room was instantly stifling. Luca Fonseca looked different. It took her sluggish brain a second to function enough for her to realise that he looked different because his hair was longer, slightly unruly. And he had a dark beard that hugged his jaw. It made him look even more intensely masculine.

He was wearing a light-coloured open-necked shirt tucked into dark trousers. For all the world the urbane, civilised businessman in his domain, and yet the vibe coming from him was anything but civilised.

He crossed his arms over that massive chest and then he spoke. 'What the hell do you think you're doing here, DePiero?'

Serena moved further into the vast office, even though it was in the opposite direction from where she wanted to go. She couldn't take her eyes off him even if she wanted to.

She forced herself to speak, to act as if seeing him again wasn't as shattering as it was. 'I'm here to start working in the fundraising department for the global communities charity.'

'Not any more, you're not,' Fonseca said tersely.

Serena flushed. 'I didn't know you were...involved until I was on my way over here.'

Fonseca made a small sound like a snort. 'An unlikely tale.'

'It's true,' Serena blurted out. 'I had no idea the charity was linked to the Roseca Foundation. Believe me, if I'd had any idea I wouldn't have agreed to come here.'

Luca Fonseca moved around the table and Serena's eyes widened. For a big man, he moved with innate grace, and that incredible quality of self-containment oozed from every pore. It was intensely captivating.

He admitted with clear irritation, 'I wasn't aware that you were working in the Athens office. I don't micromanage my smaller charities abroad because I hire the best staff to do that for me—although I'm reconsidering my policy after this. If I'd known they'd hired you, of all people, you would have been let go long before now.'

His mouth twisted with recrimination.

'But I have to admit that I was intrigued enough to have you brought here instead of just leaving you at the airport until we could put you on a return flight.'

So he hadn't even known she was working for him. Serena's hands curled into fists at her sides. His dismissive arrogance set her nerves even more on edge.

He glanced at a big platinum watch on his wrist. 'I have a spare fifteen minutes before you are to be delivered back to the airport.'

Like an unwanted package. He was firing her.

He hitched a hip onto the corner of his desk, for all the world as if they were having a normal conversation amidst the waves of tension. 'Well, DePiero? What the hell is Europe's most debauched ex-socialite doing working for minimum wage in a small charity office in Athens?'

Only hours ago Serena had been buoyant at the thought of her new job. A chance to prove to her somewhat over-protective family that she was going to be fine. She'd been ecstatic at the thought of her independence. And now this man was going to ensure that everything she'd fought so hard for was for naught.

For years she had been the *enfant terrible* of the Italian party scene, frequently photographed, with reams of newsprint devoted to her numerous exploits which had been invariably blown out of proportion. Nevertheless, Serena knew well that there was enough truth behind the headlines to make her feel that ever-present prick of shame.

'Look,' she said, hating the way her voice had got husky with repressed emotion and shock at facing this blast from her past, 'I know you must hate me.'

Luca Fonseca smiled. But his expression was hard. 'Hate? Don't flatter yourself, DePiero, *hate* is a very inadequate description of my feelings where you are concerned.'

Another poisonous memory assailed her: a battered Luca, handcuffed by Italian police, being dragged bodily to an already loaded-up van, snarling, *'You set me up, you bitch!'* at Serena, who had been moments away from being handed into a police car herself, albeit minus the handcuffs.

They'd insisted on everyone being hauled in to the police station. He'd tried to jerk free of the burly police officers and that had earned him a thump to his belly, making him double over. Serena had been stupefied. Transfixed with shock.

He'd rasped out painfully, just before disappearing into the police van, 'She planted the drugs on *me* to save herself.'

Serena tried to force the memories out of her head. 'Mr Fonseca, I didn't plant those drugs in your pockets... I don't know who did, but it wasn't me. I tried to contact you afterwards...but you'd left Italy.'

He made a sound of disgust. 'Afterwards? You mean after you'd returned from your shopping spree in Paris? I saw the pictures. Avoiding being prosecuted for possession of drugs and continuing your hedonistic existence was all in a week's work for you, wasn't it?'

Serena couldn't avoid the truth; no matter how innocent she was, this man *had* suffered because of their brief association. The lurid headlines were still clear in her mind: *DePiero's newest love interest? Brazilian billionaire Fonseca caught with drugs after raid on Florence's most exclusive nightclub, Den of Eden.*

But before Serena could defend herself Luca was standing up and walking closer, making her acutely aware of his height and powerful frame. Her mouth dried.

When he was close enough that she could make out the dark chest hair curling near the open V of his shirt, he sent an icy look from her face to her feet, and then said derisively, 'A far cry from that lame excuse for a dress.'

Serena could feel heat rising at the reminder of how she'd been dressed that night. How she'd dressed most nights. She tried again, even though it was apparent that her attempt to defend herself had fallen on deaf ears. 'I really didn't have anything to do with those drugs. I promise. It was all a huge misunderstanding.'

He looked at her for a long moment, clearly incredulous, before tipping his head back and laughing so abruptly that Serena flinched.

When his eyes met hers again they still sparkled with cold mirth, and that sensual mouth was curved in an equally cold smile.

'I have to hand it to you—you've got some balls to come in here and protest your innocence after all this time.'

Serena's nails scored her palms, but she didn't notice. 'It's true. I know what you must think...'

She stopped, and had to push down the insidious

reminder that it was what *everyone* had thought. Erroneously.

'I didn't do those kinds of drugs.'

Any hint of mirth, cold or otherwise, vanished from Luca Fonseca's visage. 'Enough with protesting your innocence. You had Class A drugs in that pretty purse and you conveniently slipped them into my pocket as soon as it became apparent that the club was being raided.'

Feeling sick now, Serena said, 'It must have been someone else in the crush and panic.'

Fonseca moved even closer to Serena then, and she gulped and looked up. She felt hot, clammy.

His voice was low, seductive. 'Do I need to remind you of how close we were that night, Serena? How easy it must have been for you to divest yourself of incriminating evidence?'

Serena could recall all too clearly that his arms had been like steel bands around her, with hers twined around his neck. Her mouth had been sensitive and swollen, her breathing rapid. Someone had rushed over to them on the dance floor—some acquaintance of Serena's who had hissed, *'There's a raid.'*

And Luca Fonseca thought... He thought that during those few seconds before chaos had struck she'd had the presence of mind to somehow slip drugs onto his person?

He said now, 'I'm sure it was a move you'd perfected over the years, which was why I felt nothing.'

He stepped back and Serena could take a breath again. But then he walked around her, and her skin prickled. She was acutely aware of his regard and wanted to adjust her suit, which felt constrictive.

She closed her eyes and then opened them again,

turning around to face him. 'Mr Fonseca, I'm just looking for a chance—'

He held up his hand and Serena stopped. His expression was worse than cold now: it was completely indecipherable.

He clicked his fingers, as if something just occurred to him, and his lip curled. 'Of *course*—it's your family, isn't it? They've clipped your wings. Andreas Xenakis and Rocco De Marco would never tolerate a return to your debauched ways, and you're still *persona non grata* in the social circles who fêted you before. You and your sister certainly landed on your feet, in spite of your father's fall from grace.'

Disgust was etched on his hard features.

'Lorenzo DePiero will never be able to show his face again after the things he did.'

Serena felt nauseous. She of all people didn't need to be reminded of her father's corruption and many crimes.

But Luca wasn't finished. 'I think you're doing this under some sort of sufferance, to prove to your newfound family that you've changed… In return for what? An allowance? A palatial home back in Italy, your old stomping ground? Or perhaps you'll stay in Athens, where the stench of your tarnished reputation is a little less…pungent? After all, it's where you'll have the protection of your younger sister who, if I recall correctly, was the one who regularly cleaned up your messes.'

Fire raced up Serena's spine at hearing him mention her family—and especially her sister. A sense of protectiveness overwhelmed her. They were everything to her and she would never, ever let them down. They had saved her. Something this cold, judgmental man would never understand.

Serena was jet-lagged, gritty-eyed, and in shock at seeing this man again, and it was evident in her voice now, as she lashed back heatedly, 'My family have nothing to do with this. And nothing to do with *you*.'

Luca Fonseca looked at Serena incredulously. 'I'm sure your family have everything to do with this. Did you drop a tantalising promise of generous donations from them in return for a move up the career ladder?'

Serena flushed and got out a strangled-sounding, 'No, of course not.'

But the way she avoided his eyes told Luca otherwise. She wouldn't have had to drop anything but the most subtle of hints. The patronage of either her half-brother, Rocco De Marco, or her brother-in-law, Andreas Xenakis, could secure a charity's fortunes for years to come. And, as wealthy as he was in his own right, the foundation would always need to raise money. Disgusted that his own staff might have been so easily manipulated, and suddenly aware of how heated his blood was, Luca stepped back.

He was grim. 'I am not going to be a convenient conduit through which you try to fool everyone into thinking you've changed.'

Serena just looked at him, and he saw her long, graceful throat work, as if she couldn't quite get out what she wanted to say. He felt no pity for her.

She couldn't be more removed from the woman of his memory of seven years ago, when she'd been golden and sinuous and provocative. The woman in front of him now looked pale, and as if she was going for an interview in an insurance office. Her abundantly sexy white-blonde hair had been tamed into a staid chignon. And yet even that, and the sober dark suit, couldn't dim her incredible natural beauty or those piercing bright blue eyes.

Those eyes had hit him right in the solar plexus as soon as she'd walked into his office, when he'd been able to watch her unobserved for a few seconds. And the straight trousers couldn't hide those famously long legs. The generous swell of her breasts pushed against the silk of her shirt.

Disgust curled through him to notice her like this. Had he learnt nothing? She should be prostrating herself at his feet in abject apology for turning his life upside down, but instead she had the temerity to defend herself: *'My family have nothing to do with this.'*

His clear-headed focus was being eroded in this woman's presence. Why was he even wondering anything about her? He didn't care what her nefarious motivations were. He'd satisfied whatever curiosity he'd had.

He clenched his jaw. 'Your time is up. The car will be waiting outside for your return to the airport. And I do sincerely hope to never lay eyes on you again.'

So why was it so hard to rip his gaze *off* her?

Anger and self-recrimination coursed through Luca as he stepped around Serena and stalked back to his desk, expecting to hear the door open and close.

When he didn't, he spun round and spat out tersely, 'We have nothing more to discuss.'

The fact that she had gone paler was something that Luca didn't like to acknowledge that he'd noticed. Or his very bizarre dart of concern. No woman evoked concern in him. He could see her swallow again, that long, graceful throat moving, and then her soft, husky voice, with that slightest hint of an Italian accent, crossed the space between them.

'I'm just asking for a chance. Please.'

Luca's mouth opened and closed. He was stunned. Once he declared what he wanted no one questioned him. Until now. And this woman, of all people? Serena DePiero had a less than zero chance of Luca reconsidering his decision. The fact that she was still in his office set his nerves sizzling just under his skin. Irritating him.

But instead of admitting defeat and turning round, the woman stepped closer. Further away from the door.

Luca had an urge to snarl and stalk over to her, to put her over his shoulder, physically remove her from his presence. But right then, with perfect timing, the memory of her lush body pressed against his, her soft mouth yielding to his forceful kiss, exploded into his consciousness and within a nano-second he was battling a surge of blood to his groin.

Damn her. Witch.

She was at the other side of his desk. Blue eyes huge, her bearing as regal as a queen's, reminding him effortlessly of her impeccable lineage.

Her voice was low and she clasped her hands together in front of her, knuckles white. 'Mr Fonseca, I came here with the best of intentions to do work for your charity, despite what you may believe. I'll do anything to prove to you how committed I am.'

Anger surged at her persistence. At her meek *Mr Fonseca*.

Luca uncrossed his arms and placed his hands on the table in front of him, leaning forward. '*You* are the reason I had to rebuild my reputation and people's trust in my charitable work—not to mention trust in my family's mining consortium. I spent months, *years*, undoing the damage of that one night. Debauchery is all very well and good, as you must know, but the stigma of possessing Class A drugs does tend to last. The truth is that once those pictures of us together in the nightclub surfaced I *had* no defence.'

It almost killed Luca now to recall how he had instinctively shielded Serena from the police and detectives who had stormed the club, which was when she must have taken the opportunity to plant the drugs on him.

He thought of the paparazzi pictures of her shopping in Paris while he'd been leaving Italy under a cloud of disgrace, and bitterness laced his voice. 'Meanwhile you were oblivious to the fallout, continuing your hedonistic existence. And after all that, you have the temerity to think that I would so much as allow your name to be mentioned in the same sentence as mine?'

If possible, she paled even more, displaying the genes she'd inherited from her half-English mother, a classic English rose beauty.

He straightened up. 'You disgust me.'

Serena was dimly aware that on some level his words were hurting her in a place that she shouldn't be feeling hurt. But something dogged deep inside had pushed her to plead. And she had.

His eyes were like dark, hard sapphires. Impervious to heat or cold or her pleas. He was right. He was the one man on the planet who would never give her a chance. She was delusional to have thought even for a second that he might hear her out.

The atmosphere in the office was positively glacial in comparison to the gloriously sunny day outside. Luca Fonseca was just looking at her. Serena's belly sank. He wasn't even going to say another word. He'd said everything. He'd just wanted to see her, to torture her. Make her realise just how much he hated her—as if she had been in any doubt.

She finally admitted defeat and turned to the door. There would be no reprieve. Hitching up her chin in a tiny gesture of dignity, she didn't glance back at him, not wanting to see that arctic expression again. As if she was something distasteful on the end of his shoe.

She opened the door, closed it behind her, and was met by his cool assistant who was waiting for her. And who'd undoubtedly been privy to the plans of her boss well before Serena had been. Silently she was escorted downstairs.

Her humiliation was complete.

Ten minutes later Luca spoke tersely into his phone. 'Call me as soon as you know she's boarded and the plane has left.'

When he'd terminated the call Luca swivelled around in his high-backed chair to face the view. His blood was still boiling with a mixture of anger and arousal. Why had he indulged in the dubious desire to see her face to face again? All it had done was show him his own weakness for her.

He hadn't even known she was on her way to Rio until his assistant had informed him; the significance of her arrival had only come to light far too late to do anything about it.

Serena DePiero. Just her name brought an acrid taste of poison to his mouth. And yet the image that accompanied her name was anything but poisonous. It was provocative. It was his first image of her in that nightclub in Florence.

He'd known who she was, of course. No one could have gone to Florence and *not* known who the DePiero sisters were—famed for their light-haired, blue-eyed aristocratic beauty and their vast family fortune that stretched back to medieval times. Serena had been the media's darling. Despite her debauched existence, no matter what she did, they'd lapped it up and bayed for more.

Her exploits had been legendary: high-profile weekends in Rome, leaving hotels trashed and staff incandescent with rage. Whirlwind private jet trips to the Middle East on the whim of an equally debauched sheikh who fancied a party with his Eurotrash friends. And always pictured in various states of inebriation and loucheness that had only seemed to heighten her dazzling appeal.

The night he'd seen her she'd been in the middle of the dance floor in what could only be described as an excuse for a dress. Strapless gold lamé, with tassels barely covering the top of her toned golden thighs. Long white-blonde hair tousled and falling down her back and over her shoulders, brushing the enticing swell of a voluptuous cleavage. Her peers had jostled around her, vying for her attention, desperately trying to emulate her golden exclusiveness.

With her arms in the air, swaying to the hedonistic beat of music played by some world-class DJ, she had symbolised the very font of youth and allure and beauty. The kind of beauty that made grown men fall to their knees in wonder. A siren's beauty, luring them to their doom.

Luca's mouth twisted. He'd proved to be no better than any other mortal man when she'd lured him to his doom. He took responsibility for being in that club—

of course he did. But from the moment she'd sashayed over to stand in front of him everything had grown a little hazy. And Luca was not a person who got hazy. No matter how stunning the woman. His whole life was about being clear and focused, because he had a lot to achieve.

But her huge bright blue eyes had seared him alive, igniting every nerve-ending, blasting aside any concerns. Her skin was flawless, her aquiline nose a testament to her breeding. Her mouth had fascinated him. Perfectly sculpted lips. Not too full, not too thin, effortlessly hinting at a dark and sexy sensuality.

She'd said coquettishly, 'It's rude to stare, you know.'

And instead of turning on his heel in disgust at her reputation and her arrogance, Luca had felt the blood flow through his body, hardening it, and he'd drawled softly, 'I'd have to be blind not to be dazzled. Join me for a drink?'

She'd tossed her head and for a second Luca had thought he glimpsed something curiously vulnerable and weary in those stunning blue eyes, but it had to have been a trick of the strobing lights, because then she'd purred, 'I'd love to.'

The wisps of memory faded from Luca's mind. He hated it that even now, just thinking of her, was having an effect on his body. Seven years had passed, and yet he felt as enflamed by anger and desire as he had that night. A bruising, humiliating mix.

He'd just left Serena DePiero in no doubt as to what he thought of her. She'd effectively been fired from her job. So why wasn't there a feeling of triumph rushing through him? Why was there an unsettling, prickling feeling of…unfinished business?

And why was there the tiniest grudging sliver of admiration for the way she had not backed down from him and the way that small chin had tipped up ever so slightly just before she'd left?

CHAPTER TWO

THE HOTEL WAS a few blocks back from Copacabana beach. To say that it was basic was an understatement, but it was clean—which was the main thing. And cheap—which was good, considering Serena was living off her meagre savings from the last year. She took off her travelling clothes, which were well creased by now, and stepped into the tiny shower, relishing the lukewarm spray.

Her belly clenched minutely when she imagined Luca's reaction to her *not* leaving Rio but she pushed it aside. She'd been standing in line for the check-in when her sister had phoned her. Too heartsore to admit that she was coming home so soon, and suddenly aware that Athens didn't even really feel like home, Serena had made a spur-of-the-moment decision to tell a white lie and pretend everything was okay.

And, even though she'd hated lying—to her sister, of all people—she didn't regret it now. She was still angry at Luca Fonseca's easy dismissal of her, the way he'd toyed with her before kicking her out of his office.

It had been enough to propel her out of the airport and back into the city. She scrubbed her scalp with unnecessary force, not liking how turbulent her emotions still were after meeting him again, and she certainly didn't like admitting that he'd roused her to a kind of anger she hadn't felt in a long time. Angry enough to rebel...when she'd thought she'd left all that behind her.

When she emerged from the bathroom she had a towel hitched around her body and another one on her head, and was feeling no less disgruntled. She almost jumped out of her skin when a loud, persistent knocking came on her door.

Scrambling around to find something to put on, Serena called out to whoever it was to wait a second as she pulled on some underwear and faded jeans and a T-shirt. The towel fell off her head so her long hair hung damply down her back and over her shoulders.

She opened the door and it was as if someone had punched her in the stomach. She couldn't draw breath because Luca Fonseca was standing there, eyes shooting sparks at her, looking angrier than she'd ever seen him.

'What the hell are you doing here, DePiero?' he snarled.

Serena answered faintly, 'You seem to be asking me that a lot lately.'

And then the fright he'd just given her faded and the anger she'd been harbouring swelled back. Her hand gripped the door.

'Actually, I might ask the same of you—what the hell are *you* doing *here*, Fonseca?' Something occurred to her. 'And how on earth did you even know where I was?'

His mouth was a tight line. 'I told Sancho, my driver, to wait at the airport and make sure you got on the flight.'

The extent of how badly he'd wanted her gone hit

her. Her hand gripped the door even tighter. 'This is a free country, Fonseca. I decided to stay and do a little sightseeing, and as I no longer work for you I really don't think you have any jurisdiction here.'

She went to close the door in his face but he easily stopped her and stepped into the room, closing the door behind him and forcing her to take a step back.

His arctic gaze took in her appearance with derision and Serena crossed her arms over her braless chest, self-conscious.

'Mr Fonseca—'

'Enough with the *Mr Fonseca*. Why are you still here, Serena?'

His use of her name made something swoop inside her. She crossed her arms tighter. It reminded her bizarrely of how it had felt to kiss him in the middle of that dance floor. Dark and hot and intoxicating. No other man's kiss or touch had ever made her feel like that. She'd pulled back from him in shock, as if his kiss had incinerated her, right through to where she was still whole. *Herself.*

'Well?'

The curt question jarred Serena back to the present and she hated it that she'd remembered that feeling of exposure.

'I want to see Rio de Janeiro before going home.' As if she would confide that she also wanted to delay revealing the extent of her failure to her family for as long as possible.

Luca snorted indelicately. 'Do you have *any* idea where you are? Were you planning on taking a stroll along the beach later?'

Serena gritted her jaw. 'I was, actually. I'd invite

you to join me, but I'm sure you have better things to be doing.'

His sheer animal magnetism was almost overwhelming in the small space. The beard and his longer hair only added to his intense masculinity. Her skin prickled with awareness. She could feel her nipples tighten and harden against the barrier of her thin T-shirt and hated the unique way this man affected her above any other.

Luca was snarling again. 'Do you realise that you're in one of the most dangerous parts of Rio? You're just minutes from one of the worst *favelas* in the city.'

Serena resisted the urge to point out that that should please him. 'But the beach is just blocks away.'

Now he was grim. 'Yes, and no one goes near this end of the beach at night unless they're out to score some drugs or looking to get mugged. It's one of the most dangerous places in the city after dark.'

He stepped closer and his eyes narrowed on her speculatively.

'But maybe that's it? You're looking for some recreational enhancement? Maybe your family have you under their watch and you're relishing some freedom? Have you even told them you've been fired?'

Serena's arms fell to her sides and she barely noticed Luca's gaze dropping to her chest before coming up again. All she felt was an incredible surge of anger and hatred for this man and his perspicacity—even if it wasn't entirely accurate.

Disgusted at the part of her that wanted to try and explain herself to him, she spat out, 'What's the point?'

She stalked around Luca and reached for the door handle, but before she could turn it and open the door an arm came over her head, keeping the door shut. She turned and folded her arms again, glaring up at Luca, conscious of her bare feet and damp hair, trying desperately not to let his sheer physicality affect her.

'If you don't leave in five seconds I'll start screaming.'

Luca kept his arm on the door, semi caging Serena in. 'The manager will just assume we're having fun. You can't be so naive that you didn't notice this place rents rooms by the hour.'

Serena felt hot. First of all at thinking of this man making her scream with pleasure and then at her own naivety.

'Of course I didn't,' she snapped, feeling vulnerable. She scooted out from under Luca's arm and put some space between them.

Luca crossed his arms. 'No, I can imagine you didn't. After all, it's not what you're used to.'

Serena thought of the Spartan conditions of the rehab facility she'd been in in England for a year, and then of her tiny studio apartment in a very insalubrious part of Athens. She smiled sweetly. 'How would you know?'

Luca scowled then. 'You're determined to stay in Rio?'

Never more so than right now. Even if just to annoy this man. 'Yes.'

Luca looked as though he would cheerfully throttle her. 'The last thing I need right now is some eagle-eyed reporter spotting you out and about, clubbing or shopping.'

Serena bit back a sharp retort. He had no idea what her life was like now. Clubbing? Shopping? She couldn't imagine anything worse.

Her smile got even sweeter. 'I'll wear a Louis Vuitton bag over my head while I go shopping for the latest Chanel suit. Will that help?'

That didn't go down well. Blood throbbed visibly in Luca's temple. 'You leaving Rio would be an even bigger help.'

Serena unconsciously mimicked his wide-legged stance. 'Well, unless you're planning on forcibly removing me, that's not going to happen. And if you even try such a thing I'll call the police and tell them you're harassing me.'

Luca didn't bother to tell her that with far greater problems in the city the police would no doubt just ogle her pale golden beauty before sending her on her way. And that such a stunt would only draw the interest of the paparazzi, who followed him most days.

The very thought of her being spotted, identified and linked to him was enough to make him go cold inside. He'd had enough bad press and innuendo after what had happened in Italy to last him a lifetime.

An audacious idea was being formulated in his head. It wasn't one he particularly relished, but it seemed like the only choice he had right now. It would get Serena DePiero out of Rio more or less immediately, and hopefully out of Brazil entirely within a couple of days.

'You said earlier that you were looking for another chance? That you'd do anything?'

Serena went very still, those huge blue eyes narrowing on him. Irritation made Luca's skin feel tight. The room was too small. All he could see was her. When she'd dropped her arms his eyes had tracked hungrily to her breasts, and he could still recall the jut of those hard nipples against her T-shirt. She was naked underneath.

Blood pooled at his groin, making him hard. *Damn.*

'Do you want a chance or not?' he growled, angry at his unwarranted response. Angry that she was still here.

Serena blinked. 'Yes, of course I do.'

Her voice had become husky and it had a direct effect on Luca's arousal. This was a mistake—he knew it. But he had no choice. Damage limitation.

Tersely, he said, 'I run an ethical mining company. I'm due to visit the Iruwaya mines, and the tribe that lives near there, to check on progress. You can prove your commitment by coming with me, instead of the assistant I'd lined up, to take notes. The village is part of the global communities network, so it's not entirely unrelated.'

'Where is the village?'

'Near Manaus.'

Serena's eyes widened. 'The city in the middle of the Amazon?'

Luca nodded. Perhaps this would be all it would take? Just the thought of doing something vaguely like hard work would have her scrambling back. Giving in. Leaving.

As if to mock his line of thought, Serena looked at him with those huge blue eyes and said determinedly, 'Fine. When do we go?'

Her response surprised Luca—much as the fact that she'd chosen this rundown flea-pit of a hotel had surprised him. He'd expected her to check into one of Rio's five-star resorts. But then he'd figured that perhaps her family had her on a tight leash where funds were concerned.

Whatever. He cursed himself again for wondering about her and said abruptly, 'Tomorrow. My driver will pick you up at five a.m.'

Once again he expected her to balk, but she didn't. He swept his gaze over the minor explosion of clothes from her suitcase and the toiletries spread across the narrow bed. The fact that her scent was clean and sweet, at odds with the sultry, sexy perfume he remembered from before, was not a welcome observation.

He looked back to her. 'I'll have an assistant stop by with supplies for the trip within the hour. You won't be able to bring your case.'

That gaze narrowed again. Suspicious. 'Supplies?'

Luca faced her squarely and said, with only the slightest twinge to his conscience, 'Oh, didn't I mention that we would be trekking through the jungle to get to the village? It takes two days from the farthest outskirts of Manaus.'

Those blue eyes flashed. 'No,' she responded. 'You didn't mention that we would be trekking through the jungle. Is it even safe?'

Luca smiled, enjoying the thought of Serena bailing after half an hour of walking through the earth's largest insect and wildlife-infested hothouse. He figured that after her first brush with one of the Amazon's countless insect or animal species she'd give up the act. But for now he'd go along with it. Because if he didn't she'd be a loose cannon in Rio de Janeiro. A ticking publicity time bomb. At least this way she'd have to admit defeat and go of her own free will.

He made a mental note to have a helicopter standing by to extract her and take her to the airport.

'It's eminently safe, once you have a guide who knows what they're doing and where they're going.'

'And that's you?' she said flatly.

'Yes. I've been visiting this tribe for many years, and

exploring the Amazon for a lot longer than that. You couldn't be in safer hands.'

The look Serena shot him told him that she doubted that. His smile grew wider and he arched a brow. 'By all means you can say no, Serena, it's entirely up to you.'

She made a derisive sound. 'And if I say no you'll personally escort me to the airport, no doubt.'

She stopped and bit her lip for a moment, making Luca's awareness of her spike.

'But if I do this, and prove my commitment, will you let me take up the job I came for?'

Luca's smile faded and he regarded her. Once again that tiny grudging admiration reared its head. He ruthlessly crushed it.

'Well, as I'm almost certain you won't last two hours in the jungle it's a moot point. All this is doing is delaying your inevitable return home.'

Her chin lifted and her arms tightened over her chest. 'It'll take more than a trek and some dense vegetation to put me off, Fonseca.'

The early-morning air was sultry, and the dawn hadn't yet broken, so it was dark when Serena got out of the back of the chauffeur-driven car at the private airfield almost twelve hours later. The first person she saw was the tall figure of Luca, carrying bags into a small plane. Instantly her nerves intensified.

He barely glanced at her as she walked over behind the driver, who carried the new backpack she'd been furnished with. And then his dark gaze fell on her and her heart sped up.

'You checked out of the hotel?'

Good morning to you too, Serena said silently, and

cursed her helpless physical reaction. 'Yes. And my suitcase is in the car.'

Luca took her small backpack from the driver and exchanged a few words with him in rapid Portuguese. Then, as the driver walked away, Luca said, 'Your things will be left at my headquarters until you get back.'

The obvious implication of *you*—not *we*—was not lost on Serena, and she said coolly, 'I won't be bailing early.'

Luca looked at her assessingly and Serena was conscious of the new clothes and shoes she'd been given. Lightweight trousers and a sleeveless vest under a khaki shirt. Sturdy trekking boots. Much like what Luca was wearing, except his looked well worn, faded with time. Doing little to hide his impressive muscles and physique.

She cursed. Why did he have to be the one man who seemed to connect with her in a way she'd never felt before?

Luca, who had turned back to the plane, said over his shoulder, 'Come on, we have a flight slot to make.'

'Aye-aye, sir,' Serena muttered under her breath as she hurried after him and up the steps into the small plane. She was glad that she'd pulled her hair up into a knot on top of her head as she could already feel a light sweat breaking out on the back of her neck.

Luca told her to take a seat. He shut the heavy door and secured it.

As Serena was closing her seatbelt she saw him take his seat in the cockpit and gasped out loud, '*You're* the pilot?'

'Evidently,' he said drily.

Serena's throat dried. 'Are you even qualified?'

He was busy flicking switches and turning knobs. He threw back over his shoulder, 'Since I was eighteen. Relax, Serena.'

He put on a headset then, presumably to communicate with the control tower, and then they were taxiing down the runway. Serena wasn't normally a nervous flyer, but her hands gripped the armrests as the full enormity of what was happening hit her. She was on a plane, headed into the world's densest and most potentially dangerous ecosystem, with a man who hated her guts.

She had a vision of a snake, dropping out of a tree in front of her face, and shivered in the dry cabin air just as the small plane left the ground and soared into the dawn-filled sky. Unfortunately her spirits didn't soar with it, but she comforted herself that at least she wasn't arriving back in Athens with her tail between her legs...just yet.

Serena was very aware of Luca's broad-shouldered physique at the front of the plane, but as much as she wanted to couldn't quite drum up the antipathy she wanted to feel for him. After all, he had good reason to believe what he did about her—that she'd framed him.

Anyone else would have believed the same...except for her sister, who had just looked at her with that sad expression that had reminded Serena of how trapped they both were by their circumstances—and by Serena's helpless descent into addiction to block out the pain.

Their father had simply been too powerful. And Siena had been too young for Serena to try anything drastic like running away. By the time Siena had come of age Serena had been in no shape to do anything drastic. Their father had seen to that effectively. And they'd been too well known. Any attempt to run would have been ended within hours, because their father would have sent his goons after them. They'd been bound as effectively as if their father had locked them in a tower.

'*Serena.*'

Serena's attention came back to the small plane and she looked forward, to see Luca staring back to her impatiently. He must have called her a couple of times. She felt raw from her memories.

'What?'

'I was letting you know that the flight will take four hours.' He pointed to a bag on the floor near her and said, 'You'll find some information in there about the tribe and the mines. You should read up on them.'

He turned back to the front and Serena restrained herself from sticking her tongue out at him. She'd been bullied and controlled by one man for most of her life and she chafed at the thought of giving herself over to that treatment again.

As she dug for the documents she reiterated to herself that this was a means to an end. She'd chosen to come here with Luca, and she was going to get through it in one piece and prove herself to him if it was the last thing she did. She'd become adept in the past few years in focusing on the present, not looking back. And she'd need that skill now more than ever.

Just over four hours later Serena was feeling a little more in control of herself, and her head was bursting with information about where they were going. She was already fascinated and more excited about the trip, which felt like a minor victory in itself.

They'd landed in a private part of the airport and after a light breakfast, which had been laid out for them in a private VIP room, Luca was now loading bags and supplies into the back of a Jeep.

His backpack was about three times the size of hers. And there were walking poles. Nerves fluttered in Serena's belly. Maybe she was being really stupid. How on earth was she going to last in the jungle? She was a city girl... That was the jungle she understood and knew how to navigate.

Luca must have caught her expression and he arched a questioning brow. Instantly fresh resolve filled Serena and she marched forward. 'Is there anything I can do?'

He shut the Jeep's boot door. 'No, we're good. Let's go—we don't have all day.'

A short time later, as Luca navigated the Manaus traffic, which eventually got less crazy as they hit the suburbs, he delivered a veritable lecture to Serena on safety in the jungle.

'And whatever you do obey my commands. The jungle is perceived to be a very hostile environment, but it doesn't have to be—as long as you use your head and you're constantly on guard and aware of what's around you.'

A devil inside Serena prompted her to say, 'Are you always this bossy or is it just with me?'

To her surprise Luca's mouth lifted ever so slightly on one side, causing a reaction of seismic proportions in Serena's belly.

That dark navy glance slid to her for a second and he drawled, 'I instruct and people obey.'

Serena let out a small sound of disdain. That had

been her father's philosophy too. 'That must make life very boring.'

The glimmer of a smile vanished. 'I find that people are generally compliant when it's in their interests to gain something…as you yourself are demonstrating right now.'

There was an unmistakably cynical edge to his voice that had Serena's gaze fixed on his face. Not liking the fact that she'd noticed it, and wondering about where such cynicism stemmed from, she said, 'You offered me a chance to prove my commitment. That's what I'm doing.'

He shrugged one wide shoulder. 'Exactly my point. You have something to gain.'

'Do I, though?' Serena asked quietly, but Luca either didn't hear or didn't think it worth answering. Clearly the answer was *no*.

They were silent for the rest of the journey. Soon they'd left the city behind, and civilisation was slowly swallowed by greenery until they were surrounded by it. It gave Serena a very real sense of how ready the forest seemed to be to encroach upon its concrete rival given half a chance.

Her curiosity overcame her desire to limit her interaction with Luca. 'How did you become interested in these particular mines?'

One of his hands was resting carelessly on the wheel, the other on his thigh. He was a good driver—unhurried, but fast. In control. He looked at her and she felt very conscious of being in a cocoon-like atmosphere with nothing but green around them.

He returned his attention to the road. 'My grandfather opened them up when prospectors found bauxite.

The area was plundered, forest cleared, and the native Indians moved on to allow for a camp to be set up. It was the first of my family's mines...and so the first one that I wanted to focus on to try and undo the damage.'

Serena recalled what she'd read. 'But you're still mining?'

He frowned at her and put both hands on the wheel, as if that reminder had angered him. 'Yes, but on a much smaller scale. The main camp has already been torn down. Miners commute in and out from a nearby town. If I was to shut down the mine completely it would affect the livelihoods of hundreds of people. I'd also be doing the workers out of government grants for miners, education for their children, and so on. As it is, we're using this mine as a pilot project to develop ethical mining so that it becomes the standard.'

He continued. 'The proceeds are all being funnelled into restoring huge swathes of the forest that were cleared—they'll never be restored completely, but they can be used for other ends, and the native Indians who were taken off the land have moved back to farm that land and make a new living from it.'

'It sounds like an ambitious project.' Serena tried not to feel impressed. Her experience with her father had taught her that men could be masters in the art of altruism while hiding a soul so corrupt and black it would make the devil look like Mickey Mouse.

Luca glanced at her and she could see the fire of intent in his eyes—something she'd never seen in her father's eyes unless it was for his own ends. Greedy for more power. Control. Causing pain.

'It is an ambitious project. But it's my responsibility. My grandfather did untold damage to this country's natural habitat and my father continued his reckless destruction. I refuse to keep perpetuating the same mistake. Apart from anything else, to do so is to completely ignore the fact that the planet is intensely vulnerable.'

Serena was taken aback at the passion in his voice. Maybe he *was* genuine.

'Why do you care so much?'

He tensed, and she thought he wouldn't answer, but then he said, 'Because I saw the disgust the native Indians and even the miners had for my father and men like him whenever I went with him to visit his empire. I started to do my own research at a young age. I was horrified to find out the extent of the damage we were doing—not only to our country but on a worldwide scale—and I was determined to put an end to it.'

Serena looked at his stern profile, unable to stem her growing respect. Luca was turning the Jeep into an opening that was almost entirely hidden from view. The track was bumpy and rough, the huge majestic trees of the rainforest within touching distance now.

After about ten minutes of solid driving, deeper and deeper into the undergrowth, they emerged into a large clearing where a two-storey state-of-the-art facility was revealed, almost completely camouflaged to blend with the surroundings.

Luca brought the Jeep to a halt alongside a few other vehicles. 'This is our main Amazon operational research base. We have other smaller ones in different locations.' He looked at her before he got out of the Jeep. 'You should take this opportunity to use the facilities while we still have them.'

Serena wanted to scowl at the very definite glint of mockery in his eyes but she refused to let him see the flicker of trepidation she felt once again, when confronted with the reality of their awe-inspiring surroundings.

She was mesmerised by the dense foliage around them. She had that impression again that the forest was being held back by sheer will alone, as if given the slightest chance it would extend its roots and vines and overtake this place.

'Serena?'

Frowning impatiently, Luca was holding open the main door.

She walked in and he pointed down a corridor.

'The bathroom is down there. I'll meet you back here.'

When Serena found the bathroom and saw her own reflection in dozens of mirrors, she grimaced. She looked flushed and sweaty, and was willing to bet that if she made it to the end of the day she'd look a lot worse.

After throwing some water on her face and tying her hair back into a more practical plait she headed back, nerves jumping around in her belly at the prospect of the battle of wills ahead and her determination not to falter at the first hurdle.

When Serena joined Luca back outside he handed her the backpack. There was a long rubber hose coming from the inside of it to sit over one shoulder. He saw her look at it.

'That's your water supply. Sip little and often; we'll replenish it later.'

She put the pack on and secured it around her waist and over her chest. She was relieved to find that it didn't feel too heavy at all. And then she saw the size of

Luca's pack, which obviously held all their main supplies and had a tent rolled up at the bottom.

Her eyes widened when she saw what looked suspiciously like a gun in a holster on his waist. He saw her expression and commented drily, 'It's a tranquilliser gun.' He sent a thorough glance up and down her body and remarked, 'Tuck your trousers into your socks and make sure your shirtsleeves are down and the cuffs closed.'

Feeling more and more nervous, Serena did as he said. When she looked at him again, feeling like a child about to be inspected in her school uniform, he was cocking a dark brow over those stunning eyes.

'Are you sure about this? Now would be a really good time to say no, if that's your intention.'

Serena put her hands on her hips and hid every one of her nerves behind bravado. 'I thought you said we don't have all day?'

CHAPTER THREE

A COUPLE OF hours later Serena was blindingly aware only of stepping where Luca stepped—which was a challenge, when his legs were so much longer. Her breath was wheezing in and out of her straining lungs. Rivers of sweat ran from every pore in her body.

She was soaked through. And it was no consolation to see sweat patches showing on Luca's body too, because they only seemed to enhance his impressive physicality.

She hadn't known what to expect, what the rainforest would be like, but it was more humid than she'd ever imagined it could be. And it was *loud*. Screamingly loud. With about a dozen different animal and bird calls at any time. She'd looked up numerous times to see a glorious flash of colour as some bird she couldn't name flew past, and had once caught sight of monkeys high in the canopy, loping lazily from branch to branch.

It was an onslaught on her senses, and Serena longed to stop for a minute to try and assimilate it all, but she didn't dare say a word to Luca, who hadn't stopped since he strode into the jungle, expecting her to follow him. He'd sent only the most cursory of glances back—presumably to make sure she hadn't been dragged into the dense greenery by one of mythical beasts that were running rampant in her imagination.

Every time the undergrowth rustled near her she sped up a little. Consequently, when Luca stopped suddenly and turned, Serena almost ran into him and skidded to a halt only just in time.

She noticed belatedly that they were on the edge of a clearing. It was almost a relief to get out of the oppressive atmosphere of the forest and suck in some breaths. She put her hands on her hips and hoped she didn't look as if she was about to burst a blood vessel.

Luca extracted something from a pocket in his trousers. It looked like a slightly old-fashioned mobile phone, a little larger than the current models.

'This is a satellite phone. I can call the chopper and it'll be here in fifteen minutes. This is your last chance to walk away.'

On the one hand Serena longed for nothing more than to see the horizon fill up with a cityscape again. And to feel the blast of clean, cool water on her skin. She was boiling. Sweating. And her muscles were burning. But, perversely, she'd never felt more energised, in spite of the debilitating heat. And, apart from anything else, she had a fierce desire to show no weakness to this man. He was the only thing that stood between her and independence.

'I'm not going anywhere, Luca.'

A glimpse of something distinctly like surprise crossed his face, and a dart of pleasure made Serena stand tall. Even that small indication that she was proving to be not as easy a pushover as he'd clearly expected was enough to keep her rooted to the spot.

He looked down then, his attention taken by something, and then back up at her. A very wicked hint of a smile was playing about his mouth as he said, with a pointed look towards her feet, 'Are you absolutely sure?'

Serena looked down and her whole body froze with fear and terror when she saw a small black scorpion crawling over the toe of her boot with its tail curled high over its arachnid body.

Without any previous experience of anything so potentially dangerous, Serena fought down the fear and took her walking pole and gently nudged the scorpion off her shoe. It scuttled off into the undergrowth. Feeling slightly light-headed at what she'd just done, she looked back at Luca.

'Like I said, I'm not going anywhere.'

Luca couldn't stem a flash of respect. Not many others would have reacted to seeing a scorpion like that with such equanimity. Men included. And any woman he knew would have used it as an excuse to hurl herself into his arms, squeaking with terror.

But Serena was staring him down. Blue eyes massive. Something in his chest clenched for a moment, making him short of breath. In spite of being sweaty and dishevelled, she was still stunningly beautiful. Helen of Troy beautiful. He could appreciate in that moment how men could be driven to war or driven mad because of the beauty of one woman.

But not him.

Not when he knew first-hand just how strong her sense of self-preservation was. Strong enough to let another take the fall for her own misdeeds.

'Fine,' he declared reluctantly. 'Then let's keep going.'

He turned his back on the provocative view of a flushed-faced Serena and strode back into the jungle.

Serena sucked in a few last deep breaths, relishing the cleared space for the last time, and then followed Luca, unable to stem the surge of triumph that he was letting her stay. And as she followed him she tried not to wince at the way her boots were pinching at her ankles and toes, pushing all thoughts of pain out of her head. Here, she couldn't afford to be weak. Luca would seize on it like a predator wearing its quarry down to exhaustion.

Serena felt as if she was floating above her body slightly. Pain was affecting so many parts of her that it had all coalesced into one throbbing beat of agony. Her backpack, which had been light that morning, now felt as if someone had been adding wet sand to it while she walked.

They'd stopped only briefly and silently for a few minutes while Luca had doled out a protein bar and some figs he'd pulled from a nearby tree—which had incidentally tasted delicious. And then they'd kept going.

Her feet were mercifully numb after going through the pain barrier some time ago. Her throat was parched, no matter how much water she sipped, and her legs were like jelly. But Luca's pace was remorseless. And Serena was loath to call out with so much as a whisper.

And then he stopped, suddenly, and looked around him, holding up a compass. He glanced back at her and said, 'Through here—stick close to me.'

She followed where he led for a couple of minutes, and then cannoned into his backpack and gave a little yelp of surprise when he stopped again abruptly. He turned and steadied her with his big hands. Serena hadn't even realised she was swaying until he did that.

'This is the camp.'

Serena blinked. Luca took his hands away and she didn't like how aware she was of that lack of touch.

Afraid he might see something she didn't want him to, she stepped back.

'Camp?'

She looked around and saw a small but obviously well-used clearing. She also noticed belatedly that the cacophony that had accompanied them all day had silenced now, and it was as if an expectant hush lay over the whole forest. The intense heat was lessening slightly.

'It's so quiet.'

'You won't be saying that in about half an hour, when the night chorus starts up.' He was unloading his backpack and said over his shoulder, 'Take yours off too.'

Serena let it drop from her aching body and almost cried out with the relief. She felt as though she might lift right out of the forest now that the heavy weight was gone.

Luca was down on his haunches, extracting things from his bag, and the material of his trousers was drawn taut over his powerful thighs. Serena found it hard to drag her gaze away, not liking the spasm of awareness in her lower belly.

He was unrolling the tent, which looked from where Serena was standing alarmingly *small*. Oblivious to her growing horror, Luca efficiently erected the lightweight structure with dextrous speed.

When the full enormity of its intimate size sank in, Serena said in a hoarse voice, 'We're not sleeping in that.'

Luca looked up from where he was driving a stake into the ground with unnecessary force. 'Oh, yes, *we* are, *minha beleza*—that is unless you'd prefer to take your chances sleeping al fresco? Jaguars are prevalent in this area. I'm sure they'd enjoy feasting on your fragrant flesh.'

Tension, fear and panic at the thought of sharing such a confined space with him spiked in Serena as Luca straightened up. She put her hands on her hips. 'You're lying.'

Luca looked at her, impossibly dark and dangerous. 'Do you really want to take that chance?' He swept an arm out. 'By all means be my guest. But if the jaguars don't get you any number of thousands of insects will do the job—not to mention bats. While you're thinking about that I'm going to replenish our water supplies.'

He started to leave and then stopped.

'While I'm gone you could take out some tinned food and set up the camping stove.'

When he walked away Serena had to resist the cowardly urge to call out that she'd go with him. She was sure he was just scaring her. Even so, she looked around nervously and stuck close to the tent as she did as he'd instructed, muttering to herself under her breath about how arrogant he was.

When Luca returned, a short while later, Serena was standing by the tent, clearly waiting for his return with more than a hint of nervousness. He stopped in his tracks, hidden behind a tree. His conscience pricked him for having scared her before. And something else inside him sizzled. *Desire*.

His gaze wandered down and took in the clothes that were all but plastered to her body after a day of trekking through the most humid ecosystem on earth. Her body was clearly defined and she was all woman, with firm, generous breasts, a small waist and curvaceous hips.

The whole aim of bringing her here had been to make her run screaming in the opposite direction, as far away as possible from him, but she'd been with him all the way.

He could still recall the terror tightening her face when she'd seen the scorpion and yet she hadn't allowed it to rise. He'd pursued a punishing pace today, even for him, and yet every time he'd cast a glance back she'd been right there, on his heels, dogged, eyes down, assiduously watching where she stepped as he'd instructed. Sweat had dripped down over her jaw and neck, making him think of it trickling into the lush valley of her breasts, dewing her golden skin with moisture.

Damn her. He hated to admit that up to now he'd been viewing her almost as a temporary irritation—like a tick that would eventually fall off his skin and leave him alone—but she was proving to be annoyingly resilient. He certainly hadn't expected to be sharing his tent with her.

The Serena DePiero he'd pegged as a reckless and wild party girl out only for herself was the woman he'd expected. The one he'd expected to leave Rio de Janeiro as soon as she'd figured she was on a hiding to nothing.

But she hadn't left.

So who the hell was the woman waiting for him now, if she wasn't the spoiled heiress? And why did he even care?

Serena bit her lip. The light was fading fast and there was no sign of Luca returning. She felt intensely vulnerable right then, and never more aware of her puny insignificance in the face of nature's awesome grandeur and power. A grandeur that would sweep her aside in a second if it had half a chance.

And then the snap of a twig alerted her to his presence. He loomed out of the gloom, dark and powerful. Sheer, abject relief that she wasn't alone made her feel momentarily dizzy, before she reminded herself that she really hated him for scaring her earlier.

Luca must have caught something of her relief. 'Worried that I'd got eaten by a jaguar, princess?'

'One can but hope,' Serena said sweetly, and then scowled. 'And don't call me princess.'

Luca brushed past her and took in the camping stove, commenting, 'I see you can follow instructions, at least.'

Serena scowled even more, irritated that she'd done his bidding. Luca was now gathering up wood and placing it in a small clearing not far from the tent. Determined not to let him see how much he rattled her, she said perkily, 'Can I help?'

Luca straightened from dumping some wood. 'You could collect some wood—just make sure it's not alive before you pick it up.'

Serena moved around, carefully kicking pieces of twigs and wood before she picked anything up. One twig turned out to be a camouflaged beetle of some sort that scuttled off and almost made her yelp out loud.

When she looked to see if Luca had noticed, though, he was engrossed in building up an impressive base of large logs for the fire. It was dusk now, and the massive trees loomed like gigantic shadows all around them.

Serena became aware of the rising sound of the forest around them as the night shift of wildlife took over from the day shift. It grew and grew to almost deafening proportions—like a million crickets going off at once right beside her head before settling to a more harmonious hum.

She brought the last of the wood she'd collected over to the pile just as Luca bent down to set light to the fire, which quickly blazed high. Feeling was returning to her feet and they had started to throb painfully.

Luca must have seen something cross her face, because he asked curtly, 'What is it?'

With the utmost reluctance Serena said, 'It's just some blisters.'

Luca stood up. 'Come here—let me see them.'

The flickering flames made golden light dance over his shadowed face. For a second Serena was too transfixed to move. He was the most beautiful man she'd ever seen. With an effort she looked away. 'I'm sure it's nothing. Really.'

'Believe me, I'm not offering because I genuinely care what happens to you. If you have blisters and they burst then they could get infected in this humidity. And then you won't be able to walk, and I really don't plan on carrying you anywhere.'

Fire raced up Serena's spine. 'Well, when you put it so eloquently, I'd hate to become more of a burden than I already am.'

Luca guided her towards a large log near the fire. Sitting her down, he went down on his knees and pulled his bag towards him.

'Take off your boots.' His voice was gruff.

Serena undid her laces and grimaced as she pulled off the boots. Luca pulled her feet towards him, resting them on his thighs. The feel of rock-hard muscles under her feet made scarlet heat rush up through her body and bloom on her face.

She got out a strangled, 'What are you doing?'

Luca was curt. 'I'm trained as a medic—relax.'

Serena shut her mouth. She felt churlish; was there no end to his talents? She watched as he opened up a complicated-looking medical kit and couldn't help asking, 'Why did you train as a medic?'

He glanced at her swiftly before looking down again. 'I was on a visit to a village near a mine with my father when I was younger and a small boy started choking. No one knew what to do. He died right in front of us.'

Serena let out a breath. 'That's awful.'

A familiar but painful memory intruded before she could block it out. She'd seen someone die right in front of her too—it was seared onto her brain like a tattoo. Her defences didn't seem to be so robust here, in such close proximity to this man. She could empathise with Luca's helplessness and that shocked her...to feel an affinity.

Luca was oblivious to the turmoil being stirred up inside Serena with that horrific memory of her own. He continued. 'Not as awful as the fact that my father didn't let it stop him from moving the tribe on to another location, barely allowing the parents time to gather up their son's body. They were nothing to him—a problem to be got rid of.'

He was pulling down Serena's socks now, distracting her from his words and the bitterness she could hear in his voice. He sucked in a breath when he saw the angry raw blisters.

'That's my fault.'

Serena blinked. Had Luca just said that? And had he

sounded ever so slightly apologetic? Together with his obvious concern for others, it made her uncomfortable.

He looked at her, face unreadable. 'New boots. They weren't broken in. It's no wonder you've got blisters. You must have been in agony for hours.'

Serena shrugged minutely and looked away, self-conscious under his searing gaze. 'I'm no martyr, Luca. I just didn't want to delay you.'

'The truth is,' he offered somewhat sheepishly, 'I hadn't expected you to last this far. I would have put money on you opting out well before we'd even left Rio.'

Something light erupted inside Serena and for a moment their eyes met and locked. Her insides clenched hard and all she was aware of was how powerful Luca's muscles felt under her feet. He looked away then, to get something from the medical box, and the moment was broken. But it left Serena shaky.

His hands were big and capable. Masculine. But they were surprisingly gentle as he made sure the blisters were clean and then covered them with thick plasters.

He was pulling her socks back up over the dressings when he said, with an edge to his voice, 'You've said a couple of times that you didn't do drugs... You forget that I was there. I saw you.'

His blue gaze seemed to sear right through her and his question caught Serena somewhere very raw. For a moment she'd almost been feeling *soft* towards him, when he was the one who had marched her into the jungle like some kind of recalcitrant prisoner.

Anger and a sense of claustrophobia made her tense. He'd seen only the veneer of a car crash lifestyle which had hidden so much more.

She was bitter. 'You saw what you wanted to see.'

Serena avoided his eyes and reached for her boots, but Luca got there first. He shook them out and said tersely, 'You should always check to make sure nothing has crawled inside.'

Serena repressed a shudder at the thought of what that might be and stuck her feet back into the boots, but Luca didn't move away.

'What's that supposed to mean? *I saw what I wanted to see.*'

Getting angry at his insistence, she glared at him. The firelight cast his face into shadow, making him seem even more dark and brooding.

He arched a brow. 'I think I have a right to know—you owe me an explanation.'

Serena's chest was tight with some unnamed emotion. The dark forest around them made her feel as if nothing existed outside of this place.

Hesitantly, she finally said, 'I wasn't addicted to Class A drugs…I've never taken a recreational drug in my life.' She tried to block out the doubtful gleam in Luca's eyes. 'But I *was* addicted to prescription medication. And to alcohol. And I'll never touch either again.'

Luca finally moved back and frowned. Serena felt as if she could breathe again. Until he asked, 'How did you get addicted to medication?'

Serena's insides curdled. This came far too close to that dark memory and all the residual guilt and fear that had been a part of her for so long. At best Luca was mildly curious; at worst he hated her. She had no desire to seek his sympathy, but a rogue part of her wanted to knock his assumptions about her a little.

'I started taking prescribed medication when I was five.'

Luca's frown deepened. 'Why? You were a child.'

His clear scepticism made Serena curse herself for being so honest. This man would never understand if she was to tell him the worst of it all. So she feigned a lightness she didn't feel and fell back on the script that her father had written for her so long ago that she couldn't remember *normal*.

She gave a small shrug and avoided that laser-like gaze. 'I was difficult. After my mother died I became hard to control. By the time I was twelve I had been diagnosed with ADHD and had been on medication for years. I became dependent on it—I liked how it made me feel.'

Luca sounded faintly disgusted. 'And your father... he sanctioned this?'

Pain gripped Serena. He'd not only sanctioned it, he'd made sure of it. She shrugged again, feeling as brittle as glass, and smiled. But it was hard. She forced herself to look at Luca. 'Like I said, I was hard to control. Wilful.'

Disdain oozed from Luca. 'Why are you so certain you're free of the addiction now?'

She tipped her chin up unconsciously. 'When my sister and I left Italy, after my father...' She stalled, familiar shame coursing through her blood along with anger. 'When it all fell apart we went to England. I checked into a rehab facility just outside London. I was there for a year. Not that it's any business of yours,' she added, immediately regretting her impulse to divulge so much.

Luca's expression was indecipherable as he stood up, and he pointed out grimly, 'I think our personal history makes it my business. You need to prove to me you can be trusted—that you will not be a drain on resources and the energy of everyone around you.'

Boots on, Serena stood up in agitation, her jaw tight with hurt and anger. She held up a hand. 'Whoa—judgemental, much? And you base this on your vast knowledge of ex-addicts?'

His narrow-minded view made Serena see red. She put her hands on her hips.

'Well?'

Tension throbbed between them as they glared at each other for long seconds. And then Luca bit out, 'I base it on an alcoholic mother who makes checking in and out of rehab facilities a recreational pastime. That's how I have a unique insight into the addict's mind. And when she's not battling the booze or the pills she's chasing her next rich conquest to fund her lifestyle.'

Serena felt sick for a moment at the derision in his voice. The evidence of just how personal his judgement was appeared entrenched in bitter experience.

Luca stepped back. 'We should eat.'

Serena's anger dissipated as she watched Luca turn away abruptly to light the camping stove near the fire. She reeled with this new knowledge of his own experience. And reeled at how much she'd told him of herself with such little prompting. She felt relieved now that she hadn't spilled her guts entirely.

No wonder he'd come down on her like a ton of bricks and believed the worst. Still...it didn't excuse him. And she told herself fiercely that she *didn't* feel a tug of something treacherous at the thought of him coping with an alcoholic parent. After all, she still bore the guilt of her sister having to deal with *her*.

Suddenly, in light of that conversation, she felt too raw to sit in Luca's company and risk that insightful mind being turned on her again. And fatigue was creeping over her like a relentless wave.

'Don't prepare anything for me. I'm not feeling hungry. I think I'll turn in now.'

Luca looked up at her from over his shoulder. He seemed to bite back whatever he was going to say and shrugged. 'Suit yourself.'

Serena grabbed her backpack and went into the tent, relieved to see that it was more spacious inside than she might have imagined. She could only do a basic toilette, and after taking off her boots and rolling out her sleeping bag carefully on one side of the tent she curled up and dived into the exhausted sleep of oblivion.

Anything to avoid thinking about the man who had comprehensively turned her world upside down in the last thirty-six hours and come far too close to where she still had so much locked away.

CHAPTER FOUR

THE FOLLOWING MORNING Luca heard movement from the tent and his whole body tensed. When he'd turned in last night Serena had been curled up in a ball inside her sleeping bag, some long hair trailing in tantalising golden strands around her head, her breathing deep and even. And once again he'd felt the sting of his conscience at knowing she'd gone to bed with no food, and her feet rubbed raw from new boots.

What she'd told him the previous evening had shocked him. She'd been taking medication since she was a child. Out of control even then. It was so at odds with the woman she seemed to be now that he almost couldn't believe it.

She'd sounded defiant when she'd told him that she'd been addicted by the age of twelve. Something inside him had recoiled with disgust at the thought. It was one thing to have a mother who was an addict as an adult. But a *child*?

Serena had given him the distinct impression that even then she'd known what she was doing and had revelled in it. But even as he thought that, something about the way she'd said it niggled at him. It didn't sit right.

Was she telling the truth?

Why would she lie after all this time? an inner voice pointed out. And if she hadn't ever done recreational drugs then maybe she really hadn't planted them on him that night... He didn't like the way the knowledge sank like a stone in his belly.

The crush and chaos of the club that night came back to him and a flash of a memory caught him unawares: Serena's hand slipping into his. He'd looked down at her and she'd been wide-eyed, her face pale. That had been just before the Italian police had separated them roughly and searched them.

The memory mocked him now. He'd always believed that look to have been Serena's guilt and pseudo-vulnerability, knowing what she'd just done. But if it hadn't been guilt it had been something far more ambiguous. It made him think of her passionate defence when he'd questioned her trustworthiness. And why on earth did that gnaw at him now? Making him feel almost guilty?

The flaps of the tent moved and the object of his thoughts emerged, blinking in the dawn light. She'd pulled her hair up into a bun on top of her head, and when that blue gaze caught his, Luca's insides tightened. He cursed her silently—and himself for bringing her here and putting questions into his head.

For possibly being innocent of the charges he'd levelled against her.

She straightened up and her gaze was wary. 'Morning.'

Her voice was sleep-rough enough to tug forcibly at Luca's simmering desire. She should look creased and dishevelled and grimy, but she looked gorgeous. Her skin was as dewy and clear as if she'd just emerged from a spa, not a night spent in a rudimentary tent in the middle of the jungle.

He thrust a bowl of protein-rich tinned food towards her. 'Here—eat this.'

There was the most minute flash of something in her eyes as she acknowledged his lack of greeting, but she took the bowl and a spoon and sat down on a nearby log to eat, barely wincing at the less than appetising meal. Yet another blow to Luca's firmly entrenched antipathy.

He looked at her and forced himself to ignore that dart of guilt he'd just felt—to remember that thanks to his mother's stellar example he knew all about the mercurial nature of addicts. How as soon as you thought they truly were intent on making a change they went and did the exact opposite. From a young age Luca had witnessed first-hand just how brutal that lack of regard could be and he'd never forgotten it.

Serena looked up at him. She'd finished her meal, and Luca felt slightly winded at the intensity of her gaze. He reached down and took the bowl and handed her a protein bar. His voice gruff, which irritated him, he said, 'Eat this too.'

'But I'm full now. I—'

Luca held it out and said tersely, 'Eat it, Serena. I can't afford for you to be weak. We have a long walk today.'

Serena's eyes flashed properly at that, and she stood up with smooth grace and took the bar from his outstretched hand. Tension bristled and crackled between them.

Serena cursed herself for thinking, *hoping* that some kind of a truce might have grown between them. And she cursed herself again for revealing what she had last night.

Luca was cleaning up the camp, packing things away, getting ready to move on. When she'd woken a while ago it had taken long seconds for her to realise where she was and with whom. A sense of exultation had rushed through her at knowing they were still in the jungle and that she'd survived the first day, that she hadn't shown Luca any weakness.

Then she'd remembered the gentleness of his hands on her feet and had felt hot. And then she'd got hotter, acknowledging that only extreme exhaustion had knocked her out enough to sleep through sharing such an intimate space with him.

Before Luca might see some of that heat in her expression or in her eyes, Serena busied herself with rolling up the sleeping bags and starting to take down the tent efficiently.

'Where did you learn to do that?' came Luca's voice, its tone incredulous.

Serena barely glanced at him, prickling. 'We used to go on camping trips while we were in rehab. It was part of the programme.'

She tensed, waiting for him to be derisive or to ask her about it, but he didn't. He just went and started unpegging the other side of the tent. Serena hadn't shared her experience of rehab with anyone—not even her sister. Even though her sister had been the one who had sacrificed almost everything to ensure Serena's care, working herself to the bone and putting herself unwittingly at the mercy of a man she'd betrayed years before and who had come looking for revenge.

Against the odds, though, Siena and Andreas had fallen in love and were now blissfully happy, with a toddler and a baby. Sometimes their intense happiness made Serena feel unaccountably alienated, and she hated herself for the weakness. But it was the same with her half-brother Rocco and his wife and children. If she'd never believed in love or genuine happiness theirs mocked her for it every time she saw them.

Without even realising it was done, she saw the camp was cleared and Luca was handing Serena her backpack.

He arched a brow. 'Ready?'

Serena took the pack and nodded swiftly, not wanting Luca to guess at the sudden vulnerability she felt to be thinking of her family and their very natural self-absorption.

She put on the pack and followed Luca for a few steps until he turned abruptly. 'How are your feet?'

Serena frowned and said, with some surprise, 'They're fine, actually.'

Luca made an indeterminate sound and carried on, and Serena tried not to fool herself that he'd asked out of any genuine concern.

As they walked the heat progressed and intensified to almost suffocating proportions. When they stopped briefly by a small stream in the afternoon Serena almost wept with relief to be able to throw some cool water over her face and head. She soaked a cloth handkerchief and tied it around her neck.

It was only a short reprieve. Luca picked up the punishing pace again, not even looking to see if Serena was behind him. Irritation rose up inside her. Would he even notice if she was suddenly pulled by some animal into the undergrowth? He'd probably just shrug and carry on.

After another hour any feeling of relief from the

stream was a distant memory and sweat dripped down her face, neck and back. Her limbs were aching, her feet numb again. Luca strode on, though, like some kind of robot, and suddenly Serena felt an urge to provoke him, needle him. Force him to stop and face her. Acknowledge that she had done well to last this far. Acknowledge that she might be telling the truth about the drugs.

She called out, 'So, are you prepared to admit that I might be innocent after all?'

She got her wish. Luca stopped dead in his tracks and then, after a long second, slowly turned around. His eyes were so dark they looked black. He covered the space between them so fast and silently that Serena took an involuntary step backwards, hating herself for the reflexive action.

He looked infinitely dangerous, and yet perversely Serena didn't feel scared. She felt something far more ambiguous and hotter, deep in her pelvis.

'To be quite frank, I don't think I even care any more whether or not you did it. The fact is that my involvement with you made things so much worse. *You* were enough to turn the incident into front-page news and put certainty into people's minds about my guilt—because they all believed that *you* did drugs, and that I was either covering for you or dealing to you. So, innocent bystander or not—as you might have been—I still got punished.'

Serena swallowed down a sudden and very unwelcome lump in her throat. She recognised uncomfortably that the need for this man to know she was innocent was futile or worse. 'You'll never forgive me for it, will you?'

His jaw clenched, and just then a huge drop of water landed on her face—so large that it splashed.

Luca looked up and cursed out loud.

'What? What is it?' Serena asked, her tension dissolving to be replaced by a tendril of fear.

Luca looked around them and bit out, 'Rain. *Damn*. I'd hoped to make the village first. We'll have to shelter. Come on.'

Even before he'd begun striding away again the rain was starting in earnest, those huge drops cascading from the sky above the canopy. Serena hurried after him to try and keep up. Within seconds, though, it was almost impossible to see a few feet in front of her nose. Genuine panic spiked. She couldn't see Luca any more. And then he reappeared, taking her hand, keeping her close.

The rain was majestic, awesome. Deafening. But Serena was only aware of her hand in Luca's. He was leading them through the trees, off the path to a small clearing. The ground was slightly higher here. He let her go and she saw him unrolling a tarpaulin. Catching on quickly, she took one end and tied it off to a nearby sapling while Luca did the same on the other side, creating a shelter a few feet off the ground.

He laid out another piece of tarpaulin under the one they'd tied off and shouted over the roar of the rain, 'Get underneath!'

Serena slipped off her pack and did so. Luca joined her seconds later. They were drenched. Steam was rising off their clothes. But they were out of the worst of the downpour. Serena was still taken aback at how quickly it had come down.

They sat like that, their breaths evening out, for

long minutes. Eventually she asked, 'How long will it last?'

Luca craned his neck to look out, his arms around his knees. He shrugged one wide shoulder. 'Could be minutes—could be hours. Either way, we'll have to camp out again tonight. The village is only a couple of hours away, but it'll be getting dark soon—too risky.'

At the thought of another night in the tent with Luca, flutters gripped Serena's abdomen. He was pulling something out of a pocket and handed her another protein bar. Serena reached for it with her palm facing up, but before she could take it Luca had grabbed her wrist and was frowning.

She was distracted by his touch for a moment—all she felt was *heat*—and then he was saying, 'What are those marks? Did you get them here?'

He was inspecting her palm and pulling her other hand towards him to look at that, too. Far too belatedly Serena panicked, and tried to pull them back, but he wouldn't let her, clearly concerned that it had happened recently.

She saw what he saw: the tiny criss-cross of old, silvery scars that laced her palms.

As if coming to that realisation, he said, 'They're old.' He looked at her, stern. '*How* old?'

Serena tried to jerk her hands away but he held them fast. Her breath was choppy now, with a surge of emotion. And with anger that he was quizzing her as if she'd done something wrong.

She said reluctantly, 'They're twenty-two years old.'

Luca looked at her, turning towards her. '*Deus*, what *are* they?'

Serena was caught by his eyes. They blazed into hers,

seeking out some kind of truth and justice—which she was coming to realise was integral to this man's nature. It made him see the world in black and white, good and bad. And she was firmly in the bad category as far as he was concerned.

But just for once, Serena didn't want to be. She felt tired. Her throat ached with repressed emotions, with all the horrific images she held within her head, known only to her and her father. And he'd done his best to eradicate them.

A very weak and rogue part of her wanted to tell Luca the truth—much like last night—in some bid to make him see that perhaps things weren't so black and white. And even though an inner voice told her to protect herself from his derision, she heard the words spill out.

'They're the marks of a bamboo switch. My father favoured physical punishment.'

Luca's hands tightened around hers and she held back a wince. His voice was low. 'How old were you?'

Serena swallowed. 'Five—nearly six.'

'What the hell....?'

Luca's eyes burned so fiercely for a moment that Serena quivered inwardly. She took advantage of the moment to pull her hands back, clasping them together, hiding the permanent stain of her father's vindictiveness.

Serena could understand Luca's shock. Her therapist had been shocked when she'd told *her*.

She shrugged. 'He was a violent man. If I stepped out of line, or if Siena misbehaved, I'd be punished.'

'You were a *child*.'

Serena looked at Luca and felt acutely exposed, recalling just how her childhood had been so spectacularly snatched away from her, by far worse than a few scars on her palms.

She noticed something then, and seized on it weakly. 'The rain—it's stopped.'

Luca just looked at her for a long moment, as if he hadn't ever seen her before. It made Serena nervous and jittery.

Eventually he said, 'We'll make camp here. Let's set it up.'

Serena scrambled inelegantly out from under their makeshift shelter. The jungle around them was steaming from the onslaught of precipitation. It was unbearably humid...and uncomfortably sultry.

As she watched, Luca uncoiled himself, and for a moment Serena was mesmerised by his sheer masculine grace. He looked at her too quickly for her to look away.

He frowned. 'What is it?'

Serena swallowed as heat climbed up her chest. She blurted out the first thing she could think of. 'Thirsty—I'm just thirsty.'

Luca glanced around them and then strode to a nearby tree and tested the leaves. 'Come here.'

Not sure what to expect, Serena walked over. Luca put a hand on her arm and it seemed to burn right through the material.

He manoeuvred her under the leaf and said, 'Tip your head back—open your mouth.'

Serena looked at him and something dark lit his eyes, making her belly contract.

'Come on. It won't bite.'

So she did, and Luca tipped the leaf so that a cascade of water fell into her mouth, cold and more refreshing than anything she'd ever tasted in her life. She coughed slightly when it went down the wrong way, but couldn't stop her mouth opening for more. The water trickled over her face, cooling the heat that had nothing to do with the humid temperature.

When there were only a few drops left, she straightened up again. Luca was watching her. They were close—close enough that all Serena would have to do would be to step forward and they'd be touching.

And then, as if reading her mind and rejecting her line of thought, Luca stepped back, letting her arm go. 'We need to change into dry clothes.'

He walked away and Serena felt ridiculously exposed and shaky. What was *wrong* with her?

Luca was taking clothes out of his pack. He straightened up and his hands went to his shirt, undoing the buttons with long fingers. A sliver of dark muscled chest was revealed, the shadow of chest hair. And Serena was welded to the spot. She couldn't breathe.

Finally sense returned. Her face hot with embarrassment, she hurried to her own bag and concentrated on digging out her own change of clothes. The last thing she needed was to let Luca Fonseca into the deepest recesses of her psyche. But, much to her irritation, she couldn't forget the way he'd looked when he'd held her hands out for inspection, or the look in his eyes just now, when she fancied she'd seen something carnal in their depths, only for him to mock her for her fanciful imagination.

Luca was feeling more and more disorientated as he pulled on fresh clothes with rough hands. *Deus*. He'd almost backed Serena into the tree just now and covered her open mouth with his, jealous of the rainwater trickling between those plump lips.

And what about those scars on her hands? The silvery marks criss-crossing the delicate pale skin? He hadn't been prepared for the surge of panic when he'd seen them—afraid she'd been marked by something on the trail—or the feeling of rage when she'd told him so flatly who had done it.

He'd met her father once or twice at social events and had never liked the man. He had cold, dead dark eyes, and the superior air of someone used to having everything he wanted.

He didn't like to admit it, but the knowledge that he'd been violent didn't surprise Luca. He could picture the man being vindictive. Malevolent. But to his own daughters? The blonde, blue-eyed heiresses everyone had envied?

Luca knew Serena was changing behind him. He could hear the soft sounds of clothes being taken off and dropped. And then there was silence for a long moment. Telling himself it was concern, but knowing that it stemmed from a much deeper desire, Luca turned around.

Her back was to him and her legs were revealed in all their long shapely glory as she stripped off her trousers. High-cut pants showed off a toned length of thigh. Firm but curvy buttocks. When she stripped down to her bra he wanted to go over and undo it, slip his hands around her front to cup the generous swells and feel her arch into him.

He was rewarded with a burgeoning erection within seconds—no better than a pre-teen ogling a woman dressing in a changing room.

The snap of her belt around her hips broke Luca out of his trance and, angry with himself, he turned away and pulled on his own trousers. The light was falling rapidly now, and Luca had been so fixated on Serena that he was risking not having the camp set up in time.

But when he turned around again, about to issue a curt command, the words died on his lips. To his surprise Serena was already unrolling the tent and staking it out, her long ponytail swinging over her shoulder.

He cursed her silently, because he was losing his footing with this woman—fast.

Serena was sitting on a log on the opposite side of the fire to Luca a short time later, after they'd eaten their meagre meal. The tent stood close by, and she couldn't stop a surge of ridiculous pride that she'd put it up herself. He'd expected her to flee back to civilisation at the slightest hint of work or danger, but here she was, day two and surviving—if not thriving. The feeling was heady, and it made her relish her newfound independence even more.

However, none of that could block out the mortification when she thought of earlier and how close she'd come to betraying her desire for him...

She caught Luca's eye across the flickering light of the fire and he asked, 'What's the tattoo on your back?'

She went still. He must have seen the small tattoo that sat just above her left shoulderblade earlier, when she'd been changing. The thought of him looking at her made her feel hot.

The tattoo was so personal to her, she didn't want to tell him. Reluctantly, she finally said, 'It's a swallow. The bird.'

'Any significance?'

Serena almost laughed. As if she'd divulge *that* to him! He'd definitely fall off his log laughing.

She shrugged. 'It's my favourite bird. I got it done a few years ago.' *The day she'd walked out of the rehab clinic, to be precise.*

She avoided Luca's gaze. Swallows represented resurrection and rebirth... Luca would hardly look that deeply into its significance, but still... She had the uncanny sense that he might and she didn't like it.

She really wanted to avoid any more probing into her life or her head. She stood up abruptly, making Luca look up, his dark gaze narrowing on her. 'I'm going to turn in now.' She sounded too husky. Even now her body trembled with awareness, just from looking at his large rangy form relaxed.

Luca stirred the fire, oblivious to her heated imaginings. 'I'll let you get settled.'

Serena turned away and crawled into the tent, pulling off her boots, but leaving her clothes on. Then she felt silly. Luca hadn't given her the slightest hint that he felt any desire for her whatsoever, and she longed to feel cooler. She took off her shirt and stripped down to her panties, and pulled the sleeping bag around her.

She prayed that sleep would come as it had last night, like a dark blanket of oblivion, so she wouldn't have to hear Luca come in and deal with the reality that he slept just inches away from her and probably resented every moment.

Luca willed his body to cool down. He didn't like how off-centre Serena was pushing him. Making him desire her; wonder about her. Wanting to know more. She was surprising him.

He'd been exposed to the inherent selfishness of his mother and women in general from a very early age, so it was not a welcome sensation thinking that he might have misjudged her.

Lovers provided him with physical relief and an escort when he needed it. But his life was not about women, or settling down. He had too much to do to undo all the harm his father and grandfather had caused. He had set himself a mammoth task when his father had died ten years ago: to reverse the negative impact of the name Fonseca in Brazil, which up till then had been synonymous with corruption, greed and destruction.

The allegations of his drug-taking had come at the worst possible time for Luca—just when people had been beginning to sit up and trust that perhaps he *was* different and genuine about making a change. It was only now that he was back in that place.

And the person who could reverse all his good work was only feet away from him. He had to remember that. Remember who she was and what she had the power to do to him. Even if she *was* innocent, any association with her would incite all that speculation again.

Only when Luca felt sure that Serena must be asleep did he turn in himself, doing his best to ignore the curled-up shape inside the sleeping bag that was far too close to his for comfort. He'd really *not* expected to have to share this tent with anyone, and certainly not with Serena DePiero for a second night in a row.

But as he lay down beside her he had to acknowledge uncomfortably that there was no evidence of the spoilt ex-wild-child. There wasn't one other woman he could think of, apart from those whose life's work it was to study the Amazon, who would have fared better than her over the past couple of days. And even some of those would have run screaming long before now, back to the safety of a research lab, or similar.

He thought of her putting up the tent, her tongue caught between her teeth as she exerted herself, sweat dripping down her neck and disappearing into the tantalising vee of her shirt. Gritting his jaw tightly, Luca sighed and closed his eyes. He'd accused her of not lasting in the jungle, but it was he who craved the order of civilisation again—anything to dilute this fire in his blood and put an end to the questions Serena kept throwing up.

A couple of hours later Luca woke, instantly alert and tensed, waiting to hear a sound outside. But it came from inside the tent. *Serena.* Moaning in her sleep in Italian.

'Papa...no, per favore, non che... Siena, aiutami.'

Luca translated the last word: *help me.* There was something gutturally raw about her words, and they were full of pain and emotion. Her voice cracked then, and Luca's chest squeezed when he heard her crying.

Acting on instinct, Luca reached over and touched her shoulder.

Almost instantly she woke up and turned her head. *'Ché cosa?'*

Something about the fact that she was still speaking Italian made his chest tighten more. 'You were dreaming.' He felt as if he'd invaded her privacy.

Serena went as tense as a board. He could see the bright glitter of those blue eyes in the gloom.

'Sorry for waking you.'

Her voice was thick, her accent stronger. He felt her pull abruptly away from his hand as she curled up again. Her hair was a bright sliver of white-gold and his body grew hot as he thought of it trailing over his naked chest as she sat astride him and took him deep into her body.

Anger at the wanton direction of his thoughts, at how easily she got under his skin and how she'd pulled away just now, almost as if he'd done something wrong, made him say curtly, 'Serena?'

She said nothing, and that wound him up more. A moment ago he'd been feeling sorry for her, disturbed by the gut-wrenching sound of those sobs. But now memories of his mother and how she'd use her emotions to manipulate the people around her made Luca curse himself for being so weak.

It made his voice harsh. 'What the hell was *that* about?'

Her voice sounded muffled. 'I said I was sorry for waking you. It was nothing.'

'It didn't sound like nothing to me.'

Serena turned then, those eyes flashing, her hair bright against the dark backdrop of the tent. She said tautly, 'It was a dream, okay? Just a bad dream and I've already forgotten it. Can we go to sleep now, please?'

Luca reacted viscerally to the fact that Serena was all but spitting at him, clearly in no need of comfort whatsoever. She pressed his buttons like no one else, and all he could think about right then was how much he wanted her to submit to him—anything to drown out all the contradictions she was putting in his head.

He reached out and found her arms, pulled her into him, hearing her shocked little gasp.

'Luca, what are you doing?'

But the defensive tartness was gone out of her voice.

He pulled her in closer, the darkness wrapping around them but failing to hide that bright blue gaze or the gold of her hair. The slant of her stunning cheekbones.

She wasn't pulling away.

Luca's body was on fire. From somewhere he found his voice and it sounded coarse, rough. 'What am I doing?'

'This...'

And then he pulled her right into him and his mouth found hers with unerring precision. Her breasts swelled against his chest—in outrage? He didn't know, because he was falling over the very thin edge of his control.

When he felt her resistance give way after an infinitesimal moment, triumph surged through his body. He couldn't think any more, because he was swept up in the decadent darkness of a kiss that intoxicated him and reminded him of only one other similar moment... with her...seven years before.

CHAPTER FIVE

SERENA WAS STILL in shock at finding herself in Luca's arms with his mouth on hers. When he'd woken her at first, she'd had an almost overwhelming instinctive need to burrow close to him, the tentacles of that horrible nightmare clinging like slimy vines to her hot skin.

And then she'd realised just who she was with—just who was precipitating such weak feelings of wanting to seek strength and comfort. Luca Fonseca, of all people? And that dream... She hadn't had it for a long time—not since she'd been in rehab. And to be having it again, *here*, was galling. As if she was going backwards. Not forwards. And it was all his fault, for getting under her skin.

Fresh anger made her struggle futilely against Luca's superior strength even after she'd let the hot tide of desire take her over, revealing how much she wanted him. She pulled back, ripping her mouth from his, mortified to find herself breathing harshly, her breasts moving rapidly against the steel wall of his chest, nipples tight and stinging.

Her body and her mind seemed to be inhabiting two different people. Her body was saying *Please don't stop* and her head was screaming *Stop now!*

'What is it, *minha beleza?*'

The gravelly tone of Luca's voice rubbed along her nerve-endings, setting them alight. Traitors.

'Do you really think this is a good idea?'

Dammit. She sounded as if she wanted him to convince her that it was, her voice all breathy.

His eyes were like black pits in his face and Serena was glad she couldn't make out their expression. She half expected Luca to come to his senses and recoil, but instead he seemed to move even closer. His hands slipped down her arms and came around her back, making her feel quivery at how light his touch was—and yet it burned.

'Luca...?'

'Hmm...?'

His mouth came close again and his lips feathered a kiss to her neck. Liquid fire spread through Serena's pelvis. *Damn him*.

She swallowed, her body taking over her mind, making her move treacherously closer to that huge hard body.

'I don't think this is a good idea. We'll regret it.'

Luca pulled back for a moment and said throatily, 'You think too much.'

And then he was covering her mouth with his again, and any last sliver of defence or righteous anger at how vulnerable he made her feel drained away. She was drowning in his strength. Mouth clinging to his, skin tightening all over as he coaxed her lips apart to explore deeper with his tongue. His kiss seven years ago had seared itself onto her memory like a brand. This was like being woken from a deep sleep. She'd never really enjoyed kissing or being touched by men…until him. And now this.

Barely aware of the fact that Luca was pulling down the zips of their sleeping bags, she only knew that there was nothing between them now, and that he was pulling her on top of him so her breasts were crushed against his broad chest.

Both hands were on her head, fingers thrust deep into her hair, and Luca positioned her so that he could plunder her mouth with devastating skill. Serena could feel herself getting damp between her legs.

Luca drew back for a moment and Serena opened her eyes, breathing heavily. With a smooth move he manoeuvred them so that Serena was on her back and loomed over her. He looked wild, feral. Exactly the way she imagined the marauding Portuguese *conquistadores* must have looked when they'd first walked on this land.

He smoothed some hair behind her ear and Serena's breath grew choppier. Her fingers itched to touch him, to feel that chest, so when his head lowered to hers again her hands went to the buttons of his shirt and undid them, sliding in to feel the dense musculature of his chest.

She was unable to hold back a deep sound of satisfaction as her hands explored, revelling in his strength. She dragged her fingers over his chest, sliding over the ridges of his muscles, a nail grazing a flat hard nipple. Her mouth watered. She wanted to taste it.

His beard tickled her slightly, but that was soon forgotten as his tongue thrust deep, making her arch up against him. He was pulling down the strap of her vest, taking with it her bra strap, exposing the slope of her breast.

When Luca pulled back again she was gasping for breath. She looked up, but everything was blurry for a moment. She could feel Luca's fingers reach inside the lace cup of her bra, brushing enticingly close to where her nipple was so hard it ached. He pulled it down and Serena felt her breast pop free of the confinement. Luca's gaze was so hot she could feel it on her bare skin.

He breathed out. *'Perfeito…'*

His head came down, and with exquisite finesse he flicked his tongue against that tip, making Serena's breath catch and her hips move of their own volition. He flicked it again, and then slowly expored the hard flesh, before placing his whole mouth around it and suckling roughly.

Serena cried out. Her hands were on his head, in his hair. She'd never felt anything like this in her life. Sex had been something to block out, to endure, an ineffective form of escape…not something to revel in like this.

His hand was on her trousers now, undoing her button, lowering the zip. There was no hesitation. She wanted this with an all-consuming need she'd never experienced before. His hand delved under her panties as his mouth still tortured her breast.

When his fingers found the evidence of her desire he tore his mouth away. She could see his eyes glitter almost feverishly as he stroked her intimately, releasing her damp heat. Serena whimpered softly, almost mindless, her hips jerking with reaction.

'You want me.'

His words sliced through the fever in her brain.

Serena bit her lip. She was afraid to speak, afraid of what might spill out. Luca was a master torturer. With his hand he forced her legs apart as much as they could go, and then he thrust a finger deep inside, where she was slick and hot. She gasped.

'Say it, Serena.'

He sounded fierce now, his finger moving intimately against her. *Oh, God...* She was going to come. Like this. In a tent in the middle of nowhere. Just from this man touching her...

Feeling vulnerable far too late, Serena tried to bring her legs together—but Luca wouldn't let her. She could see the determination on his face. The lines stark with desire and hunger. One finger became two, stretching her, filling her. She gasped, her hands going to his shoulders.

The heel of his hand put exquisite pressure on her clitoris. She was unable to stop her hips from moving, rolling, seeking to assuage the incredible ache that was building. And then his fingers moved faster, deeper, making Serena's muscles tighten against him.

'Admit you want me...*dammit*. You're almost coming. *Say it.*'

Serena was wild now, hands clutching at him. He was looking down at her. She knew what was stopping the words being wrenched from her: the fact that Luca seemed so intent on pushing her over the edge when *he* appeared to be remarkably in control. The fact that she suspected he just wanted to prove his domination over her.

But she couldn't fight it. She needed it—*him*—too badly.

'I do...' she gasped out, the words torn from her as her body reached its crescendo against the relentless rhythm of Luca's wicked hand and fingers. 'I do...want you...*damn you.*'

And with those last guttural words she went as taut as a bowstring as the most indescribably pleasurable explosion racked her entire body and broke it apart into a million pieces before letting it float back together again.

Serena had orgasmed before. But never like this. With such intensity...losing herself in the process.

Luca's brain had melted into a pool of lust and heat. Serena's body was still clamping around his fingers and he ached to be embedded within her, so that the inferno in his body might be assuaged.

But something held him back—had held him back from replacing his hand with his erection. At some point he'd become aware that he needed this woman on a level that surpassed anything he'd ever known before.

And, worse, he needed to know that she felt it too. So making her admit it, making her *come*, had become some kind of battle of wills. She'd confounded him since she'd turned up in his office, just days ago, and this felt like the first time he'd been able to claw back some control. By making her lose hers.

But now, as he extricated his hand and her body jerked in reaction, it felt like an empty triumph. Luca pulled back and gritted his jaw at the way his body rejected letting Serena go. He pulled on his shirt, feeling wild. Undone.

Serena was moving, pulling her clothes together. He saw her hands shaking and wanted to snarl. Where was the insouciant, confident woman he remembered meeting that night in Florence? She bore no resemblance to this woman, who was almost *impossibly* shy.

Luca lay back, willing down the throbbing heat in his blood. Cursing the moment he'd ever laid eyes on

Serena DePiero. She went still beside him, and even that set his nerves on edge. Sizzling.

Eventually she said hesitantly, 'You didn't...'

She trailed off. But he knew what she'd meant to say, and suddenly her unbelievable hesitance pushed him over another edge. He'd cursed this woman for a long time for sending his life into turmoil, and yet again she was throwing up another facet of her suddenly chameleon-like personality. The most in control he'd felt around her since she'd come back into his life had been just now—when she'd been surrendering to him even though she'd obviously hated it.

He would have her—completely. In his bed. On his terms. Would reveal this hesitant shyness to be the sham that it was.

And then, when he'd had her, sated himself, he would be able to walk away and leave her behind for good. One thing was certain: he'd wanted her since the moment he'd laid eyes on her, and not even his antipathy for her had put a dent in that need. If he didn't have her he'd be haunted for ever. And no woman, however alluring, retained any hold over him once he'd had her.

He came up on one elbow and looked down, saw her eyes flash blue as she looked at him. Her mouth was swollen.

Luca forced down the animalistic urge to take her there and then. He was civilised. He'd spent years convincing people that he wasn't his lush of a mother or his corrupt father.

'No, I didn't.'

He saw her frown slightly. 'Why didn't you...?'

He finished for her, 'Make love to you?'

Serena nodded her head, pulling the sleeping bag

back up over her body. Luca resisted the urge to yank it back down. *Control.*

His jaw was hard. 'I didn't make love to you, Serena, because I have no protection with me. And when we do make love it will be in more comfortable surroundings.'

He sensed her tensing.

'Don't be so sure I want to make love to you, Luca.'

He smiled and felt ruthless. '*Minha beleza*, don't even *try* to pretend that you would have objected to making love here and now. I felt your body's response and it didn't lie. Even if you don't like it.'

She opened her mouth and he reached out and put a finger to her lips, stopping her words.

'Don't even waste your breath. After that little performance you're mine as surely as if I'd stamped a brand on your body.'

She smacked his hand away, hard enough to sting. 'Go to hell, Luca.'

Luca curbed the desire to show Serena in a more subtle way that what he said was true, but it was true that he didn't have protection, and he knew that if he touched her again he wouldn't be able to stop himself.

So he lay down and closed his eyes, just saying darkly, 'Not before I take you with me, *princesa*.'

The fact that he could sense Serena fuming beside him only made him more determined to shatter her control again.

She would be his.

The following day Serena was galvanised on her walk—largely by the depth of her humiliation and her hatred for Luca. She glared at his back as he strode ahead of her and mentally envisaged a jaguar springing from the jungle to swallow him whole.

She couldn't get the lurid images out of her head—the way she'd so completely and without hesitation capitulated to Luca's lovemaking. The way he'd played her body like a virtuoso played a violin. The way he'd controlled her reactions while maintaining his own control.

His words mocked her: *'After that little performance you're mine.'* She felt like screaming. Unfortunately it had been no performance—which was galling, considering that for most of her life she'd perfected the performance of a spoilt, reckless heiress.

But on a deeper level what had happened last night with Luca terrified her.

For as long as she could remember there had been a layer between her and the world around her and she was still getting used to that layer being gone. She'd first tasted freedom when her father had disappeared and they'd been left with nothing. It had been too much to deal with, sending her spiralling into a hedonistic frenzy, saved only by her sister taking her to England and to rehab.

Since then she'd learnt to deal with being free; not bearing the constant weight of her father's presence. Her job, becoming independent, was all part of that process. Even if she still harboured deep secrets and a sense of guilt.

But when Luca had been touching her last night—watching her, making her respond to his touch—her sense of freedom had felt very flimsy. Because he'd also been touching a part of her that she hadn't yet given room to really breathe. Her emotions. Her yearning for what her sister had: a life and happiness.

And the fact that Luca had brought that to the surface made her nervous and angry. All she was to him was a conquest. A woman he believed had betrayed him. A woman he wanted to slake his desire with.

A woman he didn't like, even if he ever conceded that she might be innocent.

She'd known that the night they'd met first. He'd had a gleam of disdain in his eyes that he'd barely concealed even as she saw the burn of desire.

And yet, damn him, since she'd walked into his office the other day it was as if everything was brighter, sharper. More intense. *Bastard*.

Serena crashed into Luca's back before she'd even realised she'd been so preoccupied she hadn't noticed he'd stopped. She sprang back, scowling, and then noticed that they were on a kind of bluff, overlooking a huge cleared part of the forest.

To be out from under the slightly oppressive canopy was heady for a moment. Ignoring Luca, Serena studied the view. She could see that far away in the distance the land had been eviscerated. Literally. Huge chunks cut out. No trees. And what looked like huge machines were moving back and forth, sun glinting off steel.

Forgetting that she hated Luca for a moment, because unexpected emotion surged at seeing the forest plundered like this, she asked, a little redundantly, 'That's the mine?'

Luca nodded, his face stern when she sneaked an illicit glance.

'Yes, that's my family's legacy.'

And then he pointed to a dark smudge much closer. 'That's the Iruwaya tribe's village there.'

Serena shaded her eyes until she could make out

what looked like a collection of dusty huts and a clearing. Just then something else caught her eye: a road leading into the village and a bus trundling along merrily, with bags and crates hanging precariously from its roof along with a few live chickens.

It took a few seconds for the scene to compute and for Serena's brain to make sense of it. Slowly she said, 'The village isn't isolated.'

'I never said it was totally isolated.'

The coolness of Luca's tone made Serena step back and look up at him, her blood rapidly rising again. 'So why the hell have we been trekking through a rainforest to get to it?' She added, before he could answer, 'You never said anything about it being optional.'

Luca crossed his arms. 'I didn't offer an option.'

'My God,' Serena breathed. 'You really did do this in a bid to scare me off... I mean, I know you did, but I stupidly thought...'

She trailed off and backed away as the full significance sank in. Her stupid feeling of triumph for putting up the tent last night without help mocked her now. She'd known Luca hated her, that he wanted to punish her...but she hadn't believed for a second that there had been any other way of getting to this village.

All this time he must have been alternating between laughing his head off at her and cursing her for being so determined to stick it out. And then amusing himself by demonstrating how badly she wanted him.

Luca sighed deeply and ran a hand through his hair. 'Serena, this *is* how I'd planned to come to the village, but I'll admit that I thought you would have given up and gone home long before now.'

His words fell on deaf ears. Serena felt exposed, humiliated. She shook her head. 'You're a bastard, Luca Fonseca.'

Terrified of the emotion rising in her chest, she turned and blindly walked away, not taking care to look where she was going.

She'd landed on her hands and knees, the breath knocked out of her, before she realised she'd tripped over something. It also took a moment for her to register that the black ground under her hands was moving.

She sprang back with a small scared yelp just as Luca reached her and hauled her up, turning her to face him.

'Are you okay?'

Still angry with him, Serena broke free. And then she registered a stinging sensation on her arm, and on her thigh. She looked down stupidly, to see her trousers ripped apart from her fall, and vaguely heard Luca curse out loud.

He was pulling her away from where she'd tripped and ripping off her shirt, but Serena was still trying to figure out what had happened—and that was when the pain hit in two places: her arm and her leg.

She cried out in surprise at the shock of how excruciating it was.

Luca was asking urgently, 'Where is it? Where's the pain?'

Struggling, because it was more intense than anything she'd ever experienced, Serena got out thickly, 'My arm…my leg.'

She was barely aware of Luca inspecting her arm, her hands, and then undoing her trousers to pull them down roughly, inspecting her thigh where it was burning. He was brushing something off her and cursing again.

She struggled to recall what she'd seen. Ants. They'd just been ants. It wasn't a snake or a spider.

Luca was doing a thorough inspection of both legs and then moving back up to her arms. In spite of the pain she struggled to get out, 'I'm fine—it's nothing, really.'

But she was feeling nauseous now, with a white-hot sensation blooming outwards from both limbs. She was also starting to shake. Luca pulled her trousers back up. She wasn't even registering embarrassment that he'd all but stripped her.

She tried to take a step, but the pain when she moved almost blinded her. And suddenly she was being lifted into the air against a hard surface. She wanted to tell Luca to put her down but she couldn't seem to formulate the words.

And then the pain took over. There was a sense of time being suspended, loud voices. And then it all went black.

'Serena?'

The voice penetrated the thick warm blanket of darkness that surrounded her. And there was something about the voice that irritated her. She tried to burrow away from it.

'*Serena.*'

'What?' She struggled to open her eyes and winced at the light. Her surroundings registered slowly. A rudimentary hut of some kind. She was lying down on something deliciously soft. And one other thing registered: mercifully…the awful, excruciating pain was gone.

'Welcome back.'

That voice. Deep and infinitely memorable. And not in a good way.

It all came back.

She turned her head to see Luca looking at her with a small smile on his face. *A smile.* He was sitting down near the bed she lay on.

She croaked out, 'What happened?'

His smile faded, and it must have been a trick of the light but she could have sworn he paled slightly. 'You got stung. Badly.'

Serena recalled the ground moving under her hands and shuddered delicately. 'But they were just ants. How could ants do that?'

Luca's mouth twisted. 'They were bullet ants.'

Serena frowned. 'Should that mean anything to me?'

He shook his head. 'Not really, but they deliver a sting that is widely believed to be the most painful on record of any biting insect—like the pain of a bullet. I've been bitten once or twice; I know exactly what it's like.'

Serena felt embarrassed. 'But I passed out like some kind of wimp.'

Luca had a funny look on his face.

'The fact that you were semi-conscious till we reached the village and kept fighting to walk was a testament to your obviously high pain threshold.'

She lifted her arm and looked at it. There was only a very faint redness where she'd been bitten. All that pain and not even a scratch left behind? She almost felt cheated. And then she thought of what he'd said and her arm dropped.

'Wait a second—you carried me all the way here?'

He nodded. There was a scuffling sound from nearby

and thankfully Luca's intense focus moved off her. She looked past him to see some small curious faces peeping around the door. He said something to them and they disappeared, giggling and chattering.

Luca turned back. 'They're fascinated by the golden-haired *gringa* who arrived unconscious into their village a few hours ago.'

Serena was very disorientated by this far less antagonistic Luca. Feeling self-conscious, she struggled to sit up, moving back the covers on the bed.

But Luca rapped out, 'Stay there! You're weak and dehydrated. You're not going anywhere today, or this evening. The women have prepared some food and you need to drink lots of water.'

Luca stood up, and his sheer size made Serena feel dizzy enough to lie down again. As if by magic some smiling women appeared in the doorway, holding various things. Luca ushered them in and said to Serena over their heads, 'I have to go to the mines. I'll be back later. You'll be looked after.'

Weakly, Serena protested, 'But I'm supposed to be taking notes...'

Something flashed in Luca's eyes but he just said, 'Don't worry about that. There'll be time tomorrow, before we have to leave.'

'Before we have to leave.' She felt a lurch in her belly and an awful betraying tingle of anticipation as to what might happen once they did leave this place.

The following morning, early, Luca was trying not to keep staring at Serena, who sat at the end of a long table in the communal eating hut. She was wearing a traditional smock dress, presumably given to her by one of the women to replace her own clothes, and the simple design might have been haute couture, the way she wore it with such effortless grace.

A small toddler, a girl, was sitting on Serena's lap and staring up at her with huge, besotted brown eyes. She'd been crying minutes before, and Serena had bent down to her level and cajoled her to stop crying, lifting her up and settling her as easily as if she was her mother.

Now she was eating her breakfast—a manioc-based broth—for all the world acting as if it was the finest caviar, giving the little girl morsels in between her own mouthfuls. She couldn't have looked more innocent and pure if she'd tried, tugging remorselessly on his conscience.

A mixture of rage and sexual frustration made Luca's whole body tight. The remnants of the panic he'd felt the previous day when she'd been so limp in his arms after being stung still clung to him. She'd been brave. Even though he knew he was being completely irrational, he couldn't stop lambasting her inwardly for not behaving as he expected her to.

Their eyes met and caught at that moment and he saw her cheeks flush. With desire? Or anger? Or a mixture of both like him? Suddenly her significance wasn't important any more—who she was, what she'd done. Or not done. He wanted her, and she would pay for throwing his life out of whack not once but twice.

Resolve filling his body, he stood up and said curtly, 'We're leaving for the mines in ten minutes.'

He didn't like the way he noticed how her arm tightened around the small girl almost protectively, or how seeing a child on her lap made him feel. All sorts of things he'd never imagined feeling in his life—ever.

Her chin tipped up. 'I'll be ready.'

Luca left before he did something stupid, like take up his phone and ask for the helicopter to come early so that he could haul her back to Rio and douse this fire in his blood as soon as possible.

CHAPTER SIX

A FEW HOURS later Serena was back in her own clothes, now clean, and sitting cross-legged beside Luca in the hut of the tribal elders. She was still smarting from the intensity of his regard that morning at breakfast. As if he'd been accusing her of something. Her suspicions had been reinforced when he'd said, with a definitely accusatory tone, on their journey to the mines, 'You were good with that little girl earlier.'

Serena had swallowed back the tart urge to apologise and explained, 'I have a nephew just a little bit older. We're very close.'

She hadn't liked being reminded of that vulnerability—that from the moment she'd held Siena's son, Spiro, he and Serena had forged an indelible bond and her biological clock had started ticking loudly.

For someone who had never seen the remotest possibility of such a domestic idyll in her life, she was still surprised at how much she craved it.

And she hated it that she'd barely slept a wink in the hut because she'd missed knowing Luca's solid bulk was just inches away. She dragged her attention back to what she was meant to be focusing on: writing notes as fast as Luca translated what he wanted taken down.

They'd spent the morning at the mines and she'd seen how diplomatic he had to be, trying to assuage the fears of the miners about losing their jobs, while attempting to drag the mine and its administration into the twenty-first century and minimise further damage to the land. It was a very fine balancing act.

When he was being diplomatic and charming he was truly devastating. It gave Serena a very strong sense of just how seductive he could be if...if he actually liked her. The thought of that made her belly swoop alarmingly.

He turned to her now. 'Did you get that?'

She looked at the notes quickly. 'About coming up with ideas to actively promote and nurture growth in the local economy?'

He nodded. But before he turned back to the tribal leader Serena followed an impulse and touched his arm. He frowned at her, and she smiled hesitantly at the man Luca was talking to before saying, 'Could I make a suggestion?'

He drew back a few inches and looked at her. His entire stance was saying, *You?*

Serena fought off the urge to hit him and gritted her teeth. 'Those smock dresses that the women make—I haven't seen them anywhere else. Also, the little carvings that the children have been doing... I know that this village is twinned with another one, and they have monthly fair days when they barter goods and crops and utilise their skills and learn from each other...but what about opening it up a bit—say, having a space in Rio, or Manaus, a charity shop that sells the things they make here. And in the other village. A niche market, with the money coming back directly to the people.'

'That's hardly a novel idea,' Luca said coolly.

Serena refused to be intimidated or feel silly. 'Well, if it's not a new concept why hasn't one of these shops been mentioned anywhere in your literature about the charity? I'm not talking about some rustic charity shop. I'm talking about a high-end finish that'll draw in discerning tourists and buyers. Something that'll inspire them to help conserve the rainforest.'

Luca said nothing for a long moment, and then he turned back to the chief and spoke to him rapidly. The man's old, lined face lit up and he smiled broadly, nodding effusively.

Luca looked back to Serena, a conciliatory gleam in his eyes. 'I'll look into it back in Rio.'

The breath she hadn't even been aware of holding left her chest and she had to concentrate when the conversation started again. Finally, when Luca and the chief had spoken for an hour or so, they got up to leave. The old man darted forward with surprising agility to take Serena's hand in his and pump it up and down vigorously. She smiled at his effervescence.

Following Luca out into the slightly less intense late-afternoon heat, she could see a Jeep approach in the distance.

Luca looked at his watch. 'That'll be our lift to the airfield. We need to pack our stuff up.'

He looked at her and must have seen something that Serena had failed to disguise in time.

His eyes glinted with something indefinable. 'I thought you'd welcome the prospect of civilisation again?'

'I do,' Serena said quickly, avoiding his look. But the truth was that she didn't…exactly. Their couple of days in the rainforest...the otherworldly pace of life in the village...it had soothed something inside her. And she realised that she would miss it.

Afraid Luca might see that, she folded her arms and said, 'Are you going to give me a chance?' And then quickly, before he could interject, 'I think I deserve it. I don't want to go home yet.'

Luca looked at her. She could see the Jeep coming closer, stopping. She held her breath. His gaze narrowed on her and became...*hot*. Instantly Serena felt something spike. Anticipation.

He came closer, blocking out the Jeep arriving, the village behind him.

'I've no intention of letting you go home.'

Serena's arms clenched tighter. She didn't like the way her body reacted to that implacable statement and what it might mean. 'You're giving me a trial period?'

Luca smiled, and it made Serena's brain fuzzy.

'Something like that. I told you I wanted you, Serena. And I do. In my bed.'

Anger spiked at his arrogant tone, even as her pulse leapt treacherously. 'I'm not interested in becoming your next mistress, Fonseca. I'm interested in working.'

Luca's eyes flashed at her use of 'Fonseca'. 'I'll give you a two-week trial. Two weeks of working in the charity by day and two weeks in my bed by night.'

Serena unclenched her arms, her hands in fists by her sides, hating the betraying sizzle in her blood. Had she no self-respect?

'That's blackmail.'

Luca shrugged, supremely unconcerned. 'Call it what you want. That's the only way you'll get your trial.'

Serena swallowed a caustic rush of tangled emotions

along with the betraying hum of desire. 'And what about your precious reputation? If people see us together? What then?'

Luca moved closer. Serena's words struck him somewhere deep inside. What *was* he doing? he asked himself. All he knew was that the things that had been of supreme importance to him for a long time no longer seemed as important. There was only here and now and this woman. And *heat*. And need.

Yet he wasn't losing sight of what had driven him for all these years completely. He was cynical enough to recognise an opportunity when it arose. Having Serena on his arm would mean news, and news would mean focus on the things close to his heart. Like his foundation.

He said now, 'I have every intention of people seeing us together. You see, I've realised that seven years is like seven lifetimes in the media world. You're old news. And if anyone does make something of it I'm quite happy for you to be seen by my side as someone intent on making up for her debauched past by doing charity work. Everyone loves a redemption story, after all. And in the meantime I get what I want—which is *you*. You owe me, Serena. You don't think I'm going to give you a two-week trial without recompense, do you?'

Serena just looked at him. She was too stunned to say anything. What Luca had said was so...*cold*. And yet all she could feel was *hot*. She should be slapping him across the face and taking a bus back to Manaus and the next flight home. Maybe that was what he was doing? Calling her bluff. Goading her. She couldn't imagine that he didn't have a string of willing mistresses back in Rio.

But that only made something very dark rise up: jealousy.

'We leave in fifteen minutes.'

With that he turned and strode away, as if he hadn't just detonated a bomb between them. She watched him incredulously, and then stalked to the small hut.

As she packed up her small backpack a few minutes later she alternated between the longing to to find Luca and deliver that slap to his face which he so deserved and pausing to remember how it had felt when he'd kissed her and touched her the other night.

She'd never really enjoyed sex; it had been another route to oblivion which had invariably ended in disappointment and an excoriating sense of self-disgust.

But Luca... It was as if he was able to see right through to her deepest self, to the part of her that was still innocent, untainted by what she'd seen and experienced as a child...

'Ms DePiero?'

Serena whirled around to see a young man in the doorway of the hut.

'Senhor Fonseca is waiting for you at the Jeep.'

Serena muttered something about coming and watched the man walk away. Something inside her solidified. She could leave and go home, lose any chance of a job with the charity and start all over again. Concede defeat. Or...if she was going to admit to herself that she wanted Luca too...she could be as strategic as him.

But if she was going to stay and submit to his arrogant demands then it would be on *her* terms, and she would gain from it too.

Luca sent a wary glance to Serena, who was sitting on the other side of the plane. She was looking out of the window, so he couldn't see her expression, but he would guess that it was as stony as it had been when she'd got into the Jeep and on the silent journey to the private airfield near the airport.

He wasn't flying the plane this time. Ostensibly so he could catch up on work, but for possibly the first time in his life he couldn't focus on it.

All he could focus on was Serena, and the tense lines of her slim body, and wonder what that stony silence meant. He knew he deserved it. He was surprised she hadn't slapped him back at the village. He'd seen the moment in her expression when she'd wanted to.

He'd never behaved so autocratically with a woman in his life. If he wanted a woman he seduced her and took her to bed, and they were never under the impression that he was in the market for more than that.

But this was Serena DePiero. From the first moment he'd ever seen her he'd been tangled up into knots. The last few days had shown him a vastly different woman from the one he'd met before...and yet hadn't he seen something of this woman in her eyes that night in the club? He didn't like to admit that he *had* seen that moment of vulnerability.

His conscience pricked him. *He'd all but blackmailed her.* He wasn't so deluded that he couldn't acknowledge uncomfortably that it had been a crass attempt on his behalf to get her where he wanted her without having to let her know how badly he needed to sate this hunger inside him.

He opened his mouth to speak to her just as she turned her head to look at him and those searing blue eyes robbed him of speech. She looked determined.

'I've been thinking about your...proposal.'

Luca's conscience hit him again. He winced inwardly. Never had he imagined that she would be so diplomatic when he'd been such a bastard. 'Serena—'

She held up a hand. 'No, let me speak.'

He closed his mouth and didn't like the flutter of panic at the thought that he might just have completely mismanaged this. She could leave now and he'd never see her again.

'If I agree to stay and do this trial for two weeks... If I do well—prove that I'm capable...and...' She stopped, a dark flush staining her cheeks before she continued. 'If I agree to what you said...then I want you to assure me that you'll give me a job—whether it's here or back in Athens. A proper contracted, paying job for the charity.'

The relief that flowed through Luca was unsettling and heady. His conscience still struck him, but he was too distracted to deal with it.

He held out a hand towards Serena and growled, 'Come here.'

The flush on her cheeks got pinker. 'Luca—'

'Come here and I'll tell you.'

He saw her bite her lip, the dart of her pink tongue. After a few seconds her hands went to her belt and she undid it and pushed herself up and out of her seat. As soon as she was within touching distance Luca had closed a hand around her wrist and tugged her so that she fell onto his lap with a soft *ooph*.

'Luca, what are you—?'

He couldn't help himself. He covered her mouth with his and stopped her words. A very dangerous kind of relief flowed through him. She would be his. She wasn't leaving. Her arms crept around his neck after a moment of resistance. Her mouth softened under his. And when he swept his tongue along hers, and she sighed, he could have howled with triumph.

Before he lost it completely he drew back, his breathing laboured. He touched a hand to her jaw, cupping it, running a finger along its delicate line. He looked into her eyes and said, 'Yes, I'll give you a job.'

He could feel Serena's breath making her chest shudder against him. The pressure in his groin intensified.

'I want a signed agreement, Luca, that you'll keep your word.'

Indignation made anger flare. 'You don't trust me?' It had all been about him not trusting *her*. Luca had never considered her not trusting *him*, and it didn't sit well.

Serena's lush mouth compressed. She didn't answer directly, she said, 'A promise on paper, Luca, or I'll leave as soon as we touch down.'

Any feeling of triumph or any sense of control slipped out of Luca's grasp. His hands were around Serena's hips, holding her to him, and as much as he wanted to push her back, tell her that no woman dictated to him…he couldn't. The taste of her was on his tongue and, dammit, it wasn't enough. Not yet.

So he finally bit out, 'Fine.'

Serena took in the frankly mind-boggling three-hundred-and-sixty-degree view of Rio de Janeiro outside the glass walls of the penthouse apartment. It was at the top of the building she'd come to that first day.

She turned to face Luca. 'This is your apartment?'

He was watching her intently and inclined his head. 'Yes, but I only use it if I'm working late, or for entertaining clients after meetings.'

Or for entertaining mistresses?

Suddenly she didn't feel half as sure as she had on the plane, when Luca had pulled her into his lap to kiss her. Now her doubts and insecurities were back. Luca affected her...too much.

She crossed her arms. 'I can't stay here. It's inappropriate.'

Luca stifled an inelegant snort. 'This from the woman who was photographed at her debs in an exclusive Paris hotel in a bathtub full of champagne while dressed in a priceless gown?'

Serena flushed, recalling her father's malevolent smile and even more malevolent tone of voice: *'Good girl. We wouldn't want people to think you're becoming boring, now, would we?'*

Serena chose to ignore Luca's comment. 'What about the apartment I was meant to stay in? The one for staff?'

'It's no longer available; someone else took your place there.'

'Well, that's hardly my fault, is it?' she retorted hotly.

Luca's jaw firmed. 'It's either here, Serena, or if you insist, the charity will be put to the expense of finding you somewhere else.'

'No!' she shot out, aghast. 'But it's just—'

He cut in coolly. 'You're staying here. I'm sure you can put up with it for two weeks.'

This was what she was afraid of. He made her emotions and blood pressure see-saw out of control.

Luca looked at Serena and narrowed his gaze. She was skittish, nervy. A million miles from the woman who had melted in his arms just a short time before.

'Serena, what is it?'

She was angry, her cheeks growing pink. 'I've agreed

to sleep with you to get a job—how do you think that makes me feel?'

Luca's conscience pricked but he pointed out, 'You're not sleeping with me yet.'

She went redder.

Luca felt something give inside him and ran a hand through his hair impatiently. 'Look, I behaved like a boor earlier. The very least you deserve is a trial period. I would have given it to you anyway.'

She looked at him, surprised, and it affected him more than he'd like to admit.

'You would? And what about a job?'

Luca schooled his features. 'That depends on your trial period—as it would for anyone else.'

He moved closer then, and put his hands on her upper arms. 'And you are *not* sleeping with me to get a job. You're sleeping with me because it's what you want. What we *both* want.'

She just looked at him, and something desperate rose inside Luca. He ground out, 'The door is behind me, Serena. You can walk out right now if that's what you want and you'll still get your trial.'

For an infinitesimal moment she said nothing, and he was reminded of telling her where the door was before, willing her to use it. Now he'd launch an army if she tried to leave. He had to consciously stop his hands from gripping her arms tight, as if he could restrain her from walking out. He could see her throat work as she swallowed. Her eyes were wide, pupils as black as night.

She opened her mouth and he kept his eyes off the seductive temptation of those soft lips. He needed to hear this too badly. Needed her to stay.

'Serena...'

Her tongue moistened those lips. Luca's pulse jumped.

Her voice was husky. 'I just want a chance.'

The tension in Luca's body spiked. *Damn her.* 'And? What else?'

She turned her head away and bitterness laced her voice. 'You know I want you. In the tent…you made me show you. You humiliated me.'

Luca's chest was tight enough to hurt. An alien sensation. He cursed softly and felt as if some layer of himself was being stripped away when he admitted, 'Do you know how hard it was for me to stop myself from taking you that night?'

Those blue eyes locked with his. She whispered, 'You made me feel as if you just wanted to prove your dominance over me.'

Luca tipped her chin up with a finger and felt her jaw clench. He smiled, and it was wry. 'You credit me with far too much forethought. I needed to hear you say it…that you wanted me. You made *me* feel that much out of control.'

Instantly something flashed in those piercing eyes—something that made some of Luca's tightness ease.

'You're so in control. It's almost scary.'

Now Luca was the one to grit his jaw as he recognised that no one had ever said that to him before—certainly not a woman. Serena's gaze seemed to see right through him to where he stood as a small boy, witnessing the awesome power parents had to rip your life apart. He knew his desire for control and respectability stemmed from that chaotic, messy, tumultuous moment. And here he was, skating far too close to the edges of losing it all again. And yet…he couldn't walk away.

He said, with quiet conviction, 'If I was to kiss you right now you'd see how thin the veneer of my control is, believe me.'

Something hot flared in the bright blue depths and he stifled a groan of pure need. But he would not take her now, like this, after trekking in a jungle for days, when they were both dizzy with fatigue.

It was the hardest thing in the world, but he let her go and stepped back. 'I have work to catch up on—some conference calls to make. And I'm sure you'll appreciate a night in a real bed again. My assistant will be here in the morning to take you down to the charity offices where you'll be working. And tomorrow evening I'm taking you to a charity function.'

Serena's heart palpitated with a mixture of relief and disappointment. So he wasn't staying tonight? And then shame lanced her that she hadn't been strong enough just to walk away. That a part of her wanted to explore what this man was offering, almost more than she wanted to prove herself or ensure her independence.

The last three and a half years had been all about finding and nurturing an inner strength she'd never known she had. But Luca made her feel weak, and it scared her. But not enough to turn away from him. Damn him.

'Okay.'

Luca said nothing for a long moment and then he said quietly, '*Boa noite,* Serena. *Até amanha.*'

Till tomorrow.

He turned and walked away and the slick, modern apartment was immediately cavernous without him. They'd only spent four days together but it felt like a lifetime. Serena battled the urge to flee, once again questioning her rationale... But her decision to stay had nothing to do with being rational. That had fled out of the window as soon as Luca had pulled her onto his lap on the plane and kissed her witless.

Doubts and fears melted away. She wasn't going anywhere. She couldn't.

As soon as that registered in her body fatigue and exhaustion hit her like a freight train. Along with the realisation that she had hot water at her disposal and could finally wash.

Pushing all thoughts of Luca and what the immediate future held out of her head, she unpacked, took the longest and most delicious shower she'd ever had in her life, fell face-down onto an indescribably soft bed, and sank into oblivion.

Luca stood at the window of his office a floor below the apartment. Rio was a carpet of twinkling golden lights as far as the eye could see. He spoke into the mobile he held to his ear.

His voice was tight. 'Let's just say that I have my doubts about whether she did it or not, and I'd appreciate your help in finding out.' There was a pause, and then Luca said curtly, 'Look, Max, if it's too much trouble—' He sighed. 'Okay, yes. And, thanks, I appreciate it.'

Luca cut the connection and threw his phone down on the table behind him. It bounced off and hit the carpeted floor. He ignored it and turned back to the view. Any conversation with his brother drove his blood pressure skywards. He knew that Max didn't blame Luca specifically for the fact that they'd been split up the way they had between their parents...but guilt festered inside Luca even now. He was the elder twin and he'd always felt that responsibility keenly.

Pushing thoughts of his brother aside, Luca hated to admit it, but he felt altered in some way. As if some alchemy had taken place in his head and body since he'd stood looking at this view the last time—just before Serena had arrived almost a week ago.

He scowled at his fanciful thoughts. There was no alchemy. It was physical attraction, pure and simple. It had been between them from the moment their eyes had first locked. And now he was going to sate it. That was all.

The fact that he was prepared to allow Serena DePiero to sign an agreement which would potentially offer her employment with his company for the foreseeable future, *and* to be seen with her in public, were things that he pushed to the deepest recesses of his mind.

He focused instead on the increasing anticipation in his blood and his body at the knowledge that soon this ever-present hunger would be assuaged.

CHAPTER SEVEN

THE FOLLOWING EVENING Serena waited on the outdoor terrace that wrapped around the entire apartment, a ball of nerves in her gut. The fact that Luca had said he was taking her to a charity function had been conveniently forgotten when she'd succumbed to exhaustion the previous evening—and in the whirlwind of the day she'd just had.

She'd woken early and had some breakfast just before his sleek assistant Laura had arrived, cracking a minute smile for once. She'd handed Serena a sheaf of papers and hot embarrassment had risen up when she'd seen it was the contract assuring her of work if she completed her trial period successfully. The contract she'd demanded.

To her relief there was no mention of the more personal side of their agreement. Luca's cool efficiency was scary.

After she'd signed, Laura had taken her down to the first floor, where the offices for the charity were based, and introduced her to the staff. Serena had spent such a pleasant day with the friendly Brazilians, who had been so nice and patient with her rudimentary Portuguese that she'd almost fooled herself into forgetting what else awaited her.

But she couldn't ignore it any longer. Not when she'd returned to the apartment to find a stylist and a troupe of hair and make-up people waiting to transform her for Luca's pleasure. Or *delectation* might be a better word. She felt like something that should be on display.

An entire wardrobe of designer clothes seemed to have materialised by magic during the day, and this whole process brought back so many memories of her old life—when her father had insisted on making sure his daughters had the most desirable clothes...for the maximum effect.

The thought of the evening ahead made her go clammy. Right now, weakly, she'd take a jungle full of scorpions, snakes, bullet ants and even an angry Luca Fonseca over the social jungle she was about to walk into.

And then she drew herself up tall. She was better than this. Was she forgetting what she'd survived in the past few years? The intense personal scrutiny and soul-searching? The constant invasion of her privacy as she'd faced her demons in front of strangers? And not only that—she'd survived the jungle with Luca, who'd been waiting for her to falter at every step.

Although right now that didn't feel so much of a triumph as a test of endurance that she was still undergoing. They'd exchanged the wild jungle for the so-called civilised jungle. And this time the stakes were so much higher.

At that moment the little hairs all over her body stood up a nano-second before she heard a noise behind her. She had no time to keep obsessing over whether or not she'd picked out the right dress. Squaring her shoulders, and drawing on the kind of reserves that she hadn't had to call on in years, Serena turned around.

For a second she could only blink to make sure she wasn't dreaming. Her ability to breathe was severely compromised. Memories of Luca seven years ago slammed into her like a punch to the gut. Except this Luca was infinitely harder, more gorgeous.

'You've shaved...' Serena commented faintly. But those words couldn't do justice to the man in front of her, dressed in a classic tuxedo, his hard jaw revealed in all its obduracy, the sensual lines of his mouth even more defined.

His thick dark hair was shorter too, and Serena felt an irrational spurt of jealousy for whoever had had his or her hands on his head.

She was too enflamed and stunned by this vision of Luca to notice that his gaze had narrowed on her and a flush had made his cheeks darken.

'You look...incredible.'

Luca's eyes felt seared, right through to the back. She was a sleek, beautiful goddess. All he could see at first was bare skin, arms and shoulders. And acres of red silk and gold, sparkling with inlaid jewels. A deep V drew his eye effortlessly to luscious curves. There was some embellishment on the shoulders and then the dress fell in a swathe of silk and lace from her waist to the floor. He could see the hint of one pale thigh peeping out from the luxurious folds and had to grit his jaw to stop his body from exploding.

She'd pinned her hair back into a low bun at the base of her neck. It should have made the outfit look more demure than if her hair had been around her shoulders in a silken white-golden tumble, but it didn't. It seemed to heighten the provocation of the dress.

Luca registered then that she looked uncomfortable.

Shifting minutely, those long fingers were fluttering near the V of the dress, as if to try and cover it up. The woman Luca had seen in Florence had been wearing a fraction of this much material and revelling in it.

She was avoiding his eye, and that made Luca move closer. She looked up and his pulse fired. He came close enough to smell her clean, fresh scent. Suddenly it felt as if he hadn't seen her in a month, when it had been just a day. A day in which he'd had to restrain himself from going down to the charity offices.

Danger.

He ignored it.

He might have expected her scent to be overpowering, overtly sensual, but it was infinitely more subtle.

Familiar irritation that she was proving to be more difficult to grasp than quicksilver made him say brusquely, 'What's wrong? The dress? You don't like it?'

She looked up at him and need gripped Luca so fiercely that his whole body tensed. But something very cynical followed. He'd had an entire wardrobe of clothes delivered to the apartment—and she wasn't happy?

Her eyes flashed. 'No, it's not the dress.' Her voice turned husky. 'The dress is beautiful. But what were you thinking, sending all those clothes? I'm not your mistress, and I don't want to be treated like one.'

Surprise lanced him, but he recovered quickly. 'I thought you'd appreciate being prepared for a public event.'

Serena looked down and muttered, 'You mean public humiliation.'

Something shifted in Luca's chest. He tipped up her chin, more concerned than he liked to admit by her uneasiness. Colour stained her pale cheeks and Luca almost gave in to the beast inside him. *Almost*. With a supreme effort he willed it down. 'What I said before… about exposing you to public scrutiny…that won't happen, Serena. I won't let it.'

Her eyes were wide. *Wounded*? Her mouth thinned. 'Isn't that part of the plan, though? A little revenge?'

Luca winced inwardly. What did this woman do to him? She called to his most base instincts and he could be as cruel as his father ever had been. Shame washed through him.

He shook his head, something fierce erupting inside him. 'I'm taking you out because I want to be seen with you, Serena.'

As he said it he realised it was true. He genuinely wanted this. To have her on his arm. And it had very little to do with wanting to punish her. At the thought of adverse public reaction a protective instinct nearly bowled him over with its force.

Before he could lose his footing completely, he took her by the hand and said gruffly, 'We should leave or we'll be late.'

In the lift something caught his eye, and he looked down to see Serena's other hand clutching a small bag which matched her dress. Her knuckles were white, and when his gaze travelled up he could see the tension in her body and jaw.

The lift jerked softly to a halt and almost against his will Luca found his hand going to the small of Serena's back to touch her. The minute his hand came into contact with the bare, warm, silky skin left exposed by the backless design she tensed more.

He frowned as something had dawned on him. 'Are you…*nervous*?'

Serena's eyes flashed with some indefinable emotion and she quickly stepped out of the open doors of the elevator, away from his touch, avoiding his narrowed gaze.

'Don't be ridiculous. It's just been a while since I've gone to anything like this, that's all.'

Luca sensed that there was a lot more to it than that, but he gestured for her to precede him out of the building, realising too late what awaited them outside when a veritable explosion of light seemed to go off in their faces. Without even realising what he was doing he put his arm around Serena and curved her into his body, one hand up to cover her face, as they walked quickly to his car, where a security guard held the passenger door open.

In the car, Serena's heart was pumping so hard she felt light-headed. The shock of that wall of paparazzi when she hadn't seen it in so long was overwhelming. And she couldn't help the fierce pain of betrayal. Everything Luca had just said was lies...and she hated that she wouldn't have expected it of him.

She was a sap. Of *course* he was intent on—

Her hand was taken in a firm grip. She clenched her jaw and looked at Luca in the driver's seat. His face was dark...*with anger?*

'Serena, I had nothing to do with that. They must have been tipped off.'

He looked so grim and affronted that Serena felt something melt inside her. Felt a wish to believe him.

'It won't happen again.'

She took her hand from Luca's and forced a smile. 'Don't worry about it.'

The imprint of Luca's body where he'd held her so close was still making her treacherous skin tingle all over. The way he'd drawn her into him so protectively had unsettled her. She'd felt unprotected for so long that it was an alien sensation. Maybe he *hadn't* planned it. She recalled him biting off a curse now, as if he'd been as surprised as her...

Once they'd left the paparazzi behind she pushed a button to lower her window, relishing the warm evening Rio breeze and the tang of the sea.

'Are you okay?'

Serena nodded. 'Fine—just needed some air.'

The setting sun was bathing the sky in a pink glow, and from somewhere distant Serena could hear cheers and clapping.

She looked at Luca. 'What's that?'

Luca's mouth twitched. 'Every evening sunset-worshippers applaud another stunning sunset from the beaches.'

Serena couldn't take her eyes off the curve of Luca's mouth. 'I love that idea,' she breathed. 'I'd like to see the sunset.'

She quickly looked away again, in case that dark navy gaze met hers when she felt far too exposed. Her cheeks were still hot from that moment when she'd been captivated by the way he filled out his suit so effortlessly. The obviously bespoke material did little to disguise his sheer power, flowing lovingly over defined muscles.

'Where do you live when you don't stay at the apartment?' Serena blurted out the first thing she could think of to try and take her mind off Luca's physicality.

He glanced at her, his hands strong on the wheel of the car.

'I have a house in Alto Gavea—it's a district in the Tijuca Forest, north of the lake…'

She sneaked a look. 'Is it your family home? Where you grew up?'

He shook his head abruptly, and when he answered his voice was tight. 'No, we lived out in the suburbs. My parents wouldn't have approved of living so near to the beaches and *favelas*.'

Serena thought of what he'd told her about his parents so far and asked, 'You weren't close to them?'

His mouth twisted. 'No. They split up when we were six, and my mother moved back to her native Italy.'

Serena had forgotten about that Italian connection. 'You said *we*… Do you have brothers and sisters?'

She could sense his reluctance to answer, but they weren't going anywhere fast in the evening traffic. Luca sighed. 'Yes, I have a twin brother.'

Serena's eyes widened. 'Wow—a twin? That's pretty amazing.' Her mind boggled slightly at the thought of *two* Lucas.

He slid her a mocking look and said, 'We're non-identical. He lives in Italy; he moved there with our mother after the divorce.'

Serena processed this and turned in her seat to face him. 'Wait…you mean you were split up?'

The thought of anyone splitting her and Siena up at that young age made her go cold. Siena had been the only anchor in her crazy world.

Luca faced forward, his voice emotionless. 'Yes, my parents decided that each would take one of us. My mother chose me to go to Italy with her, but when my brother got upset she swapped us and took him instead.'

Serena gasped as that scenario sank in. 'But that's... horrific. And your father just let her?'

Luca looked at her, face hard. 'He didn't care which son he got as long as he got one of us to be his heir.'

Serena knew what it was to grow up under a cruel tyrant, but this shocked even her. 'And are you close now? You and your brother?'

Luca shrugged minutely. 'Not particularly. But he was the one who bailed me out of jail, and he was the one who arranged for the best legal defence to get me out of Florence and back to Rio, avoiding a lengthy trial and jail time.'

His expression hardened to something infinitely cynical.

'A hefty donation towards "the preservation of Florence" was all it took to get the trial mysteriously dismissed. That money undoubtedly went to corrupt officials—one of whom was probably your father—but I was damned if I was going to hang for a crime I wasn't even responsible for. But they wouldn't clear me completely, so every time I fly to Europe now I come under the radar of Europe's law enforcement agencies.'

Serena felt cold. She turned back to the front, staring unseeingly out of the window, knowing it was futile to say anything. She'd protested her innocence till she was blue in the face, but Luca was right—his association with her *had* made things worse for him.

They were turning into a vast tree-lined driveway now, which led up to a glittering colonial-style building. When Luca pulled up, and a valet parker waited for him to get out, Serena took several deep breaths to calm her frayed nerves.

Luca surprised her by not getting out straight away.

He turned to her. 'I'm not interested in the past any more, Serena. I'm interested in the here and now.'

Serena swallowed. Something fragile seemed to shimmer between them...tantalising. And then he got out of the car and she sucked in another shaky breath.

He came around and opened her door, extended a hand to help her out. She took it, and when his gaze tracked down her body and lingered on her breasts a pulse throbbed between her legs.

He tucked her arm into his as they moved forward and joined similarly dressed couples entering a glittering doorway lit by hundreds of small lights. It was a scene Serena had seen a million times before, but never heightened like this. Never *romantic*.

She asked herself as Luca led her inside, greeting someone in Portuguese, if they really could let the past go. Or was that just what Luca was willing to say so that he could bed her and then walk away, with all that resentment still simmering under the surface?

'Do you think you could crack a smile and not look as if you're about to be subjected to torture?'

Serena glanced at Luca, who had a fixed social smile on his face. She sent up silent thanks that he couldn't read her thoughts and said sweetly. 'But this *is* torture.'

Something flared in his eyes—surprise?—and then he said, 'Torture it may well be, but a few hours of social torture is worth it if it means that a *favela* gets a new free school staffed by qualified teachers.'

Serena felt immediately chastened. 'Is that what this evening's ball is in aid of?'

Luca looked at her assessingly. 'Among some other causes. The global communities charity too.'

Serena thought of that sweet little girl in the village—a million miles away from here...and yet *not*.

'I'm sorry,' she said huskily. 'You're right—it *is* worth it.'

Serena missed Luca's speculative look because a waiter was interrupting them with a tray of champagne. Luca took a glass and looked at her when she didn't.

She shook her head quickly and said to the waiter, 'Do you have some sparkling water, please?'

The waiter rushed off and Luca frowned slightly. 'You really don't drink any more?'

Serena's belly clenched. 'No, I really don't.' She made a face. 'I never liked the taste of alcohol anyway. It was more for the effect it had on me.'

'What was that?'

She looked at him. 'Numbing.'

The moment stretched between them...taut. And then the attentive waiter returned with a glass of water on a tray for Serena. She took it gratefully. Luca was getting too close to that dark place inside her.

To her relief someone came up then, and took his attention, but just as Serena felt hopeful that he might forget about her she felt her heart sink and jump in equal measure when she felt him reach for her hand and tug her with him, introducing her to the man.

Luca was finding it hard to concentrate on the conversation around him when he usually had no problem. Even if he *was* with a woman. He was aware of every tiny movement Serena made in that dress, and acutely aware of the attention she was attracting.

He was also aware that she seemed ill at ease. He'd expected her to come back into this kind of environment and take to it like the proverbial duck to water, but when they'd first come in she'd looked *pained*. It was just like in the jungle, when she'd proved him resoundingly wrong in his expectations of her.

Now her head was bent towards one of the executive team who managed his charities abroad, and they were engaged in an earnest conversation when Luca would have fully expected Serena to look bored out of her brains.

At that moment her head tipped back and she laughed at something the other woman had said. Luca couldn't breathe, and the conversation stopped around them as she unwittingly drew everyone's eye. She literally... *sparkled*, her face transformed by her wide smile. She was undeniably beautiful...and Luca realised he'd never seen true beauty till that moment.

His chest felt tight as he had a vision of what he'd subjected her to: dragging her into the jungle on a forced trek. She'd endured one of the most painful insect bites in the world. She'd stayed in a rustic village in the depths of the Amazon without blinking. She'd endeared herself to the tribespeople without even trying. It had taken him *years* to be accepted and respected.

And the miners—some of the hardest men in Brazil—weathered and rough as they came—they'd practically been doffing their caps when Serena had appeared with him, as if she was royalty.

Luca could see the crowd moving towards the ballroom and took Serena's hand in his. She looked at him with that smile still playing about her mouth and a sense of yearning stronger than anything he'd ever felt kicked him in the solar plexus. A yearning to be the cause of such a smile.

As if she was reading his mind her smile faded on cue.

'Come on—let's dance,' Luca growled, feeling unconstructed. Raw.

He tugged Serena in his wake before he remembered that he didn't even *like* dancing, but right now he needed to feel her body pressed against his or he might go crazy.

When they reached the edge of the dimly lit dance floor Luca turned and pulled her with him, facing her. The light highlighted her stunning bone structure. That effortlessly classic beauty.

Unbidden, he heard himself articulate the question resounding in his head. 'Who *are* you?'

She swallowed. 'You know who I am.'

'Do I really?' he asked, almost angry now. 'Or is this all some grand charade for the benefit of your family, so you can go back to doing what you love best—being a wild society princess?'

Serena went pale and pulled free of Luca's embrace, saying angrily, 'I've told you about me but you still don't have the first clue, Luca. And as for what I love best? You'll never know.'

She turned and was walking away, disappearing into the vast lobby, before Luca realised that he was struck dumb and immobile because no woman had ever walked away from him before.

Cursing under his breath, he followed her, but when he got to the lobby there was no sign of a distinctive red dress or a white-blonde head. The way she'd stood out in the crowd mocked him now. His gut clenched with panic.

He got to the open doors, where people were still arriving. He spotted the valet who had taken his car and accosted him, asking curtly, 'The woman I came with—have you seen her?'

The valet gulped, visibly intimidated by Luca. 'Yes. Sir. I just saw her into a taxi that had dropped off some guests.'

Luca swore so volubly that the valet's ears went red. He stammered, 'Do—do you want your car?'

Luca just looked at him expressively and the young man scurried off.

They were on a hill overlooking the city. Luca looked out onto the benignly twinkling lights of Rio and the panic intensified. He recalled Serena saying she wanted to see the sunset... Would she have gone to the beach? At this time of night?

Panic turned to fear. He took out his phone and made a call to Serena's mobile but it was switched off. Rio was a majestic city, but at night certain areas were some of the most dangerous on earth. Where the *hell* had she gone?

Serena stalked into the apartment and the door slammed behind her with a gratifyingly loud bang. She was still shaking with anger, and her emotions were bubbling far too close to the surface for comfort.

She kicked off her shoes and made her way out to the terrace, taking deep breaths. Damn Luca Fonseca. It shouldn't matter what he thought of her...but after everything they'd been through she'd foolishly assumed that he'd come to see that she *was* different.

This was the real her. A woman who wanted to work and do something worthwhile, and never, ever insulate herself against life again. The girl and the young woman she'd been had been born out of the twisted machinations of her father.

Her hands wrapped around the railing. Self-disgust rose up inside her. To think that she was willing to go to bed with a man who thought so little of her. Where was the precious self-esteem she'd painstakingly built up again?

She knew where… It had all dissolved in a puddle of heat as soon as Luca came within feet of her. And yet she knew that wasn't entirely fair—he'd treated her as his exact equal in the jungle, and earlier, in the charity offices, she'd been surprised to find that he'd already put in motion discussions on her idea for a high-end tourist shop showcasing products from the villages and credited her with the plan.

She heard a sound behind her and tensed. Panic washed through her. She wasn't ready to deal with Luca yet. But reluctantly she turned around to see him advancing on her, his face like thunder, as long fingers pulled at his bow-tie.

She still got a jolt of sensation to see him clean-shaven. It should have made him look more urbane. It didn't.

CHAPTER EIGHT

Luca threw aside his bow-tie just before he came onto the terrace and bit out, 'Where the hell were you? I've been all over the beachfronts looking for you.'

His anger escalated when he saw Serena put her hands on her hips and say defiantly, 'What was it? Did you think I'd hit some nightclub? Or that I'd gone to find some late-night pharmacy so I could score some meds?'

Luca stopped. He had to acknowledge the relief that was coursing through his veins. She was here. She was safe. But the rawness he felt because she'd walked out on him and looked so upset when he'd suggested she was acting out a charade was still there.

An uncomfortable truth slid into his gut like a knife. Perhaps this *was* her. No charade. No subterfuge.

And just like that, Luca was thrown off-centre all over again.

He breathed deeply. 'I'm sorry.'

Serena was surprised. She blinked. 'Sorry for what?'

Honesty compelled Luca to admit, 'For what I said at the function. I just... *You...*'

He looked away and put his hands on his hips. Suddenly it wasn't so hard to say what he wanted to say—as if something inside him had given way.

He dropped his hands, came closer and shook his head. 'You confound me, Serena DePiero. Everything I thought I knew about you is wrong. The woman who came to Rio, the woman who survived the jungle, the woman who gave those villagers the kind of courtesy not many people ever give them...she's someone I wasn't expecting.'

Serena's ability to think straight was becoming compromised. Emotion was rising at hearing this admission and knowing what it must be costing him.

Huskily she said, 'But this *is* me, Luca. This has always been me. It was just...buried before.' Then she blurted out, 'I'm sorry for running off. I came straight here. I wouldn't have gone near the beaches—not after what you said. I do have *some* street-smarts, you know.'

Luca moved closer. 'I panicked. I thought of you being oblivious to the dangers.'

Now Serena noticed how pale Luca was. *He'd been worried about her.* He hadn't assumed she'd gone off the rails. The anger and hurt drained away, and something shifted inside her. A kind of tenderness welled up. *Dangerous.*

She had to physically resist the urge to go to him and touch his jaw. Instead she said, 'I'm here...safe.'

His hands landed on her hips and he tugged her into him. She was shorter without her heels. He made her feel delicate. Her skin was tingling now, coming up in goosebumps in spite of the warm air. Emboldened by his proximity, and what he'd just said, she lifted her own hands and pushed Luca's jacket apart and down his arms.

He let go of her so that it could fall to the ground.

Without saying anything, Luca took her by the hand and led her into the apartment, stepping over his coat.

Serena let herself be led. She'd never felt this connection with anyone else, and a deep-rooted surge of desire to reclaim part of her sexuality beat like a drum in her blood.

Yet when Luca led her into what she assumed was his bedroom, because of its stark, masculine furnishings, trepidation gripped her. Perhaps she was being a fool? Reading too much into what he'd said? Didn't men say *anything* to get women into bed? There was so much in her past that she was ashamed of, that she hadn't made peace with, and Luca seemed to have an unerring ability to bring all of those vulnerabilities to the fore. What would happen when he possessed her completely?

Her hand tightened around Luca's and he stopped by the bed and turned to face her. Serena blurted out the first thing she could think of, as if to try and put some space between them again. 'I lost my virginity when I was sixteen...does that shock you?'

He shrugged, his expression carefully veiled, 'Should it? I lost mine at sixteen too—when one of my father's ex-mistresses seduced me.'

Serena's desperation rose, in spite of her shock at what he'd just revealed so flatly. 'It's what men expect, though, isn't it? For their lovers to be somehow...innocent?'

Luca made a face. 'I like my lovers to be experienced. I've no desire to be some wide-eyed virgin's first time.'

A wide-eyed virgin she certainly was *not*. Innocence had been ripped from her too early.

Luca pulled her closer and heat pulsed into Serena's lower body. She could feel his arousal between them, thick and hard. It scattered painful thoughts and she welcomed it like a coward.

'I want you, Serena, more than I've ever wanted anyone. I've wanted you from the first moment I laid eyes on you...'

For a heady moment Serena felt an overwhelming sense of power. She reassured herself that the emotions rising inside her were transitory; sex had never touched her emotionally before, so why should it now?

When he reached for her Serena curled into him without even thinking about it. It felt like the most necessary thing. The world dropped away and it was just them in this tight embrace, hearts thudding, skin hot.

His fingers spread out over her back, making her nipples harden almost painfully against the material of the dress. And then he lowered his head and his mouth was on hers, fitting like the missing piece of a jigsaw puzzle. Serena's lips opened to his on a sigh, tongues touching and tasting, stroking intimately. Her hands wound up around his neck, fingers tugging the short strands of hair, exploring, learning the shape of his skull.

Luca's wicked mouth and tongue made her strain to get even closer. After long, drugging moments he drew back, breathing harshly. Serena had to struggle to open her eyes.

'I want to see you,' he muttered thickly. 'Take down your hair.'

Serena felt as if she was in a dream. Had she, in fact, had this dream more often than once in the past seven years? She lifted her hand to the back of her head, feeling incredibly languid, and removed the discreet pin. Her hair tumbled around her shoulders, making her nerve-ends tingle even more.

Luca reached out and ran his fingers through it, then fisted it in one hand as the other reached around her to draw her into him again, kissing her with ruthless passion, tongue thrusting deep.

Serena's legs were starting to wobble. Luca's mouth was remorseless, sending her brain into a tailspin.

His hands came to the shoulders of her dress and pulled with gentle force, so the material slipped down her arms, loosening around her chest. She broke away from his mouth and looked up into dark pools of blue, feeling insecure.

Her arms came up against her breasts. Luca drew back and gently tugged them away, pulling the front of the dress down, leaving her bared to him.

She wore no bra, and Luca's gaze was so hot her skin sizzled. He reached out a hand and cupped the weight of one breast, a thumb moving over one puckered nipple. She bit her lip to stop from moaning out loud.

And then Luca put his hands on her hips and pulled her into him, hard enough to make her gasp, and replaced his thumb with his mouth, suckling on that hard peak roughly, making her back arch.

His erection was insistent against her and Serena's hips moved of their own volition.

Luca lifted his head. *'Feiticeira.'*

Her tongue felt heavy in her mouth, 'What does that mean?'

'Witch,' Luca replied succinctly.

And he kissed her again before her mind could catch up with the fact that his hands were now pushing her dress down over her hips so that it fell to the floor in a silken swish.

He put one hand between their bodies and Serena

held her breath when he explored down over her belly and lower, until he was gently pushing her legs apart so that he could feel for himself how ready she was.

Serena felt gauche, but wanton, as Luca moved his hand between her legs, over her panties. She lowered her head to his shoulder when her face got hot, and her breathing grew harsher when his wicked fingers moved against her insistently.

He slipped a finger under the gusset of her panties and touched her, flesh to flesh. Serena bit her lip hard enough to make tears spring into her eyes. She wanted to clamp her thighs together—the sensation was too much—but Luca's hand was too strong.

Her legs finally gave way and she collapsed back onto the bed, heart thumping erratically.

Luca started to undo his shirt, revealing that broad and exquisitely muscled chest. A smattering of dark hair covered his pectorals, leading down in a silky line under his trousers to where she could see the bulge of his arousal.

Serena's brain melted and she welcomed it. She didn't want to think or analyse—only feel.

His hands moved to his trousers and he undid them and pushed them down, taking his underwear with them. His erection was awe-inspiring. Long and thick and hard, a bead of moisture at the tip.

'Seven years, Serena,' he said throatily, 'For seven years I've wanted you above any other woman. No one came close to how I imagined this.'

She looked up at him, taken aback. She watched as he reached for something in a drawer in the side table. He rolled protection over his length. There was something unashamedly masculine about the action.

'Lie back,' he instructed gruffly.

Serena did, glad he was giving instructions because she couldn't seem to formulate a single coherent thought.

Luca curled his fingers under the sides of her panties and gently took them off. Now she was naked. And even though she'd been naked in front of men before it had never felt like this. As if she was being reborn.

Luca came down over her on strong arms, their bodies barely touching. He kissed her, and those broad shoulders blocked everything out. Serena reached up, desperate for contact again, her hands touching his chest and moving down the sides of his body, reaching around to his back, sliding over taut, sleek muscles.

Luca broke away. 'You're killing me. I need you... *now*. Spread your legs for me.'

Serena's entire body seemed to spasm at that husky entreaty. She moved her legs apart and Luca came down over her, his body pressing against hers. She could feel the thick blunt head of him pushing against her, seeking entrance.

She opened her legs wider, every cell in her body straining towards this union. Aching for it. She looked up at him, her whole body on the edge of some unknown precipice.

As if some lingering tension shimmering between them had just dissolved, Luca thrust in, hard and deep, and Serena cried out at the exquisite invasion.

It was sore...he was so big...but even as she had that thought the pain was already dissipating to be replaced by a heady sensation of fullness.

'Serena?'

She opened her eyes. Luca was frowning. She hadn't realised that she was biting her lip.

He started to withdraw. 'I've hurt you.'

There was a quality to his voice Serena had never heard before. She gripped him tight with her thighs, trapping him. 'No,' she said huskily. 'You're not hurting me… It's…been a while.'

He stopped, and for an infinitesimal moment Serena thought he was going to withdraw completely. But then he slowly thrust in again and relief rushed through her.

Luca reached under her back, arching her up into him more as he kept up a steady rhythm that made it hard to breathe. She could feel her inner muscles tight around him, saw his gritted jaw, the intense look of concentration on his face.

Luca pressed a searing kiss to her mouth before trailing his lips down, closing them over one nipple and then the other, forcing Serena's back to arch again as spasm after spasm of tiny pleasures rushed through her core.

She locked her feet around the back of Luca's body and he went deeper, but she couldn't break free of that sliver of control that kept her bound, kept her from soaring to the stars. A blinding flash of insight hit her like a smack in the face: she recognised now why she couldn't let go in this moment of intense intimacy—the reason why she'd never let herself feel this deeply before—it was because she'd always been too afraid of losing control.

Which was ironic. But being out of control on drink and medication had been—perversely—*within* her control. This wasn't. This was threatening to wrench her out of herself in a way that was frankly terrifying.

A small sob of need escaped Serena's mouth as that elusive pinnacle seemed to fade into the distance. The turmoil in her chest and body was burning her. But she couldn't let go—even as she heard a guttural sound coming from Luca's mouth and felt his body tense within her before deep tremors shook his big frame and his body thrust against her with the unconscious rhythm of his own release.

She felt hollowed out, unsatisfied.

Luca withdrew from her body, breathing harshly, and Serena winced minutely as her muscles relaxed their tight grip. As soon as Luca released her from the prison of his arms she felt the need to escape and left the bed.

She barely heard him call her name as she shut the bathroom door behind her, locking it. Her legs were shaking and tears burned the back of her eyes as the magnitude of what had just happened sank in. There was something fundamentally flawed, deep inside her. She'd been broken so long ago that she couldn't function normally now. And Luca had to be the one to demonstrate this to her. The ignominy was crushing.

Serena blindly reached into the shower and turned the spray to hot, stepping underneath and lifting her face up to the rush of water. Her tears slid and fell, silent heaves making her body spasm as she let it all out.

She heard banging on the door, her name. She called out hoarsely, 'Leave me alone, Luca!'

And then, mercifully, silence.

Serena sank down onto the floor of the shower as the water beat relentlessly down over her body. She drew her knees up to her chest and dropped her head onto them and tried to tell herself that what had just happened *wasn't* as cataclysmic as she thought it was.

* * *

Luca looked at the locked door. He wasn't used to feeling powerless, but right now he did. He cursed volubly, knowing it wouldn't be heard because he could hear the spray of the shower and something that sounded suspiciously like a sob.

His chest hurt. Was she crying? Had he hurt her?

Luca cursed again and paced. He went to his wardrobe and took out some worn jeans, pulled them on, paced again.

Dammit. No woman had ever reacted like that after making love with him. Running to the bathroom. *Crying.* And yet...

Had he really made love to Serena? Luca asked himself derisively. Or had he been so overcome with lust that he'd not taken any notice of the fact that she clearly hadn't been enjoying herself?

He winced now when he thought of how tight she'd been. And her husky words...*It's...been a while.* To be so tight he'd guess a lot longer than 'a while'. Which meant what? That her reputation for promiscuity was severely flawed, for a start. And she'd been awkward, slightly gauche. Not remotely like the practised seductress he might have expected.

He'd seen how her face had tightened, become inscrutable. She'd shut her eyes, turned her head away... But Luca had been caught in the grip of a pleasure so intense that he'd been unable to hold himself back, releasing himself into her with a force unlike anything he'd known before.

For the first time in his memory Luca was facing the very unpalatable fact that he'd behaved with all the finesse of a rutting bull.

The spray of the shower was turned off and Luca became tense. He felt a very real urge to flee at the prospect of facing Serena now. But that urge stemmed from some deep place he wouldn't acknowledge. She hadn't reached him there. No one had.

When Serena emerged from the bathroom, dressed in a voluminous terrycloth robe, she still felt raw. The bedroom was empty, and a lurch of something awfully like disappointment went through her belly to think that Luca had left.

And then she cursed herself. Hadn't she told him to *'leave me alone'*? Why on earth would he want to have anything to do with a physically and emotionally wounded woman when there had to be any number of willing women who would give him all the satisfaction he might crave without the post-coital angst?

Still…it hurt in a way that it shouldn't.

Serena belted the robe tightly around her waist and, feeling restless, went out to the living area. Her hair lay in a damp tangle down her back.

But when she looked out through the glass doors she saw him. He hadn't left. Her heart stopped as something very warm and treacherous filled her chest.

As she came closer to the open doors she could see that he'd pulled on soft faded jeans. His back was broad and smooth, his hair ruffled. From her hands or the breeze? Serena hovered at the door, on the threshold.

And then Luca said over his shoulder, 'You should come and see the view—it's pretty spectacular.'

Serena came out and stood not far from Luca, putting her hands on the railing. The view was indeed exquisite. Rio was lit up with a thousand lights, the Sugar Loaf in the distance, and the beaches just out of sight. It was magical. Other-worldly.

'I've never seen anything like this,' she breathed, curiously soothed by Luca's muted reaction to her re-appearance.

He said lightly now, 'I find that hard to believe.'

Serena's hands tightened on the railing. 'It's true. Before...I wouldn't have noticed.'

She could sense him turning towards her and her skin warmed. Just like that. From his attention. She glanced at him and his face looked stark in the moonlight.

'Did I hurt you? You were with me all the way and then...you weren't.'

'*No!*' Serena blurted out, horrified that he would think that. 'No,' she said again, quieter, and looked back at the view. 'Nothing like that.'

'Then...what?'

Why wouldn't he let it go? Serena wasn't used to men who gave any consideration to how much she'd enjoyed sex—they'd usually been happy just to say they'd *had* her. The wild child.

Luca's voice broke in again. 'You've already come in my arms, so I know what it feels like, but you shut down.'

Serena got hot, recalling the strength of her orgasm when he'd been touching her in the jungle... But that had been different... He hadn't been *inside her*.

And she hadn't been falling for him.

The realisation hit her now, as if she'd been blocking it out. She *was* falling for him—tumbling, in fact. No wonder her body had shut down. It had known before she did. She'd been right to fear his total possession.

She looked at him, shocked, terrified it might be written over her head in neon lights. But he was just raising a brow, waiting for an answer. Oblivious.

Her mind whirling with this new and fragile knowledge, she whispered, 'I told you…it's been a while.'

'What's "a while"?'

Serena stared at him, wanting him to let it go. 'Years—okay? A long time.'

Something in his eyes flashed. 'You haven't had any lovers since you left Italy?'

She shook her head, avoiding his eye again, and said tightly, 'No—and not for a while before that.'

God, this was excruciating!

'The truth is I've never really enjoyed sex. My reputation for promiscuity and sexual prowess was largely based on the stories of men who'd been turned down. I'm afraid I'm not half as debauched as you might think…a lot of talk and not a lot of action.'

Luca was quiet for a long time, and then he said, 'I could tell you weren't that experienced. But you were touted as one of Europe's most licentious socialites and you didn't do much to defend yourself.'

She sent him a dark glance. 'As if anyone would have believed me.' She looked out over the view and felt somehow removed, suspended in space. 'Do you know how I learned to French kiss?'

She could sense Luca going still. 'How?'

Serena smiled but it was bitter, hard. 'One of my father's friends. At a party. He came into my room.'

She let out a shocked gasp when Luca grabbed her

shoulders and pulled her around to face him. His face was stark, pale. His reaction took her aback.

'Did he touch you? Did he—?'

Serena shook her head quickly. '*No*. No. My sister Siena was there…we shared a room. She woke up and got into bed beside me and the man left. After that we made sure to lock our door every night.'

Luca's hands were still gripping her shoulders. '*Deus*…Serena.'

He let her go and ran a hand through his hair, looking at her as if she was a stranger. On some deep level Serena welcomed it. The other thing was too scary. Luca looking at her with something approximating gentleness…

She saw a lounger nearby and went over and sat down, pulling her knees up to her chest. Luca stood with his back to the railing, hands in his pockets. Tense.

As if the words were being wrung out of him, he finally said, 'It's not adding up. *You're* not adding up.'

'What's not adding up?' Serena asked quietly, her heart palpitating at Luca's intent look.

'You've had nothing but opportunities to be difficult since you got here and you haven't been. No one can act that well. A child who is medicated for being difficult, wilful…who grows into a wild teenager hell-bent on causing controversy wherever she goes…that's not you.'

Serena's heart beat fast. She felt light-headed. Faintly she said, 'It *was* me.'

Luca was grim. '*Was?* No one changes that easily, or that swiftly.'

He came over and pulled a chair close, sat down. Serena knew her eyes had gone wide. She felt as if she were standing on the edge of a precipice, teetering, about to fall.

'I want to know, Serena... Why were you put on medication so young?'

'I told you...after my mother died—'

Luca shook his head. 'There has to be more to it than that.'

Serena just looked at him. No one had ever been interested in knowing her secrets before. In rehab the professionals had been paid to delve deep, and she'd let them in the interests of getting better.

Luca was pushing her and pushing her—and for what? As if he'd welcome her darkest secrets...

The desire to be vulnerable and allow herself to confide in him in a way she'd never done before made her scared. It was too much, coming on the heels of what had just happened. Realising she was falling in love with him when he was only interested in bedding her. She'd been at pains to let Luca know that this was the real her, and yet she knew well it wasn't. There was a lot more to her. And she couldn't let it out. She felt too fragile.

Acting on a blind instinct to protect herself, Serena stood up abruptly, making Luca tip his head back.

Coldly she said, 'There's nothing more to it—and I thought men didn't like post-coital post-mortems. If we're done here for the evening I'd like to go to bed. I'm tired.'

She went to walk around Luca, her heart hammering, but he grabbed her wrist, stopping her in her tracks. He stood up slowly, eyes narrowed on her.

'What the hell…? *If we're done here for the evening?* What's *that* supposed to mean?'

Serena shrugged and tried to affect as bored a demeanour as possible. 'We've been to the function, we've slept together…' She forced herself to look at him and mocked, 'What more do you want? For me to tuck you in and read you a story?'

Luca's face flushed. He let her wrist go as if it burnt him. He seemed to increase in size in front of her, but instead of intimidating her it only made her more aware of him. He bristled.

'No, sweetheart, I don't want you to tuck me in and read me a story. I want you in my bed at my convenience for as long as I want you.'

He was hard and cruel. And more remote than she could remember ever seeing him. Something inside her curled up tight. But still that instinct to drive him away from seeing too much made her say nonchalantly, 'Well, if it's all the same to you, I'd appreciate spending the rest of the night on my own.'

Liar, her body whispered. Even now between her legs she was getting damp with the desire to feel him surge deep inside her.

So that she could shut down all over again? More humiliation? No, she was doing the right thing.

He came close…close enough to make sweat break out over Serena's skin… If he touched her he'd know how false she was being.

But he stopped just inches away and said, 'We both know that I could have you flat on your back and begging me for release in minutes…a release that you *will* give me next time, Serena.'

He stepped back and Serena felt disorientated. He thought she'd *wilfully* kept herself from being pleasured just to thwart him in some way?

He swept her up and down with a scathing glance. 'But right now I find that my desire has waned.'

He turned and strode back into the apartment and Serena started to shake in reaction. Everything in her wanted to call out to him.

But wasn't this what she wanted? To push him back? The shackles of her past had never felt so burdensome as they did right then. She recognised that they were protecting her, but also imprisoning her.

She could imagine Luca getting changed, walking out through the door, and her gut seized in rejection. Luca was the only person she'd come close to telling everything. She could remember the look on his face just before she'd turned cold. He'd been *concerned*. Until she'd convinced him that she had nothing to say except that she wanted him to leave.

And why wouldn't he leave? He was proud enough to take her at face value. She knew how quickly he damned people—after all he'd damned her for long enough… But that had been changing.

A sense of urgency gripped her—so what if he *did* just want her in his bed? Suddenly Serena knew that in spite of how terrified it made her feel, she desperately wanted to lean on Luca's inherent strength and face these last demons that haunted her still. She was sick of letting her past define her, of being afraid to get too close to anyone in case they saw inside her.

After all, what was the worst that could happen? Luca couldn't look at her any more coldly than he just had. And if he didn't believe her…? Then at least she would have been totally honest.

She heard a movement and saw Luca stride towards the front door, dressed now in black trousers and a black top.

He looked utterly intimidating, but Serena gathered all of her courage, stepped into the apartment again and said, 'Wait, Luca, please. Don't go.'

CHAPTER NINE

Luca stopped at the door, his hand on the knob. Had he even heard that? Or was it his imagination conjuring up what he wanted to hear from a siren who had him so twisted inside out that he barely knew which way was up any more?

He didn't turn around and forced out a drawl. 'What is it, *minha beleza*? You're ready to come this time?'

He felt dark inside, constricted. He'd really thought he'd seen something incredibly vulnerable in Serena—he'd finally believed that she truly was exactly as she seemed—and then...*wham!* She couldn't have made more of a fool of him if she'd professed undying love and he'd believed her.

There was no sound behind him and he whirled around, anger like a molten surge within him. When he saw the pallor of Serena's cheeks and how huge and bruised her eyes looked he pushed down the concern that rose up to mock him and said scathingly, 'Nice try, *namorada*, but I'm not falling for whatever part you want to play now. Frankly, I prefer a little consistency in my lovers.'

Luca went to turn and leave again, but Serena moved forward jerkily. 'Please, just wait—hear me out.'

He sighed deeply, hating the ball of darkness in his gut. The darkness that whispered to him to run fast and far away from this woman.

He turned around and crossed his arms, arching a brow. 'Well?'

Serena swallowed. Her hair was like a white-gold curtain over her shoulders, touching the swells of her breasts under the robe. Breasts that Luca could taste on his tongue even now.

Incensed that she was catching him like this, and yet still he couldn't walk away, he strode past her over to his drinks cabinet and delivered curtly, 'Spit it out, will you?'

He poured himself a glass of whisky and downed it in one. Hating that she'd even made him feel he needed the sustenance. His hand gripped the glass. He wouldn't look at her again.

'Serena, so help me—'

'You were pushing me to talk…and I didn't want to. So I pretended just now…pretended that I wanted to be alone. I didn't mean what I said, Luca.'

Luca went very still. An inner voice mocked him. *She's still playing you.* But he recalled the way she'd looked so hunted…just before something had come over her expression and she'd morphed into the ice queen in front of his eyes.

Slowly he put the glass down and turned around. Serena looked shaken. Pale. Yet determined.

'I'm sorry.'

Her voice was husky and it touched on his skin like a caress he wanted to rail against.

He folded his arms. 'Sorry for what?'

She bit her lip. 'I wanted you to think that I'd had enough so you'd leave, but that's not true.'

'Tell me something I *don't* know,' Luca drawled, and saw how she went even paler.

He cursed out loud and went over to her, taking her by the arm and leading her to a couch to sit down.

'Serena, so help me God, if this is just some elaborate—'

'It's not!' she cried, her hands gripped together in her lap. 'It's not,' she said again. 'You were just asking me all these things and I felt threatened… I've never told anyone what happened. I've always been too ashamed and guilty that I didn't do something to stop it. And for a long time I doubted that it had even happened…'

Luca knew now that this was no act. Serena was retreating, her mind far away. Instinctively he reached out and took her hands, wrapping them in his. She looked at him and his chest got tight. *Damn her*.

'What happened?'

Her hands were cold in his and her eyes had never looked bigger or bluer.

'I saw my father kill my mother when I was five years old.'

Luca's mouth opened and closed. 'You *what*?'

Serena couldn't seem to take her eyes off Luca, as if he was anchoring her to something. Her throat felt dry.

'When I was five I heard my parents arguing…nothing new…they argued all the time. I sneaked downstairs to the study. When I looked in through the crack of the door I could see my mother crying. I couldn't understand what they were arguing about, although in hindsight I know it was most likely to do with my father's affairs.'

Luca was grim. 'What happened?' he asked again.

'My father backhanded my mother across the face and she fell... She hit her head on the corner of his desk.'

Serena went inward.

'All I can remember is the pool of blood growing around her head on the rug and how dark it was. And how white she was. I must have made a sound, or something. The next thing I remember is my father dragging me back upstairs. I was crying for my mother...hysterical. My father hit me across the face...I remember one of my baby teeth was loose and it fell out... A doctor arrived. He gave me an injection. I can still remember the pain in my arm... The funeral...everything after that... was blurry. Siena was only three. But I can remember the doctor coming a lot. And once the police came. But I couldn't speak to them. I wanted to tell them what I'd seen but I'd been given something that made me sleepy. It didn't seem important any more.'

Her voice turned bitter.

'He got it covered up, of course, and no one ever accused him of her death. That's when it started. By the time I was twelve my father and his doctor were feeding my medication habit. They said I had ADHD—that I was difficult to control. Wilful. That it was for my own good. Then my father started saying things like *bi-polar*. He was constantly perpetuating a myth of mental uncertainty around me—even to my sister, who always believed that I tried to take my own life.'

'Did you?' Luca's voice was sharp.

Serena shook her head. 'No. But even though I denied it my sister was programmed by then to believe in my instability just like everyone else. My father even made a pretence of not allowing me to take drugs for the condition—while he was maintaining a steady supply to me through the doctor on his payroll.'

Luca shook his head. 'But why didn't you leave when you could?'

Serena pushed down the guilt. She had to start forgiving herself.

'I couldn't see a way out. By the time I was sixteen I was living the script my father had written for me years before.'

She reeled off the headlines of the time.

'I was a *wild child. Impossible to tame. Out of control.* And I was addicted to prescription drugs... Siena was innocent. The good girl. Even now Siena still retains an innocence I never had. My father played us off against each other. If Siena stepped out of line I got the punishment...never her. She was being groomed as the perfect heiress. I was being groomed as the car crash happening in slow motion.'

Luca's hands had tightened over hers and it was only then that Serena realised how icy she'd gone.

'Why haven't you ever gone to the police about your mother's death?'

Shame pricked Serena. 'Who would have believed disgraceful, unstable Serena DePiero? It felt hopeless. *I* felt hopeless. And in a way I had begun to doubt myself too...had it really happened? Maybe I was dreaming it up? Maybe I *was* just some vacuous socialite hooked on meds?'

Luca was shaking his head and Serena instantly went colder. She'd been a fool to divulge so much. She pulled her hands back.

'You don't believe me.'

Luca's gaze narrowed and his mouth thinned. 'Oh, I

believe you, all right. It just about makes sense. And I met your father—he was a cold bastard.' He shook his head. 'He turned you into an addict, Serena.'

Something fragile and treacherous unfurled inside Serena. *Acceptance.*

She said huskily, 'I'm sorry about before. I didn't want to tell you everything.'

'So what changed?'

Serena felt as if she was being backed into a corner again, but this time she fought the urge to escape or to push him away. 'You deserved to know the truth, and I was being less than honest.'

'Less than honest about what?'

He was going to make her say it.

Serena was captivated by Luca's gaze. Time seemed to have slowed to a throbbing heartbeat between them. In the same moment she was aware of a giddy rush through her body—a sense of weightlessness. She'd told someone her innermost secrets and the world hadn't crashed around her.

Serena's belly swooped and she took a leap into the void. 'I didn't want to spend the rest of the night alone. It was just an excuse.'

Luca looked at her and something in his eyes darkened. *Desire.* He cupped her face in his hands and slanted his mouth over hers in a kiss so light that it broke Serena apart more than the most passionate kisses they'd exchanged.

When he pulled back she kept him close and whispered shakily, 'Will you stay, Luca?'

She suddenly needed him desperately—needed a way to feel rooted when she might float off altogether and lose touch with the earth.

Luca kissed her mouth again and said throatily, 'Yes.'

He stood and pulled Serena up with him, and then he bent and scooped her into his arms as if she weighed no more than a feather. Her arms moved around his neck but she couldn't resist trailing her fingers along his jaw, and then reaching up to press a kiss against the pulse she could see beating under his bronzed skin.

His chest swelled against her breasts and her whole body pulsed with heat and awareness.

He put her down gently by the rumpled bed, where the scent of their bodies lingered in the air, sultry… Even though they'd already made love Serena was trembling as if they hadn't even touched for the first time.

They came together in a kiss of mutual combustion.

There was no time for Serena to worry about her body letting her down again because she was too feverish for Luca—hands spreading out over his bare chest, nails grazing his nipples, causing him to curse softly. Her hands moved to his trousers, and she unzipped them, freeing his erection. She took him in her hand, relishing the steely strength.

Luca's hands were busy too, opening the belt of the robe and sliding it over her shoulders. Serena looked up at him and took her hands away from his body so that the robe could fall to the floor.

His gaze devoured her…hot. Dark colour slashed his cheeks as he tugged his trousers down and off completely, kicking them aside.

He pushed her gently onto the bed. Serena was shocked at how fast her heart was racing, how ragged her breath was.

Gutturally he said, 'I want to take this slow—not like before.'

But Serena was desperate to feel him again. She was ready. She shook her head and whispered, 'I don't want slow. I want *you*.'

He caught her look and said rawly, 'Are you sure?'

She nodded again, and saw his jaw clench as if he was giving up some thin shred of control. He reached for protection and she watched him smooth it onto his erection, an almost feral look on his face.

Serena's sex pulsed with need. She lifted her arms and beckoned him, spreading her legs in a mute appeal.

His eyes flashed and he muttered something indistinct. He leant down to place his hand on her sex, cupping its heat. Serena found his wide shoulders and gripped him, biting her lip.

He spread his fingers and explored her secret folds, releasing the slick heat of her arousal.

His voice was rough. 'You're so ready for me.'

'Please…' said Serena huskily. 'I want you, Luca.'

Every cell in her body felt engorged with blood as he came down over her, pressing her into the bed, his body hard next to her softness. Crushing it deliciously.

He bent his head and took one pebbled nipple into his mouth, his teeth capturing it for a stinging second before letting go to soothe it with his tongue. This teasing was almost unbearable.

Serena was about to sob out another plea when he pushed his thick length inside her. Her eyes widened and she sucked in a breath as he pushed in, relentless, until he was buried inside her.

'You're so tight…like a vice.' He pressed a kiss to her mouth, hot and musky. 'Relax, *preciosa*…'

The endearment did something to Serena. She felt her body softening around him. He slid even deeper and a look of deep carnal satisfaction crossed his face, making something exult inside her. A sense of her own innately feminine power.

Her nipples scraped against his hair-roughened chest with a delicious friction as Luca started to move in and out, each powerful glide of his body reaching deeper inside Serena to a place she'd locked away long ago. She couldn't take her eyes off him. It was as if he was holding her within his gaze, keeping her rooted in the inexorable building of pleasure.

He reached around to her thigh and brought it up over his hip, his hand smoothing her flesh, then gripping it as his movements became harder, more powerful. That hand crept up and cupped her bottom, kneading, angling her hips, so that he touched some part of her that made her gasp out loud as a tremor of pleasure rocked through her pelvis.

Unconsciously Serena tilted her hips more and Luca moaned deeply. His thrusts became faster and Serena could feel the tight coil of tension inside her, tightening and tightening unbearably, to a point of almost pain.

She was incoherent, only able to stay anchored by looking into Luca's eyes. When she closed hers briefly he commanded roughly, 'Look at me, Serena.'

She did. And something broke apart deep inside her.

Her whole body tautened against his, nerves stretched to screaming point. Luca moved his hand between them, his fingers finding the engorged centre of her desire, and he touched her with a precision that left her nowhere to hide or hang on to. She imploded. Her control was shattered—the control she'd clung to all her life. Since her world had fallen apart as a child, when being *out* of control had become her control.

In one instant it was decimated, and Serena soared high on a wave of bliss that was spectacular. The definition of an orgasm being a *petit mort*, a small death, had never felt so apt. She knew that a part of her had just died and something else incredibly fragile and nebulous was taking its place.

She floated back down to reality, aware of her body milking Luca's own release as he shuddered and buried his head in her shoulder, his body embedded deep within hers. Her legs wrapped around him, and the pulsations of their mutual climaxes took long minutes to die away.

Luca was in the kitchen the following morning, making breakfast, before he realised that he'd never in his life made breakfast for a lover. In general he liked being in a situation where he could extricate himself rather than have to deal with the aftermath and unwelcome romantic projections.

But here he was, cooking breakfast for Serena without half a second's hesitation or any desire to put as much space between them as possible. His head was still fuzzy from an overload of sensual pleasure and the revelations she'd made.

He couldn't help thinking of her: a little girl, traumatised by the violent death of her mother, with a sadistic and mercurial father who tried to discredit her as soon as he could. Somehow it wasn't that fantastical to believe her father capable of such things.

He thought back to that night when he'd watched Siena come to bail Serena out of jail. The way she had tended to Serena like a mother to her cub…the way Serena had leant on her as if it was a familiar pattern.

Both had been manipulated by their father's machinations. Both had been acting out their parts. The good girl and the bad girl.

It all made a sick kind of sense now, because Luca knew he hadn't imagined the vulnerability he'd sensed about her that night he'd first met her...

A sound from behind him made him tense and he turned around to see Serena, tousle-haired and dressed in the robe, standing in the doorway. She looked hesitant, shy, and Luca was falling, losing his grip. Everything he thought he'd known about her...*wasn't*.

His hands gripped the bowl he was using to whisk eggs. 'Hungry?'

'Starving.'

Serena's voice was husky, and it fired up Luca's blood, reminding him of how she'd shouted out his name in the throes of passion just short hours before. How she'd begged and pleaded with him. How she'd felt around him.

Deus.

Serena came into the kitchen feeling ridiculously shy. Luca looked stern, intense.

'I didn't know you cooked.'

Luca grimaced in a half-smile, some of the intensity in his expression diminishing slightly as he continued whisking. 'I don't...I have a very limited repertoire and scrambled eggs is about as haute cuisine as it gets.'

Serena sat up on a stool by the island and tried not to let herself melt too much at seeing Luca in such a domestic setting in worn jeans and a T-shirt, his hair mussed up and a dark growth of stubble on his jaw.

'Where did you learn?'

He was taking thin strips of bacon now, and placing them under a hot grill. He didn't look at her. 'When my mother left, my father let the housekeeper go; he always felt it was an unnecessary expense.'

Serena felt indignation rise. 'But how did you cope? Did your father cook?'

Luca shook his head. 'I was at boarding school outside Rio for most of the time, so it was only the holidays when I had to fend for myself.' His mouth twisted. 'One of my father's many mistresses took pity on me when she found me eating dry cereal. She taught me some basics. I liked her—she was one of the nicer ones—but she left.'

More sharply than she'd intended, Serena said, 'She wasn't the one who seduced you?'

Luca looked at her, a small smile playing around his hard mouth. 'No.'

Embarrassed by the surge of jealousy, Serena said, 'Your father never married again?'

'No.'

Luca poured some delicious-smelling coffee out of a pot into big mugs, handing her one. Serena bent her head to smell deeply.

'He learnt his lesson after my mother walked away with a small fortune. She'd come from money in Italy, but by then it was almost all gone.'

Serena thought of his parents not even caring which boy went with who and felt sad. She remarked almost to herself, 'I can't imagine how I would have coped if Siena and I had been separated.'

Luca put a plate full of fluffy scrambled eggs and crispy bacon in front of Serena. He looked at her as he settled on his own stool. 'You're close, aren't you?'

Serena nodded, emotional for a second at the thought of her sister and her family. 'Yes, she saved me.'

Luca's gaze sharpened. 'It sounds to me like you saved yourself, as soon as you could.'

Serena shrugged minutely, embarrassed again under Luca's regard. 'I guess I did.' She swallowed some of the delicious food and asked curiously, 'Is your twin brother like you? Determined to right the wrongs of the world?'

Luca sighed heavily. 'Max is…complicated. He resented me for a long time because my father insisted on leaving everything to me—even though I tried to give him half when our father died. He was too proud to take it.'

Serena shook her head in disbelief, and was more than touched to know that Luca had been generous enough to do that.

'He had a tougher time than me—our mother was completely unstable, lurching from rich man to rich man in a bid to feather her nest, and in and out of rehab. Max went from being enrolled in an exclusive Swiss boarding school to living on the streets in Rome…'

Serena's eyes widened.

'He pulled himself out of the gutter with little or no help; he wouldn't accept any from me and he certainly wouldn't take it from my father. It was only years later, when he'd made his first million, that we could meet on common ground.'

Serena put down her knife and fork. Luca had shown signs of such intransigence and an inability to forgive when she'd first come to Rio, but now she was seeing far deeper into the man and realising he'd had just as much of a complicated background as she had in many respects. And yet he'd emerged without being tainted by the corruption of his father, or by the vagaries of his mother—vagaries that she understood far too well.

For the first time Serena had to concede that perhaps she hadn't done too badly, considering how easy it would have been to insist on living in a fog, not dealing with reality.

Luca was looking at her with an eyebrow raised. He was waiting for an answer to a question she hadn't heard. She blushed. 'Sorry. I was a million miles away.'

'You said when you first got here that you wanted to see Rio?'

Serena nodded, not sure where this was going or what might happen after last night.

'Well…'

Luca was exhibiting a tiny glimmer of a lack of his usual arrogance and it set Serena's heart beating fast.

'It's the weekend. I'd like to show you Rio.'

The bottom seemed to drop out of Serena's stomach. She felt ridiculously shy again. Something bubbled up inside her—lightness. *Happiness*. It was alien enough to take her by surprise.

'Okay, I'd like that.'

CHAPTER TEN

'Had enough yet?'

Serena mumbled something indistinct. This was paradise. Lying on Ipanema Beach as the fading rays of the sun baked her skin and body in delicious heat. There was a low hum of conversation from nearby, the beautiful sing-song cadence of Portuguese, people were laughing, sighing, talking. The surf of the sea was crashing against the shore.

And then she felt Luca's mouth on hers and her whole body orientated itself towards his. She opened her eyes with an effort to find him looking down at her. Her heart flip-flopped. She smiled.

'Can we stay for the sunset?'

Luca was trying to hang on to some semblance of normality when the day that had just passed had veered out of *normal* for him on so many levels it was scary.

'Sure,' he said, with an easiness belying his trepidation. Serena's open smile was doing little to restore any sense of equilibrium.

One day spent walking around Rio and then a couple of hours on the beach was all it had taken to touch her skin with a luminous golden glow. Her hair looked blonder, almost white, her blue eyes were standing out even more starkly.

That morning they had taken the train up through the forest to the Cristo Redentor on Corcovado and Serena had been captivated by every tiny thing. Standing at the railing, looking down over the breathtaking panorama of Rio, she'd turned to him and asked, with a look of gleaming excitement that had reminded him of a child, 'Can we go to the beach later?'

Luca's insides had tightened ominously. She didn't want to go shopping. She wanted to see Rio. Genuinely.

Before they'd hit the beach they'd eaten lunch at a favourite café of Luca's. At one point he'd sat back and asked, with an increasing sense of defeat, 'Your family really aren't funding you…are they?'

Immediate affront had lit up those piercing eyes. Luca wouldn't have believed it before. But he did now, and it had made something feel dark and heavy inside him.

'Of course not.' She'd flushed then, guiltily, and admitted with clear reluctance, 'My sister and her husband paid for an apartment for me in Athens…when I was ready to move on. But I'm going to pay them back as soon as I've made enough money.'

Darkness had twisted inside Luca. People got handouts all the time from family, yet she clearly hated to admit it. And this was a woman who had had everything…a vast fortune to inherit…only to lose it all.

She'd flushed self-consciously when she'd caught him looking at her cleared plate of *feijoãda*, a famous Brazilian stew made with black beans and pork. 'My sister is the same. It's a reaction to the tiny portions of food we were allowed to eat by our father, growing up.'

Her revelation had hit him hard again. The sheer abuse her father had subjected her to. Anger still simmered in his belly. Luca had felt compelled to reach out and take her hand, entwining his fingers with hers—something that had felt far too easy and necessary.

'Believe me, it's refreshing to see a woman enjoy her food.'

Her hand had tensed in his and she'd said, far too lightly, while avoiding his eyes, 'I'm sure the women you know are far more restrained.'

Was she jealous? The suspicion had caught at Luca somewhere deeply masculine. And that deeply masculine part of him had been triggered again when he'd insisted on buying her a bikini so she could swim at the beach, as they hadn't been prepared.

He took her in now, as she lay beside him, the three tiny black triangles doing little to help keep his libido in check. He was just glad that the board shorts he'd bought to swim in were roomy enough to disguise his rampant response.

As if aware of his scrutiny Serena fidgeted, trying to pull the bikini over her breasts more—which only made some of the voluptuous flesh swell out at the other side.

Luca bit back a groan.

She'd hissed at him in the shop, 'I'm not wearing that—it's indecent!'

Luca had drawled wryly, 'Believe me, when you see what most women wear on the beaches here you'll feel overdressed.'

And when they'd hit the sand Serena's reaction had been priceless. Mouth open, eyes popping out of her head, she'd watched the undeniably sensual parade of beautiful bodies up and down the beach.

Luca hadn't been unaware of the blatant interest her pale blonde beauty had attracted, and had stared down numerous men.

The sun was setting now, and people were starting to cheer and clap as it spread out in a red ball of fire over the horizon, just to the left of one of Rio's craggy peaks.

Serena sat up and drew her legs to her chest, wrapping her arms around them. She smiled at Luca, before taking in the stunning sunset and clapping herself. 'I love how they do that.'

Her pleasure in something so simple mocked his deeply rooted cynicism. And then Luca realised then that he was enjoying this too, but it had been a long time since he'd taken the time to appreciate it. Even when he'd been younger he'd been so driven to try and counteract his father's corrupt legacy that he'd rarely taken any time out for himself. He'd fallen into a pattern of choosing willing women who were happy with no-strings-attached sex to alleviate any frustration.

He'd never relaxed like this in a typical *carioca* way, with a beautiful woman.

The sun had set and she looked at him now, and all he could see was the damp golden hair trailing over her shoulders, close to the full thrust of her breasts. Her mouth, like a crushed rose petal, was begging to be tasted. And those wide eyes were looking at him with a wariness that only fired his libido even more.

He said roughly, 'Let's get out of here.'

Serena couldn't mistake the carnal intent in Luca's eyes. He'd been looking at her all day as if he'd never seen her before. And today…today had been like a dream.

Her skin felt tight from the sun and sea, and she

didn't know if it was just Luca's unique effect on her, or the result of watching the Rio natives embrace their sensuality and sexuality all afternoon, but right now she trembled with the sexual need that pulsed through her very core and blood.

'Yes,' she said.

She stood up, and Luca stood too, handing her the sundress she'd put on that morning.

They walked the short distance back to Luca's car and when he took her hand in his, Serena's fingers tightened around his reflexively. He wore an open shirt over his chest, still in his shorts, and her heart clenched because he looked so much younger and more carefree than the stern, intimidating man she'd met again the day she'd arrived in Rio.

When they began winding up through the hills, away from the beaches, Serena asked, 'Where is this?'

Luca glanced at her. 'We're going to my home in Alto Gavea. It's closer.'

Serena's heart beat fast. *His home.*

The rest of the drive was in silence, as if words were superfluous and might not even penetrate the thick sensual tension between them.

This part of Rio was encased in forest, reminding Serena of the rainforest with a sharp poignancy. And Luca's home took her breath away when he turned in to a long secluded drive behind fortified gates.

It was an old colonial house, two-storey, white, with terracotta slates on the roof, and it was set, literally, in the middle of the lush Tijuca Forest.

He pulled the car to a stop and looked at her for a long moment. They were suspended in time, with no sounds except for the calls of some birds.

Then he broke the spell and got out of the car, helping Serena out of the low-slung seat. She let out a small squeal of surprise when he scooped her up into his arms and navigated opening the front door with commendable dexterity.

He took the stairs two at a time and strode into a massive bedroom. Serena only had time to take in an impression of a house that was cool and understated. In his room, the open shutters framed a view showcasing the illuminated Christ the Redeemer statue in the far distance on its hill overlooking Rio.

Everything became a little dream-like after that, and Serena knew that on some level she was shying away from analysing the significance of the day that had passed.

Luca put her down, only to disappear into a bathroom, where she heard the sound of a shower running. When he emerged he was taking off his clothes until he stood before her naked, unashamedly masculine and proud.

'Come here.'

She obeyed without question. When she stood before him he reached down for the hem of her dress and pulled it up and off. Then he turned her around and undid her flimsy bikini top so that it fell to the floor.

He turned her back and hooked his fingers into the bottoms, and pulled them down until she could step out of them at her feet. In that moment, naked, she'd never felt more womanly or more whole. Or more free of the shadows that had dogged her for as long as she could remember. They weren't gone completely, but it was enough for now.

He took her hand and led her into the bathroom,

which was fogged with steam that curled over their sticky, sandy bodies. Standing under the hot spray, Serena lifted her face and Luca covered her mouth with his, his huge body making the space tiny.

When he took his mouth off hers she opened her eyes to see his hot gaze devouring her. And just like that she was ready, her body ripening and moistening for him, ravenous at the sight of Luca's gleaming wet and aroused body. He lifted her and instructed her to put her legs around him—then groaned and stopped.

She looked at him, breathless with anticipation. 'What's wrong?'

'No protection, *preciosa*. We need to move.'

Serena was dazed as he carried her out of the shower, her legs still wrapped around his waist. She could see the pain on his face at the interruption but she was glad… She'd been too far gone to think about protection herself.

He put her down on the bed and reached for a condom from his cabinet, ripping the foil and sheathing himself with big, capable hands. Serena felt completely wanton as she watched this display of masculine virility.

And then he was coming back down over her, pushing her legs apart, settling between them, asking huskily, 'Okay?'

She nodded, her chest tightening ominously, and then Luca was thrusting in so deep her back arched and her legs went around his waist. It was fast and furious, his gaze holding hers, not letting her look away.

Bliss broke over her after mere minutes. She was so primed—as if now it was the easiest thing in the world and not something that had been torturously elusive when they'd first made love.

Serena bit into Luca's shoulder as powerful spasms racked her body just as he reached his own climax, his body thrusting rhythmically against hers until he was spent. He collapsed over her and she tightened her arms and legs around him, loving the feel of him pressing her into the bed, his body still big inside hers.

Eventually he withdrew, and Serena winced as her muscles protested. Luca collapsed on his back beside her, his breathing as uneven as hers. She looked at him to find him watching her with a small enigmatic smile playing around his mouth.

He came up on one arm and touched his fingers to her jaw. 'You make me lose my mind every time…' he admitted gruffly.

Serena looked at him. Somehow his confession wasn't as comforting as she'd thought it might be. It left her with a definite sense that Luca did not welcome such a revelation.

And then he was kissing her again, wiping everything from her mind, and she welcomed it weakly. She was far too afraid to face the suspicion that she had fallen in love with this man and there was no going back.

Three days later

'Miss DePiero? Senhor Fonseca said to let you know that he's been unavoidably detained and you should eat without him.'

'Okay, thank you.' Serena put down the kitchen phone extension and looked at the chicken stew she'd made, bubbling on the state-of-the-art cooker. *Unavoidably detained*. What was that code for?

Crazy to feel so disappointed, but she did. She'd spent her lunch hour buying ingredients, and as soon as she'd finished work at the charity office she'd rushed back to start cooking.

And now she felt ridiculous—because wasn't this such a cliché? The little woman at home, cooking dinner for her man and getting all bent out of shape because it was spoiled?

Mortified at the thought of what Luca's reaction would have been to see this attempt at creating some kind of domestic idyll, and losing any appetite herself, Serena took the chicken stew off the cooker. When it had cooled sufficiently she resisted the urge to throw it away and put it into a bowl to store in the fridge.

Feeling antsy, she headed outside to the terrace. The stunning view soothed her in a way that Athens had never done, even though she now called it home.

'Maledire,' she cursed softly in Italian. And then she cursed Luca, for making her fall for him.

The weekend had been...*amazing*. She remembered Luca kissing the tattoo on her shoulder. He'd murmured to her, 'You know the swallow represents resurrection?'

Serena had nodded her head, feeling absurdly emotional that he *got it*.

When they'd woken late on Sunday Luca had told her that he had to visit a local *favela* and she'd asked to go with him. She had seen first-hand his commitment to his own city. The amazing Fonseca Community Centre that provided literacy classes, language classes, business classes and a crèche so that everyone in the community could learn.

When she'd gone wandering, left alone briefly, she'd found Luca in the middle of a ring of men, doing *capoeira*, a Brazilian form of martial arts. He'd been stripped to the waist, his torso gleaming with exertion, making graceful and unbelievably agile movements to the beat of a drum played by a young boy.

She hadn't been the only woman ogling his spectacular form. By the time he'd finished, a gaggle of women and girls had been giggling and blushing. But a trickle of foreboding had skated over her skin… That had been the moment when he'd caught her eye and she'd seen something indecipherable cross his face. By the time he'd caught up with her again there had been something different about him. He'd shut down.

He'd brought her back here, to this apartment, and even though he'd stayed the night and made love to her, something had been off. When she'd woken he'd been gone, and she hadn't seen him again until late that evening, when he'd arrived and, with an almost feral look on his face, had kissed her so passionately that all tendrils of concern had fled, to be replaced with heat, distracting her from the fact that he clearly hadn't been interested in anything else.

The truth was that every moment she spent with Luca was ripping her apart internally. Especially when he looked at her as if she were some kind of unexploded device, yet kissed her as if his life depended on it. Clearly he was conflicted about her. He'd admitted that it was hard for him to come to terms with the fact that she wasn't what he'd believed her to be. And Serena had the gut-wrenching feeling that Luca would have almost preferred it if she *had* been the debauched, spoilt princess he'd expected.

She had to face the fact that her confession, while

liberating for her, had not proved to be so cataclysmic for Luca.

And of *course* it wouldn't have been, Serena chided herself. For Luca this was just...an affair. A slaking of desire. The fact that it had brought about her own personal epiphany was all Serena would have to comfort her when it was over, and that would have to be enough.

When Luca walked into the apartment it was after midnight. He felt guilty. He knew Serena had been making dinner because she'd told him earlier, when he'd seen her on a visit to the charity offices. It was a visit that had had his employees looking at him in surprise, because he usually conducted meetings in his own office and had little cause to visit them.

The apartment was silent, but he could smell the faint scent of something delicious in the air. When he went into the kitchen it was pristine, but he opened the fridge and saw the earthenware bowl containing dinner. The thought that perhaps she hadn't eaten because he hadn't been there made him feel guiltier. He hadn't even known that Serena could cook until she'd told him she'd taken lessons in Athens.

And he hadn't known how deeply enmeshed he was becoming with her until he'd looked at her in the *favela* and the enormity of it all had hit him. It had taken seeing her against that dusty backdrop—Serena DePiero, ex-socialite and wild child, looking as comfortable in the incongruous surroundings as if she'd been born into them like a native. In spite of the white-blonde beauty that had set her apart. He'd certainly been aware of the men looking at her, and the same black emotion that had gripped him at the beach had caught him again.

Jealousy. For the first time.

It was in that moment that a very belated sense of exposure had come over him and made him pull back from a dangerous brink. Luca knew better than anyone how fickle people were—how you couldn't trust that they wouldn't just pull your world out from under your feet within seconds.

His own parents had done it to him and his brother—setting them on different paths of fate almost as idly as if they were Greek gods, playing with hapless mortals. For years he'd had nightmares about his parents pulling them limb from limb, until their body parts were so mixed up that they didn't even know who was who any more.

Serena was getting too close—under his skin. Everything kept coming back to how badly he'd misjudged her—and never more so than now. He'd just had a conversation with his brother, who was in Rio on business.

And yet as he stood in the doorway of her bedroom now and saw the shape of her under the covers, the bright splash of white-blonde hair, he was taking off his clothes before he even realised what he was doing, sliding in behind her, wrapping himself around her and trying desperately to ignore the way his soul felt inexplicably soothed.

Even as she woke and turned towards him, her seeking sleepy mouth finding his, Luca was steeling himself inside—because this would all be over as soon as she knew what his brother had just told him. Because then everything that had bound them from the past would be gone.

But just...not yet.

When Serena woke in the dawn light, the bed was empty. But the hum in her body and the pleasurable ache between her legs told her she hadn't dreamt that Luca had come into her bed last night. Or dreamt the mindless passion he'd driven her to, taking her over the edge again and again, until she'd been spent, exhausted, begging for mercy.

It was as if Luca had been driven by something desperate.

She blinked, slowly coming awake. And even though her body was sated and lethargic from passion, her heart was heavy. She loved Luca, and she knew with cold certainty that he didn't love her. But he wanted her.

His love was his commitment to the environment, to making the world a better place in whatever small way he could, born from his zeal not to be like his predecessors—a zeal she could empathise with.

And Serena knew that she wouldn't be able to continue falling deeper and deeper without recognising that the heartbreak would be so much worse when she walked away.

It was only when she sighed deeply and moved her head that she felt something, and looked to see a note on the pillow beside her.

She reached for the thick paper and opened it to read:

Please meet me in my office when you wake. L.

A definite shiver of foreboding tightened Serena's skin. No wonder there had been something desperate in Luca's lovemaking last night. This was it. He was going to tell her it was over. The signs had been there for the last few days, since the *favela*.

Anger lanced her. To think that he would just send her away so summarily after sating his desire, which was obviously on the wane, and after she'd enjoyed working in the charity office so much. But, as much as she'd come to love Rio de Janeiro, she didn't relish the thought of being in such close proximity to him in the future—seeing him get on with his life, take another lover.

She wasn't going to let him discard her completely, though; no matter what had happened between them personally he owed her a job. In any event, she knew now that she had to go home. So, while Luca might be preparing to let her go, Serena told herself stoutly that she was ready.

It was only when she noticed her hands trembling in the shower that she had to admit her anger was stemming from a place of deep fear that she was about to feel pain such as she'd never felt before—not even when she'd been at her lowest ebb, trapped by her addictions. Before, she'd anaesthetised herself against the pain. Now she would have nothing to cling on to, and she wasn't sure how ready she was to cope with that.

CHAPTER ELEVEN

WHEN SERENA KNOCKED on Luca's office door about an hour later she felt composed, dressed in plain trousers and a silk shirt. Hair tied back. It had been a mere two weeks since she'd come here for the first time, but she was a different person.

Damn him.

His assistant opened the door and ushered her in, and it took a second after the girl had left for Serena to realise that there was another man in the room. He was standing on the other side of Luca's desk, and Luca stood up now from his high-backed chair.

'Serena—come in.'

Her heart lurched. So formal. For a crazy moment Serena wondered if the other man was a solicitor, so that Luca could get out of the contract?

When she came closer, though, she saw a resemblance between the two men, even though this man had tawny eyes and dark blond messy hair. They were almost identical in size and build. The stranger was as arrestingly gorgeous as Luca, but in a more traditional way—in spite of the scar she could see running from his temple to his jaw. He oozed danger, even though he looked as if he might have stepped from the pages of Italian *Vogue* in an immaculate dark suit.

She sensed a subtle tension in the air, and had just realised herself who he was when Luca said, 'This is my brother—Max Fonseca Roselli.'

She came forward and took the hand offered to her, suffering none of the physical reaction Luca caused within her with only a look. Even so, she saw the unmistakably appreciative gleam in his unusual golden-green eyes and could well imagine that he must leave a trail of bleeding hearts wherever he went. He had that same indomitable arrogance that Luca wore so well.

'Nice to meet you.'

His hand squeezed hers. 'You too.'

Serena pulled away, getting hot, sensing Luca's intense focus on them and Max's desire to needle his brother. When she looked at Luca, though, he gave nothing away and she cursed herself. Of *course* he wouldn't be proprietorial or jealous.

Luca indicated for them to sit down and said heavily, 'Max has some news for you…and me. I thought I owed it to you to let him tell you face to face.'

Now Serena was nervous, and she looked from him to Max and back. 'What is it?'

Luca explained. 'I asked Max to look into what happened at the club that night—to do some digging.'

Before she could properly assimilate that information, Max drawled in a deep voice, 'My brother knows I have some…less than legitimate connections.'

Serena looked at him and her heart went out to both of them for what they'd been through as children. The way their parents had all but rolled the dice to decide their fate.

Huskily she admitted, 'I… Luca told me what happened.'

Max's eyes flared and he shot his brother a scowl.

Luca said warningly, 'This isn't about *us*.'

For a second Serena could have laughed. They might not be identical, but right then she could see how similar they were—and they probably didn't even know it themselves.

Max looked back to her. 'I did some digging and discovered who did plant the drugs on Luca that night. He was a small-time dealer and in the crush he spotted you together. He knew that if he could plant the drugs on you or Luca no one would ever dispute that you had been involved.'

Shame lanced Serena to be reminded that everyone knew of her exploits and how tarnished her reputation was, even as her heart beat fast and she wondered why Luca had asked his brother to do this.

Max continued. 'He's actually in jail at the moment on another charge, and he's been bragging to anyone who will listen about how he set you and Luca up—it would appear that he couldn't bear to keep such a coup to himself. He's been charged with the offence and hasn't a leg to stand on because he's confessed to so many witnesses.'

For a moment the relief was so enormous that Serena felt dizzy, even though she was sitting down. She looked at Luca, whose face was stern. 'You can clear your name.'

He nodded, but he didn't look happy about it. He looked grim.

Max stood up, rising with athletic grace. 'My flight leaves in a couple of hours. I have to go.'

Serena stood up too. 'Thank you so much. This means…a lot.'

Max inclined his head before sending an enigmatic look to his brother. 'I'll be in touch.'

Luca nodded. They didn't embrace or shake hands before Max left, striding out with that same confident grace as his brother.

When he was gone, Serena sank down onto the chair, her head in a spin. She looked at Luca, barely taking in that he looked a little pale, his face all lean lines. 'How…? Why did you ask him to do this?'

He sighed heavily. 'Because I owed it to you to find out the truth. After all, you've been nothing but honest with me. The fact is that I think I suspected you were innocent in the jungle. This just proves that you were as much a victim as I was. You deserve to have your life back, Serena. And you deserve to have the slate cleared too. My lawyers and my PR team will make sure this is in all the papers.'

Serena felt an almost overwhelming surge of emotion to think that Luca was going out of his way to clear her name too. Perhaps now people wouldn't always associate her with feckless debauchery.

Treacherously, this made her hope for too much, even when *The End* was written into every tense line of Luca's body. Clearly he just wanted to move on now.

It made her want to push him away again, for making her feel too much. For making her fall in love. *Damn him*.

'And if Max hadn't found the culprit so easily? Would you have believed me anyway?'

Luca stood up and paced behind his desk, his white shirt pulled across his chest, trousers hugging slim hips. Just like that, heat flared in Serena's solar plexus.

He stopped and looked at her. 'Yes.'

Serena cursed herself for pushing him. She hated

herself for the doubt, for thinking that he was lying. And then she had to concede that Luca *didn't* lie. He was too moral. Too damn good.

She stood up again, her legs wobbly. 'Well, thank you for finding out.'

Luca looked at her for a long moment, and then he said, 'Serena—'

She put up her hand, because she couldn't bear for him to say it. 'Wait. I have something I need to tell you first.'

His mouth closed and he folded his arms across his chest. Serena knew she couldn't be anything else other than completely honest. She had been through too much soul-searching to ever want to hide away from pain again. She might never see him again. The urge to tell him how she felt was rising like an unstoppable wave.

'I've fallen in love with you, Luca.'

He looked at her, and as she watched, the colour leached from his face. She broke apart inside, but was determined not to show it.

'I know it's the last thing you want to hear. We were only ever about...' she stalled '...not *that*...and I know it's over.'

She gestured with a hand to where Max had been sitting.

'After this...we owe each other nothing. And I'm sorry again that your association with me made things bad for you.'

Luca unfolded his arms and slashed a hand in the air, looking angry. 'You don't have to apologise—if I hadn't been so caught up in blaming you, I would have ensured a proper investigation was carried out years ago. You had to suffer the stigma of those accusations too.'

Serena smiled bitterly. 'I was used to it, though. I had no reputation to defend.'

'No—your father took care of that.'

Responsibility weighed heavily on her shoulders. 'I have to go home... I have to tell people about my father—see that he's brought to justice finally.'

'If there's anything you need help with, please let me know.'

Her heart twisted. So polite. So courteous. A million miles from their first meeting in this office. And even though she knew her own family would be there to back her up, she felt an awful quiver of vulnerability—because, really, the only person she wanted by her side the day she faced her father again was Luca.

But that scenario was not to be part of her future.

She hitched up her chin and tried to block out the fact that she'd told Luca she loved him and had received no similar declaration in return. That fantasy belonged deep where she harboured dreams of the kind of fulfilment and happiness she saw her sister experiencing with her family. But at least she could take one good thing with her.

'Are you still going to give me a job?'

'Of course—wherever you want,' Luca said quickly, making another piece of Serena's heart shatter. He was obviously *that* eager to see her go.

'I'd like to go back to Athens today.'

Luca said tightly, 'Laura will arrange it for you.'

'Thank you.'

So clipped, so polite.

Before anger could rise at Luca's non-reaction to her baring her soul to him, she turned to leave.

She was at the door before she heard a broken-sounding, 'Serena...'

Heart thumping, hope spiralling, Serena turned around. Luca looked tortured.

But he said only two words. 'I'm sorry.'

Her heart sank like a stone. She knew he didn't love her, but she marvelled that the human spirit was such an irrepressibly optimistic thing even in the face of certain disappointment.

She forced a smile. 'Don't be. You've given me the gift of discovering how strong I am.'

You've given me the gift of discovering how strong I am.

Luca was stuck in a state of paralysis for so long after Serena left that he had to blink and focus to realise that Laura was in his office and speaking to him, looking worried.

'Senhor Fonseca? Are you all right?'

And as if he'd been holding something at bay, it ripped through him then, stunning and painful in its intensity, like warmth seeping into frozen limbs. Burning.

'No,' he issued curtly, going over to his drinks cabinet and helping himself to a shot of whisky.

When he turned around, Laura's eyes were huge and she was pale. And Luca knew he was coming apart at the seams.

He forced himself not to snarl at the girl, but the pain inside him was almost crippling. 'What is it?'

Laura stuttered, making him feel even worse. 'It's—it's Miss DePiero. I just thought you'd want to know she's on her way to the airport. She's booked first class on a flight to Athens this afternoon.'

'Thank you,' Luca bit out. 'I'm going to be unavailable for the rest of the day. Please cancel all my appointments. Go home early if you want.'

Laura blinked and said faintly, 'Yes, sir.' And then backed away as if he might explode.

He waited until Laura had left and then left himself, knowing nothing more than that he needed to get out—get away. Because he felt like a wounded animal that might lash out and cause serious harm.

He was aware of one or two people approaching him as he walked out of the building, but they quickly diverted when they saw his face. He walked and walked without even knowing where he was going until he realised he was at Ipanema Beach. Where he'd taken Serena just a few days ago.

The scene was the same, even during the week. The beautiful bodies. The amorous couples. The crashing waves. But it mocked him now, for feeling so carefree that day. For believing for a moment that he could be like those people. That he could *feel* like them.

Anger rose up as he ripped off his tie and jacket, dropping them on a bench and sitting down. That was the problem. He knew he couldn't feel. The ability had been cut out of him the day he and his brother had been torn apart.

As young boys they'd been close enough to have a special language that only they understood. It had used to drive their father crazy. And Luca could remember that they'd sensed something was happening that day when their parents had brought them into their father's study.

Luca's mother had bent down to his level and said, with the scent of alcohol on her breath, 'Luca, darling,

I love you so much I want to take you to Italy with me. Will you come?'

He'd looked at Max, standing near his father. Luca had known that Max loved their mother—he had too—but he didn't like it when she came home drunk and falling down. He and Max would fight about it—Max hating it if Luca said anything critical, which he was more liable to do.

He'd looked back at his mother, confused. 'But what about Max? Don't you love him too?'

She'd been impatient. 'Of course I do. But Max will stay here with your father.'

Panic had clutched at his insides, making him feel for a moment as if his bowels might drop out of his body. 'For ever?'

She'd nodded and said, slurring slightly, 'Yes, *caro,* for ever. We don't need them, do we?'

Luca had heard a noise and looked to see Max, ashen, eyes glimmering with tears. 'Mamma…?'

She'd made an irritated sound and said something in rapid Italian, taking Luca by the hand forcibly, as if to drag him out. Luca had felt as if he was in some kind of nightmare. Max had started crying in earnest and had run to their mother, clutching at her waist. That was when Luca had felt some kind of icy calm come over him—as if Max was acting out how he felt deep inside, but he couldn't let it out. It was too huge.

His mother had issued another stream of Italian and let Luca go, shoving him towards his father, prising Max off her and saying angrily, *'Bastante!* Stop snivelling. I'll take you with me instead. After all,' she'd said snidely over Max's hiccups, 'your father doesn't care *who* he gets…'

The black memory faded. His mother had told him she loved him and then minutes later she'd demonstrated how empty her words were. Swapping one brother for the other as if choosing objects in a shop.

Serena had told him she loved him.

As soon as she'd said the words, Luca had been transported back to that room, closing in on himself, waiting for the moment when she'd turn around and show him that she didn't mean it. Not really. She was only saying it because that was what women did, wasn't it? They had no idea of the devastation they could cause when the emptiness of their words was revealed.

But she hadn't looked blasé. Nor as if she hadn't meant it. She'd been pale. Her blue eyes had looked wounded when he'd said, 'I'm sorry.'

He thought of her words: *You've made me see how strong I am.*

Luca felt disgusted. And how strong was *he*? Had he ever gone toe-to-toe with his own demons? No, because he'd told himself building up trust in the Fonseca name again was more important.

He heard a sound and looked up to see a plane lifting into the sky from the airport. He knew it couldn't be her plane, but he had a sudden image of her on it, leaving, and panic gripped him so acutely that he almost called out.

It was as clear as day to him now—what lay between him and his brother. He should have ranted and railed that day when their parents had so cruelly split them up. He should have let it out—not buried it so deep that he'd behaved like a robot since then, afraid to feel anything. Afraid to face the guilt of knowing that he could have done more to protect them both.

If he'd let out the depth of his anger and pain, as Max had, then maybe they wouldn't have been split apart. Two halves of a whole, torn asunder. Maybe their parents would have been forced to acknowledge the shallow depths of their actions, their intent of scoring points off each other.

It all bubbled up now—and also the sick realisation that he was letting it happen all over again. That while he'd had an excuse of sorts before, because he'd only been a child, he was an adult now—and if he couldn't shout and scream for what he wanted then he and Max had been pawns for nothing.

And, worse, he'd face a life devoid of any meaning or any prospect of happiness. Happiness had never concerned him before now. He'd been content to focus on loftier concerns, telling himself it was enough. And it wasn't. Not any more.

Serena stood in line for the gate in the first-class lounge. She was grateful for it, because there was enough space there for her to feel numb and not to have to deal with a crush of people around her.

She couldn't let herself think of Luca, even though her circling thoughts kept coming back to him and that stark look on his face. *I'm sorry.*

She was sorry too. Now she knew how he'd felt when he'd told her that he wished he'd never set eyes on her.

She wanted to feel that way too—she actively encouraged it to come up. But it wouldn't. Because she couldn't regret knowing him. Or loving him. Even if he couldn't love her back.

For a wild moment Serena thought of turning around and going back, telling him she'd settle for whatever he could give her… And then she saw herself in a few years…months…? Her soul shrivelled up from not being loved in return.

The man ahead of her moved forward and the airline steward was reaching for her boarding pass.

She was about to take it back and go through when she heard a sort of commotion, and then a familiar voice shouting, 'I need to see her!'

She whirled around to see Luca being restrained by two staff members a few feet away, dishevelled and wild-looking in shirt and trousers.

'What are you *doing*?' she gasped in shock, stepping out of the way so that people could continue boarding.

She wouldn't let her heart beat fast. She couldn't. It didn't mean anything.

His eyes were fierce. 'Please don't go. I need you to stay.'

A feeling of euphoria mixed with pain surged through her. 'Why do you want me to stay, Luca?'

The men holding him kept a tight grip. Luca didn't even seem to notice, though. He looked feverish, as if he was burning up.

His voice was rough with emotion. 'When you told me you loved me…I couldn't believe it. I was too afraid to believe. My mother said that to me right before she swapped me for my brother…as if we were nothing.'

Serena's belly clenched. 'Oh, Luca…' She looked at the security men, beseeching, 'Please let him go.'

They finally did, but stayed close by, ready to move in again. Serena didn't care. She was oblivious.

He took her hand and held it to his chest, dragging her closer. She could feel his heart thudding against his chest.

'You say you love me…but a part of me can't trust it…can't believe it. I'm terrified that you'll turn around one day and walk away—confirm all my twisted suspicions that when people say they love you, they'll annihilate you anyway.'

Serena felt an incredible welling of love and reached out her other hand to touch Luca's face. She knew he was scared.

'Do you love me?'

After a long moment—long enough for her to see how hard this was for him to admit—he said, 'The thought of you leaving, of life without you…is more than I can bear. If that's love then, yes, I love you more than I've loved anyone else.'

Serena's heart overflowed. 'Are you willing to let me prove how much I love you?'

Luca nodded. 'The pain of letting you go is worse than the pain of facing my own pathetic fears. You've humbled me with your strength and grace.'

She shook her head, tears making her vision blurry. 'They're not pathetic fears, Luca. I'm just as scared as you are.'

He smiled, and it was shaky, all that arrogant bravado replaced by raw emotion. He joked, 'You? Scared? Not possible. You're the bravest person I know. And I have no intention of ever letting you out of my sight again.'

Serena smiled and fought back tears as Luca pulled her in to him and covered her mouth with his, kissing her with unrestrained passion.

When they separated, the crowd around them clapped and cheered. Giddy, Serena blushed and ducked her head against Luca's neck.

He looked at her. 'Will you come home with me?'

Home. Her own place—with him.

The ferocity and speed with which they'd found each other terrified her for a moment. *Could she trust it?* But she saw everything she felt mirrored in Luca's eyes, and she reached out and snatched the dream before it could disappear.

'Yes.'

The next day when Serena woke up she pulled on a big T-shirt and went looking for Luca in his house in Alto Gavea. She still felt a little dizzy from everything that had happened. She and Luca had come back here from the airport, and after making love they'd talked until dawn had broken. He'd promised to go to Athens with her to start the lengthy process of telling her family everything and pursuing her father.

She heard a noise as she passed his study and went in to see him sitting behind his desk in only jeans. Stubbled jaw. He looked up and smiled, and Serena couldn't help smiling back goofily.

He held out a hand. 'Come here.'

She went over and let him catch her, pulling her onto his lap. After some breathless kisses she moved back. 'What are you doing?'

A glint of something came into his eyes and he said, 'Catching up on local news.'

He indicated with his head to the computer and Serena turned to look. When she realised what she was seeing, she tensed in his arms. The internet was filled with photos of them kissing passionately in the airport—obviously taken by people's mobile phones. One headline screamed: *Has Fonseca tamed wild-child DePiero at last*? Another one: *Fonseca and DePiero rekindle their scandalous romance!*

She felt sick and turned to Luca, who was watching her carefully. 'I'm sorry. This is exactly what you were afraid of.'

But he just shrugged, eyes bright and clear. No shadows. 'I couldn't care less what they say. And they have it wrong—you tamed *me*.'

Serena let the past fall away and caressed Luca's jaw, love rising to make her throat tight. 'I love you just as you are.'

Luca said gruffly, 'I want to take you to every beach in South America to watch the sunset—starting with the ones here in Rio.'

Serena felt breathless. 'That could take some time.'

Luca kissed her and said, 'At least a lifetime, I'm hoping.'

He deliberately lifted up her left hand then, and pressed a kiss to her ring finger, a question in his eyes and a new tension in his body. Serena's heart ached that he might still doubt her love.

She nodded her head and said simply, 'Yes. The answer will always be yes, my love.'

Three years later.

The wide-eyed American reporter was standing in front of Rome's supreme court and saying breathlessly, 'This is the trial of the decade—if not the century. Lorenzo DePiero has finally been judged and condemned for his brutality and corruption, but no one could have foreseen the extent to which his own children and his wife suffered. His landmark sentencing will almost certainly guarantee that he lives out the rest of his days in jail.'

The press were still stunned to have discovered that the privileged life they'd assumed the DePiero heiresses to have lived had all been a lie.

Behind the reporter there was a flurry of activity as people streamed out of the majestic building. First was Rocco De Marco, the illegitimate son of Lorenzo DePiero, with his petite red-haired wife Gracie. Quickly on their heels were Siena Xenakis and her husband Andreas.

But the press waited with hushed reverence for the person they wanted to see most: Serena Fonseca. She had taken the stand for four long days in a row and had listed a litany of charges against her father. Not least of which had been the manslaughter of his wife, their mother, witnessed by her when she was just five years old.

If anyone had been in doubt about the reliability of a witness who had been only five at the time, the further evidence of her father's systematic bullying and collusion with a corrupt doctor to get her hooked on medication had killed those doubts.

Her composed beauty had been all the more poignant for the fact that she hadn't let her very advanced pregnancy stop her from taking on such an arduous task: facing down her father every day. But then, everyone agreed that the constant presence by her side of her husband, Luca Fonseca, had undoubtedly given her strength.

They finally emerged now—a striking couple. Luca Fonseca had an arm curved protectively around his wife and the press captured their visible smiles of relief.

Lawyers for the respective parties gave statements as the family got into their various vehicles and were whisked away with a police escort to a secret location, where they were all due to celebrate and unwind after the previous taxing months.

Luca looked at Serena in the back of the Land Rover, their hands entwined. He lifted them up and pressed a kiss to her knuckles. 'Okay?'

Serena smiled. She felt as if a weight had finally been lifted off her shoulders for the first time in her life. She nodded. 'Tired…but happy it's finally done and over.'

Luca pressed a long, lingering kiss to her mouth, but when he pulled back, Serena frowned and looked down. Immediately concerned, Luca said, 'What is it?'

Serena looked at him, a dawning expression of shock and wonder on her face. 'My waters have just broken… all over the back seat.'

The driver's eyes widened in the rearview mirror and he discreetly took out a mobile phone to make a call.

Serena giggled at the comic look of shock and pure fear on Luca's face. He'd been on high alert for weeks now, overreacting to every twinge Serena felt. And then it hit her—along with a very definite cramping of pain.

Her hand tightened on his. 'Oh, my God, we're in labour.'

Luca went into overdrive, instructing the driver to go to the nearest hospital.

Their police escort was already peeling away from the rest of the convoy and the driver reassured him in Italian, 'I'm on it—we'll be there in ten minutes.'

Luca sat back, heart pumping with adrenalin, a huge ball of love and emotion making his chest full. He drank in his beloved wife, her beautiful face, and those eyes that never failed to suck him in and make him feel as if he were drowning.

'I love you,' he whispered huskily, the words flowing easily from his heart.

'I love you too.'

Serena smiled, but it was wobbly. He could see the emotion in her eyes mirrored his own. He spread his hand over her distended belly, hard with their child who was now starting the journey to meet them.

His wife, his family...*his life*. He was enriched beyond anything he might have believed possible.

And eight hours later, when he held his newborn baby daughter in his arms, her tiny face scrunched up and more beautiful than anything he'd ever seen in his life—after his wife—Luca knew that trusting in love was the most amazing revelation of all.

* * * * *

AWAKENED BY HER DESERT CAPTOR

This is for Iona, Heidi, Fiona and Susan...my support network. Love you ladies.

PROLOGUE

THE PRIEST'S EYES widened as he took in the spectacle approaching down the aisle, but to give him his due he didn't falter in his words, which came as automatically to him as breathing.

It was a slim figure, dressed from head to toe in black leather, the face obscured by a motorcycle helmet's visor. The person stopped a few feet behind the couple standing before the priest, and his eyes widened even further as a young woman emerged from under the motorcycle helmet as she took it off and placed it under one arm.

Long red hair cascaded dramatically over her shoulders just as he heard himself say the words, '…or for ever hold your peace…' a little more faintly than usual.

The woman's face was pale, but determined. And also very, very beautiful. Even a priest could appreciate that.

Silence descended, and then her voice rang out loud and clear in the huge church. 'I object to this wedding. Because last night this man shared my bed.'

CHAPTER ONE

Six months previously...

SYLVIE DEVEREUX STEELED herself for what was undoubtedly to be another bruising encounter with her father and stepmother. She reminded herself as she walked up the stately drive that she was only making an appearance for her half-sister's sake. The one person in the world she would do anything for.

Lights spilled from the enormous Richmond house, and soft classic jazz came from the live band in the back garden, where a marquee was just visible. Grant Lewis's midsummer party was an annual fixture on the London social scene, presided over each year by his smiling piranha of a wife, Catherine Lewis—Sylvie's stepmother and mother to her younger half-sister, Sophie.

A shape appeared at the front door and an excited squeal presaged a blur of blonde as Sophie Lewis launched herself at her older sister. Sylvie dropped her bag and clung on, struggling to remain upright, huffing a chuckle into her sister's soft, silky hair.

'I guess that means you're pleased to see me, Soph?'

Sophie, younger by six years, pulled back with a grimace on her pretty face. 'You have *no* idea. Mother is even worse than usual—literally throwing me into the arms of every eligible man—and Father is holed up in his study with some sheikh dude who is probably the grimmest guy I've ever seen, but also the most gorgeous—pity it's wasted on—'

'*There* you are, Sophie—'

The voice broke off as Sylvie's stepmother realised who

her sister's companion was. They were almost at the front door now, and the lights backlit Catherine Lewis's slender Chanel-clad figure and blonde hair, coiffed to within an inch of its life.

Her mouth tightened with distaste. 'Oh, it's you. We didn't think you'd make it.'

You mean you'd hoped I wouldn't make it, Sylvie desisted from saying. She forced a bright smile and pushed down the hurt that had no place here any more. She should be over this by now, at the grand age of twenty-eight. 'Delighted as ever to see you, Catherine.'

Her sister squeezed her arm in silent support. Catherine stepped back minutely, clearly reluctant to admit Sylvie into her own family home. 'Your father is having a meeting with a guest. He should be free shortly.'

Then her stepmother frowned under the bright lights, taking in what Sylvie was wearing. Sylvie felt a fleeting sense of satisfaction at the expected wave of disapproval. But then she also felt incredibly weary...tired of this constant battle she fought.

'You're welcome to change in Sophie's room if you wish. Clearly you've come straight from one of your... er...shows in Paris.'

She had actually. A matinée show. But she'd left work dressed in jeans and a perfectly respectable T-shirt. She'd changed on the train on the way. And suddenly her weariness fled.

She stuck a hand on her hip and cocked it out. 'It was a gift from a fan,' she purred. 'I know how much you like your guests to dress up.'

The dress really belonged to her flatmate, the far more glamorous Giselle, who was a couple of bra sizes smaller than her. Sylvie had borrowed it, knowing full well the effect it would have. She knew it was childish to feel this urge to shock constantly, but right now it was worth it.

Just then there was movement nearby, and Sylvie followed her stepmother's look to see her father standing outside his office, which was just off the main entrance hall. She barely registered him, though. He was with a man—a tall, very broad, very dark man. The most arresting-looking man she'd ever seen. His face was all sculpted lean lines, not a hint of softness anywhere. Dark slashing brows. Grim indeed, if this was who Sophie had been talking about.

Power and charisma was a tangible force around him. And a very sexual magnetism. He was dressed in a light grey three-piece suit. Dark tie. Pristine. The white of his shirt made the darkness of his skin stand out even more. His hair was inky black, and short. His eyes were equally dark, and totally unreadable. She shivered slightly.

The two men were looking at her, and Sylvie didn't even have to see her father's face to know what his expression would be: a mix of old grief, disappointment and wariness.

'Ah, Sylvie, glad you could make it.'

She finally managed to drag her mesmerised gaze from the stranger to look at her father. She forced a bright smile and moved forward. 'Father—good to see you.'

His welcome was only slightly warmer than her stepmother's. A dry kiss on her cheek, avoiding her eyes. Old wounds smarted again, but Sylvie pushed them all down to erect the *don't care* façade she'd honed over years.

She looked up at the man and fluttered her eyelashes, flirting shamelessly. 'And who do we have *here*?'

With evident reluctance, Grant Lewis said, 'I'd like you to meet Arkim Al-Sahid. We're discussing a mutual business venture.'

The name rang a dim bell, but Sylvie couldn't focus on how she knew it. She put out her hand. 'Pleasure, I'm sure. But don't you find discussing business at a party so *dull*?'

She could almost feel the snap of her stepmother's censure from behind her, and heard something that sounded like a strangled snort from her sister. The man's expression had a faint sneer of disapproval now, and suddenly something deep inside Sylvie erupted to life.

It goaded her into moving even closer to the man, when every instinct urged her to turn and run fast. Her hand was still held out and his nostrils flared as he finally deigned to acknowledge her. His much bigger hand swallowed hers, and she was surprised to feel that his skin was slightly calloused as long fingers wrapped around hers.

Everything suddenly became muffled. As if a membrane had been dropped around the two of them. A pulse throbbed violently between her legs and a series of out-of-control reactions gripped her so fast she couldn't make sense of them. Heat, and a weakness in her lower belly and limbs. A melting sensation. An urge to move even closer and wind her arms around his neck, press herself against him, along with that urge to run, which was even stronger now.

Then he broke the connection with an abrupt move, extricating his hand from hers. Sylvie almost stumbled backwards, confused by what had happened. Not liking it at all.

'Pleasure, indeed.'

The man's voice was deep, with a slight American accent, and his tone said that it was anything but a pleasure. The sensual lines of his mouth were flat. That dark gaze glanced over her, dismissing her.

Immediately Sylvie felt cheaper than she'd ever felt in her life. She was very aware of how short her gold dress was—skimming the tops of her thighs. Her light jacket didn't provide much coverage. She was too voluptuous for the dress, and she felt every exposed inch of it now. She was also aware of the fall of her unruly hair, its natural red hue effortlessly loud and attention-seeking.

She made a living from wearing not much at all. And

she'd grown a thick skin to hide her innate shyness. Yet right now this man's dismissal had blasted away that carefully built-up wall. Within mere seconds of meeting him—a total stranger.

Aghast to note that she was feeling a sense of rejection, when she'd developed an inbuilt defence mechanism against ever experiencing it again, Sylvie backed away.

Relief surged through her when her sister appeared, slid an arm through their father's and said with forced brightness, 'Come on, Daddy, your guests will be wondering where you are.'

She watched as her father, stepmother and sister walked off—along with the disturbing stranger who sent her barely a glance of acknowledgement.

On legs that felt absurdly shaky Sylvie finally followed the group outside and determined to stay out of that man's dangerous orbit, sticking close to Sophie and her group of friends.

A few hours later, though, she found herself craving a moment's peace—away from people getting progressively drunker, and away from the censorious gaze of her stepmother and the tension emanating from her father.

She found a quiet spot near the gazebo, where a river ran at the end of the garden. After sitting down on the grass and taking off her shoes she put her feet in the cool rushing water and breathed out a sigh.

It was only after she'd tipped her head back and had been contemplating the full moon, low in the sky, for a few seconds that she felt a nerve-tingling awareness that she wasn't alone.

She looked around just as a tall, dark shape moved in the shadows of a nearby tree. Stifling a scream, Sylvie sat up straight, heart pounding, and asked, 'Who's there?'

The shadow detached itself, revealing the other reason for her need to escape: so she could find an opportunity to dwell on why she'd had such a confusing and forcible reaction to the enigmatic stranger.

'You know exactly who's here,' came the arrogant response.

Sylvie could make out the glitter of those dark eyes. Feeling seriously at a disadvantage, sitting down, she stood again and shoved her feet back into her shoes, her heels sinking into the soft earth, making her wobble.

'How much have you had to drink?' He sounded disgusted.

Anger at the unjust question had Sylvie putting her hands on her hips. 'A magnum of champagne—is that what you expect to hear?'

She'd actually had nothing to drink, because she was still on antibiotics to clear up a nagging out-of-season chest infection. Not that she was about to furnish *him* with that little domestic detail.

'For your information,' she said, 'I came here because I believed I'd be alone. So I'll leave you to your arrogant assumptions and get out of your way.'

Sylvie started to stalk off, only noticing then how close they were—close enough for Arkim Al-Sahid to reach out and touch her. Which was exactly what he did when her heel got caught in the soft earth again and she pitched forward into thin air with a cry of surprise.

He caught her arm in such a firm grip that she went totally off balance and was swung around directly into his chest, landing against him with a soft *oof*. Her first impression was of how hard he was—like a concrete block.

And how tall.

Sylvie forgot why she'd been leaving. 'Tell me,' she asked, more breathily than she would have liked, 'do you hate everyone on sight, or is it just me?'

She could make out the sensual line of his mouth, twisting in the moonlight.

'I know you. I've seen you... Plastered all over Paris on those posters. For months.'

Sylvie frowned. 'That was a year ago—when the new show opened.' *And that wasn't really me.* She'd been chosen for the photo shoot as she was more voluptuous than the other girls...but in truth she was the one who bared the least of all of them.

She knew she should pull back from this man, but she seemed to be unable to drum up the necessary motor skills to do so—and why wasn't he pushing her away? He was obviously one of those puritans who disapproved of women taking their clothes off in the name of entertainment.

His silent condemnation angered her even more.

She arched a brow. 'So that's it? Seeing me in the flesh has only confirmed your worst suspicions?'

She saw how his gaze dropped down between them, to where she could feel her breasts pressed against him. Her skin grew hot all over.

His voice sounded husky. 'Admittedly, there is a lot of flesh to see.' His gaze rose again and bored into hers. 'But then I guess not half as much as is usually on show.'

That ripped away the illusion of any cocoon. Sylvie tugged herself free of his grip and pushed against him to get away. She was too angry, though, not to give him a piece of her mind before she left.

'People like you make me sick. You judge and condemn and you've no idea what you're talking about.'

She took a step back towards him and stuck a finger in his chest, hating how aware she was of his innate masculinity.

'I'll have you know that the L'Amour revue is one of the most upmarket cabaret acts in the world. We are world-class trained dancers. It's not some seedy strip joint.'

His tone was dry. 'Yet you *do* take off your clothes?'

'Well...' The truth was that Sylvie's act didn't actually require her to strip completely. Her breasts were slightly too large, and Pierre preferred the flatter-chested girls to do the full nudity. It provided a better aesthetic, as far as he was concerned.

Arkim Al-Sahid emitted a sound of disgust. Sylvie wasn't sure if it was directed at her or himself.

And then he said, 'I couldn't care less if you stripped naked and hung upside down on a trapeze in your show. This conversation is over.'

Sylvie refrained from pointing out that that was actually Giselle's act, assuming he wouldn't appreciate it.

He'd turned and was stalking away before she could say anything more anyway, and Sylvie bubbled with futile indignation and hurt pride. And something else—something deeper. A need to not have him judge her so out of hand when his opinion shouldn't matter.

She blurted out the words before she could stop herself—an irritating side effect of her red hair: her temper. She hated being a cliché, but sometimes she couldn't help it.

He halted in his tracks, his broad frame silhouetted by the lights of the party and the house in the distance.

Slowly he turned around, incredulity visible on his face.

For a moment Sylvie had to choke back a semi-hysterical giggle, but then he said in an arctic tone, '*What* did you say?' and any urge to giggle died.

She refused to let herself be intimidated and drew back her shoulders. 'I believe I said that you are an arrogant, uptight prat.'

Arkim Al-Sahid prowled back towards her. Deep in the garden as they were, he was like a jungle cat, in spite of his still pristine three-piece suit. All predatory and menacing. There was a thrill in her blood that was extremely inappropriate as she found herself backing away... Until her back slammed into something solid. The gazebo.

He loomed over her now...larger than life. Larger than anyone she'd ever known. He caged her in with his hands either side of her head. Suddenly her heart was racing, her skin prickling with anticipation. His scent was exotic and musky. Full of dark promise and danger and wickedness.

'Are you going to apologise?'

Sylvie shook her head. 'No.'

For a long second he said nothing, and then, almost contemplatively, 'You're right, you know...'

Her breath stopped... Was he *apologising*? 'I am?'

He nodded slowly, and as he did so he lifted a hand and trailed one finger down over Sylvie's cheek and jaw to where the bare skin of her shoulder met her dress.

She was breathing so hard now she felt as if she might hyperventilate. Her skin was on fire where he touched her. *She* was on fire. No man had ever had this effect on her. It was overwhelming, and she was helpless to rationalise it.

'Yes,' he said in a low voice. 'I'm very *uptight*. All over. Maybe you could help me with that?'

Before she could react his arm had snaked around her waist, pulling her into him, and his other hand was deep in her hair, anchoring her head so that he could plunge his mouth down onto hers, stealing what little breath she had left along with her sanity.

It was like going from zero to one hundred in a nanosecond. This was no gentle, exploratory kiss. It was explicit and devastating. Sylvie's tongue was entwined with Arkim Al-Sahid's before the impulse to let him in had even registered. And there wasn't one part of her that rejected him—which was so out of character for her that she couldn't appreciate the significance right now.

Her hands were on his chest, fingers curling into his waistcoat. Then they were climbing higher to curl around his neck, making her reach up on tiptoe to get closer.

Adrenalin and a kind of pleasure she'd never experienced before coursed through her blood. It radiated out from the core of her body and to every extremity, making her tingle and tighten with need.

His hand was on her dress now, at her shoulder, fingers tucking under the fabric, pulling it down.

There was something wild and earthy beating inside her as his mouth left hers and trailed down over her jaw, down to where her shoulder was now bare.

Sylvie's head tipped back, her eyes closed. Her entire world was reduced to this frantic, urgent beat that she had no will to deny as she felt her dress being pulled down, and cool night air drifting over hot skin.

Her head came up. She felt dizzy, drugged. 'Arkim...' She was dimly aware that she didn't even know this man. Yet here she was, entreating him to...to stop? Go on?

When he looked at her, though, those black eyes—like hard diamonds—robbed her of any ability to decide.

'Shh...let me touch you, Sylvie.'

His mouth wrapped around her name...it made her melt even more. His other hand was on her thigh, between them, inching up under her dress, pushing it up. This was more intimate than she'd ever been with any man, because she didn't let many get close, but it felt utterly right. Necessary. As if she'd been missing something her whole life and a key had just been slotted into place, unlocking some part of her.

Tacitly, her legs widened. She saw a glimmer of a smile on Arkim's face and it wasn't cruel, or judgemental. It was *sexy*.

He lowered his head to her now bared breast and closed his mouth over the pouting flesh, sucking her nipple deep and then rolling and flicking it with his tongue. Sylvie nearly shot into orbit. Electric shocks pulsed through her and tugged between her legs, where she was wet and aching...

And where Arkim's fingers were now exploring… Pushing aside her panties and sliding underneath, searching between slick folds and finding where her body gave him access, then thrusting a finger deep inside.

Sylvie's hands tightened, and it was only then that she realised she had them clasped on Arkim's head as his mouth suckled her and his finger moved in and out of her body, making a strange and new tension coil unbearably tight within her. Was this what he'd meant about being uptight? Because she felt it too. Deep in her core. Tightening so much it was almost unbearable.

Overcome with emotion at all the sensations rushing through her, she lifted Arkim's head from her breast, looking into those dark, fathomless eyes. 'I can't… What are you…?'

She couldn't speak. Could only feel. One minute she'd thought he was the devil incarnate, and now…now he was taking her to heaven. She was confused. His whole body was flush against hers, his leg pushing hers apart, his fingers exploring her so intimately…

Frustrated by her lack of ability to say anything, she leant forward and pressed her mouth to his again. But he went still. And then suddenly he was pulling away so fast Sylvie had to stop herself from falling forward. He stood back and looked at her as if she'd grown two heads, his horrified expression clear in the moonlight. His tie was askew and his waistcoat was undone. His hair mussed up. Cheeks flushed.

'What the hell…?'

Sylvie wanted to say, *My thoughts exactly*, but she was still struck mute.

Arkim backed away and said harshly, 'Don't *ever* come near me again.' And then he stalked off, back up the garden and into the light.

Three months ago...

Sylvie couldn't believe she was back at the house in Richmond again so soon. She usually managed to avoid it, because Sophie lived in central London in the family's *pied-à-terre*.

But the *pied-à-terre* wasn't suitable for this occasion: a party to celebrate the announcement of her little sister's engagement...to Arkim Al-Sahid.

Sylvie could still hear the shock in her sister's voice when she'd phoned her a few days ago: *'It's all happened so fast...'*

Nothing would have induced Sylvie to come into the bosom of her family again except for this. No way was she going to let her little sister be a pawn in her stepmother's machinations. Or *that* man's.

The man she'd been avoiding thinking about ever since that night. The man who had at first dismissed her and then... She shivered even now, her skin prickling with awareness at the thought of meeting him again.

The memory of what had happened was as sharp and humiliating as if it had happened yesterday. His voice. The disgust. *'Don't* ever *come near me again.'*

The shrill tones of Sylvie's stepmother hectoring some poor employee nearby stopped her thoughts from devolving rapidly into a kaleidoscope of unwelcome images.

Her hands closed over the rim of the sink in the bathroom as she took in her reflection.

Despite her best efforts she could still remember the excoriating wave of humiliation and exposure when she'd watched Arkim Al-Sahid walk away and realised that her breast was bared and her legs still splayed in wanton abandonment. Panties pulled aside. One shoe on, one off. And she'd been complicit—every step of the way. She couldn't even say he'd used force.

He'd crooked his finger and she'd all but come running. Panting. Practically begging.

The true magnitude of how easily she'd let him—more or less a complete stranger—reduce her to a quivering wreck was utterly galling.

Sylvie cursed herself. She was here for Sophie—not to take a trip down memory lane. She stood up straight and checked her appearance. A far cry from the gold dress she'd worn that night. Now she was positively respectable, in a knee-length black sleeveless shift and matching high heels, her hair pulled back into a low bun. Discreet make-up.

She didn't like to think of the reaction in her body when her sister had informed her of the upcoming nuptials. It had been a mix of shock, incomprehension, anger—and something far more disturbing and dark.

Sylvie made her way into the huge dining room, which had been set up for a buffet-style dinner party. She was acutely aware of Arkim Al-Sahid, looking as grimly gorgeous as ever, and made sure to stay far away from him. It meant, though, that she couldn't get Sophie to herself. And she needed to talk to her.

The evening was interminable. Several times, as Sylvie made mind-numbingly boring small talk, she felt the back of her neck prickle—as if someone was staring at her... or more likely *glaring* at her. But each time she looked around she couldn't see him.

Not seeing her sister anywhere now, Sylvie determined to find her and went looking. The first place she thought to look was in her father's study/library, and she opened the door carefully, seeing nothing inside the oak-panelled room filled with heaving shelves of books but the fire, which was dying down low.

The warmth and peace called to her for a minute, and she slipped in and closed the door behind her.

Then she saw a movement coming from one of the high-backed chairs near the fire. 'Soph? Is that you?' The room had always been her little sister's favourite hiding place when she was younger, and Sylvie felt a lurch near her heart to think of her sister retreating here.

But it wasn't Sophie—which became apparent all too quickly when a tall, dark shape uncoiled from the chair to stand up.

Arkim Al-Sahid.

Instinctively Sylvie backed away, and said frigidly, 'At the risk of being accused of following you I can assure you I wasn't.' She turned to go, then stopped and turned back. 'Actually, I have something to say to you.'

He folded his arms. 'Do you, now?'

He was as implacable as a stone pillar. It infuriated Sylvie that he could so effortlessly arouse seething emotions within her. She stalked over to the chairs and gripped the back of the one he'd been sitting in. She hated it that he looked even more enigmatic and handsome. As if the intervening months had added more hard muscle to his form. Made his features even more saturnine.

He was dressed in similar pristine fashion to last time—in a three-piece suit. He sent a dismissive look up and down her body, and then said with a faint sneer, 'Who are you trying to fool? Or are we all going to be treated to an exclusive performance, in which you reveal the truth of what lies beneath your pseudo-respectable façade?'

Sylvie's anger spiked in a hot rush. 'At first I couldn't understand why you hated me on sight, but now I know. Your father is one of America's biggest porn barons, and you've made no secret of the fact that you disowned him *and* his legacy to forge your own. You don't even share his name any more.'

Arkim Al-Sahid's body vibrated with tension, his dark eyes narrowing on her dangerously. 'As you said, it's no secret.'

'No...' Sylvie conceded, slightly thrown off balance by his response.

'And your point?'

She swallowed. Lord, but he was intimidating. Not a hint of humanity anywhere in his whipcord form or on that beautiful face.

'You're marrying my sister purely to gain social acceptance, and she deserves more than that. She deserves love.'

Arkim emitted a short, curt laugh. It was so shocking to see his face transformed by a smile—albeit a mocking one—that she almost lost her train of thought.

'You're for real? Since when does anyone marry for *love*? Your sister has a lot to gain from this union—not least a lifetime of security and status. At no point has she indicated that she's not happy for this engagement to proceed. Your father is keen to secure her future—which is no surprise, considering how his eldest daughter turned out.'

Sylvie kept her expression rigid. Amazing how this man's opinion sneaked under her guard with such devastating effect and struck far too close to the heart of her—which was the last place he should be impacting.

He continued. 'I'm not stupid, Miss Devereux. This is as much a business transaction for him as it is a chance to secure his daughter's future. It's not a secret that his empire took a big hit during the downturn and that he's doing all he can to bolster his coffers again.'

Business transaction. She felt nauseous. Sylvie knew vaguely that her father's fortune had taken a dip...but she also knew perfectly well that her stepmother was the real architect behind this plan. She was a firm believer that a woman's place was by her rich husband's side, and no doubt had convinced Grant Lewis that this was their ticket to security for the future.

She ungritted her teeth and desisted from belabouring the point of whether or not love existed. Clearly in his world it didn't.

'Sophie's not right for you—and you are certainly not right for *her*.'

An assessing look came over that starkly handsome face. 'She's perfect for me. Young, beautiful, intelligent. Accomplished.' He looked her up and down. 'And above all she's refined.'

Sylvie held up a hand, hating it that that stung. 'Please—save your insults. I'm perfectly aware where I come on your scale of condemnation. Clearly you have issues with certain industries, and you've deemed me worth judging on the basis of what I do.'

'What you *are*,' he said harshly.

Her hands clenched into fists. 'You didn't seem to have much of an issue with what I *am* the last time we met.'

His face flushed dark red and Sylvie felt the bite of his self-condemnation as sharply as if he'd just slapped her.

'That was a mistake—not to be repeated.'

Something about that lash of recrimination made her want to curl up and protect herself. The look on his face was pure...disgust. And it would have been worse if it was solely for her. But she could tell it wasn't. It was for himself.

Hurt lodged deep in her belly like a dark, malevolent thing, tugging on other hurts, reopening old wounds. Reminding her of the disgust on her father's face when he'd looked at her after her mother had died...

She desperately wanted to lash back and see this man's icy condemnatory control snap. Acting on blind instinct, and on that hurt, she stepped out from behind the chair and right up to Arkim Al-Sahid. She pressed her body to his, lifting her arms to wind them around his neck.

His nostrils flared and those black eyes flashed. His hands were on her arms, his grip tight. 'What the hell do you think you're doing?'

But he didn't pull her arms down. Sylvie's entire body was quivering with adrenalin at her bravado.

'I'm proving that you're a hypocrite, Mr Al-Sahid.'

And then, in the boldest move she'd ever made in her life, she reached up and pressed her mouth to his. She moved her lips over his and through the frantic thumping of her heart she could feel excitement flooding her at the sheer proximity of their bodies. Brain cells were scrambled in a rush of heat.

She could feel the tension holding his body rigid... But what he couldn't disguise was the explicit thrust of his arousal against her belly. That evidence was enough to send a thrill of exultation through Sylvie and help her block out the memory of how he'd pushed her away the last time.

Except then she started to forget why she'd even started this. Her body moved against him, closer. Arms locked tighter. And after a heart-stopping infinitesimal moment his hands loosened from her arms and slid down the length of her torso to her hips, gripping her there as his mouth started to move on hers—slowly at first and then, like a storm gathering strength, with an almost rough intensity.

For a long moment everything faded into the distance as the kiss became hotter and more intense. Arkim Al-Sahid's hands pulled Sylvie even closer—so close that she could feel his heart beating. And then something shifted. He went very still, before abruptly breaking the kiss.

Sylvie was left grasping air when he thrust her away from him. She stumbled backwards and found herself landing heavily in the chair behind her, her breathing laboured, her heart out of control. Dizzy.

Arkim's mouth twisted and his voice was rough. '*No. I will not do this.* You *dare* to try and seduce me on the evening of the announcement of my engagement to your sister? Is there no depth to which you won't descend?'

Sylvie was going cold all over. The lust which had risen up like wildfire dissipated under his murderous gaze. Her brain felt woolly...it was hard to think. Why had it been so important to kiss him like that? What had she been trying to prove? How did this man have the ability to make her act so out of character?

She looked up at him. 'It wasn't like that. I'd never do anything to hurt Sophie.'

Arkim made a rude sound just as a knock sounded at the door and it was opened.

Sylvie heard a voice say, 'Sorry to disturb you, Mr Al-Sahid, but they're ready to make the announcement.'

Sylvie realised that whoever was at the door wouldn't be able to see her in the chair just as Arkim Al-Sahid answered with a curt, 'I'll be right there.' The door closed again and he looked down at her, black eyes glittering with disgust and condemnation. 'I think it would be best for all of us if you left now, don't you?'

CHAPTER TWO

Present day—a week after the ruined wedding...

ARKIM AL-SAHID LOOKED out over the view from his palatial office and apartment complex, high in the London skyline. And even though the past week had brought to life a lot of his worst nightmares all he could think about right at that moment was of how he'd only met Sylvie Devereux twice in the past six months—three times if you counted her memorable appearance in the church—and yet each time he'd let his legendary control slip.

And now he was paying for it. More than he'd ever thought possible.

Anger was a constant unquenchable fire within him. He was paying for the fact that she was a privileged spoilt brat, who didn't take rejection well. Who had acted out of her poisonous jealousy of her younger sister to ruin their wedding.

Yet his conscience pricked him. It had been *him* who had fallen for her all too obvious charms. He'd had to fight it from the moment he'd laid eyes on her, when she'd stood in the reception hall of her father's house with her hand on her hip, her beautiful body flaunted to every best advantage.

He could still see her eyes landing on him, widening, the familiar glitter of feminine awareness, the scenting of his power. Sensing a conquest. And then she'd sashayed over as if she owned the world. As if she could own him with a mere flutter of her eyelids. And, dammit, he had almost fallen right then—as soon he'd seen those amazing eyes up close.

One blue and the other green and blue.

An intriguing genetic anomaly in a perfect face—high cheekbones, patrician nose and a mouth so lush it could incite a man to sin.

His body had come to hot, pulsing life under that knowing feline gaze, showing him that any illusion that he mastered his own impulses was just that: a flimsy illusion.

His mouth compressed now as he stared unseeingly out of the window, as if he could try to compress the memories.

The full repercussions of his weakness sat like lead in his belly. The marriage to Sophie Lewis was off. And Arkim's very substantial investment in Grant Lewis's extensive industrial portfolio was teetering on the brink of collapse. Losing the deal wouldn't put much of a dent into Arkim's finances, but the subsequent loss of professional standing *would*.

He was back to square one. Having to prove himself all over again. His team had been fielding calls from clients all week, expressing doubts and fears that Arkim's solid business reputation was as shaky as his personal life. Stocks and shares were in freefall.

The tabloids had salivated over the story, featuring a caricaturised cast of characters: the stoical and long-suffering father; the scandalous daughter bent on revenge borne out of jealousy; the sweet innocent bride—the victim—and the ruthless social-climbing mother.

And Arkim—son of one of the world's richest men, who was also one of its most infamous, dominating the world's porn industry.

Saul Marks lived a life of excess in Los Angeles, and Arkim hadn't seen him since he was seventeen. He'd made a vow a long time ago to crawl out from under his father's shameful reputation, even going so far as to change his name legally as soon as he'd been able to—choosing a name that had belonged to a distant ancestor of his mother's as he hadn't thought her present-day immediate family would appreciate their bastard relative making a claim on their name.

Arkim's mother had come from a wealthy and high-born family in the Arabian country of Al-Omar. She'd been studying in the States at university when she'd met and been seduced by Saul Marks. Naive and innocent, she'd been bowled over by the handsome charismatic American.

When she'd become pregnant, however, Marks had already moved on to his next girlfriend. He'd supported Arkim's mother, but wanted nothing to do with her or the baby…until she'd died in childbirth and he'd been forced to take his baby son into his care after Zara's family in Al-Omar had expressed no interest in their deceased daughter's son.

Arkim's early life had been a constant round of English boarding schools and impersonal nannies, interspersed with time spent with a reluctant father and his dizzying conveyer belt of lovers, who invariably came from the porn industry. One of whom had taken an unhealthy interest in Arkim and given him an important life lesson in how vital it was to master self-control.

But a week ago, when the society wedding of the decade had imploded in scandalous fashion, all those ambitions and his efforts to distance himself from shame and scandal had turned to dust.

And all because of a red-haired witch.

A witch who had somehow managed to sneak under his impenetrable guard. It was galling to recall how hard it had been to let her go that night in the study. How hard *he'd* been. From the moment he'd first seen her appear. Looking like a schoolteacher. With her hair pulled back, her face pale. Covered up.

He'd only come to his senses because there had been

something in the way she'd kissed him—something he hadn't believed... Something innocent. Gauche. But it was a lie—as if she'd been trying to figure out what he liked. Acting sweet and innocent after she'd just been completely brazen. Attempting to seduce him away from her sister.

The only thing that had got Arkim through the past week of ignominy and public embarrassment had been the prospect of making Sylvie Devereux pay. And the kind of payment he had in mind would finally exorcise her from his head, and his body, once and for all.

For months she'd inhabited the dark, secret corners of his mind and his imagination. She'd been the cause of sleepless nights and lurid dreams. Even during his engagement to her far sweeter and infinitely more innocent sister.

Apart from the injury Sylvie had caused to Arkim with her selfish behaviour, she'd also recklessly played with her sister's life. The young woman had been inconsolable, absolutely adamant that she wouldn't give Arkim another chance. And could he blame her? Who would believe the son of a man who lived his life as if it was a bacchanal?

The words Sylvie Devereux had said in the church still rang in his head: *'This man shared my bed.'* And yet even now his body reacted to those words with a surge of frustration. Because she most certainly had *not* shared his bed. It had been a bare-faced lie. Conjured up to create maximum damage.

Sylvie Devereux wanted him so badly? Well, then, she'd have him—until he was sated and he could throw her back in the trash, where she belonged.

But it would be on *his* terms, and far out of the reach of the ravenous public's gaze. The damage to his reputation stopped right here.

Sylvie looked out of the small private plane's window to see a vast sea of sand below her, and in the distance, shimmering in a heat haze, a steel city that might have come directly from a futuristic movie.

The desert sands of Al-Omar and its capital city, B'harani.

Some called it the jewel of the Middle East. It was one of its most progressive countries, presided over by a very dynamic and modern royal couple. Sylvie had just been reading an article about them in the in-flight magazine: Sultan Sadiq and his wife Queen Samia, and their two small cherubic children.

Queen Samia was younger than Sylvie, and she'd felt a little jaded, looking at the beaming smile on the woman's face. She was pretty, more than beautiful, and yet her husband looked at her as if he'd never seen a woman before.

She'd seen her father look at her mother like that.

Sylvie ruthlessly crushed the small secret part of her that clenched with an ominous yearning. The cynicism she'd honed over years came to the fore. Sultan Sadiq might well be reformed now, but she could remember when he'd been a regular visitor to the infamous L'Amour revue and had cut a swathe through some of its top-billed stars.

Not Sylvie, though. Once she was offstage and dressed down, with her hair tied back, she slipped unnoticed past all her far more glamorous peers. She courted endless teasing from the other girls—and from the guys, who were mostly gay—having earned the moniker of 'Sister Sylvie', because of the way she would prefer to go home and curl up with a book or cook a meal rather than head out to party with their inevitably rich and gorgeous clientele. A clientele that appreciated the very discreet ethos of the revue *and* any liaisons that ensued out of hours.

But even they—her friends, who were more like her family now—didn't know the full extent of her duality... how far from her stage persona she really was.

'Miss Devereux? We'll be landing shortly.'

Sylvie looked up at the beautiful olive-skinned stewardess, with her dark brown eyes and glossy black hair. She forced a smile, suddenly reminded of someone with similar colouring. Someone infinitely more masculine, though, and more dangerous than this courteous flight attendant.

That fateful day almost two weeks ago rushed back with a garish vividness that took her breath away. Reminding her painfully of the searing public scrutiny, judgement and humiliation. And *his* face. So dark and unforgiving. Those black eyes scorching the skin from her body.

He'd moved towards her, his anger palpable. But her stepmother had reached her first, slapping Sylvie so hard that her teeth had rattled in her head and the corner of her lip had split. It was still tender when she touched her tongue to it now.

And then she saw in her mind's eye her sister's face. Pale and tear-streaked. Eyes huge. Shocked. *Relieved*. That relief had made it all worthwhile. Sylvie didn't regret what she'd done for a second. Sophie hadn't been right for Arkim Al-Sahid.

Her feeling of vindication had been fleeting, though. The truth was, when she'd stood behind them in that church her motivation for stopping the wedding had felt far more complex than it should have.

Arkim was the only man who'd managed to breach the defences Sylvie hadn't even been aware she'd erected so high. She'd bared herself to him in a way she'd never done with anyone else—which was ironic, considering her profession—only to be cruelly pushed aside...as if she was a piece of dirt on his shoe. Not worthy to look him in the eye.

But her sister *was* worthy. Her beautiful blonde, sweet sister. Just as Sophie was worthy of their father's affections. Because *she* didn't remind him of his beloved dead first wife.

Maybe it was this stark landscape that was making her think about all of that—and *him*. Forcing him up into her consciousness. She buckled her seat belt, diverting her mind away from painful memories and towards what lay ahead. The problem was that she wasn't even entirely sure what lay ahead.

She and some of the other girls from the revue had been invited over to put on a private show for an important sheikh's birthday celebrations. Sylvie wasn't flying with the others because they'd travelled before her. She'd only been asked to join them afterwards—hence her solo trip on the private jet.

It wasn't unusual for this kind of thing to happen. Their revue had performed privately for A-list stars around the world, much as a pop star might be asked to perform, and they'd done a residency one summer in Las Vegas. But this… Something about this made Sylvie's skin prickle uncomfortably.

She tried to reassure herself that she was being silly. The other girls would be waiting for her, they'd rehearse and perform, and then they'd be home before they knew it.

They were landing now, and she noticed that they were quite far outside the city limits, with nothing but desert as far as the eye could see. The airport didn't look like a busy capital city's airport. Just a few small buildings and a runway carved into the arid landscape. She pushed the nervous flutters down.

Once the small jet had taxied to a gentle stop Sylvie was escorted to the door of the plane—and the heat of the desert hit her so squarely that she had to suck in a breath of hot, dry air. Sweat instantly dampened the skin all over her body. But along with the trepidation she felt at what lay ahead was a quickening of something like exhilaration as she took in the clear blue vastness of the sky and the rolling dunes in the distance.

She was so far away from everything that was familiar in this completely alien landscape, but it soothed her a little after the last tumultuous couple of weeks. It was as if nothing here could hurt her.

'Miss, your car is waiting.'

Sylvie looked down to see a sleek black car. She put on her sunglasses and went down the steps and across the scorching runway to where a driver was holding the back door open. He was dressed in a long cream tunic, with close-fitting trousers underneath and a turban on his head. He looked smart and cool, and she felt ridiculously underdressed in her jeans, ballet flats and loose T-shirt. Like a gauche westerner.

Someone was putting her cases into the boot, and Sylvie smiled as the driver bowed deferentially, indicating for her to get in.

She did so—with relief. Already craving the cool balm of air-conditioning. Already wanting to twist her long, heavy hair up and off her neck.

The door was closed quickly behind her and then a lot of things seemed to happen simultaneously: she heard the snick of the door locking, the driver slid into the front seat and the privacy partition slid up, and Sylvie realised that she wasn't alone in the back of the car.

'I trust you had a pleasant flight?'

The voice was deep, cool—and instantly, painfully, recognisable. Sylvie turned her head and everything seemed to go into slow motion.

Arkim Al-Sahid was sitting at the far side of the luxurious car, which was now moving. A fact she was only vaguely aware of. She went hot and cold all at once. Her belly dropped near her feet. Her breath was caught in her chest. Shock was seizing at her ability to respond.

He was dressed in his signature three-piece suit. As if they were in Paris or London. En route to some civilised place. Not here, in the middle of a harsh sun-beaten land. Here in the middle of nowhere. Here where she'd just thought nothing could touch her.

Arkim Al-Sahid looked so dark, and his face was etched in lines of cruelty.

A small voice jeered at Sylvie, *Did you really think he would do nothing?* And underneath the shock was the pounding of her heart that told her that perhaps, in some very deep and hidden secret space, she *hadn't* thought he would do nothing. But she'd never expected this...

He reached forward and her sunglasses were plucked off her face and tucked away into his pocket before she could react. She blinked, and he came into sharp, clear focus. Dark hair brushed back from a high forehead. Deep-set eyes over sharp cheekbones. His patrician nose giving him a slightly hawk-like aspect.

And that mouth... That cruel and taunting mouth. The mouth that even now she could recall being on hers. Hard and demanding, sending her senses into overdrive. It was curved up into the semblance of a smile, but it was a smile unlike anything Sylvie had ever seen. It was a smile that promised retribution.

When she remained mute with shock, one dark brow arched up lazily. 'Well, Sylvie? I'll be exceedingly disappointed over the next two weeks if you've lost the ability to do anything with your tongue.'

Arkim tried to ignore the frantic rate of his pulse, which had burst to life as soon as he'd seen her distinctive shape appear in the doorway of the plane. Slim, yet womanly. Even in casual clothes.

Her glorious red hair glowed like the setting sun over the Arabian sea. Her face was as pale as alabaster, her skin perfect and flawless. Her eyes were huge and almond-shaped, giving her that feline quality, her left eye with that distinctive discolouration. It did nothing to diminish her appeal—it only enhanced it.

Irritation rose at her effortless ability to control his libido.

Arkim was about to say something else when she got out a little threadily, 'Where are the other girls?'

He felt a twinge of guilt, but pushed it down deep. He glanced briefly at his watch. 'They're most likely performing, as arranged, for the birthday celebrations of one of the Sultan's chief advisors—Sheikh Abdel Al-Hani. They'll be on a plane first thing tomorrow morning.'

If possible, Sylvie paled even more. It sent a jolt of something horribly like concern through him, reminding him of when her stepmother had slapped her in the church and how his first instinctive reaction had been to put himself between them. *Not* something he relished remembering now.

But now the shocked glaze was leaving her face, colour was surging back into her cheeks and her eyes were sparking. 'So why am I not there too? What the hell *is* this, Arkim?'

Nurturing the sense of satisfaction at having Sylvie where he wanted her, rather than his other more tangled emotions, Arkim settled back into his seat. 'Believe it or not, people here call me Sheikh too—a title conferred upon me by the Sultan himself...an old schoolfriend. But I digress. This is about payback. It's about the fact that your jealous little tantrum had far-reaching consequences and you aren't going to get away with it.'

Sylvie put out a hand and Arkim noticed it was trembling slightly. He ruthlessly pushed down his concern. Again. This woman didn't deserve anything but his scorn.

'So...what? You're kidnapping me?'

Arkim picked a piece of lint off his jacket and then looked at her. 'I'd call it a...a *holiday*. You came here of

your own free will and you're free to go at any time…
It's just not going to be that easy for you to leave when
there's no public transport and no mobile phone coverage,
so I'm afraid you'll have to wait until I'm leaving too. In
two weeks.'

Sylvie clenched her hands into fists on her lap, her jaw
tight. 'I'll damn well walk across the desert if I have to.'

Arkim was calm. 'Try it and you'll be lucky to last
twenty-four hours. It's certain death for anyone who
doesn't know the lie of this land—not to mention the fact
that someone as fair as you would fry to a crisp.'

Sylvie was reeling, and trying hard not to show it. She
felt as if she'd fallen through a wormhole and everything
was upside down and inside out. Panic tightened her gut.

'What about my job? I'm expected back—it was only
supposed to be a one-night event.'

Arkim's face was scarily expressionless. It made her
want to reach across and slap him, to see some kind of
reaction.

'Your job is unaffected. Your boss has been recompensed very generously for the use of your time. So much
so, in fact, that I believe he can finally start the renovations he's been wanting to do for years. As a result of my
generous donation the revue is actually closing for a month
from next week, while they do the work.'

She had to choke back a lurch of even greater panic;
it was common knowledge how much Pierre wanted to
renovate—he'd been begging for loans from banks for
months. And this would be perfect timing…before the
high tourist season.

She spluttered. 'Pierre would never let one of his girls
go off on an assignment alone. He'll raise hell when I don't
return, no matter how much you've offered him!'

Arkim smiled, and it was cold. 'Pierre is like anyone
else in this world—mesmerised when large sums of money

are mentioned. He's been assured that your services are required as dance teacher to one of the Sheikh's daughters and her friends, who want to learn the western way of dancing. The fact that you're here with me instead is something he doesn't need to be aware of.'

Sylvie folded her arms, trying to not let on how scared she was. She injected mockery into her voice. 'I'm surprised. I would have thought your morals wouldn't allow you to come within ten feet of me—much less arrange a private performance.'

Arkim was no longer smiling. 'I'm prepared to risk a little moral corruption for what I want—and I want you.'

She sucked in a breath at hearing him declare it so baldly. 'I should have known you'd have no scruples. So you've effectively *bought* me? Like some kind of call girl?'

Arkim's mouth curled up into that cruel smile again. 'Come now...we both know that that's not so far from the truth of what you are.'

This time Sylvie couldn't hold back. She was across the seat and launching herself at Arkim, hand outstretched, ready to strike, when he caught her wrists in his hands. They were like steel manacles, and she fell heavily against his body.

Instantly awareness sparked to life, infusing her veins with heat and electricity. Even now, when she was in the grip of panic and anger.

'Let me *go*.'

Arkim's jaw was like granite, and this close she could see the depths of anger banked deep in his eyes. He was livid. She felt a quiver of real fear—even though, perversely, she knew he wouldn't hurt her physically.

'No way. We have unfinished business and we're not leaving this place until it's done.'

Sylvie was excruciatingly aware of her body, pressed to Arkim's much harder and more powerful one. Of the way her breasts were crushed against him, as they'd been crushed against him once before…when he'd thrust her back from him and looked at her as if she'd given him a contagious disease.

'What are you talking about?' she asked, hating the tremor in her voice.

The expression in his eyes changed for the first time, flashing with a heat that Sylvie felt deep in her belly.

'What I'm talking about is the fact that I'm going to have you—over and over again—for however long it takes until I can think straight again.' A note of unmistakable bitterness entered his voice. 'You've done it, Sylvie—you've got me.'

She finally broke free from Arkim's grip and sat back, as far away as she could. 'I don't want you.' *Liar*, whispered an inner voice. She ignored it. She hated Arkim Al-Sahid. 'As soon as this car stops I'm out of here, and you can't stop me.'

Arkim merely looked amused. 'Each time we've met you've demonstrated how much you want me, so protesting otherwise won't work now. Where we're going has no public transport, and it would take you about a week to walk to B'harani—days in any other direction before you hit civilisation.'

Sylvie crossed her arms over her chest, a feeling of claustrophobia threatening to strangle her. 'This is ridiculous.' The thought of being alone with this man in some remote desert for the next two weeks was overwhelming. 'You can't force me to do anything I don't want to do, you know.'

He looked at her, and there was something so explicit in his gaze that she felt herself blushing.

'I won't need to use force, Sylvie.'

And just like that the humiliation she'd felt that night in the study of her father's house came back and rolled over her like a wave.

She fought it. 'This just proves how little you really felt for my sister. Hurting me will only hurt *her*.'

The expression on Arkim's face became incredulous at the mention of Sophie 'You *dare* speak to me of hurting your sister? When *you* were the one who callously humiliated her in public?'

Words of defence trembled on Sylvie's tongue, but she bit them back. She would never betray her sister's confidence. Sophie had just been a pawn to him. It never would have worked. She had to remember that. She'd done the right thing.

But then she saw something in the distance and became distracted.

Arkim followed her gaze and said, 'Ah, we're here.'

Here was another, even smaller airfield, with a sleek black helicopter standing ready.

Slightly hysterically Sylvie remembered something she'd learnt when she'd taken self-defence classes after a—luckily—minor mugging in Paris. The tutor had told the class the importance of not letting an attacker take you to another location at all costs. Because if he did get you to another place, then your chances of survival were dramatically cut down.

It would appear to be common sense, but the tutor had told them numerous stories of people who had been so frightened they'd just let themselves be taken to another place, when they should always have tried to get away during the initial attack.

And okay, so technically Arkim wasn't attacking Sylvie, but she knew that if she got into that helicopter her chances of emerging from this encounter unscathed were nil.

The car came to a stop and he looked at her. 'Time to go.'

Sylvie shook her head. 'I'm not getting out. I'm staying in this car and it's going to take me back to wherever we landed. Or to B'harani. I hear it's a nice city—I'd like to visit.'

She hoped the desperation she was feeling wasn't evident.

He turned to face her more fully. 'This car is driven by a man who speaks only one language, and it's not yours. He answers to me—no one else.'

The sheer hardness of Arkim's expression told her she was on a hiding to nothing. A sense of futility washed over her. She wouldn't win this round.

'Where is it that you're proposing to take me?'

'It's a house I own on the Arabian coast. North of B'harani and one hundred miles from the border of Burquat. Merkazad is in a westerly direction, about six hundred miles.'

The geographical details somehow made Sylvie feel calmer, even though she still had no real clue where they were. She'd heard of these places, but never been.

Something occurred to her. 'This...' her mouth twisted '...this fee you've paid Pierre. I assume it's conditional on my agreeing to this farcical non-existent dance tuition?'

Arkim nodded. 'That's good business sense, I think you'll agree.'

Sylvie wanted to tell him where he could stick his business sense, but she refrained. She didn't doubt that there really was no option but to go with Arkim. For now.

'Once we're at this...this place, you won't force me to do anything I don't want to?'

Arkim shook his head, eyes gleaming with a disturbing light. 'No, Sylvie. There will be no force involved. I'm not into sadism.'

His smug arrogance made her want to try and slap him again. Instead, she sent him a wide, sunny, smile. 'You know, work has been so crazy busy lately I'm actually looking forward to an all-expenses-paid break. The fact that I have to share space with *you* is unfortunate, but I'm sure we can stay out of each other's way.'

Arkim just smiled slowly, and with an air of sensual menace, as if he knew just how flimsy her bravado was.

'We'll see.'

Sylvie had never been in a helicopter before, and she'd been more mesmerised than she cared to admit by the way the desert dunes had unfolded beneath them, undulating into the distance like the sinuous curves of a body. It all seemed utterly foreign and yet captivating to her.

Her stomach was only just beginning to climb back down from her throat when she heard a deep voice in her ear through the headphones.

'That's my house, Al-Hibiz, directly down and to your left.'

Sylvie looked down and her breath was taken away. *House?* This was no house. It looked like a small but formidable castle, complete with ramparts and flat roofs. It was distinctly Arabic in style, with ochre-coloured walls. Within those walls she could see lush gardens, and in the distance the Arabian sea sparkled. What looked like an oasis lay far off in the distance, a spot of deep green. It was like something out of a fairytale.

It distracted her from the shock she still felt after realising that Arkim was co-piloting the helicopter, and the way his hands had lingered as he'd strapped her in, those fingers resting far too close to her breasts under her thin T-shirt.

He should have looked ridiculous, getting into the cockpit still dressed in his suit, against the backdrop of the stark desert, but he hadn't. He'd looked completely at home, powerful and utterly in control.

And now the helicopter was descending onto a flat area

just outside the walls of the castle, which looked much bigger from this vantage point.

Sylvie could see robed men waiting, holding on to their long garments and the turbans on their heads as the helicopter kicked up sand and wind. When the craft bounced gently onto the earth she breathed out a deep sigh of relief, unaware of how tense she'd been.

The helicopter blades stopped turning and a delicious silence settled over them for a moment, before Arkim got out and the men approached. She watched as he greeted the men heartily in a guttural language that still managed to sound melodic, a wide smile on his face.

It took her breath away. It was the first genuine smile she'd ever seen on his face. Admittedly their previous encounters hadn't exactly been conducive to such a reaction. Not unless she counted that sexy smile when his hand had explored between her legs—

'Time to get out, Sylvie. I'm afraid the chopper has to go back and you're not going to be in it.'

She scowled, hating to be caught out in such a memory. She fumbled with the seat belt and swatted his hand away when he would have helped. Eventually it came undone and she extricated her arms, unaware of how the movement pulled her T-shirt taut over her breasts, or of how Arkim's dark gaze settled there for a moment with a flash of hunger. If she'd seen that she might well have barricaded herself into the helicopter, come hell or high water.

But then she was out, and swaying a little unsteadily on the firm sun-baked ground.

Staff dressed in white rushed to and fro, loading luggage into the back of a small people carrier, and then Arkim was leading Sylvie over to what looked like a luxurious golf buggy. He indicated for her to get in, and after a moment's futile rebellion she did so.

She really was stuck here now—with him.

He got in beside her and drove the small open-sided vehicle to the entrance of the castle, where huge wooden doors were standing open. They entered a beautiful airy courtyard, with a fountain in the centre. A deliciously cool gentle mist of moisture settled on her skin from the spray.

But the vehicle had stopped now, and Arkim was at her side, holding out a hand. Sylvie ignored it and stepped out, not wanting to see what would undoubtedly be a mocking look on his face.

When he didn't move, though, she had to look at him. He gestured with a hand and—damn him—a mocking smile.

'Welcome to my home, Sylvie. I expect our time here to be…cathartic.'

CHAPTER THREE

SYLVIE PACED BACK and forth in the rooms she'd been shown to by Arkim. *Cathartic! The arrogant, patronising son-of-a—*

A knock sounded on the door and she halted, her breathing erratic. Her hands balled into fists at her sides—she wasn't ready to see Arkim again.

Cautiously she approached the ornately decorated door and opened it, ready to do battle, only to find two pretty, smiling women on the other side. They had her two wheelie suitcases. One filled with now redundant dance costumes, the other with her own clothes.

She forced a smile and stood back. They entered meekly and she observed their pristine white dresses. Like long tunics. They wore white head coverings too, but not veils obscuring their faces. They looked cool and fresh, and Sylvie felt sticky and gritty after the tumultuous day.

As they were leaving again one of the girls stopped and said shyly, 'I'm Halima. If you need anything just pick up the phone and I will come to you.'

She ducked her head and then was gone, leaving Sylvie feeling a little slack-jawed. She had her own *maid*?

Arkim had left her here with a curt instruction to rest and said that he'd let her know when dinner would be ready. Sylvie could see the sky outside turning blood-red from the setting sun, and for the first time took in the sheer opulence of the rooms.

She was in a reception area that would have housed her small Parisian apartment three times over. It was a huge octagonal space, with a small pond in the centre with a tiled bottom and sides, where exotic fish swam lazily.

There were eight rooms off this main area. Two guest bedrooms, a dining room, and a living room complete with state-of-the-art sound system and media centre which had had all channels available when Sylvie had flicked it on.

The decor throughout was subtle and understated. The stone walls of the castle had been left exposed. and modern artwork and an eclectic mix of antiques enhanced the rather austere ancient building. Huge oriental rugs adorned the floors, softening any sharp edges further. The windows were all open to the elements, and even though it was sweltering outside, the castle had been designed so that balmy breezes wafted through the open rooms.

There was also a gym, and an accompanying thermal suite with hot-tub and sauna/steam room. And then there was the main bedroom suite, dressed in tones of dark red and cream. A fan circled overhead, distributing the air to keep it cool.

She'd never considered herself much of a sensualist, beyond tapping into her inner performer for her work, but right now her senses were heightened by everything she'd seen since she'd arrived in this country.

The bed was situated in the middle of the room, and strewn with opulent coverings and pillows. It had four posters and luxurious drapes, which were held back in place by delicately engraved gold curtain ties. The bed looked big enough to hold a football team with room to spare, let alone one person... *Or two*, inserted a snide voice, which Sylvie ignored.

One thing she was sure of: Arkim Al-Sahid would *not* be sharing her bed. Yet something quivered to life deep inside her and she couldn't seem to take her eyes off it... an image filled her brain of naked pale limbs entwined with much darker ones.

For years Sylvie had seen her peers indulge in casual sexual relationships and on some level had envied them that ease and freedom. She'd gone on dates...but the men involved had all expected her to be something she wasn't. And when they'd pushed for intimacy she'd found herself shutting down. The prospect that they'd somehow 'see' the real her and reject her was a fear she couldn't shake.

It was galling that she seemed to be hardwired to want more than casual sex—based on a fragile memory of the happiness and joy that had existed between her parents before her mother had so tragically died. She'd somehow clung to it her whole life, letting it sink deep into her unconscious.

It was even more galling, though, that Arkim Al-Sahid could look at her with explicit intent and have the opposite effect from making her shut down. When he looked at her she felt as if something was flowering to life deep inside her.

Irritated with the direction of her thoughts, and telling herself she was being ridiculous, Sylvie walked over to the French doors of the main bedroom and stepped outside. Heat washed over her like a dry caress, sinking into her bones and melting some of the tension away in spite of her wish to stay rigid at all costs.

She had her own private terrace, complete with a sparkling lap pool, its turquoise tiles illuminating the water. Low seats were scattered in twos and threes around low tables, with soft raw silk cushions. Lanterns hung from the walls, but weren't lit. Sylvie could imagine how seductive it might be at night, with only the flickering lights and the vast expanse of a star-filled night sky surrounding her.

And then she berated herself for getting sucked into a daydream so easily. Pushing the images out of her head, she walked over to the boundary wall, with its distinctive Arabic carvings. Outside she could see nothing but desert and dunes. A bird of prey circled lazily against the intense blue of the sky.

It compounded her sense of isolation and entrapment, and yet…much to her chagrin…Sylvie couldn't seem to drum up any sense of urgency. She realised that she was exhausted from the shock and adrenalin of the day.

A sound made her whirl around from the wall, her heart leaping into her throat. But it was only Halima again, with her shy smile.

'Sheikh Al-Sahid has sent me to tell you that he would be happy for you to join him in an hour for dinner. He said that should give you time to freshen up.'

Sylvie felt grim. 'Did he, now?' She thought of something and said, 'Wait here a moment—I'd like you to give him something, please.'

When she came back she felt unaccountably lighter. She handed the girl a folded-up note and said sweetly, 'Please give this to Sheikh Al-Sahid for me.'

The girl scurried off and Sylvie closed the door. A wave of weariness came over her, dousing any small sense of rebellious triumph. She set about unpacking only the most necessary items from her case, having no intention of staying here beyond a night. Whatever she had to do to persuade Arkim to let her go, she'd do it.

She was disappointed but unsurprised to see that her mobile phone didn't work. Exactly as he'd told her. She put it down and sighed, then took off her clothes, finding a robe. When she got to the door leading into the bathroom she had to suck in a breath. The sinks and the bath seemed to be carved out of the stone itself, with gold fittings that managed to complement the stark design without being tacky.

The bath was more like a small pool. When she'd filled it up, and added some oils she'd found in a cleverly hidden cabinet, exotically fragrant steam wrapped around her in a caress.

She drew off the robe and took the few steps down into

the bath, trying not to feel too overwhelmed by the sheer luxury. The water closed over her body and as she tipped her head back she closed her eyes and pushed all thoughts of Arkim Al-Sahid out of her mind, trying to pretend she was on a luxury mini-break and not in the middle of an unforgiving desert, cut off from civilisation with someone who hated her guts.

Arkim stood looking out over the view, at the fading twilight casting the dunes into mysterious shadows. He had claimed this part of his maternal ancestral home for himself. His mother's family had no interest in him, and he'd told himself a long time ago that he didn't care. They'd rejected her and he wanted nothing to do with them—even if they came begging.

He'd come here initially as an exercise in removing himself from his father's sphere. He'd never expected this land to touch him as deeply as it had done on first sight. Almost with a physical pull. His mind automatically felt freer, less constrained, when he was here. He felt connected with something primal and visceral.

When he'd made his first million this property had been his first purchase, and he'd followed it up with properties in Paris, London and New York. He'd surpassed his goals one by one. All of them. Only to fall at the last hurdle: gaining the stamp of social approval and respect that would show everyone that he was *not* his father's son. That he was vastly different.

He thought of Sophie Lewis now and his conscience twinged. He hadn't thought of her very often. In truth, he'd had his doubts—their relationship had been very… platonic. But Arkim had convinced himself that it suited him like that. Her father had been the one to suggest the match, and the more Arkim had thought about it the more the idea had grown on him.

In contrast to her flame-haired provocative sister, Sophie had been like a gentle balm. Shy and innocent. Arousing no hormone-fuelled lapses of character. He'd courted her. Taken her for dinner. To the theatre. Each outing had soothed another piece of his wounded soul, making him believe that marriage to her would indeed offer him everything he'd ever wanted—which was the antithesis of life with his father.

He would be one of those parents who was respectable—respected—who came to school to pick up his son with his beautiful wife by his side. A united front. There would be no scandals. No children born out of wedlock. No mistresses. No sordid rumours and sniggering behind his back. No child of *his* would have to deal with bullying and fist fights when another kid taunted him about the whores his father took to his bed.

But the gods had laughed in his face at his ambitions and shown him that he was a fool to believe he could ever remove the stain of his father's legacy from his life.

He looked at the crumpled piece of paper in his hand and opened it out again to read.

Thank you for the kind 'invitation' to dinner, but I must decline. I've already made plans for this evening.
Sincerely, Sylvie Devereux.

Arkim had to battle both irritation and the lust that had held his body in an uncomfortable grip since he'd seen Sylvie earlier that day. He fought the urge to go straight to her room to confront her. No doubt that was exactly what she wanted.

He'd annoyed her by bringing her here and she was toying with him to get her own back. His mouth tipped up in a hard smile. No matter. He didn't mind being toyed with as long as she ended up where he wanted her—underneath him, naked and pliant and begging for mercy. Begging forgiveness.

When Sylvie woke it was dawn outside. She felt as if she'd slept for a week, not just the ten or so hours she *had* slept. Strangely, there was no disorientation—she knew exactly where she was.

She was still in the robe and she sat up, looking around warily, as if she might find Arkim lurking in a corner, glaring at her. She wondered how he'd reacted when she hadn't shown for dinner. She wasn't sure she wanted to know...

She got up and opened the French doors, the early morning's cool breeze a balm compared to the stifling heat which would no doubt come once the sun was up. She walked to the boundary wall again and sucked in a deep breath. The intense silence wrapped around her. She couldn't remember the last time she'd experienced this level of stillness—if ever. It seemed to quiet something inside her...some sense of restlessness. It was disconcerting—as if she was betraying herself by finding an affinity with any part of this situation.

She went back inside and dressed in jeans and a clean T-shirt, loath to make any kind of effort with clothes or to leave her rooms in case it showed acquiescence to Arkim. But she was also feeling somewhat trapped, and she didn't like it.

In the end Halima appeared, fresh-faced and smiling, with a tray of breakfast, bringing it into the dining room.

Sylvie's stomach rumbled loudly and she realised that because she'd turned down dinner the previous evening she'd not eaten since she'd been on the plane the day before. She was starving, and when Halima pulled back a cloth napkin to reveal a plate of fragrant flat breads Sylvie had to bite back of a groan of appreciation. It was a mezze-style feast, with little bowls of olives and different cheeses, hard and soft. And a choice of fragrant coffee or sweet tea.

Before she left, Halima said, 'Sheikh Al-Sahid sends his apologies. He's been detained by a business call otherwise he would have joined you. He said he will meet you for lunch.'

Sylvie forced a smile. She couldn't shoot the messenger. 'Thank you.'

After Halima left and Sylvie had eaten her fill, she wandered around her rooms for a bit, feeling increasingly claustrophobic. She knew she should really do some exercises to keep herself flexible, especially after travelling, but she was feeling too antsy to focus. She left her rooms and walked down long stone corridors that gave glimpses into intriguing courtyards and other open spaces.

Through one open courtyard she saw a terrace with tall ornate stone columns and a vast pool that stretched around the side of the castle. It was breathtaking. Idyllic.

Sylvie backed away from the seductive scene and explored further. Some doors were closed, and she refrained from opening them in case she stumbled into Arkim.

Eventually she found herself at the main door, which led out to the central courtyard. Adrenalin flooded her system when she saw the golf buggy that Arkim had used to bring them into the castle the previous day. The key was in the ignition. And from here she could see that the main doors to the castle complex were open.

She had a sudden vision of Arkim wearing down her defences, slowly but surely. If he kissed her again she was very much afraid that she'd melt—just as she had before, when she'd lost all control of her rational functions.

The truth was that she didn't have an arsenal of experience to fend off someone like Arkim, and the thought of him ever discovering how flimsy her façade was made her go cold with terror.

She didn't think. She reacted. She got into the golf buggy and turned the key, setting it in motion. Her heart was clamouring as she sped out of the castle complex.

Less than an hour later Sylvie's feet sank into the sand. She was on top of a dune, with the now dead golf buggy in front of her. Futile anger made her kick ineffectually at the inanimate object. It had started sputtering and slowing down about ten minutes before, eventually conking out.

The sun beat down mercilessly and there was nothing as far as the eye could see except sand, sand and more sand. Heat waves shimmered in the distance.

Of course it was only now that Sylvie realised just how stupid she'd been to react to her own imagination like that and set off in a panic. She had no water. No food. No idea where she was. Even if she'd had the means she wasn't sure which way she'd come!

Her T-shirt was stuck to her skin and her jeans felt red-hot and too tight. Right now she would have given anything for a cool white tunic and a head-covering. She could feel her skin prickling uncomfortably under the sun, and the roof of the buggy offered scant protection.

She gulped and, absurdly, tears pricked her eyes. Arkim Al-Sahid had driven her to this desperate measure. She wished she'd never laid eyes on the man. She wished he'd never kissed—

Something caught at her peripheral vision and she looked. For a second she wondered if she was seeing things, and then as the image became more distinct her eyes widened.

It was a man on top of a horse... Except this looked like no ordinary horse. It was a huge black stallion. And the man...

Sylvie felt as if she might have slipped back a few centuries. At first she thought it must be one of Arkim's staff, because he was dressed in white robes, with a *keffiyeh* around his head. His face was obscured by the material, leaving only his eyes and dark skin visible. And was that a jewelled dagger stuck into the roped belt around his waist?

He drew up alongside her, the horse rearing up, making Sylvie back away skittishly. Even now—even though her accelerated pulse told her otherwise—she was hoping she was mistaken.

But the man who jumped off the horse had such grace and innate athleticism that her mouth dried.

He tied the horse to the buggy and then stalked towards her, growing bigger and taller as he did so. Right up until the moment that he ripped aside the material covering his mouth and face Sylvie was still hoping it was anyone but...*him*. Of course he'd found her. This man seemed to have a heat-seeking radar, able to pin her to the spot no matter where she was.

'You damned little fool. What the *hell* did you hope to achieve by this stunt?'

She tried to ignore how Arkim's almost savage appearance made her feel as if she was losing it completely. He looked even more ridiculously handsome against this unforgiving backdrop.

She shouted back. 'I was trying to get away from *you*, in case it wasn't completely obvious.'

Arkim's eyes glittered like obsidian. 'In a golf buggy? With none of your things?' He was scathing. 'Did you really think you could just bounce merrily across hundreds of miles of desert and roll into the nearest petrol station to refuel?'

Humiliated beyond measure, Sylvie launched herself at Arkim, hands balled into fists and beating against his chest.

He caught her arms easily and held her immobile. Tension crackled between them, and for a heart-stopping moment Sylvie thought he was going to kiss her—but then a piercing sound shattered the air and they both looked up to see two Jeeps coming towards them over the top of the dune, horns blasting.

Sylvie felt so jittery all she wanted was to escape back to the castle as quickly as possible and lock herself in her rooms. She was caught between a rock and a hard place. Literally. The thought didn't amuse her.

The Jeeps pulled up and concerned-looking staff spilled out. Sylvie immediately felt guilty for having precipitated this search.

Arkim wordlessly led her over to the nearest vehicle and said a few words to the driver. Then he opened up the back door for her. When she would have expected to get in, he handed her a bottle of water. She looked at him and he was grim.

'Drink, you'll be dehydrated.'

Sylvie couldn't argue with that, and she was thirsty, so she took several large gulps. Then Arkim reached into the back of the Jeep again and pulled out a long white robe. He thrust it at her.

'I'm supposed to put this on?' Sylvie said waspishly.

Arkim's expression darkened. 'Yes. You're already burning.'

Her skin *was* still prickling, but Sylvie was afraid that it was more to do with his effect on her than the sun—even though when she looked her arms were ominously pink.

Mutinously she pulled on the long-sleeved robe, and was surprised at how much cooler she felt instantly—which was crazy when she was pulling on *more* clothes.

Then he was unwinding his *keffiyeh* from his head, and before she could stop him he'd placed it over her hair, like a shawl. He started to wind it around her head, tucking it in, until there was only one long piece left that he drew across her mouth and tucked in at the back.

She was effectively swaddled. And it was only then that she realised that the Jeeps were driving off into the distance, towing the buggy behind them. Arkim's scent was disturbing, and all around her. The thought that this fabric had been across his mouth was almost too intimate to take in.

He held his horse by the reins and was leading it over. Sylvie pulled down the material covering her mouth. 'What are you doing? Where are the Jeeps going?'

He stopped in front of her, the huge horse prancing behind him. 'We are going for a little trip.'

Before she could ask more, Arkim had his hands around her waist and was lifting her effortlessly onto the horse. His sheer strength took her breath away and she clung to the saddle, her brain reeling at being so high up. She hadn't been on a horse since she was a teenager...

Arkim put his foot in the stirrup and vaulted on behind her, his agility awesome. And suddenly he was all around her. Strong muscled thighs gripping hers, his torso against her back, his arms coming around her to take the reins.

'Cover your mouth.'

Sylvie was too stunned to move. 'Wh—where are we going?'

Arkim angled himself so he could see her and made a rude sound. 'Don't you *ever* do anything you're told?' The material was firmly pulled back over her mouth and he said, 'It'll stop sand getting in.'

Sylvie couldn't say anything else, because Arkim was turning the horse around and they were galloping in the opposite direction from where the Jeeps had gone. For a semi-hysterical moment Sylvie thought that perhaps she'd pushed Arkim so far he was just going to dump her in the desert and leave her to die a slow, painful death.

Gradually, though, as they galloped into the seeming nothingness of the sandy landscape, almost against her will she felt herself relaxing into Arkim's body, letting him take her weight. One of his arms was around her torso, holding her to him, and she felt the intimate space between her legs soften and moisten.

She was fast losing all sense of reality. The real world and civilisation felt very far away.

After about twenty minutes Arkim drew the stallion to a stop, its muscles quivering under Sylvie's legs. He got off the horse and Sylvie looked down to see his arms outstretched towards her. His mouth was stern.

'Bring your leg over the horse, Sylvie.'

She wanted to disobey, but she knew Arkim would pull her off the horse anyway. Better to do it with a modicum of decorum and not let him see how intimidated she was. And she was scared... Even though she knew—in some way she didn't like to investigate—that he wouldn't harm her.

Her hands landed on Arkim's wide shoulders and his hands clamped around her waist as he lifted her down as effortlessly as before. She saw the reins on the ground and said nervously, 'Won't the horse just go?'

'Aziz won't move unless I say so. And we won't be long.' Arkim's tone brooked no disobedience—from her or the horse.

Sylvie broke away from Arkim's hands. The *keffiyah* was still around her mouth and she pulled it down as she looked around at a sea of nothing but blue sky and dunes.

'Why are we here?'

Arkim planted himself in front of her, hands on hips. 'Because this is where you would have ended up if the buggy hadn't run out of fuel. This is where we might have found you in two days, if we were lucky enough, dehydrated and burnt to a crisp.'

Sylvie looked at him and shivered. 'You're exaggerating.'

Arkim looked livid. He grabbed her arms with his hands. 'No, I'm not. Men who know this area, who have lived here for years, can still get caught out by the desert. Right now it looks calm, wouldn't you agree?'

Sylvie nodded hesitantly.

Arkim's mouth thinned. 'It's anything but. There's a sandstorm due to hit any day now. Have you ever been in a sandstorm?'

She shook her head.

'Imagine a tidal wave coming towards you—except in this case it's made of sand and debris, not water. You'd be obliterated in seconds. Suffocated.'

Genuine horror and fear finally made her realise just how reckless she'd been. She seized on the surge of anger. He made her feel as if she was a tiny ship bobbing about in a huge raging sea.

'Okay, fine—I get it. What I did was foolish and reckless and silly. I didn't know. I didn't mean to put everyone to so much trouble...' A very unwelcome sense of vulnerability made her lash out. 'But, in case you don't remember, it's *your* fault I'm even here!'

Arkim looked down at that beautiful but defiant face and felt such a mix of things that he was dizzy. He shook his head, but nothing rational would come to the surface. All he could see was *her*.

He gave in to the urgent dictates of his blood and lowered his mouth to the lush contours of hers—and drowned.

His tongue swept into her mouth in a marauding move and he quickly became oblivious to everything except the rough stroke of his tongue against Sylvie's, demanding a response.

She resisted him for long seconds, but he felt her

gradually relax, as if losing a battle with herself. Once again there was an almost unbelievable hesitance—as if she didn't know what to do. The thought that she could do this—get under his skin so easily, make him doubt himself—made Arkim's blood boil.

He held the back of her covered head and put his hand to where her neck met her shoulder in an unashamedly possessive move, his thumb reaching for and finding that hectic pulse-beat, which was telling him that no matter how ingrained it was in her to act, she couldn't control *everything*.

And finally he felt her arms relax and start to climb around his neck, bringing her body into more intimate contact with his. Her mouth softened and she...acquiesced. The triumph was heady. Her tongue stroked his sweetly, sucking him deep—as deep as he imagined the exquisite clasp of her body would be around his in a more intimate caress.

He wanted to throw her down on the ground right here and pull up that robe, yank down her jeans, until he could find his release. The desire was so strong he shook in a bid to rein it in. And that brought him back from the brink of losing it completely.

Reality slammed into him. He was in the middle of the desert, under the merciless sun, about to ravage this woman. Make her his...brand her like some kind of animal.

He wanted to push her away from him and yet never let her go.

He hated her. He wanted her.

He pulled back from the kiss even though everything in his body and his blood protested at the move. He felt the unrelenting beat of the sun on his head. Her eyes opened after a moment, wide and blue...and that intriguing blue-green. Her cheeks were flushed. Lips swollen.

And then suddenly she tensed and scrambled free of

his arms. Arkim might almost have laughed—even now she was intent on playing this game of push and pull. Acting her little heart out.

'Have you forgotten that you're a civilised man?'

Even her voice sounded suitably shaky. But Arkim barely cast her a glance as he reached for the horse's reins. 'I don't have to be civilised here.'

That was why he'd brought her here in the first place—because he didn't trust himself around her in more civilised surroundings. It was as if he'd known the desert was the only place big enough to contain what he felt for her.

He picked up the reins, ignoring the dull throb of unsatisfied desire in his system...the way his arousal pressed against his trousers under his robe.

'You really can't turn it off, can you?'

Sylvie scowled at him. She should have looked ridiculous. The *keffiyah* was askew on her head, and slivers of bright red curling tendrils of hair peeped out from under its folds. She crossed her arms. 'Turn what off?'

'Your constant need to act out some role—pretend you don't want this.'

'I'm *not* acting. And I *don't* want this! I don't know what happened there...a moment of sunstroke...but it won't be happening again.'

Arkim almost felt pity for her. He reached out and rubbed a thumb back and forth over her plump lower lip. 'Oh, don't worry—it'll be happening again, and you'll be fully participant in it when it does.'

Sylvie slapped his hand away. She might have screamed at his arrogance, but he was lifting her up onto the horse again before she could take another breath. And, in any case, what could she say after she'd just melted all over him?

It was pathetic. *She* was pathetic. She turned to mush

when he came near her. So she'd just have to keep him at a distance.

But then he got up on the horse behind her again, and predictably Sylvie's body went into a paroxysm of anticipation as one arm snaked around her torso, holding her to him, and his other hand expertly gathered the reins to urge the horse on. Of course he would *have* to be an expert horseman too. Was there anything this man *couldn't* do? Apart from act in a civil manner to her?

His lower body was pressed against her backside now, and she could feel the thrust of something unmistakably hard. Her face flamed, and it had nothing to do with the sun. She yanked the material of the *keffiyah* back over her mouth. He wouldn't have to ask her to cover up. She'd never uncover herself again in this man's presence.

CHAPTER FOUR

SYLVIE SAT CURLED up on one of the vast couches in the living area of her suite. When she'd returned to her rooms a couple of hours ago she'd found Halima waiting for her, with ointment for her sun-tender skin and some lunch snacks—and plenty of water. Arkim's efficiency at work. Afterwards she'd changed into loose pants and layered on a couple of her sleeveless workout tops to keep her arms bare.

On their return Arkim had taken her into an expansive stables area at the back of the castle, and when he'd helped Sylvie off the horse she'd felt wobbly-legged and suitably chastened after being shown the very real dangers of the desert.

Arkim hadn't accompanied her back to the castle; he'd sent for one of his staff to do it. Sylvie had recognised him as one of the drivers of the Jeeps and had apologised to him for having dragged them out to look for her. She wasn't even sure if he'd understood her, but he'd shaken his head and looked embarrassed, as if it was nothing.

The night was falling outside now: the sky was a stunning deep violet colour and stars were appearing. Questions abounded in her head. Questions about Arkim. Seeing him against this backdrop was more intriguing than she liked to admit. And she hated to acknowledge it but she was also fascinated by the barely repressed emotions below the surface of his urbanity. He was different here. More raw. It should be intimidating. But it excited her.

What was his connection to this place? And if he had a connection here, how could he—a man who had this desert in his blood, so timeless and somehow base—agree to marry purely for business and strategic reasons?

A noise made her tense and she looked round to see the object of her thoughts in the doorway to her living room. Dressed in a robe again, with his head bare, he looked... powerful. Mysterious.

Sylvie's belly tightened. 'Come to check your prisoner is still here?'

Arkim's mouth lifted slightly at one corner, as if he were wryly amused, and Sylvie felt it like a punch to the gut.

'Somehow I don't think even *you* would be so foolish as to try and escape again.'

Sylvie scowled. 'Next time I'll prepare better.'

His smile faded. 'There won't be a next time—believe me. You won't be leaving until I do.'

She stood up, frustration running through her blood. 'Look, this is crazy. I need to get back to Paris. I have to—'

Arkim interrupted her. 'You have to eat.'

She could see staff now, coming up behind him, carrying things.

He stood aside and said, 'I've arranged for dinner to come to you this evening. We'll have it on the terrace.'

She felt completely impotent. What could she do? Storm off to another part of the castle in protest?

She preceded Arkim out to where the staff were setting up on the terrace, and when she saw lanterns being lit, sending out soft golden light, her heart flipped. She'd imagined this seductive scenario...

Plates of fragrant steaming food were being placed on a low table and the scents teased Sylvie's nostrils. She was an unashamed foodie, and the prospect of an exotic feast was too much temptation to resist.

Halima arrived then, with a bottle of champagne which she put in an ice bucket by the table. Sylvie scowled at it, just as Arkim came into her line of vision and held out a hand.

'Please, take a seat.'

Sylvie sat down cross-legged on a low chair, and watched as Arkim lowered himself athletically into a similar pose on the other side of the delicately carved table. It should have made him look less manly, but of course it didn't.

'How are your arms?'

She glanced down, noting with relief that the vivid pink had faded and they weren't so hot. In this day and age of knowledge of sun damage she'd been very stupid.

She said, 'Much better. Halima's ointment was very effective.'

She looked at Arkim and words of apology for running off earlier trembled on her tongue. But he wasn't looking at her—he was piling a plate high with different foods before handing it to her. Like a coward, she swallowed the words back and took the plate, telling herself that he would only spurn an apology.

There was a faint popping sound as he expertly opened the champagne and poured her a glass of the sparkling wine. She accepted it after a moment's hesitation.

Arkim arched a brow. 'You don't like champagne?'

'I don't drink much of any alcohol, I never really acquired the taste.'

Arkim made a noise and she looked at him, seeing him fill his own glass as he said, 'You forget that I've seen you inebriated.'

Sylvie frowned, and then that night in the garden flooded back. Hotly she defended herself. 'My shoe got stuck in the ground. I was still on antibiotics from a chest infection that night—the last thing I'd have done was drink alcohol.'

He just looked at her, eyes narrowed, and she glared at

him. After a long moment he shrugged and said, 'It hardly matters now, in any case.'

Sylvie was disconcerted by how much it *did* matter to her. She looked away from him and put down her glass without taking a sip, choosing to focus on the food instead and trying to block him out. *Ha!* As if *that* was possible.

Arkim could see how tense Sylvie's body was as she resolutely avoided his eye and picked at the food. Her jaw was so tight he thought she might break it if she had to chew. Her vibrant hair was piled high in a haphazard bun, tendrils trailing down to frame her face. His fingers itched to undo the knot and let her hair fall around her shoulders and down her back.

He diverted his attention from the urge he felt to undo that knot and watched with growing incredulity, and something much earthier, as Sylvie seemed to be absorbed by the food—spearing large morsels and evidently taking extreme pleasure out of the discovery of the various tastes. It was incredibly sensual to watch.

She seemed to be completely oblivious to Arkim and he sat back slightly, the better to observe her. He knew she *wasn't* oblivious to him, though—it was there in the tension of her body, and in the pulse beating under the delicate pale skin of her throat.

He'd noticed for the first time this evening that his impression of her being tall actually wasn't correct. He might have registered it before if she hadn't distracted him so easily, but she'd always seemed a lot taller. Maybe it was because she consistently stood up to him in a way no one else did.

That revelation wasn't welcome. It made him think of the fact that he'd overheard her trying to apologise to a member of his staff earlier. He'd have assumed it was for show, but she had been almost out of his earshot, so patently not doing it for his benefit.

Sylvie was actually only just above average height, and her whole frame was on the petite side. He didn't like the way this fact made his conscience smart a little. It made him see a vulnerability he'd blocked out before, and reminded him of the way her stepmother had slapped her in the church...

She leaned forward at that moment, to get some bread, and her full breasts swayed with the movement. Arkim's whole body seemed to sizzle, and he was reminded of exactly who he was dealing with here—a mistress of selfishness and manipulation.

'You like the food?' he asked now, in some kind of effort to wrench his mind off Sylvie's physical temptations, angry with himself.

She glanced at him—a flash of blue and green. She nodded and swallowed what she was eating. Her voice was low, husky, when she said, 'It's delicious. I've never tasted flavours like this before.'

'The lamb is particularly good.'

He speared a morsel of succulent meat with his fork and held it across the table. When she reached for it with her hand he pulled it back and looked at her. She scowled.

'Coward,' Arkim said softly.

Something in him exulted when he saw the fire flash in her eyes as she took the bait and leant across the table to take the piece of meat off his fork and into her mouth.

Her loose tops swayed, giving Arkim an unrestricted view of her lace-clad breasts. Full and perfectly shaped. She moved back before he could make a complete fool of himself by grabbing her and hauling her across the table.

Her cheeks were flaming. And he didn't think it was from the spices in the lamb. Their mutual chemistry was obvious. So why would she fight it like this?

He leant back on one arm again. She took a sip of champagne and he watched the long, graceful column of her throat work, jealous of even that small movement. She might have passed for eighteen, with her face free of make-up.

Something niggled at him—where was the *femme fatale*? So far he had to admit that the Sylvie he had here was nothing like the woman who had provoked him beyond measure each time he'd seen her before. Not least when she'd appeared in the church, dressed from head to toe in motorcycle gear. The soft black leather jacket and trousers had moulded to her body in a way that had been indecent—and even more so in a church.

He'd expected her to be a lot more sophisticated, knowing... Giving in to her situation and manipulating him as much as she could. That was how the women he knew operated—ultimately they would follow the path of least resistance and take as much as they could.

That was what had attracted him to Sophie Lewis and made him believe he could marry her—her complete lack of guile or artifice. A rare thing in this world.

And that was as far as the attraction had gone.

Arkim ignored the voice. But he had to acknowledge uncomfortably that if the wedding had gone ahead and he'd married Sophie Lewis he wouldn't be here now with her sister. And for a sobering and very unpalatable moment Arkim couldn't regret that fact.

A deeper, darker truth nudged at his consciousness—the very real doubts he'd had himself about the wedding as it had come closer and closer. But he wasn't a man who spent fruitless time wondering about what might have been. And he didn't entertain doubts. He made decisions and he dealt in reality, and this was now his reality.

Sylvie was avoiding looking at him and he hated that.

He said, 'Your eyes... I've never seen that before.'

***

Sylvie was straining with every muscle she had not to let Arkim see how much he was getting to her, lounging on the other side of the table as he was, like some kind of robed demigod. When she'd leant across the table—provoked into taking that food off his fork—and she'd seen him looking down her top, she'd almost combusted.

Distracted, and very irritated, she said, 'They're just eyes, Arkim. Everyone has them. Even you.'

She risked a look and saw that half-smile again. *Lord.*

'Yes, but none as unusual as you. Blue and blue-green.'

Sylvie hated the frisson she felt to think of him studying her eyes. 'My mother had it too. It's a condition called heterochromia iridum. There's really nothing that mysterious about it.'

Arkim frowned now. 'Your mother was French, wasn't she?'

Sylvie nodded, getting tenser now, thinking of Arkim's judgmental gaze turning on her deceased mother. Sophie must have mentioned it to him.

'Yes, from just outside Paris.'

'And how did your parents meet?'

Sylvie glared at him. 'You're telling me you don't know?'

He shrugged lightly and asked, 'Should I?'

For a moment she processed that nugget. Maybe he genuinely didn't.

From what she'd learnt of this man, he would not hesitate to take advantage of another excuse to bash her—so, anticipating his scathing reaction, she lifted her chin and said, 'She was a dancer—for a revue in Paris that was in the same building where I now dance. It had a different name when she was there and the show was…of its time.'

'What does that mean?' he drawled derisively. 'Not so much skin?'

Sylvie cursed herself for being honest. Why couldn't she just have said her mother had been a nurse, or a secretary? Because, her conscience answered her, her mother would never have hidden her true self. And neither would Sylvie.

'Something like that. It was more in the line of vintage burlesque.'

'And how did your father meet her? He doesn't strike me as the kind of man who frequents such establishments.'

Sylvie pushed down the hurt as she recalled sparkling memories full of joy—her father laughing and swinging her mother around in their back garden. She smiled sweetly and said, 'Just goes to show that you can't always judge a book by its cover.'

Arkim had the grace to tilt his glass towards her slightly and say, 'Touché.'

She played with her champagne glass, which was still half full. She grudgingly explained, 'He was in Paris on a business trip and went with some of his clients to the show. He saw my mother...asked her out afterwards... that was it.'

Sylvie would never reveal the true romance of her parents' love story to this cynical man, but the fact was that her father had fallen for Cécile Devereux at first sight—a *coup de foudre*—and had wooed her for over a month before her mother had finally deigned to go out with him— an English businessman a million miles removed from the glamorous Cécile Devereux's life. Yet she'd fallen in love with him too. And they'd been happy. Ecstatically.

Familiar emotion and vulnerability rose up inside Sylvie now and she knew she didn't want Arkim to probe any further into her precious memories.

She took a sip of champagne and looked at him. 'What about *your* parents?'

Arkim's expression immediately darkened. It was visible even in the flickering light of the dozens of candles and lanterns.

'As you've pointed out—you know very well who my father is.'

Sylvie flushed when she recalled throwing that in Arkim's face in her father's study. She refused to cower, though. This man had judged her from the moment he'd laid eyes on her.

She thought of how he was doing everything he could to distance himself from his parent and she was doing everything to follow in her mother's footsteps. The opposite sides of one coin.

'I don't know about your mother—were they married?'

His look could have sliced through steel. Clearly this wasn't a subject he relished, and it buoyed her up to see him lose that icy control he seemed to wield so effortlessly. It reminded her of how she'd wanted to shatter it when she'd first met him. Well, it had shattered all right—taking her with it.

Arkim's tone was harsh. 'She died in childbirth, and, no, they weren't married. My father doesn't *do* marriage. He's too eager to hang on to his fortune and keep his bedroom door revolving.'

Sylvie didn't like the little dart of sympathy she felt to hear that his mother had died before he'd even known her. She moved away from that kernel of information. 'So, you grew up in America?'

His mouth tightened. 'Yes. And in England, in a series of boarding schools. During holidays in LA I was a captive audience for my father's debauched lifestyle.'

Sylvie winced inwardly. There was another link in the chain to understanding this man's prejudices.

Hesitantly she said, 'You've never been close, then?'

Arkim's voice could have chilled ice. 'I haven't seen him since I was a teenager.'

Sylvie sucked in a breath.

Before she could think how to respond, Arkim inserted mockingly, 'Living with him taught me a valuable lesson from an early age: that life isn't some fairytale.'

The extent of his cynicism mocked Sylvie's tender memories of her own parents. 'Most people don't experience what you did.'

His eyes glittered like black jewels. He looked completely relaxed, but she could sense the tension in his form.

The question was burning her up inside. 'Is that one of the reasons why you agreed to marry Sophie? Because you don't believe real marriages can exist?'

'Do you?' he parried.

Sylvie cursed her big mouth and glanced away. She longed to match his cynicism with her own, but the truth was that even after witnessing how grief had torn her father apart she *had* seen real love for a while.

She looked back. 'I think sometimes, yes, they can. But even a happy marriage can be broken apart very easily.' *By devastating illness and death.*

He looked at her consideringly for a long moment and she steeled herself. But then he asked, 'What was your mother like?'

Sylvie's insides clenched harder. She looked at her glass.

'She was amazing. Beautiful, sweet…kind.' When Arkim didn't respond with some cutting comment, she went on, 'I always remember her perfume…it was so distinctive. My father used to buy it in the same shop for her whenever he was in Paris. It was opposite the Ritz hotel, run by a beautiful Indian woman. He took me with him once. I remember she had a small daughter…' Her mouth quirked as she got lost in the memory. 'I used to sit at my mother's feet and watch her get ready to go out with my father. She used to hum all the time. French songs. And she would dance with me…'

'Sounds just like one of those fairytales—too good to be true.'

Arkim's voice broke through the memories like a rude klaxon. Sylvie's head jerked up. She'd forgotten where she was for a moment, and with whom.

'It *was* true. And good.'

She hated it that her voice trembled slightly. She wouldn't be able to bear it now if Arkim was to delve further and ask about her mother's death. That excruciating last year, when cancer had turned her mother into a shadow of her former self, would haunt Sylvie for the rest of her life. She'd lost both her parents from that moment.

She felt prickly enough to attack. 'Why did you agree to marry my sister? Really?'

Arkim was expressionless. 'For all the reasons I have already explained to you.'

Beyond irritated, and frustrated at the way he made her feel, Sylvie put down her napkin and stood up, walking over to the wall. She heard him move and turned around to face him, feeling jittery.

He stood a few feet away. Too close for comfort. Before she could say anything, Arkim folded his arms and said, 'I won't deny I had my doubts…'

Sylvie went still.

'That night in the study, when you found me… I wasn't altogether certain that I was going to go through with it. But then you appeared…' Something like anger flashed in his eyes. 'Let's just say that you helped me make up my mind.'

Sylvie reeled. He might have called it off? And then his words registered. Anger flared. 'So it was *my* fault?'

He ignored that. 'Why did you break up the wedding? Was it purely for spite?'

The realisation that Arkim might have called the whole thing off was mixing with her anger, diluting it. Making her heart beat faster. Words trembled on her lips. Words that would exonerate her. But she couldn't do it; she'd promised her sister.

She lifted her chin. 'All you need to know is that if I had to do it over again I wouldn't hesitate.'

Arkim's face hardened even more. He didn't like that. But his drawling voice belied his expression. 'The motorbike was a cute touch. Did you learn how to ride one especially for dramatic effect?'

Sylvie flushed. 'I used to have one in Paris—to get around. Until it got stolen. I hired one that day...more for expediency than anything else.'

He sneered now. 'You mean a quick, cowardly getaway so you didn't have to deal with the fallout...?'

Before Sylvie could formulate a response, Halima and some other discreet staff appeared at that moment, defusing the tension a little, and removed the remains of their dinner from the table.

When they were gone Sylvie was still facing Arkim, like an adversary in a boxing ring. The revelation that she'd inadvertently influenced his decision to marry Sophie was crowding everything else out of her head. Presumably it had been because she'd reminded him of exactly the kind of woman he *didn't* want. And that stung.

She pushed down her roiling emotions and tried to appeal to his civilised side. 'Arkim...you've made your point. You need to let me go now.'

His expression remained as hard as granite. Unforgiving. Sylvie shivered. This man wasn't civilised here.

And then he said, 'I've paid a substantial sum of money for your presence and I believe that I'd like to see you dance for me.' The shape of his mouth turned bitter. 'After all, thousands have seen you dance, so why shouldn't I?'

The thought of performing in front of this man made

Sylvie go cold, and then hot. 'Now?' Her voice squeaked slightly.

A ghost of a smile touched his lips. 'No, tomorrow evening. You'll perform a very *private* dance. Just for me.'

She straightened her spine. 'If you're expecting a lap dance, I hate to disappoint you but I really don't do that kind of thing.'

He moved close enough to reach out and trail a finger down over her cheek and jaw, and said softly, 'I'm looking forward to seeing what you *do* do.'

She slapped his hand down, terrified of the way his touch made her melt so easily. Terrified he'd kiss her again. 'And why on earth should I do anything you ask me to?'

Arkim's jaw clenched, and then he said baldly, 'Because you owe me, and I'm collecting.'

The following evening Halima held up one of Sylvie's rhinestone-encrusted outfits and stroked it reverently. 'This is so beautiful.'

The thought of the robed young woman wearing it, baring her skin so comprehensively, made Sylvie feel a little uncomfortable, and she gently took the garment out of Halima's hands to hang it up, along with the other costumes the girl had insisted on taking out of her suitcase.

She hadn't been able to eat since breakfast that morning, and her belly had been doing somersaults all day at the thought of dancing for Arkim. She'd realised that of course he'd be expecting her to rebel, refuse. And then maybe he'd initiate another cosy dinner and tell her more things about himself that would put her on uneven ground where her feelings towards him were concerned.

As she'd lain in bed last night and gone over everything he'd told her she had found her antipathy hard to cling on to. So she'd decided to keep him at arm's length and do the opposite of what he was expecting and dance for him.

She realised with some level of dark irony that if he was reverse psychoanalysing her, then it was working.

And if Sylvie was being completely honest with herself, a part of her still wanted to provoke Arkim—make him admit that he was just like everyone else.

It was that damned icy façade of his that had sneaked under her skin and made her want to break it apart as soon as he'd looked at her for the first time with such disdain. And where had breaking that control apart got her? To one of the hottest places on earth. About to strip herself bare in front of a man who wanted her, yet despised her.

Words trembled on Sylvie's tongue. Words to instruct Halima to go and tell the Sheikh that she wasn't available this evening after all. But she couldn't back down now.

She surveyed herself in the mirror as Halima clipped a veil behind her head, obscuring her mouth, so only her heavily kohled eyes were visible. Her hair was tucked and hidden under another veil.

Sylvie wondered if Arkim would appreciate the fact that the act she'd decided to do was based on the story of *Scheherazade*. Somehow, she didn't think he'd be amused.

She took a deep breath and turned to Halima. 'Now all I need is a sword...do you think you can find one here?'

The young girl thought for a moment, then brightened. 'Yes!'

Anticipation lay heavy and thick in Arkim's bloodstream as he waited for Sylvie to appear. He'd given instructions for her to be brought to one of the ceremonial rooms, where traditionally the Sheikh would greet and entertain his important guests. The room was open to the elements behind Arkim. Lanterns lit the space with golden flickering shadows.

Just then he noticed that a strong gust of wind whipping through the open space had almost put out one of the candles. The storm. It was coming. It made Arkim feel reckless. Wild. He'd gone out on Aziz earlier that day, tracking it, seeing the wind pick up. The stallion had moved skittishly, wanting to get back to cover.

There was a raised marble dais in the centre of the room, where the Sheikh would usually sit to greet his guests, and it was also sometimes used for ceremonial performances and dances. Arkim didn't doubt that he was about to bring this space into serious disrepute by having Sylvie dance here, but he couldn't seem to care too much.

He took a sip of his wine. *Where was she?* He tensed at the thought that she was defying him again.

Just as he was about to put down his glass and stand up and go to her, his blood fizzing, she appeared. She was slight and lissom…in bare feet. Arkim blinked as blood roared up into his head and south to another part of his anatomy.

She didn't look in his direction or acknowledge him as she stepped up onto the dais. He wasn't sure what he'd been expecting, but it wasn't this. She was wearing gold figure-hugging trousers that were flared at the ends and partially slit up the sides, embellished with jewels and lace. They sat low on her hips, along with a belt from which tassels dropped and moved and swayed with her body.

Her middle was toned and bare, and encircled with a delicate gold chain that sat just above the curve of her hips. A cropped black top with long trailing sleeves was tied in the front, between her breasts, worn over a gold-coloured and very ornate-looking bra.

Her breasts were…perfection. Full and luscious, beautifully shaped. Her provocative cleavage was framed by the top.

She still hadn't even so much as flicked a glance in his direction, and he noticed properly for the first time that the lower half of her face was obscured by a black veil, and that a black covering also hid her hair. Arkim wanted to rip it off and see those red tresses tumbling around her shoulders.

All that was visible of her face were her heavily kohled eyes. She was bending down now, doing something with speakers, and then a slow, sultry and distinctly Arabic beat filled the space.

Arkim's eyes widened when he saw her pick up a large curved sabre—he'd been too distracted to notice it before. He frowned. It looked disturbingly like the one that hung in the exhibition room that housed all his precious antiques and old weapons.

Sylvie faced away from him now, and all he could see was the tempting curve of her buttocks, the tantalising line of her waist and hips, and that gold chain glinting in the flickering glow of the lamps. And then she lifted the sword high in her hands over her head and slowly turned to face him. Those distinctive eyes met his, and she started to move sinuously to the beat of the music.

And Arkim's brain stuttered to a halt.

He was aware of pale skin, dips and hollows, a toned belly. She played with the huge sword as if it was a baton—twirling it in one hand and then in the other. She was on her knees now, one leg raised at a right angle, and arching her body backwards like a bow, with the sword resting on its tip behind her and her free arm stretched out in front of her. The line of her throat was long and graceful, and curiously vulnerable.

The music seemed to be pounding in time with Arkim's blood. And then it changed and became a little faster, with a different beat.

Sylvie straightened up and bent forward with impressive flexibility, bringing the sword back in front of her to place it on the ground and push it away. And then, still bending forward, she lifted the veil and head covering off her head. She undid the tie on her black top and removed that too.

Now her hair tumbled down, free and wild, and the ornately decorated gold bra was revealed. He could see the faint sheen of perspiration on her pale skin and his insides tightened with pure, unadulterated lust. Would her skin be sheened like that when he joined their bodies for the first time?

She came onto her knees, facing Arkim again, and started undulating her body in a series of movements—hips, arms, chest—disconnected but connected. He'd seen belly dancers before, but never like this. Bright red hair trailed over her shoulders and down to her breasts. He wanted to reach out and curl a tendril around his hand, pull her towards him.

She was looking at him now, but blankly. A sizzle of irritation ran through his blood. When women looked at him, they *looked*.

She moved lithely to her feet and brought her whole body into the dance. This should be boring him to tears. But it wasn't. He hated to realise that he was most likely in the kind of thrall that had mesmerised men for hundreds of years when a woman danced like this for him.

And then he realised it was *her*. There was something profoundly captivating about Sylvie and the way she moved. It was knowing, and yet there was something Arkim couldn't put his finger on…something slightly *off*. As if a piece of the jigsaw was missing.

She'd stopped dancing now, her chest moving rapidly with her breath, her hair tangled in waves and falling down her back as she stood with one hand on her hip and the other stretched out towards him, as if she were offering him something.

She hadn't even stripped. But arousal sat heavy in Arkim's body and bloodstream. He felt like a fool. Sylvie had told him that she didn't do lap dances, but somehow that was exactly what he had expected. Something tawdry and fitting for the picture he'd built up of her in his head.

But this whole performance had been sweetly titillating—like a throwback to a more innocent time. A time that Arkim had never had the pleasure of knowing. He'd never really experienced innocence. His own had been corrupted when he had been so young.

Anger rushed through him and he stood up. He did a slow hand-clap and then said, as equably as he could, 'Who exactly are you trying to fool with a routine suited to the top of a table in a restaurant?'

Sylvie's arm dropped and she looked at him, cheeks flushed. Arkim's body throbbed all over. But he held on to what tiny bit of control he had—rigidly.

Her gaze narrowed on him. 'I take it that you didn't care for it, then? Too bad you can't get your money back.'

Her voice was breathy, and there was something defiant in those flashing blue-green eyes. It sent his churning cauldron of emotions into overdrive. She was taunting him. He thought of all the people she'd bared herself to, and yet she wouldn't for him. The thought that she might have an inkling of just how badly he wanted her scored him deep inside.

He didn't want to go near Sylvie for fear of what might happen if he did. As if some beast inside him might be unleashed and she'd see just how close to the edge of his control he was. He felt feral. As if he needed desperately to prove to himself that she was who he believed she was.

'You'll dance again, Sylvie. And this time you'll perform exactly as you do for the thousands of people who have seen *all* of you. I won't accept anything less. Be back here in half an hour.'

CHAPTER FIVE

SYLVIE WATCHED ARKIM stalk out of the huge space, adrenalin still fizzing in her blood. Vulnerability and frustration vied with her anger at his high-handedness. And a need to wipe the disdainful look off his face.

More anger coursed through her when she thought of what Arkim had been expecting and what he clearly still expected: *You'll perform exactly as you do for the thousands of people who have seen* all *of you.*

She was surprised he hadn't had a pole installed so she could shimmy up and down it. Clearly she'd done such a good job of doing absolutely *nothing* to amend Arkim's bad opinion of her, she'd merely raised his expectations.

It had taken more nerve than she'd thought she possessed to come in here and dance for him. It had taken all her strength to look at him and through him—even though he'd sat there like some kind of lord and master, surveying her as if she was some morsel for his delectation.

But she'd still been acutely aware of that powerful body, its inherent strength barely leashed. He'd dressed in western style, in dark trousers and an open-necked shirt. And somehow, after seeing him in nothing but pristine three-piece suits and then the traditional Arabic tunic, it was a little shocking—as if he was unravelling, somehow.

Suddenly there was a flurry of movement as staff entered the cavernous space and rushed to close the huge open doors.

Sylvie had been so caught up in her own thoughts that she hadn't noticed how the sky had darkened outside—dramatically. There was so much electricity in the air she could swear it was sparking along her skin.

And then Halima appeared, a look of excitement on her pretty face. 'The Sheikh has told me to help you. We must close all your doors and windows—the storm is coming.'

As Halima ushered her out of the room, eager to do her Sheikh's bidding, Sylvie's rage spiked—as if in tandem with the escalating weather outside. If Arkim wanted a damn lap dance so badly, then maybe she should give him exactly what he wanted.

They got back to Sylvie's rooms, and Halima was about to close the French doors but turned around, eyes wide. 'You can see the sandstorm coming!'

'Really?' Curiosity distracted Sylvie momentarily and she went to the doors to look outside. She sucked in a breath when a powerful gust of wind made the curtains flap. She hadn't noticed how strong the winds had become.

'Look—see there? In the distance?'

Sylvie followed Halima's finger and saw what looked like a vast cloud against the darkening sky. It took her eyes several seconds to adjust to the fact that it was a bank of sand, racing across the desert towards them. It was like a special effect in a movie.

'My God...' she breathed, more in awe than in fear at the sight. 'Will we be okay?'

Halima shut the doors firmly and nodded. 'Of course. This castle has withstood much worse. We will be quite safe inside, and by morning it will be gone. You'll see.'

Sylvie shivered at the thought of all that energy racing across the desert—the fury she'd seen in the cloud-like shape. Not unlike the fury she'd seen in Arkim's eyes...

Halima left Sylvie to get ready, telling her she must make sure all the other doors and windows were closed.

Sylvie was grateful for that when she surveyed her outfit in the mirror a short time later. She might have winced if she hadn't still been so angry.

She'd customised one of her short skirts and now it barely grazed the tops of her thighs. The rest of her legs were covered in over-the-knee black socks. She wore a simple white shirt, knotted just under her bust, leaving her midriff bare. Underneath the skirt she wore a pair of black dance shorts, embellished with costume gems sewn into the edges, and under the shirt she wore a glittering black bra top.

She tied her hair back now, in a high ponytail. Her eyes were still heavily kohled, lashes long and dark. Lips bright red.

She felt like a total fraud, just aping what she'd seen in a million images and movies as to what constituted a lap dance outfit. It was ridiculously similar to something a famous pop-star had worn in one of her videos.

The fact was that the L'Amour revue prided itself on doing avant-garde strip routines, burlesque in nature. They didn't do anything as hokey as this. Sylvie's mouth firmed—Arkim clearly wasn't appreciative of the more subtle side of her profession.

Just then there was a knock at the door and Sylvie grabbed for her robe, slipping it on over her clothes. She didn't want Halima to see her like this. She felt tawdry.

The girl appeared. 'The Sheikh is ready for you, Miss Devereux.'

Sylvie tightened the belt of her robe and took a deep breath. 'Thank you.'

But as she walked to the ceremonial room again, behind the young girl, she felt the anger start to drain away. Doubts crept in. She was *not* what Arkim thought she was, and yet here she was—letting him goad her into pretending to be something she wasn't.

Because he'd never believe you, inserted a small voice.

She was at the door now, and her circling thoughts faded as Halima gently nudged her over the threshold.

The door closed behind her. The interior was darker than it had been, with the encroaching storm turning the world black outside. Too late to back out now. Girding her loins, Sylvie straightened her shoulders and walked in.

Arkim was sitting in his chair again, with a table beside him holding more wine and food. The anger surged back. He was so arrogant. Demanding. Judgemental. Cold.

She did her best to avoid his eyes, but she was burningly aware of him. He looked dark and unreadable when she sneaked a glance at his face. He seemed so in control. As if nothing would ruffle his cool.

Sylvie *badly* wanted to ruffle his cool.

She put on her music again, aware of the tension spiking in the room when the slow, sultry, sexy beat filled the space. She saw the chair that she'd asked Halima to provide in the centre of the dais, and she slowly unbelted her robe and then slid it off, throwing it to one side.

Did she hear an intake of breath coming from his direction?

She ignored it and walked up to the chair, turning to face Arkim with her hands on the back of it. And now she looked him straight in the eye. Unashamed. Exuding confidence even if she was quivering on the inside.

She started to move, using a mixture of what she'd seen some of the other girls do for their routines and her own modern dance moves. And a hefty dose of inspiration from one of her favourite movies of all time: *Cabaret*.

She kept eye contact with Arkim, even though her confidence threatened to dissolve when his gaze moved down, over her body, over her splayed legs as she sat in the chair. She dipped her head down between her legs before coming back up, deliberately making sure her cleavage would be visible, and running her hands up her bare thighs.

His gaze was so black it seemed to suck all the light out of the room—or was that the storm? Sylvie didn't know. She only knew that as his eyes tracked her movements she became more and more emboldened. She felt as if she was becoming one with the music. The throbbing bass beat was deep in her blood...telling her where to move next. Telling her to stand up, to put her hands on the seat of the chair and bend over, while sending a sideways look to Arkim. Telling her to straighten and then arch her back as she pulled her hair tie off so her hair tumbled down around her shoulders.

And telling her to open the buttons on her shirt, down to where it was tied under her breasts, so that they would be revealed.

Something dangerous was pounding through her blood—the same something that had coursed through it that night in the garden, when Arkim had pressed against her, letting her feel how aroused he was by her...even though he disapproved of her.

Sylvie felt powerful—because she could sense his control cracking. Arkim's cheeks were flushed, eyes glittering darkly. Jaw clenched. This was what she wanted...to make him admit he was a hypocrite.

Without really thinking about what she was doing, Sylvie stepped down from the dais and walked over to Arkim. His chin tipped up and their gazes clashed—just as the music faded away and stopped, bursting the bubble of illusion around them.

She knew instantly that she'd made a tactical error. Desperate to try and regain her sense of power, she started to walk away from his chair—but a big hand shot out and gripped her wrist, stopping her in her tracks.

She looked down at him, heart bumping violently. That obsidian gaze glittered up at her, and she saw the fire in their depths. The knowledge that she'd managed to ruffle him wasn't as satisfying as she'd expected when she was this close to him.

He stood up and they were almost touching. The air sizzled.

'What the *hell*,' he said in a low voice, 'do you think you're doing?'

The disgust Sylvie read in his eyes made her pull her wrist free of his grip with a jerk. She was aware that the huge sand cloud was approaching closer and closer through the massive windows behind Arkim, about to envelop them totally, blotting everything out. It made her feel reckless—as if everything was about to be altered for ever.

'Isn't this what you expected of me?' she asked tauntingly. 'I'm giving you exactly what you want.'

'*Exactly* what I want?' he asked.

And before she could say anything, just before the sandstorm inexorably claimed the castle in its path, Arkim speared both hands into her hair, angling her face up to his.

'I'll show you exactly what I want,' he said gutturally.

Arkim crushed Sylvie's mouth under his, his need too great to be gentle or finessed. He wanted to devour her.

Her lips were soft, but she kept her mouth closed and there was tension in her body. Damn her. She would *not* deny him. Not after that cheap little show. Yet even in spite of the tackiness he'd still been turned on. *Again.* And she was right—he'd asked for this.

That knowledge wasn't welcome.

Neither was her resistance.

Arkim was aware of the changing quality of sound around them. How everything was muffled. The sandstorm must have enveloped them by now. But all of that was secondary to the woman in his arms. The woman who would pay for turning his life upside down.

He took his mouth off hers and looked down to see those extraordinary eyes glaring at him. If he wasn't acutely aware of how her body quivered against his he would have let her go, been done with her. A reluctant lover was not something he was interested in—not that he had much experience of that.

But Sylvie wanted him. It had sparked between them from the moment their eyes had met—from the moment he'd rejected her outright. And in spite of that rejection they were here now, as if this course had always been inevitable.

There was no turning back until this was done and she'd paid. And he was sated.

He relaxed his hands in her hair, started to subtly massage her skull. It felt fragile under his hands.

'What are you doing?' she said huskily.

Her hands were against his chest, but she wasn't pushing him away. His arousal was so hard he ached with the need to sheathe himself inside her body, feel her contract around him. But her innate fragility did something to him...it tempered his anger, turned it into a need to seduce. To make her acquiescent.

'I'm making love to you.'

Her hands pushed against his chest now. 'Well, I don't want to be made love to.'

Arkim shook his head, his fingers all the while massaging her skull in slow, methodical movements. 'You've admitted you want me. And I think you *do* want to be made love to—very much. After all, you're a highly sexed woman...aren't you, Sylvie?'

Sylvie looked up into his eyes. Even in heels she felt tiny next to him. Puny. Weak. His fingers were in her hair, massaging her... She felt like purring. Not like pushing him away. But she had to. *Highly sexed?* If he found out what she really was—

She went cold at the thought and pushed him again, but his chest was like a steel wall. Immovable. At the same time she was aware that she wasn't scared; the fight to get away from him was as much a fight with herself as it was with him. More so. And he knew it—the bastard.

His hands were moving now…down to her jaw, cradling her face. Something dangerous lurched inside Sylvie—some emotion that had no place there. It seemed to be the hardest thing in the world to free herself completely and move away.

Arkim's scent was heady, masculine. It enticed her on a very basic female level. He didn't even say anything this time. He just bent his head and kissed her again, those sensual lips moving over hers with masterful precision and an expertise she couldn't resist even though she tried.

She tried to keep her mouth closed, like before. But Arkim was biting gently on her lower lip, making it tingle, making her want more… She felt some of her resistance give way, treacherously, and he took advantage like the expert he was—slipping his tongue between her lips, finding hers and setting her world on fire.

His hands moved over her shoulders, down her back, urging her into him, against the hard contours of his body. Her scanty costume offered little protection. She was helplessly responding to his kiss, to the tantalising slide of his tongue against hers, urging her to mimic him, initiate her own contact.

Sylvie couldn't think. Everything was blurry, fuzzy. Except for this decadent pleasure, seeping into her veins and making her feel languorous. Treacherously, she didn't want this moment to stop. *Ever.*

Her hands were moving, lifting of their own volition, sliding around Arkim's neck so that she could press closer. She was aware of her breasts, crushed to his chest, tightening into hard points. One of his hands was on her lower back and it dipped down further, cupping one buttock, squeezing gently. Between her legs she felt hot, moist…

But as Arkim's hand slipped even lower, precariously close to where Sylvie suddenly wanted to feel him explore her, she had a startling moment of clarity—this man hated her. He believed that she was little more than a common tart, debauched and irredeemable, and she was about to let him be more intimate with her than anyone else had ever been.

Disgusted with her lack of control, Sylvie took Arkim by surprise and pushed herself free of his embrace. For a second when he opened his eyes they looked glazed, unfocused, and then they cleared and narrowed on her. She felt hot and dishevelled. And exposed.

She put her arms around herself. 'I told you. I don't want this.'

Colour slashed Arkim's cheekbones. He was grim. 'You want this, all right—you're just determined to send me crazy for wanting it too.'

Something enigmatic lit his eyes, and for a split-second Sylvie had the uncanny impression that it was vulnerability.

That impression was well and truly quashed when he said coldly, 'I don't play games. Go to bed, Sylvie.'

He turned on his heel, and he was walking away when something rogue goaded her to call after him, 'You don't know a thing about me. You think you do, but you don't.'

Arkim stopped and turned around, his face etched in stern lines. It made Sylvie want to run her fingers over them, see them soften. She cursed herself.

'What don't I know?' he asked, with a faint sneer in his tone.

'Things like the fact that I'd never sleep with someone who hates me as much as you do.'

He walked back towards her slowly and Sylvie regretted saying anything. He stopped a few feet away.

'I thought I hated you...especially after what you did

to ruin the wedding...but actually I don't feel anything for you except physical desire.'

Sylvie was surprised how strong the dart of hurt was, but she covered it by saying flippantly, 'Oh, wow—thanks for the clarification. That makes it all *so* much better.'

To her surprise, Arkim just looked at her for a long moment, and then he reached for the robe that lay on the ground near their feet and handed it to her, saying curtly, 'Put it on.'

Now he wanted her to cover up... Why didn't that make her feel vindicated in some way?

She slipped her arms into the sleeves and belted the thick material tightly around her waist. Arkim was still looking at her intently, but it had a different quality to any expression she'd seen before. She felt exposed, and a little disorientated. For a moment when he'd handed her the robe she could have sworn he'd seemed almost...apologetic.

As much as she didn't want to hear his scathing response again, she was tired of playing a role that wasn't really her. 'There's something else you don't know.'

Arkim arched a brow.

She took a deep breath. 'I've never actually...stripped. The main act I do in the show is the one with the sword. I do other routines too, but I've never taken all my clothes off. What I did just now... I made it up... I was just proving a point.'

He frowned, shook his head as if trying to clear it. 'Why don't I believe that?'

Sylvie lifted her chin. 'Because you judged me before you even met me, and you have some seriously flawed ideas about what the revue actually is. Why would I lie? It's not as if I have anything to lose where you're concerned.'

She saw a familiar flash of fire come into Arkim's eyes and went on hurriedly.

'The man who runs the revue—Pierre—he knew my

mother. They were contemporaries. When I arrived in Paris I was seventeen years old. He took me under his wing. For the first two years I was only allowed to train with the other dancers. I wasn't allowed to perform. I cleaned and helped keep the books to pay my way.' Sylvie shrugged and looked away, embarrassed that she was telling Arkim so much. 'He's protective of me—like a father figure. I think that's why he doesn't allow me to do the more risqué acts.'

When she glanced back at Arkim his face was inscrutable. Sylvie realised then that he probably resented her telling him anything of the reality of her life.

When he spoke his voice was cool, with no hint of whether or not he believed her. 'Go to bed Sylvie, we're done here.'

She felt his dismissal like a slap in the face and realised with a sense of hollowness that perhaps she should have been honest from the beginning. Then they could have avoided all of this. Because clearly Arkim had no time for a woman who didn't match up to his worst opinions.

He turned to walk away again and she blurted out before she could stop herself, 'What do you mean, "we're done"?'

Arkim stopped and looked at her. He seemed to be weighing something up in his mind and then he said, 'We'll be leaving as soon as the storm has passed.'

Then he just turned and walked out, leaving Sylvie gaping. *'We'll be leaving...'* She'd done it. She'd provoked him into letting her go. She'd finally made him listen to her—made him listen as she tried to explain who she really was. And now he didn't want to know. Yet instead of relief or triumph all Sylvie felt was...deflated.

'I don't feel anything for you except physical desire.' Arkim's own words mocked him. He couldn't get the flash

of hurt he'd seen in Sylvie's eyes out of his head. And he tried. He couldn't deny that it made him feel...guilty. Constricted.

He'd lied. What he felt for her was much more complicated than mere physical desire. It was a tangled mess of emotions, underscored by the most urgent lust he'd ever felt.

He didn't ever say things to hurt women—he stayed well away from any such possibility by making sure that his liaisons were not remotely emotional. Yet he seemed to have no problem lashing out and tearing strips off Sylvie Devereux at every opportunity.

It should be bringing him some sense of pleasure, or satisfaction. But it wasn't. Because he had the skin-prickling feeling that there was something he was missing. Something in Sylvie's responses. He would have expected her to be more petulant. Whiny. More obviously spoilt.

She'd shown defiance, yes, and even though her dash into the desert had been foolhardy she'd shown resilience.

Arkim sat in his book-lined study with its dark, sophisticated furniture and classic original art. He'd always liked this room because it was so far removed from what he remembered of his childhood in LA: his father's vast modern glass mansion in the hills of Hollywood. Everything there was gaudy and ostentatious, the infinity swimming pool full of naked bodies and people high on drugs.

And now he felt like a total hypocrite. Because when Sylvie had stood in front of him in some parody of what strippers wore—because *he'd* all but goaded her into it— he'd been as hard and aching as he could ever remember being. The insidious truth that he really was not so far removed from his father whispered over his skin and made him down a gulp of whisky in a bid to burn it away.

He'd brought her here and asked for it—and she'd called his bluff spectacularly. She was turning him upside down and inside out with her bright blue and green gaze that seemed to sear right through him and tear him apart deep inside. Showing up everything he sought to hide.

The fact that she'd seemed intuitively to sense the maelstrom she inspired within him had galvanised him into kissing her into submission. And yet she'd been the one who had stood there proudly and told him she wouldn't sleep with someone who hated her.

He'd walked away from her just now because she'd shamed him. The irony mocked him.

Arkim couldn't deny it any more: Sylvie made no excuses for what she did and she had more self-worth than most of the people he encountered, who would look down their noses at her. As he had.

When she'd mentioned going to Paris at seventeen he'd felt a tug of empathy and curiosity that no other woman had ever evoked within him. He'd been seventeen when he'd last seen his father. When he'd told him he wasn't coming back to LA and when he'd decided that he would do whatever it took to make it on his own.

Arkim stood up and paced his study. It felt claustrophobic, with the shutters closed against the storm which raged outside—not unlike the turmoil he felt within.

The truth was that he wanted to know more about Sylvie—more about why she did what she did. About her in general. And he'd never felt that same compulsion to know about her sister.

He'd told Sylvie that they'd be leaving as soon as the storm was over—a reflexive reaction to the fact that she affected him in a way he hadn't anticipated. He'd thought it would be easy, that she'd be easy. The truth was that the storm might pass outside, but it would rage inside him until he quenched it.

If he left this place without having her she would haunt him for the rest of his life.

* * *

When Sylvie woke the next morning everything was dark and quiet. She got up and padded to the shutters over her windows, not sure what to expect. Maybe the castle would be completely buried in sand? But when she opened them she squinted as beautiful bright blue skies were revealed. What looked like just a thin layer of sand lay over the terrace—the only clue to the formidable weather of the previous evening.

Her mind skittered away from thinking of what else had happened. She wanted to cringe every time she thought of how she must have made such a complete fool of herself—prancing around in those stupid clothes. Even more cringeworthy was recalling how for a few moments she'd got really into it, and had seriously thought she might be turning Arkim on.

But he'd been disgusted. Yet not disgusted enough not to kiss her. And she'd responded—which said dire things about her own sense of self-worth.

Thank God she'd managed to pull back. To show some small measure of dignity. If she hadn't, she could well imagine that Arkim might have laid her down on that stone floor and had her there and then—and discovered for himself just how innocent she was. Sylvie balked at that prospect.

The sunlight streaming into the room reminded her of the fact that Arkim had said they'd be leaving. She sank back on the bed. She'd done it. She'd managed to resist him and disgust him so completely that he was prepared to take her home. In spite of the mutual physical lust that sparked between them like crackling fire whenever they got close.

She hated to admit it, but that sense of deflation hadn't lifted. Had she enjoyed sparring with Arkim so much? Had she wanted him to take her in spite of what he thought of her? In spite of her brave words last night?

Yes, said a small voice, deep inside. *Because he's connected with you on a level that no other man ever has.*

Sylvie felt disgusted with herself. Was she so wounded inside after her father's rejection of her that this was the only way she could feel desire? For a man who rejected her on every level but the physical?

Someone knocked on the door and she reached for her robe, pulling it on. Halima appeared, smiling, with breakfast on a tray. She set it up on a table near the French doors and opened them wide.

'The storm has passed! It will be good weather for your trip with the Sheikh.'

'My trip…?' Sylvie said quietly, assuming Halima meant her trip home.

The other girl chattered on. 'Yes, the oasis is so beautiful this time of year…and the way it emerges from the desert—it's like a lush paradise.'

Sylvie frowned, confused. 'Wait—the oasis? Arkim—I mean, the Sheikh isn't leaving to go home today?'

Now Halima looked confused. 'No, he is preparing for his trip and you are going with him. I am to pack enough things for a few days.'

Sylvie's heart-rate picked up pace, along with her pulse. What was Arkim up to now?

She rushed through her breakfast and got washed, and when she re-emerged into the suite Halima was waiting with her bag packed.

Sylvie had dressed in simple cargo pants and a T-shirt. Halima took one look and tutted, saying something about more suitable clothing. Sylvie followed the girl into the dressing room, which Sylvie hadn't explored fully yet, having been intent on using her own clothes. But now Halima was opening the wardrobe doors, and Sylvie gasped when she saw what looked like acres of beautiful fabric: dresses, trousers… All with designer labels.

'Whose are these?' she breathed, letting the silk of one particularly beautiful crimson dress move through her fingers. The thought of them belonging to another woman—or women—was stinging Sylvie in a place that was not welcome.

'They're yours, of course. The Sheikh had them delivered especially for you before your arrival.'

Shock made Sylvie speechless for a moment, and then she said carefully, 'Are you sure they aren't left over from the last woman he had here?'

Halima turned and looked at her, incomprehension clear on her pretty face. 'Another woman? But he's never brought anyone else here.'

Sylvie knew she wasn't lying—she was too sweet... innocent. Her heart started beating even harder. She'd assumed this exotic remote bolthole was one of Arkim's preferred places to decamp with a mistress. She would never have guessed she was the first woman he'd brought here.

'Here—you should change into this.'

Sylvie blinked and saw Halima holding out a long cream tunic with beautiful gold embroidery. Like a more elaborate version of the tunic Arkim had put on her when he'd found her in the desert. *'You're burning.'* His reprimand came back.

'Is this a cultural thing?' Sylvie asked Halima as she slipped out of her trousers.

'Well, yes. Where you're going *is* more rural, and conservative. But it's also practical. It protects you from the heat and sun.'

'Where you're going.' Sylvie was very aware that she had given no indication to the girl that she was *not* going on this trip. Was she going to just...*go*? Acquiesce? Her pulse tripped again at the thought, and a wave of heat seemed to infuse her skin from toe to head.

The tunic was matched with close-fitting trousers in a

beautiful soft cotton material. They too were embroidered with gold. And then Halima was placing a gossamer-light matching shawl around her shoulders. Soft flat shoes completed the outfit.

Sylvie caught sight of herself in a mirror and sucked in a breath. Her hair stood out vibrantly against the light colours of the clothes. She looked…not like herself—but perversely *more* like herself in a way she'd never seen before.

Halima tweaked Sylvie's shawl over her head, and then they were walking down the corridor. She felt a little like a bride being walked to face her fate.

Sylvie chastised herself for being so compliant. Of course she wanted to leave. Of course she had no intention of going off to this admittedly, intriguing-sounding oasis with a man who felt nothing for her and yet made her body come alive in a way that made her want to descend with him into a pit of fire.

She was going to tell Arkim she had no intention of—

All her thoughts faded to nothing when they rounded the corner into the main hall and Sylvie saw Arkim waiting for her.

CHAPTER SIX

HE SIMPLY TOOK her breath away. It was as if she'd never seen him before. He was so tall and exotic, in a long dark blue tunic. Still stern...

It made her yearn for things: to see him smile, unbend. To know more about him. Dangerous things.

The staff left their bags between two Jeeps and melted away into the shadows. Sylvie was aware that this was the moment when she should make it absolutely clear that she had no intention of going with Arkim to this oasis. But she was rooted to the spot—caught and mesmerised by those obsidian eyes.

There was an intense silent conversation happening between them. He was issuing a direct challenge with that fathomless gaze. A challenge that she felt in every pulsing, throbbing beat of her blood. A challenge of the most sensual kind. A challenge to step up and own her femininity in a way she'd never done before. A challenge to go with him.

She felt giddy...breathless. The palms of her hands were damp with perspiration that had nothing to do with the heat.

It came down to this: did she want this man enough to throw her self-respect to the winds and risk the bitter sting of self-recrimination for ever? Did she want to give him the satisfaction of knowing that he was right? That ultimately she couldn't resist him? And did she want to risk the worst kind of rejection?

He moved, and her breath hitched at the sheer grace and beauty of his masculinity. He stopped in front of her. She could see the tension in his form and on his face. It made something inside her soften, uncoil. Closer, like this, he was infinitely more seductive, less formidable. And infinitely harder to resist.

'There are two Jeeps behind me.'

Sylvie had seen them. She nodded.

'The one on the left will take you back to the airfield where we landed the other day—if you want it to. The one on the right is the one I'm taking to the oasis. I told you last night that we'd both be leaving, but I've decided to stay. I want you to stay with me, Sylvie. I think there are things about you that I don't know...that I want to know. And I want *you*. This isn't about the past or the wedding any more. I've made my point. This is about...*us*. And it's been about us since the moment we met.'

His mouth twisted.

'Perhaps our failing all along has been that we didn't pursue this attraction at the time. If we had we wouldn't be standing here now.'

Sylvie's chest contracted with a mixture of volatile emotions. 'Because you'd be married to my sister? That's heinous—'

His finger against her lips stopped her words. He looked disgusted. He took his finger away, but not before Sylvie had the strongest urge to take it into her mouth.

'No. I *never* would have pursued your sister with marriage in mind if we had had an affair.'

Affair. The word hit her hard. Arkim didn't need to clarify the fact that Sylvie would never in a million years be a contender for marriage or a relationship.

Right now she felt very certain that she would be getting into the Jeep on the left. But then his mouth softened into those dangerously sensual lines and he slid a hand around her neck, under her hair. Suddenly she couldn't think straight.

'If we don't do this...explore our mutual desire...it'll

eat us up inside like acid. If you're strong enough to walk away, to deny this, then go ahead. I won't come after you, Sylvie. You'll never see me again.'

She wanted to pour scorn on Arkim's words. The sheer *arrogance*! As if she *wanted* to see him again! She should be pulling away from him and saying *good riddance*. But there was a quality to his voice... Something almost... rough. Pleading. And the thought of never seeing him again made her want to reach out and grip the material of his tunic in her fist. Not walk away.

God. What did that mean? What did that make *her*?

Arkim took his hand away and stepped back. Sylvie almost reached out for him. She teetered on the cliff-edge of a very scary and precipitous drop into the unknown. His words seduced her: *There are things about you that I don't know...that I want to know.*

A fluttering started low in her belly. Nerves, excitement. The thought of going with him...getting to know him more...letting him be intimate with her...was terrifying. But the thought of leaving...going back to her life and not knowing him...was more terrifying.

Sylvie's gut had been guiding her for a long time now—taking her out of the toxic orbit of her stepmother and her father's black grief at the age of seventeen—and it was guiding her towards the Jeep on the right-hand side before she could stop herself.

Arkim displayed no discernible triumph or sanctimony. He just held the passenger door open for her to get in, closed it, and got in at the other side. Sylvie was aware of the staff re-materialising, to put their bags in the back of the Jeep, and once that was done Arkim was pulling away and out of the castle.

She tried to drum up a sense of shame for her easy capitulation but it eluded her. All she felt was a fizzing sense of illicit anticipation.

Endless rolling desert and blue skies surrounded them. It should have been a boring landscape but it wasn't. And the silence that enveloped them was surprisingly easy as Arkim navigated over a road that was little more than a dirt track.

Eventually, though, Sylvie had to say the words beating a tattoo in her brain. She looked at him, taking in his aristocratic profile. 'Halima told me you've never brought anyone else to the castle.'

His hands tightened on the steering wheel momentarily and his jaw twitched. 'No, I haven't taken anyone else there.'

She hated it that she cared, because it meant nothing, and the feeling of exposure after having mentioned it made her say frigidly, 'I should have guessed that you'd prefer to keep this…*situation* well out of the prying gaze of the media. The last thing you want is to be publicly associated with someone like *me*.'

Arkim glanced at Sylvie, and she was surprised to see his mouth tip up ever so slightly at one side. 'I think our association became pretty public when you broke apart the wedding and claimed that I'd spent the night in your bed.'

She flushed. She'd conveniently forgotten that. She never had been a good liar. Afraid he'd ask her again about her motive for doing such a thing, she said hurriedly, 'This oasis—it's yours?'

Arkim finally looked away again to the road—but not before Sylvie's skin had prickled hotly under his assessing gaze. 'Yes, it's part of the land I own. However, nomads and travellers use it, and I would never disallow them access as some others do. It's really their land.'

There was unmistakable pride in Arkim's tone, and it made Sylvie realise that, whatever their tangled relationship was, this man was not without integrity.

Genuinely curious, she asked, 'What's your connection to Al-Omar?'

Arkim's jaw tightened. 'This is where my mother is from—hence my name. The land belonged to a distant ancestor. She grew up in B'harani; her father was an advisor to the old Sultan, before Sadiq took over.'

'And do you see any of your family here?'

Before he'd even answered Sylvie might have guessed the truth from the way his face became stern again.

'They disowned my mother when she brought shame on the family name—in their eyes. They've never expressed any interest in meeting me.'

Sylvie felt a surge of emotion and said quietly, 'I'm sorry that she had to go through that. She must have felt lonely.'

How bigoted and cruel of them, to just leave her. But she didn't think Arkim would appreciate any further discussion on the subject, or hearing her saying she felt sorry for him.

She looked out of the window and took the opportunity to move things on to a less contentious footing. 'It is beautiful here...so different to anything I've ever seen before.'

There was a mocking tone to his voice. 'You don't miss the shops? Clubs? Busy city life?'

She immediately felt defensive. 'I love living in Paris, yes. But I actually hate shopping. And I work late almost every night, so on the nights I *do* have off the last thing I want to do is go out to a club.'

Arkim seemed to consider this for a moment. Then he settled back into his seat and angled his body towards her, one hand relaxed on the wheel and the other on his thigh.

'So tell me something else about yourself, then... How did you end up in Paris at seventeen?'

Sylvie cursed herself. She'd asked for it, hadn't she? By changing the subject. She looked at him and there was something different about him—something almost conciliatory. As if he was making an effort.

Because he wants you in his bed.

She ignored the mocking voice. 'I left home at seventeen because I was never the most academic student and I wanted to dance.'

She deliberately avoided going into any more detail.

'So why not dance in the UK? Why did you have to go to Paris? Surely your aspirations were a little higher?'

Arkim sounded genuinely mystified instead of condemning, and Sylvie felt a rush of emotion when she remembered those tumultuous days. Her hands clenched into fists in her lap without her realising what they were doing.

Suddenly one of his hands covered hers. He was frowning at her. 'What is it?'

Shocked at the gesture, she looked at him. The warmth of his hand made her speak without really thinking. 'I was just remembering… It was not…an easy time.'

Arkim took his hand away to put it on the wheel again, in order to navigate an uneven part of the road. When they were through it, he said, 'Go on.'

Sylvie faced forward, hands clasped tightly in her lap. She'd never spoken of this with anyone—not really. And to find that she was about to speak of it now, to this man, was a little mind-boggling.

Yet even *his* judgement could never amount to the self-recrimination she felt for behaving so reactively. Even though she couldn't really regret it. She'd learnt so much about herself in the process.

'As is pretty obvious, my stepmother and I don't get on. We never have since she married my father. And my father… Our relationship is strained. I rebelled quite a bit—against both of them. And Catherine, my stepmother, was making life…difficult for me.'

'How?' Arkim's voice was sharp.

'She wanted me to be sent to a finishing school in Switzerland—a way to get rid of me. So I left. I went to Paris to find some old contacts of my mother's. I'd always wanted to dance, and I'd taken lessons as a child... But after my mother died my father lost interest. And when Catherine came along she insisted that dance classes weren't appropriate. She had issues with keeping my mother's memory alive.'

That was putting it mildly. Her father had had issues too, and his had had more far-reaching consequences for Sylvie. Her stepmother was just a jealous, insecure woman. She'd never known Sylvie well enough for her rejection to really hurt. But her father *had* known her.

'So you took off to Paris on your own and started working at the revue?'

Sylvie nodded and settled back into her seat, the luxurious confines of the vehicle making it seductively easy to relax a little more. 'I had about one hundred pounds in my pocket when I met up with Pierre and found a home at the revue. I had to pay my way, of course. He let me take dance classes, but only if I cleaned in my spare time.'

'You took no money from your father?'

Sylvie glanced at Arkim's frown and slightly incredulous expression and wondered why she was surprised at his assumption that she would have. 'No, I haven't taken a penny from my father since I left home. I'm very proud of the money I make—it's not much, but it's mine and it's hard-earned.'

He schooled his expression. This information put everything he knew about Sylvie on its head and pricked his conscience. It was so completely opposite to everything he'd always assumed about her: that she was a trust fund kid, petulant and bored, seeking to disgrace her family just because she could. It sounded as if she'd sought refuge in Paris out of rebellion, yes, but also because she'd more or less been pushed away.

Very aware of that direct gaze on him, he said a little gruffly, 'You should rest for a bit—it'll take another hour or so to get there.'

Sylvie's eyes flashed at his clear dismissal of the subject, but gradually the tense lines of her body relaxed and she curled her legs up on the seat. Her head drifted to one side, long red hair trailing down over her shoulder.

Her lashes were long and dark against her cheeks. She wore no make-up, and Arkim noticed a smattering of small, almost undetectable freckles across the bridge of her nose. Had that been the sun? Because he didn't remember seeing them before. They gave her an air of innocence that compounded the naivety he'd seen in her dancing.

His chest felt tight. He looked back to the desert road, feeling slightly panicked. He shouldn't have indulged his base desire like this. He'd already behaved completely out of character by bringing her to Al-Omar in the first place—like some medieval overlord. He should have called the helicopter and got them both back to civilisation. He'd made his point—he'd demonstrated his anger.

But his hands gripped the steering wheel tight and he kept on driving. Because he wasn't ready to call it quits, to let her go. And she'd made a very clear choice to stay, and the triumph he'd felt in that moment still beat in his blood. Why would he turn back now, when they could exorcise this lust between them and get on with their lives?

'We're here.'

Sylvie opened her eyes and looked out of her window, straightening up in her seat as wonder and awe filled her. Maybe she was still dreaming? Because this was paradise. They were surrounded by lush greenery—greener than anything she'd ever seen before.

Arkim had got out of the Jeep and was opening her door. She got out on wobbly legs, eyes on stalks.

Two big tents were set up nearby—dark and lavishly decorated, with their tops coming to a point in the centre. Smaller tents sat off at a distance, separated from the others by trees. Sand dunes rose up around the camp, almost encircling it on one side, and on the other side was a rocky wall. When Sylvie shaded her eyes to look, she saw the most exquisite natural pool.

She walked over, stunned. The water was so clear she could see right down to the rocks at the bottom. The air was warm and soft—a million miles from the harsh heat she'd experienced since she'd arrived.

She felt Arkim's presence beside her but was afraid to look at him because her emotions were all over the place—especially so soon after waking up. It was as if she was missing a layer of skin.

'This is obviously a very special place,' she finally managed to get out, without sounding too husky.

'Yes, it is. I think it's the most peaceful spot on this earth.'

Sylvie looked at him at last and saw that he was staring down into the water. When he lifted his head and looked at her his gaze was so direct that it took her breath away. It was the most unguarded she'd ever seen him, and she could see so many things in his eyes. But the one that hit her right in the belly was desire.

She had a feeling that whatever lay tangled between them—all the animosity, misjudgement and distrust—it was slipping away and becoming irrelevant. What was relevant was here and now. Just the two of them—a man and a woman.

It was so primal that Sylvie was almost taking a step towards Arkim before she realised that someone was interrupting them, telling him something.

Arkim's gaze slipped from Sylvie's and she held herself rigid, aghast that she'd come so close to revealing herself like that. Was she really so ready to jump into his arms? Even though she'd already tacitly capitulated by coming here?

Sylvie composed herself as Arkim talked to the man, and then he was turning towards her. 'Lunch has been prepared for us.'

She welcomed the break in the heightened tension and followed him as he led her to an open area outside the tents, where a table had been set up under a fabric covering held up by four posts. It was rustic, but charming.

The table was low, covered in a deep red silk tablecloth, and there was no cutlery. Arkim indicated a big cushion on one side of the table for Sylvie and she sat down, mesmerised by the mouth-watering array of foods laid out on platters. The smell alone was enough to get her stomach growling.

Arkim settled himself opposite her and handed her a plate with an assortment of food which she surmised she was meant to eat with her hands. Silver finger bowls were set by their plates.

Sylvie experimented with something that looked like a rice ball, closing her eyes in appreciation as warm cheese melted into her mouth. When she opened them again she saw Arkim taking a sip of golden liquid and watching her. There was something very sensual about eating with her hands. And then she looked at Arkim's strong hands and imagined them tracing her body... Heat suffused her face.

'Try your drink—it's a special brew of the region. Not exactly wine, but a relation.'

Sylvie hurriedly took a sip, hoping it might cool her down. It was like nectar—sweet but with a tart finish. 'It's delicious.'

Arkim's mouth tipped up. 'It's also lethal, so just a few sips is enough.'

She frowned. 'I thought people didn't really drink in this part of the world?'

'They don't... But there are nomads from this region who have made a name for themselves with this brew. It's a secret recipe, handed down over hundreds of years and made from rare desert berries.'

Sylvie took another sip and relished the smooth glide of the cold liquid down her throat. She realised that she'd always known what sensuality was in an abstract and intellectual way, and that she could exude it when she wanted to, but she'd never really embodied it herself. She felt as if she embodied it now, though, when this man looked at her. Or touched her.

She put the glass down quickly, shocked at how easily this place was entrancing her. And at how easily Arkim was intriguing her by making her believe that things had somehow shifted. They had...but in essence nothing much had changed. She was who she was, and *he* was who he was.

When this man set his mind to seduction it was nigh impossible to resist him, and Sylvie had a sense that she was far more vulnerable to him than she even realised herself. She knew it was irrational, because she'd already agreed to come here, but she felt she had to push him back.

She heard herself saying, 'Why go to the trouble of bringing me here when we both know this isn't about romance? You say you don't hate me, but what you do feel for me isn't far off that.'

Arkim looked at Sylvie from where he lounged across the table. Her hair glowed so bright it almost hurt to look at. Her skin was like alabaster—like a pearl against the backdrop of this ochre-hued place.

He replied with an honesty he hadn't intended. 'You've

turned my life upside down. You irritate me and frustrate me...and I want you more than I've ever wanted another woman. What I feel for you is...ambiguous.'

Sylvie looked at him, and this time there was no mistaking the hurt flashing in her eyes. Before Arkim could react she stood up and paced away for a moment, and then she swung round, hair slipping over one shoulder, tunic billowing around her feet.

She crossed her arms. 'This was a mistake. I should never have come here with you.'

Arkim cursed his mouth and surged to his feet. Yet again Sylvie was exposing all his most base qualities. He couldn't believe how uncouth he was around this woman. He moved towards her and she took a step back. He controlled his impulse to grab her.

'You're here because you want to be, Sylvie—plain and simple. This isn't about what's happened. This is about us—here and now. Nothing else. I won't dress it up in fancy language. There is a physical honesty between us which I believe has more integrity than any fluctuating and fickle emotions.'

He saw how she paled, but how her pulse stayed hectic. Arkim felt as if he held the most delicate of brightly coloured humming-birds in his palm and it was about to fly away, never to be seen again.

He wanted her full acquiescence—for her to admit she wanted him. It unnerved him how much he wanted that when he hadn't given much consideration to her feelings before now.

Another truth forced its way out. 'You were right last night. I don't know you, but I want to. Sit down...finish eating. Please.'

Arkim was tense, waiting. But eventually Sylvie moved jerkily and sat down again. None of her usual grace was evident. She avoided his eyes as he took his seat again and they ate some more, awareness and tension crackling between them like a live wire.

After a minute she wiped her mouth with a napkin and took another sip of her drink. Then she looked at Arkim, her blue-green gaze disturbingly intense.

'So...what was it like growing up in LA?'

Relief that she was engaging stripped away Arkim's guardedness. His inner reaction to her question was a list of words. *Brash. Artificial. Excessive.* But he said, 'I hated it. So much so that I've never been back.'

Sylvie assimilated that, and then said, 'I've been to Las Vegas and I hated it there. It's so fake—like a film set.'

A spurt of kinship surprised Arkim. 'LA is massive—sprawling. Lots of different areas separated by miles of freeway...no real connection. Everyone is looking for a place in the spotlight—striving to be skinnier, more tanned, more perfect than the next person. There's no soul.'

'They say no one walks in LA.'

Arkim smiled and it felt odd—because he wasn't used to smiling so spontaneously in the presence of anyone, much less a woman.

'That's true. Unless you go somewhere like Santa Monica, and then it's like a catwalk.'

'You really haven't seen your father since you left?'

He shook his head. 'Not since I was seventeen.' Then he grimaced. 'That's not entirely accurate. I would have left voluntarily, but I was still too young. He threw me out.'

'Why?'

Arkim steeled himself. 'Because he caught me having sex with his mistress—a famous porn actress.'

He saw myriad expressions cross Sylvie's face: shock, hurt, and then anger.

She put her napkin down, eyes flaming, jaw tight. 'You absolute hypocrite! You have the gall to subject me to your judge and jury act and all the time—'

'Wait.' Arkim's voice rang out harshly.

He hadn't even been aware of the impulse to lean across the table and capture Sylvie's wrist in his hand before he realised that was what he was doing. Panic made his gut clench. For the first time in his life he found that his words were tripping out before he could stop them—along with an urge to make her understand.

Because if Sylvie damned him then there truly was no hope for his redemption at all...

'I didn't seduce her. She seduced me.'

Sylvie looked at Arkim, her wrist still caught in his firm grip. There was something almost desperate in his eyes. Her anger, which had flared so quickly, started to fizzle out. 'What do you mean?'

He let her wrist go and stood up, moving away from the table to pace, running a hand through his hair. Sylvie had never seen him like this. On the edge of his control.

He turned to face her, his face etched in stark lines. 'I was back from England for the summer holidays. My father had refused to let me stay in Europe for the summer, even though I'd offered to pay my own way by working. I'd done my A levels. I was just biding my time until I had to go to college. My father knew I hated LA, so he taunted me with it.'

His mouth twisted. 'Cindy was everywhere I was. Especially when my father wasn't around. And invariably she was half-naked.'

Self-disgust was evident in his voice.

'I thought I could resist her... I tried for the whole summer. I was only a few days from returning to the UK and she found me by the pool. I was too weak. The worst thing was that she stayed in control the whole time while I lost it. My father found us in the pool house.'

He didn't have to elaborate on what had happened next

for Sylvie to join the dots. She shouldn't be feeling anything other than what he'd dished out to her—judgement and condemnation... But she couldn't help it. Sympathy surged in her breast. She could well imagine that whatever judgement she might hurl at Arkim, he'd already judged himself a thousand times over—and far more harshly than anyone else could have.

'You were seventeen, Arkim. There's probably not a straight teenage hormonal boy on the planet who could have resisted the seduction of an older and more experienced woman—much less a porn star whose job is controlling sex.'

Arkim's harsh lines didn't relax. 'She only did it because she wanted to make my father jealous...to push him into some kind of commitment. She gambled the wrong way, though. He threw her out too.'

He turned away from her then, to look out at the view. His back was broad, formidable. As if he didn't want her to look at him.

'Do you know I saw my first orgy when I was eight?'

Sylvie put a hand to her mouth, glad he wasn't looking at her reaction. She took her hand down after a moment. 'Arkim...that's—'

He turned around again. He was harsh. 'That was my life. Someone saw me watching, and of course I couldn't really understand what was happening. It was after that that my father sent me to school in England. He got off on the idea of sending me to school with English royalty. But it saved me, I think. I only had to survive the holidays, and I learned to avert my eyes from the debauched parties he liked to throw.'

The thought of such a small child witnessing such things and then being sent away... Sylvie stood up. 'That was abuse, Arkim. And what that woman did to you— seducing you like that—it was a form of abuse too.'

Arkim smiled, but it was infinitely cynical and Sylvie suddenly loathed it.

'*Was* it abuse? When it was the most exciting moment of my life at that point? She showed me how much pleasure a man can feel. I submitted to her. Even though I hated myself for it.'

For a second Sylvie felt a blinding flash of jealousy so acute she nearly gasped. The thought of this man being helpless, submitting to a woman who had given him pleasure… and who was not *her*…was painful.

Thankfully he didn't seem to notice her seismic reaction and he said, 'Do you know what it's like to grow up under the influence of someone with no moral compass?'

Sylvie shook her head, clawing back control.

He was grim. 'It's like you're tainted by his deeds—no matter what you do to try and distance yourself. It's a tattoo on your skin—for ever. And I failed the test. I proved I was no better than my father—a man who debased a sweet, innocent woman from a foreign country and all but dumped her by the road when she needed him most.'

His words sank heavily into the silence, and just like that Sylvie saw Arkim's intense personal struggle. Saw why he'd always reacted so strongly to her. She understood now how very attractive a respectable marriage would be—it would offer him everything he'd never had. It all made sense. And her heart ached.

The approach of another staff member broke the bubble surrounding them. The man said something to Arkim that Sylvie couldn't understand. She was reeling with all this new information, feeling such a mix of things that she hardly knew how to assimilate it all.

The man left and Arkim turned to her, his face expressionless again, as if he *hadn't* just punched a hole in her chest with his revelations.

'There are some nomads who want to meet with me. You should rest for a while—it's the hottest part of the day.'

Sylvie felt his dismissal like a glancing blow, but before she could say a word Arkim was striding away. A middle-aged woman dressed all in black appeared by her side. She had a smiling face and kind eyes. She said something Sylvie couldn't understand and gestured for Sylvie to follow her. With no other choice, she did, and was led to the smaller of the two big tents.

The woman slipped off her shoes before she went in so Sylvie copied her, not wanting to cause any offence.

It took her eyes a moment to adjust to the darker interior, and when they had her jaw dropped. It was refreshingly cooler inside, and the entire floor area was covered in oriental rugs, each in a more lavish design than the last. Her toes curled at the sensation of the expensive material under her feet...it was like silk.

The tent was simply the most decadent thing Sylvie had ever seen. Dark and full of lustrous materials. Huge soft cushions around a low coffee table; a dressing screen with intricate Chinese drawings. Beautiful lamps threw out soft lights...drawing the eye to the most focal point of the tent: the bed.

It was on a raised platform in the centre of the room. It was a four-poster, with heavy drapes pulled back at each corner. More cushions in lush jewel colours were strewn artfully across the pillows, and the sheets—Sylvie reached out to touch them—they were made of satin and silk. The bed was a byword in shameless opulence.

Sylvie caught the older woman's eye. She was looking at her with a very knowing glint. There was obviously only one reason for Sylvie to be here with the Sheikh.

She blushed furiously, squirming on the spot, and suffered through being shown the bathroom—another eye-poppingly sensual space, complete with a huge copper claw-footed bath—and tried not to die of embarrassment.

When the woman had left, Sylvie paced back and forth, expecting to see Arkim darken the tent's doorway at any moment. She felt panic at the thought of seeing him again. When he didn't appear she sank down into a chair near the bottom of the bed and glared balefully at the entrance of the tent for a few minutes. She realised that Arkim had really meant her to have a nap. He wasn't coming.

A sense of disappointment cut through all the other emotions, mocking her. The last thing she felt like doing was napping—she was so keyed up, her mind racing. But when she got up and sat down on the edge of the sumptuous bed it seemed to draw her into the centre, cushioning her like a cloud.

The last thing she remembered before sleep claimed her was vowing to herself that she would absolutely *not* think again about what he'd just told her—because that way lay all sorts of danger, and feelings that made her far too susceptible to the man.

CHAPTER SEVEN

SYLVIE WOKE SOME time later with a jolt. She'd been having a horrible dream about hundreds of naked faceless people with bare limbs entwined—so much so that she couldn't tell where one person ended and another began. She was tiny in the dream, and trying to find a way out, but gradually getting more and more suffocated...

She scowled and stretched out her stiff limbs. So much for not thinking about what Arkim had told her. She shook off the disturbing tendrils of the dream and looked around, taking in the fact that someone must have come into the tent and lit some more lights. *Arkim?* The thought made her heart beat faster.

She went into the bathing area and, feeling sticky, took off her clothes and dropped them to the floor. She stepped under the shower, which was in a large private cubicle near the bath and open to the elements. Twilight was just starting to turn the sky dusky, and Sylvie couldn't help but be affected by the magic of the place as the deliciously warm water sluiced down over her head and body.

Eventually she switched off the shower, dragged a towel around herself and twisted up her damp hair. She found a robe hanging on the back of the dressing screen. It was a beautiful emerald-green colour, silk—light as a feather. Slipping it on, she relished its coolness against her skin.

And then she went to the door of the tent and looked out. Twilight was descending around the camp in earnest now, bathing it in a gorgeous lilac light. She didn't see anyone moving, but could hear low voices in the distance and smell something cooking. No sign of Arkim. She didn't like the hollow feeling that brought with it. Only a couple of hours ago she'd been ready to leave, and then he'd told her...so much.

She thought of the pool she'd seen when they'd arrived and slipped her shoes on to explore. The air was sultry and warm, even though the intensity of the day had diminished. When she came close to the beautifully peaceful pool she pushed aside foliage and then she stopped dead in her tracks, her heart in her mouth, because it was occupied.

By a butt-naked Arkim.

He stood in the shallows, and all she could see were the firm globes of a very muscular bottom as he bent and threw water over his head. Water ran in rivulets down his back. And then he stood straight and tensed. He'd sensed her. Sylvie stopped breathing. She knew she should turn and run. Do something. But she couldn't move.

And then he turned around.

His hair was slicked back, and he was...*magnificent*. Sylvie had seen plenty of naked male bodies—working at the revue and helping people change between numbers meant personal modesty quickly became a thing of the past. But she'd never seen a man like this. He looked as if he'd been carved out of rock. His chest was broad and leanly muscled. His chest hair was dark and dusted over his pectorals before dissecting his chest and abs to lead down to slim hips and...

Sylvie's heart was beating so fast she wasn't sure how she was still standing. Arkim's penis twitched under her gaze, the shaft getting harder as she watched, rising from the thicket of dark hair between his powerfully muscled thighs.

Somehow she dragged her gaze up and his dark eyes were on her, molten... The very air seemed to contract around them.

When she'd first seen him he'd been dressed in that

three-piece suit, all buttoned up. Here, now, he was stripped bare. Without the armour that told the world he was different, respectable. To Sylvie there was something very poignant about finding Arkim like this, naked.

He stepped out of the pool and gracefully bent down to pick up a piece of material and wrap it around his waist. Sylvie was barely aware. Her entire body and mind was focused solely on this man, on this moment. It throbbed with potential.

She realised with a stunning flash of clarity that she wanted to give herself to him—this man who had never had a moment of purity in his life. Who'd seen things at a young age that had darkened his view of the world for ever.

It was the one thing she had—her innocence. And with every fibre of her being she wanted to gift it to *him*. As if she could assuage the raw edges she'd seen earlier.

Arkim walked up to her and Sylvie's eyes stayed on his, unblinking. She was drawing confidence from his obvious arousal and his intentness on her.

He looked almost ferocious, every line of his body and face unyielding. 'What do you want, Sylvie?'

It wasn't just a question. It was almost a demand.

Sylvie spoke what was in her heart and soul. And in her body. 'I want *you*, Arkim.'

He came closer and lifted a hand, undoing the pin holding up her damp hair, letting it fall loose around her shoulders. He put his hands on her arms and pulled her closer. Closer to that bare wet chest. Until they were touching. Until the points of her breasts hurt with the need to press against him more fully. His erection pushed against her lower belly and excitement flooded her, making her ready.

'Arkim...' she said, not even sure what she was asking for. Why wasn't he taking her right now? Making the most of his conquering?

'You're sure you want this?'

Sylvie hadn't been expecting this consideration. Another dangerously tender emotion ran through her. She didn't hesitate. She moved closer, feeling the delicious press of her breasts against him.

'Yes.'

Just one word. Simple, but devastating.

In a rush of emotion she said, 'I want to give you—' But she stopped, not sure how to articulate exactly what she *did* want to give him. So she just said a little lamely, 'I want to give you myself.'

Arkim's hands were so tight on her arms it almost hurt, but then they relaxed marginally and he bent down for a moment. She felt herself being lifted into his arms, against his chest, and he walked back the way she'd come.

One of her arms was tight around his neck and she ducked her head into his chest, eyes shut tight. Her other hand was on her robe, holding it together. She didn't want to catch the knowing eyes of that woman, or anyone else. She felt too raw and needy.

And also dangerously cosseted, held in his arms like this.

She pushed down all the tangled emotional implications of how she was feeling and focused on the urgent hunger racing through her blood.

When everything felt cooler and darker Sylvie knew that they'd entered an interior space and opened her eyes again. It had to be Arkim's tent—similar to hers, but bigger, more masculine, with bolder colours. And the bed in the centre of the tent was…huge.

Arkim carried her over and put her down on her feet by the side of it. She avoided looking at it by looking at him.

He cupped her face with his hand. 'I've wanted you from the moment I saw you. I saw it as a weakness, as something to be denied…but not any more.'

Sylvie felt vulnerable. She believed him, and his words had all sorts of implications she couldn't think about right now.

Acting on impulse, she raised herself on tiptoe and put her arms around his neck. 'Stop talking…you're ruining the moment.'

Arkim smiled, and it was devilish. It made something soar inside her.

He tugged the belt on Sylvie's robe and it fell open. She unwrapped her arms from his neck and stood before him, heart palpitating wildly as Arkim pushed the robe apart, revealing her naked body to his dark gaze.

He looked at her for a long moment, until Sylvie could start to feel herself trembling lightly. She was someone who knew her own body intimately, as any dancer would, but right now it felt foreign, and she was insecure.

'You're shaking.'

She looked at him and tried a smile. 'You're quite intimidating.'

Arkim's answer to that was to take off the material around his waist before he pushed her robe off her shoulders so that it fell down her arms and to the floor.

'Now we're equal.'

Those words impacted deep inside her. All along she'd fought a battle with this man not to let him make her feel inferior, less than him. The moment was heady.

Arkim turned then, taking her with him as he moved closer to the bed. Sylvie was unbalanced and fell against him, but he caught her easily and drew her down with him, so they landed on the soft surface in a sprawl of limbs.

She was lying on top of his hard body, every inch of her flesh coming into contact with his. She felt dizzy. And then Arkim's hands were smoothing down her bare back and cupping her buttocks, pulling her thighs apart so that they lay either side of his hips.

His mouth reached up to hers and Sylvie felt her hair fall over her shoulders, screening them as she fell into the kiss...wet and rough and intoxicating.

After more long, languorous kisses Arkim moved, so that Sylvie was now the one on her back, and he loomed over her, huge and awe-inspiring in the gloom of the tent. One of his thighs was between her legs and he moved it against her, making her body twitch and ache. The friction caused a delicious tension to coil inside her and she bit her lip.

Arkim's gaze roved over her body hungrily. 'You are more beautiful than I could ever have imagined.'

Sylvie shook her head, feeling breathless because of what was happening between her legs. 'No...*you're* beautiful.'

But he didn't seem to be listening. He was transfixed by her breasts, cupping one now, so that the hard point pouted upwards wantonly. He lowered his head and blew gently on it, making her tingle and ache for more, and then his mouth was on her, and that wicked tongue, flicking and sucking on the turgid flesh.

Her hands were in his hair, fingers funnelling deep, holding him to her. Her back was arched and she was fast losing any sense of reason. Or maybe she'd lost it when she'd laid eyes on this man for the first time. Anyway, it was gone.

He lavished attention on both breasts until they ached and felt swollen, and then his mouth was moving down... over her belly and lower. Sylvie only realised her hands were still on his head when he reached up to take them away. Taking both her hands in one of his, he held them captive over her belly.

Now she really was at his mercy. He moved lower, the bulk of his body forcing her legs apart.

Sylvie lifted her head and looked down. 'Arkim...' Her voice sounded rough, broken. Taut with need.

He looked up at her and said, 'Shh...'

Sylvie's head was too heavy. She let it fall back just as he released her hands, and then both of his hands were on her buttocks, lifting her to his mouth, where his tongue explored the damp folds of her sex, laying her so open she couldn't bear it.

She had to bite down on a fist when she felt his tongue surge deep inside her, and then his teeth were nipping... The tension was coiling so tightly now she thought she might have to scream to release the pressure, and he was relentless.

Sylvie was vaguely aware of bucking towards him mindlessly—and then he reached up and squeezed her breast, and she exploded into a million tiny pieces of pleasure so intense that she couldn't breathe or see.

She'd orgasmed before—you couldn't work in her industry and remain completely unaware of taking pleasure—but it had always been by her own hand, and never this...*mind-blowing*. She'd actually thought it was overrated. Evidently she'd been doing it all wrong, she thought dreamily as her body floated back to earth slowly, lusciously.

She was aware of him moving aside momentarily, with an intense focus in his movements, and then he was back, coming over her and leaning on both arms, the muscles bunched and taut.

Sylvie felt him lodge himself between her legs, and then the potent thrust of his erection against the sensitised folds of her sex. For a moment she thought it might be too soon, that she couldn't possibly— But then he hitched himself against her, the head of his erection sliding tantalisingly between those folds, and her whole body quivered with anticipation.

Instinctively she put her hands on Arkim's arms, as if to hold on for the ride, and her legs opened wider in tacit acceptance.

Sylvie's eyes were huge, staring up at him as if he knew all the secrets of the universe. Arkim didn't know how he hadn't already spilled onto the sheets, like the virginal teenager he'd been all those years ago, when he'd felt her body convulse in spasms of pleasure. But somehow he hadn't…and now he was on the very edge of his control as he felt her body accept his.

He started to sink into her tight, silken hot sheath.

Her *very* hot and *very* tight sheath.

In fact as Arkim's body sought to go deeper he realised that Sylvie's body was tight against him in a way he'd never encountered before…

His brain was overheating, his body screaming for a release of the tension, and those huge limpid eyes were still staring up at him. The hard tips of her breasts scraping against his chest.

Arkim was about to lose it…the heady scent of musk and sex urged him on. He gritted his jaw and thrust hard—and went nowhere.

He heard Sylvie's swift, sharp intake of breath and looked down. His brain was feeling too hot, too fuzzy to try and figure out what was wrong. But something *was* wrong. Very wrong.

Moments ago Sylvie had been flushed with pleasure. Now she looked pale and clammy. Shocked. She was biting her lip and her eyes shone with…*tears*?

Arkim's insides seemed to drop from a height. But even as suspicion crept in he fought the knowledge… She was just small—that was it. A lot smaller than he'd realised she was.

He clenched his buttocks, trying to forge a passage, and

Sylvie's hands gripped his like steel clamps, her nails digging into his muscles.

'Stop—please! It *hurts*.'

And the truth resounded in Arkim's head like a klaxon going off. *Virgin. Innocent.*

It was too much to take in. But he had to. *She was a virgin.*

Arkim pulled back from Sylvie's resisting body, her wince of obvious pain making him feel as if someone had just punched him in the gut. Somehow he got off the bed, stood up… His legs were shaky. He stared at Sylvie but didn't really see her, and then he acted on autopilot, going to the bathing area to take care of the protection.

He caught the expression on his face in the mirror and stopped. He looked dark, feral. He looked…*like his father.* With that insatiable glint in his eye. Narcissistic and intent only on his own self-satisfaction. Uncaring if someone might be innocent, pure. Like his mother. *Like Sylvie.*

He was no better than his father. This proved it more than any teenage humiliation with a porn actress. Something cold settled down over Arkim's heart. Something hard and familiar.

He went back out to the main area of the tent and saw Sylvie sitting on the side of the bed, the sheet wrapped around her body. She looked at him over her shoulder and the dark hardness inside Arkim nearly split apart because she looked so forlorn.

He reached for his trousers and pulled them on, irrational anger growing deep down inside him and crawling upwards to catch him in its hot grip.

'Why didn't you tell me?' He walked around to stand in front of her.

She looked shell-shocked. Arkim drove the emotion down.

'Why?' It burst out of him like the firing of a rifle.

Sylvie flinched, her hands clutching the sheet to her chest. 'I wasn't sure you'd notice. I almost told you...but I didn't know how.'

Arkim felt as if all of his ugliness was exposed. He sneered. 'How about, *Hey, Arkim, I'm a virgin, by the way... be gentle with me.*'

Sylvie stood up then, and Arkim could see how she trembled. The exposed skin of her shoulder and upper chest was very white. Delicate. Fragile. And he'd been like a rutting bull in a china shop.

He wanted to smash something.

'I didn't think you'd notice and I didn't think it was important.'

'Well, I *did* notice and it *is* important.' Arkim stalked away and then back, folding his arms across his chest. 'You're twenty-eight and you work in a strip club—how the hell are you still a virgin?'

Sylvie hitched her chin. 'It's *not* a strip club. And I just...was never interested before now.'

She started to look around for her things and Arkim caught her by the arm. The anger inside him was a turbulent mass. Everything in him wanted to lash out, to blame someone—blame *her*. If she'd told him...

What? asked a snide voice. *Would you have let her go?* Never.

'Why, Sylvie? And it's not just because you weren't interested. You're a sexual being—it oozes from you. I had no idea. If I had—'

She wrenched her arm free, fire flashing in her eyes now, any hint of vulnerability gone. 'You'd have what? Declined the offer?'

She spied her robe on the ground and grabbed it, letting the sheet fall as she tugged it on—but not before Arkim saw that luscious body and his own reacted forcibly.

Then she stopped and glared at him. 'You want to know

the psychological motivation behind my still being a virgin? Really?'

Suddenly he didn't. But she went on.

'My father rejected me as a child. My mother had died—his beloved wife—and I resembled her so much that he couldn't bear to look at me. So he sent me away. He's never been able to look at me since then without pain or grief. The truth is he would have switched me for her any day of the week.'

Arkim's chest ached. 'How can you know that?'

'Because I overheard him talking to someone. I heard him say how he couldn't bear the sight of me—that I was a constant reminder that she was gone and that if he could he'd have her back instead of me.'

Arkim reached out, but she slapped his hand away.

'And as for why I decided to let you be my first lover…? Well, maybe I felt bizarrely secure in the fact that you'd already rejected me on pretty much every level that counts. When you've protected yourself against rejection your whole life, it's almost a relief not to have to fear it any more.'

She stepped back, the robe pulled so tightly around her that every curve was lovingly delineated, and then she left.

Sylvie was so angry and humiliated she could have cried. But her anger kept the tears at bay. What on earth had possessed her to spill her soul to Arkim like that? As if he cared about the sob story of her relationship with her father. Or about her deepest inner fears of being rejected. She'd never even spoken to Sophie of any of this, not wanting to burden her sister with a negative view of their father.

Sylvie paced back and forth, her emotions vying between humiliation and anger, very aware of the dull throb and stinging between her legs. She stopped in her tracks when she thought of the excruciating pain of Arkim trying to penetrate her—his shock when he'd realised why he couldn't.

She sat down gingerly on the side of her own bed. She'd never expected it to be that bad. Up till that moment it had been the most incandescently pleasurable experience of her life. And she'd truly thought that he wouldn't know—that it would always be her own secret.

The tender feelings that had led Sylvie to want to soothe him in some way mocked her now. All the while she'd been thinking she was giving Arkim the supreme gift of her innocence he'd been ready to reject it outright. Evidently her lack of experience was a huge turn-off.

What she'd told Arkim wasn't entirely true—his outright rejection of her hadn't really prepared her for this. Or for how much it would hurt. Far more than the physical pain.

She reminded herself that she'd knowingly risked this when she'd chosen to come here. She had no one to blame but herself. It wasn't a comfort.

Arkim was undoubtedly done with her and his little plan of retribution. He would let her go and she would never see him again.

Feeling raw and weary, Sylvie stood and picked up her bag, started to fill it with the clothes that must have been unpacked when she'd been sleeping. She couldn't see Arkim doing such a menial task, so it hadn't been him in her tent.

Now she felt doubly foolish.

Packing her things with more force than necessary, Sylvie didn't hear anything until a deep and infinitely familiar voice spoke from behind her.

'What are you doing?'

Sylvie's entire body hummed in response. She cursed her reaction and didn't turn around. 'I'm leaving—what does it look like?'

'Why?'

There was some note in Arkim's voice that made her insides flutter dangerously but she ignored it. She steeled herself and dropped the clothes from her hands and turned around. In the dim flickering lights of the tent Arkim looked huge. He'd put a tunic on over his trousers.

'Your reaction just now was hardly indicative of wanting us to spend more time together.'

She thought Arkim winced, but couldn't be sure it wasn't a trick of the light and her imagination.

Then he said, 'I could have handled that better. Did I hurt you?' His voice had turned gruff.

The fluttering in her belly intensified, but Sylvie pushed it down ruthlessly. 'I'm okay.'

And she was. As soon as he'd pulled out the pain had faded and all that was left was some tenderness.

Then she said tartly, 'You obviously weren't prepared for me to be a virgin because all along you've assumed I'm some kind of a sl—'

'Do *not* even say that word.' Arkim stepped forward, the lines in his face harsh.

The hurt was back and more painful. Why was he doing this? Bothering? Sylvie crossed her arms, wishing she'd had the foresight to change out of the robe, which felt very flimsy now.

'Look, you don't have to do this…apologise, or whatever it is you're doing. I get it. Me being a virgin was not a welcome surprise, and I understand that you have no desire to be the one to initiate me.'

Arkim came closer and shook his head, a look of incredulity coming over his face. It was only now that she noticed the growth of stubble on his jaw, remembered how it had felt against her softer skin…*between her thighs*.

'That's not it at all. I didn't handle my reaction well

and I'm sorry for that. I had no right to take out my anger on you. It was just a shock when I expected—' Arkim stopped and ran a hand through his hair and stepped back. He cursed and walked to the door of the tent.

For a heart-stopping second Sylvie thought he was leaving, and her brave façade was just about to crumble when he stopped and put his hand up over the top of the doorway.

He spoke into the inky darkness outside. 'My mother was a virgin. My father seduced her and took her virginity from her. She didn't even enjoy the experience. He was rough...'

Arkim turned around and Sylvie felt her heart beating too fast. She sank down onto the bed. 'How can you know this?'

He was grim. 'She kept a diary. It was in a box of her personal items that my father somehow miraculously kept. I read it when I was a teenager.' His voice was rough. 'When it became obvious you were...innocent I realised that I was doing to another woman exactly what he'd done to her.'

Sylvie shook her head and stood up again, compelled to go over to Arkim with a fierceness she'd never felt before. 'You didn't know... I could have explained, but I didn't.' She bit her lip. 'This is going to sound really stupid, but when you told me about what had happened to you... I wanted you to be the one...'

Arkim reared back slightly. 'You wanted to sleep with me because you felt sorry for me?'

'No.' She stopped, and then admitted sheepishly, 'Maybe, in a way...'

Arkim looked ready to bolt, but Sylvie put a hand on his arm. He stopped, his face etched with injured pride.

'Not like that.' Her mouth twitched slightly. 'Believe

me, you don't inspire *pity* in people, Arkim—anything but. I wanted to sleep with you because you truly are the first person who has connected with me on that level... From the moment I saw you, I wanted you. Even when you looked at me with disdain it made me want to make you notice me.'

'I noticed you...' His tone was wry.

Sylvie's cheeks grew hot as she remembered that first time they'd met. The erroneous impression she'd made.

She let his arm go and shrugged lightly, avoided his eye. 'I thought that I could somehow gift you something... pure. The purest thing I have to give. To show you that not everything is tainted.' She looked at him again. 'You are nothing like your father. And I am nothing like your mother. This is *not* the same. You are considerate...you stopped when you knew I was in pain. It sounds like your father wasn't even aware of that.'

Something in the air between them changed...sizzled. The tension shifted to one full of awareness. Wanting.

Arkim lifted a hand and cupped Sylvie's jaw. 'What do you say we start again?'

Her breath hitched. Start again...? As in from the beginning or just from tonight? But she was too afraid to ask it out loud, to break this fragile spell. She'd bared herself completely to him and he was still here. Still wanted her.

'Yes...' she breathed.

Arkim moved closer and Sylvie's skin tingled all over. Her breasts, still sensitive, peaked to hard points.

'And, for the record, I don't reject you... I absolutely accept you.' His voice became fervent. 'You are *mine*, Sylvie. No one else's on this earth.' Something dark crossed his face. 'If I was a better man I'd let you go, but I'm too selfish to let anyone else have you.'

And then he kissed her, before she could say a word, and there was nowhere left to run or hide.

The fire swept up around them faster than before, and then he was carrying Sylvie over to the bed, putting her down and sweeping her clothes and bag away with one hand.

He took off his clothes and her hungry gaze roved over him, as if it was her first time seeing him. His erection strained from his body, thick and long. She felt a glimmer of fear, remembering the pain.

But as if reading her mind Arkim came down over her and said, 'I'll make it good…don't worry. It won't hurt again.'

She looked at him and felt her heart turn over. The thought of this man not taking the opportunity to hurt her…she'd never expected it. She couldn't speak. So she just nodded.

He carefully opened her robe and peeled it off her, laying her bare. And then he came alongside her on the bed and proceeded to do everything he'd done before, and more, until Sylvie was writhing, begging… Her sex was hot and damp, aching to feel him again, pain be damned.

'Touch me first,' he said hoarsely, poised above her, his powerful body between her legs.

Sylvie was nearly incoherent, her vision blurry. She looked down to see Arkim's sheathed erection and put a hand down to encircle him. She lamented the protection—she wanted to feel him skin to skin—but even like this… it was awe-inspiring. *He* was awe-inspiring.

She squeezed him gently, moved her hand up and down experimentally, and then she looked at him and saw the huge strain on his face. He was holding back, going slowly for her. Letting her get used to him.

Tenderness welled inside her. She took her hand from him and then placed both her hands on his hips, drawing her legs up in an instinctive feminine move as old as time.

'Now, Arkim—I need you now.'

She saw him struggle, and then give in. His body fused with hers and inch by inch he slowly sank into her. To the point of resistance.

'Sweetheart, relax…let me in.'

The endearment made something melt inside Sylvie and she could feel all the muscles that were clamping so hard against him relax.

Arkim slid a little deeper. She felt so full…almost uncomfortable. But also…*amazing*. Arkim kept going until Sylvie could barely breathe and his hips touched hers. She felt impaled…but *whole*. It was such a new and alien sensation. And then he started to pull out, beginning a dance of movement between their bodies that Sylvie had never known existed. Just when she thought he was withdrawing from her completely he'd thrust back in, and each time it felt a little more imperative that he did so.

Her legs were wrapped around his waist and her hands were on his buttocks now, silently commanding his movements to be stronger, more forceful.

Arkim huffed out laboured-sounding words. 'Should have known you'd be a fast learner…'

Sylvie smiled up at him—but then her smile got stuck as Arkim touched something deep inside her that sent shockwaves and thrills through her. His movements became faster, wilder, as if he couldn't control them any more, and the delicious tension Sylvie had felt before coiled tight within her again, and tighter. Until she begged for release.

Arkim put a hand between them and pressed his thumb against her, and Sylvie couldn't hold back her cry as she broke into shards of light and sensation. Her whole body convulsed with pleasure around Arkim's, her skin damp and slick.

Powerful shudders shook Arkim's body as he finally

took his own release, and through the cataclysm Sylvie could feel the contractions of her body around his. In that moment she'd never felt so complete.

CHAPTER EIGHT

Sylvie floated on her back, naked in the warm water, and looked up into an endless violet-hued sky. Early evening was practically the only time Arkim would let her out, for fear of the sun damaging her skin, even though she faithfully slathered on factor fifty.

The silky water lapped between her legs. Soothing the tenderness. She couldn't keep back a small smile… The last week had been the most illuminating, mind-blowing week of her life. It had been an intense tutorial in the sensual arts, with a master teacher.

She'd never known… She'd heard people talk about it, but had never really understood just what they'd been going on about. And that deep-rooted fear of rejection had made her shy away from any intimacy.

Not here, though. Every night and most of the day Arkim laid Sylvie bare, over and over again, until she was reduced to a mass of sensation and lusting and craving—no longer a human being. He'd turned her into some kind of animal.

That thought made something tighten inside her and Sylvie flipped over, lazily swimming to the far end of the pool. She wasn't worried about being seen—the staff knew not to come to the pool at this time, and used it only during the day.

She sat on a natural stone ledge in the water, the tops of her breasts exposed, and blushed when she imagined Arkim taking her here—pressing between her legs, urging her to wrap them around his waist as he thrust so deep inside her she'd have to bite down on his skin to contain her cries of ecstasy.

She wasn't entirely sure someone hadn't slipped a drug into her drink or food, and that this wasn't all some kind of crazy hallucination. But the air was warm on her wet skin, and the water was real enough. As was the smell of cooking. And the sounds of people in the distance, laughing and talking softly.

Sylvie hadn't seen much of the nomads—they kept themselves to themselves. And anyway...how could she notice anyone else when Arkim filled her vision larger than a twenty-foot statue?

Physically Sylvie had never been more replete or happy. Emotionally, however... Her insides tightened again.

Since she and Arkim had started sleeping together there had been no more intensely personal confessionals. She had no idea what he thought of her now, beyond the very physical evidence that he wanted her. And she wanted him. *Oh, God.* She wanted him more and more each day. As if the more she had of him the tighter would be the bonds holding them together.

For her.

Sylvie knew one thing: even though he'd said he accepted her, this was a moment out of time for Arkim. He didn't have to say it. Whatever he'd once thought of her—and whatever he thought of her now—was irrelevant. This was just a slaking of lust for him. And when they left here he would turn his back and walk away. Because a man like Arkim Al-Sahid, with all his dark secrets and troubled past, would never choose a woman like Sylvie.

Even if she *had* been a virgin, and that had changed his perception of her, she was still unpalatable in his real world. Sylvie had to remember that, and not get caught up in this interim magic and madness.

In spite of everything that had brought them here he'd given her an incredible gift. The gift of her own sensuality and sexuality. Which was ironic, considering she'd been successfully projecting it for years. He'd taken the broken pieces inside her and forged a new wholeness. And that was what she would take with her when this was over...

She heard a movement and looked up to see Arkim standing at the edge of the pool, with only a towel around his waist. Hair slicked back. He'd obviously just showered. Instantly Sylvie could feel the effect of his presence on her body—blood flowing to erogenous zones, flesh swelling, tingling, becoming engorged.

With his hands on his hips and a scowl on his face he looked truly intimidating. He was looking for her, and Sylvie's breath quickened as his gaze came closer and closer... *Zing!* Eye contact. Heat. Pulsing awareness.

The scowl faded and was replaced by a look of carnal intent. With one hand Arkim undid the towel and twitched it to the ground. He stepped into the pool—gloriously, unashamedly naked.

Like a little wanton, Sylvie had her legs open and ready for him when he came close enough to touch her. He registered her acquiescence with a feral smile that curled her insides.

The head of his erection notched against her sex, slipping between slick folds. His hands cupped and moulded her breasts, teasing the hard points, before he lowered his head so that he could tease first one, then the other, with his hot mouth and tongue and teeth.

Then his mouth was on hers, swallowing her cry as he seated himself with one smooth thrust, deep inside her. Everything quickened. She was so primed she couldn't hold back a series of shattering orgasms, and she felt Arkim's struggle as he fought to hang on... But it was too much. He pulled free of her clasping body at the last moment and the hot spurt of his seed landed on her belly and breasts. His face was drawn back into a silent scream of ecstasy.

The lash of his essence on her skin felt like a brand,

and intensely erotic. But as suddenly as she felt that, Sylvie felt cold, in spite of the heat and languor in her bones. Because she ached with wanting to feel his seed lodged deep inside her, where it might create life, connecting her to this man for ever.

'Are you planning on dropping off the radar for good?'

Arkim scowled into the satellite phone and answered his executive assistant. 'Of course not.'

'Good, because the deal with Lewis is still on—just about. But you need to be here to deal with it.'

After a few more minutes of discussion Arkim ended the call. He was on a horse, on a sand dune, looking down over the oasis.

He could see Sylvie's bright red hair as she played with a group of the nomad children, chasing them. He could hear their squeals of delight from here. Her skin had taken on a golden glow and more delicate freckles, in spite of the high-factor sun cream he insisted she wear every day.

He felt himself smiling, and a sense of deep contentment was flowing over him and through him. Along with that piquant edge of desire never far from the surface whether Sylvie was in sight or not.

His smile faded when he thought of that first night again. He'd been convinced he'd have to take them both back to civilisation after she'd walked out on him—justifiably—with all the hauteur of a queen. What she'd told him about the legacy of her father had eaten away at his guts like acid: *'When you've protected yourself against rejection your whole life it's almost a relief not to have to fear it any more.'* But ultimately he hadn't been strong enough to walk away. Or to send her away. So he'd been selfish. And taken her for himself.

And even though she'd told him so fiercely, *'You're not your father...'* he was afraid that he was. That he still had some deep flaw inside him. Yet somehow, right now, looking down at that bright head, the assertion didn't sting as much as it usually did.

He'd always ensured his lovers never strayed beyond the firm boundaries he laid down. He always went to their places, or met them in hotels. He never brought them to his personal space. Never encouraged them to talk of personal matters.

And he never spirited them away to a desert oasis to lose himself in their bodies before he went crazy...

'Are you planning on dropping off the radar for good?'

It suddenly struck him: *what the hell was he doing?* His smile faded completely and he went cold inside. His reputation still hung in the balance, and it was thanks to that woman's actions. He'd meted out his vengeance. He'd had her under him, begging for release. *But not for forgiveness.* At what point had Arkim forgotten that?

Around the first time Sylvie opened her legs to you...

It started hitting him like a series of blows about the head and face. Just how much he'd let her in. Just how much he'd told her. And all because since the moment she'd arrived she'd been nothing like he'd expected. The biggest revelation of all having been her innocence. Her physical innocence.

He had to force himself to acknowledge now that that was as far as her innocence went. She still hadn't told him her reasons for disrupting the wedding that day.

Something trickled down his neck and spine. A sense of having been monumentally naive. Moments ago—before Arkim had had that phone conversation—he'd been contemplating what might happen after Al-Omar. He'd contemplated keeping Sylvie on as his lover. Because he didn't see an end in sight to this ravenous desire. The more he had of her, the more he wanted.

From his vantage point now he could see the children scattering as someone called them, the cry lifted on the wind.

Sylvie stood and looked up to where he was, shaded her eyes. Arkim felt her pull even from here as the breeze moulded the long tunic she wore to her body, showing off the curves of her high, full breasts.

He imagined a scenario of returning to civilisation and allowing Sylvie to slip under his skin even more indelibly. She was the last woman he needed in his life right now—right when everything hung in the balance *because of her*.

With a sharp kick of his heel on his horse's flank he made his way back to the oasis. He knew what he had to do.

'Look! It's a puppy with eyes like mine!'

Sylvie was sitting cross-legged outside Arkim's tent, more happy than she cared to admit to see him returning from his satellite phone call, even if he did look very grim. She held up a squirming bundle of white fur with a tail, yapping intermittently.

Arkim crouched down and Sylvie held it so he could see the puppy's brown and blue eyes. There was something about Arkim's grimness that made her say nervously, 'Sadim, one of the younger boys, showed him to me. They were excited because of the similarity...the eye discolouration.'

He straightened up again. 'You shouldn't be handling it—dogs around here are feral.'

Sylvie's sense of something being wrong increased. Arkim's tone was harsh in a way she hadn't heard in days.

She stood up too, cradling the dog against her chest, feeling at a disadvantage. 'He's not feral...he's gorgeous.'

The small boy Sylvie had spoken of hovered nearby. With a brusque movement Arkim gestured him over. He took the puppy out of Sylvie's arms, his hands brushing against her breasts perfunctorily, and handed it back to the boy, saying something that made the boy look at him as if he'd just kicked the puppy before he ran off.

Sylvie stared at him. 'What did you do that for?'

Arkim was definitely harsh now. 'Because we don't have time for this. It's time to leave... I have to return to London.'

'Oh, is everything okay?' Sylvie struggled to assimilate Arkim's change in mood and this news.

'I've arranged for the helicopter to come for you in a couple of hours. Halima will ensure your bags from the castle are on board.'

'For me?' Sylvie repeated faintly, aware that Arkim hadn't really answered her question.

His face was expressionless, and it made Sylvie think of the passionate intensity he'd shown in bed only a few hours before. It suddenly felt like a long time ago. Not hours.

'Yes, for you,' Arkim reiterated. 'The helicopter will take you to the international airport in B'harani, where one of my staff will meet you and see you on to a plane back to France. I'm taking the Jeep back to the castle as I've some business to attend to there before I return to Europe.'

When she said nothing, feeling cold inside, and as if she'd been hit with a bat, Arkim asked almost accusingly, 'Did you think we could stay here for ever?'

Yes, came a rogue voice. And Sylvie felt like such a fool. She'd been weaving daydreams and fantasies out of something that didn't exist. This oasis and what had happened here was as much of a mirage as the kind a dying man in the desert might see through the heat waves in the distance. For ever unreachable.

She forced herself to look Arkim in the eye. 'No, of course not.'

His voice was stark, stripped of anything remotely soft.

'This can't ever be anything more than what's happened here. You *do* know that, don't you?'

Sylvie felt her old cynical walls—badly battered and crumbled—start to resurrect themselves. What Arkim really meant was, *You didn't really think I'd ever want to be associated with you outside of this remote outpost, did you?*

She couldn't believe she'd let herself fall so hard and so fast for someone who would only ever hold her in mediocre esteem. Who had only seduced her as a form of retribution. And she'd been fully complicit.

'Of course I know that, Arkim.' She tried to inject as much nonchalance into her voice as possible.

She felt brittle. If someone so much as brushed past her now she might shatter. She stepped back—out of the pull Arkim exerted on her with such effortless ease.

'I should pack my things. I don't want there to be any delay when the helicopter gets here.'

'Mariah will bring you some lunch.'

Sylvie forced a smile. 'That's considerate—thank you.'

She turned and walked away before he could see the rise of tumultuous emotions within her. Anger and hurt and self-recrimination. She should have left when she had the chance. She should have protected herself better. She should have known that he would just drop her from a height when he was done with her... She just hadn't expected it to be so soon, so cold, and so brutal.

A month later, London...

Arkim stood at his office window, gazing out on a scene of unremitting grey skies and rain. An English summer in all its glory.

He realised, somewhat moodily, that he seemed to be spending an inordinate amount of time looking out of his window across the iconic cityscape, with an inability to focus.

Since he'd come back to London he'd been braced for the fallout from his very public humiliation. But, to his shock and surprise, when he'd requested a debriefing from his PR team he'd been informed that there *was* no discernible fallout. Yes, he'd lost some business initially, and the tabloid reports in the immediate aftermath had been bruising. Stocks had fallen sharply, but it had been very temporary. And ultimately not damaging.

Arkim was not a little stunned to realise that in the wake of his ruined wedding, the world hadn't stopped turning. The reputation he'd spent so long building up hadn't crumbled to pieces, as he'd feared. Many more scandals had come and gone. He was already old news. People couldn't care less if he'd really slept with Sylvie Devereux.

The deal with Grant Lewis had been signed off on, and the old man appeared to feel no rancour towards Arkim, despite what had happened. Lewis had been in straits far more dire than he'd led anyone to believe, and his eagerness to keep the deal on the table only reminded Arkim of how eroded his well-worn cynicism had become. Lust for power and wealth trumped even scandal.

A hum of ever-present frustration pulsed in his blood. Despite his best efforts to resist the urge, he'd had his team checking the papers and media daily for any news of Sylvie, but to all intents and purposes she'd vanished back into her life.

An image of her face, wide open and smiling, her skin lightly golden from the sun and dusted with freckles, came back to him so vividly that he sucked in a breath.

An ache had settled deep into his being from the moment he'd watched her helicopter take off from the oasis that day and it hadn't subsided. The truth could no longer be ignored or denied. *He still wanted her.*

In the last month he'd been to functions with the most beautiful women in the world, and they'd left him cold. Dead inside. But all he had to do was conjure up a memory of Sylvie—*that day in the pool*—and he was rewarded with a surge of arousal. About which he could do nothing unless he wanted to regress to being the age of fourteen in a shower stall.

The intercom sounded from his desk and Arkim welcomed the distraction, turning around. 'Yes, Liz?'

'There's a young lady downstairs to see you…'

Even before Arkim could ask her name, blood was rushing to his head and heat to his groin.

'Who did you say?' He had to ask, after his assistant had said the name. Surely he'd misheard—?

'Sophie Lewis…your…er…ex-fiancée.'

Disappointment was acute. So acute that Arkim knew he had a problem. And what on earth could Sophie Lewis possibly want with the man who had—allegedly—been unfaithful to her with her own sister?

'Send her up,' he said grimly.

Sylvie had finished rehearsals with Pierre and the rest of the revue for the day and had stayed behind at the dance studios to practise on her own for her modern dance class.

She focused on the music and the athletic movements of her body, clad in dance leggings and a cropped tank top. Her hair was up in a high ponytail and her skin was sheened with perspiration from the exertion. But the burn of her muscles and the intense focus was good. Anything to block *him* and the fact that she would never see him again out of her mind. Block out the fact that he wanted nothing to do with her. That what had happened meant nothing to him…

Sylvie made an awkward move and landed heavily on her foot. Damn. *Damn him for invading her thoughts.*

She bent down over her foot, but thankfully she hadn't strained it. They were close to the opening night for the relaunch of the club—Pierre would never forgive her if she injured herself now...especially when she wasn't even practising the revue's routines.

She stood up straight in front of the long mirror that spanned one whole wall and stretched her neck. She was about to start at the beginning again when she saw something move, and she looked towards where the door was reflected in the mirror to see a big dark shape.

Arkim.

This was really getting to be too much. Now she was seeing things. She blinked. But he didn't go away.

The door was pushed open and he walked in. Dressed in dark trousers and a light shirt, sleeves rolled up, top button open. As if he'd just strolled in from a nearby office.

Slowly, eyes widening, Sylvie turned around, half expecting him not to be there when she faced him. But he was. He was real.

To her utter horror she felt a welling of emotion: a mixture of anger, relief and the sheer need to run to him and wrap herself so tightly around him he wouldn't be able to breathe.

She took a deep, steadying breath, and curled her hands into fists. Had she already forgotten the brutality with which he'd let her go that day at the oasis? Coldly. Summarily.

Praying her voice wouldn't betray her, and lamenting her less than pristine physical state, she said coolly, 'Hello, Arkim.'

'Hello, Sylvie.'

That voice. *His* voice. It reached inside her and squeezed tight. She remembered him saying *Sylvie* with a guttural groan as his climax had made his whole body go taut over hers.

'I can't imagine that you were just passing.'

Arkim put his hands in his pockets and walked into the room, his every step gracefully athletic. Masculine. He was clean-shaven. And he'd had a haircut.

He was still quite simply the most astoundingly handsome man she'd ever seen.

He stopped a couple of feet away. Close enough for his scent to tickle her nostrils and for her body to go into meltdown at his proximity. Her heart seemed to have been in shock, because it started again at about triple its normal rate.

'No, I wasn't just passing. I came especially. To see you.'

She dampened down the surge of excitement. Her hurt at the way he'd sent her off was still acute. She lifted her chin. 'Why? Did I leave something behind?'

Arkim's face was impassive, but she saw a muscle work in his jaw. His throat moved. Sylvie could have spent hours just studying every minute part of his olive-skinned anatomy. *She had.*

'You could say that. *Me.*'

Her eyes clashed with the darkest brown. Incredulity made her mouth gape before she found the wherewithal to say, 'I left *you* behind?'

'Yes…' he breathed, and moved even closer.

His eyes were roving hungrily over her now, making a hot flush spread out all over Sylvie's body from between her legs. This man had changed her utterly, in so many ways. So much so that the minute Pierre had seen her again the older patriarchal man had looked her up and down and said accusingly, 'Something's different…what's happened to you?'

Sylvie had been mortified beyond belief to think that someone might be able to *see* what had happened to her. But she could feel it even when she danced. A new awareness of her body…her sexuality.

She crossed her arms over her chest and glared at Arkim, the architect of all of this. His eyes met hers again and she saw the fire in them. But before she could say anything—not even sure what she *wanted* to say—he asked, 'What was that dancing you were just doing? It was different to the way you danced for me.'

Taken aback, Sylvie said, 'It's something I'm working on for my contemporary dance class.'

'I liked it...it was beautiful.'

And just like that Sylvie's jagged emotions stopped pricking her. 'You did?'

Arkim reached out and touched a loose tendril of hair. He nodded. 'You looked as if you were lost in another world.'

She was finding it hard to breathe. 'I choreographed the dance.'

It was only when she said it that she felt totally exposed. A lot of that dance had been born out of the pain she'd felt for the past month.

She stepped back and his hand fell away. His eyes flashed. Still the same arrogant Arkim. And what had he meant when he'd said she'd left him behind?

'What do you want, Arkim? I haven't finished practising, and I only have this space for another twenty minutes.'

'I want to talk to you. And I have something for you at my apartment.'

'Your apartment?'

'I have an apartment here in Paris. I'm working here for the next few weeks—in my Paris office.'

Of *course* he had an office and an apartment here. He *would*.

But still, she resisted. 'Why, Arkim? Why do we have to talk? I think we said everything, don't you? Or you certainly did, anyway.'

He looked for a moment, as if he didn't want to say

anything, but then he did. 'Your sister came to see me... I *know*, Sylvie.'

Sylvie could feel her blood draining south so quickly that she swayed. Immediately Arkim's hand was on her arm. To her awful shame, her first thought was not of Sophie but of the fact that Arkim hadn't come because he wanted her back at all...

'Sophie...came to see you?' Sylvie was vaguely aware that her phone had been off all day during rehearsals, so she'd been uncontactable.

He nodded. Grim. 'Look, finish your practice. I'll wait, and then you'll come with me...yes?'

There was no way Sylvie could focus now. She'd break her ankle. And that was just at the thought of Arkim waiting for her. She shook her head. 'No, I'll change now and come with you.'

She had no choice. She had to know what Sophie's visit to him meant. And that was *all* Arkim wanted to talk to her about. As long as she remembered that she'd be okay.

He let her go. 'I'll wait for you downstairs. My car is at the door.'

As Arkim waited in the back of his chauffeur-driven car he couldn't dampen down the swell of triumph...or the swell of his erection. His whole body had gone on fire as soon as he'd seen Sylvie through the door...her lithe dancer's body moving with such grace and power...in a way he'd never seen before. Beautiful, elegant...passionate. He'd been mesmerised. In awe. In lust.

She'd looked wary at seeing him again, even though he'd felt the resurgence of the powerful sexual connection between them. Yet could he blame her for being wary? He'd behaved like an idiot that last day at the oasis... He'd been acting on a knee-jerk reflex to get rid of Sylvie before she slid herself even more indelibly under his skin...but it had been too late.

He had to concede that even if Sophie hadn't come—

His thoughts stopped working as Sylvie walked out through the door, her vibrant hair tied back in a knot—damp from a shower? She wore faded skinny jeans that showed her long legs off to perfection, ballet flats and a loose off-the-shoulder T-shirt, with the straps of a vest visible underneath. Her skin was pale again...like a pearl.

Arkim let his driver get out to open the door for her. He literally couldn't move for fear of making a complete idiot of himself.

When she slid into the back seat on the other side she didn't look at him, putting her slouchy bag firmly on her lap as she strapped her seat belt on. Arkim wanted to reach across and force her to meet his eyes, force her to know how much he wanted her before he crushed that soft mouth under his and found some sense of peace for the first time in a month.

A flutter of panic at the strength of how much he wanted her made his gut tighten. How relieved he'd been as soon as he'd laid eyes on her...

Sylvie Devereux was still completely wrong for him on so many levels. This was lust. Pure and simple. Unprecedented, but not without its sell-by date.

Then she looked at him with those wide eyes, blue and blue-green, and Arkim's thoughts scattered to pieces.

'Why did Sophie come to see you?'

Arkim dragged his brain back into some kind of functioning order. 'She told me everything.'

CHAPTER NINE

THE CAR WAS moving at a snail's pace in the early-evening Paris traffic as Arkim's words sank in. And even though Sylvie was preoccupied by what he was saying, and what it meant, she was acutely aware of that big, powerful body so close to hers. Legs spread, chest broad.

She had to get it together. *Sophie.* Hesitantly she asked, 'When you say "everything", do you mean—?'

'I mean,' Arkim said, cutting her off, 'I know that she's gay, Sylvie. She told me everything. About how she was afraid to come out. About how she was railroaded into marriage by her parents because they thought it would sweeten the deal for me. I'd made no attempt to hide the fact that I wanted to settle in England, and I wasn't averse to settling down with a suitable wife.'

The kind of wife who would remove Arkim permanently from his sordid past... Sylvie thought to herself, with a lurch of pain near her heart.

He continued, 'She told me about her girlfriend in college, and how she was too terrified to stand up to her mother...that she's always had trouble standing up to her.' Arkim's mouth twisted. 'I can understand why.'

Sylvie reeled. 'My God...she really *did* tell you everything.'

Arkim nodded. 'She also told me that she'd refused to let you do anything at first, because she didn't want you to damage your already contentious relationship with your father and stepmother, and they'd inevitably blame you even though it had nothing to do with you... But the week of the wedding she was panicking so much that she accepted your offer to step in at the last minute if she needed it. Which is what you did...in your own inimitable way.'

Sylvie blushed, thinking of that daring moment again. Arkim looked equable enough right now, but she knew how deep his emotions went, and how he simmered.

Trepidation gripped her. 'Were you angry with her?'

For a second he just looked at her, and then he said with faint incredulity, 'Even now your first concern is whether or not I got angry with her?'

Sylvie squirmed. 'Well, I know how intimidating you can be.'

Arkim's mouth thinned. 'At first I was angry, yes.' He reacted to the look that crossed Sylvie's face. 'I had a right to be. Both of you made me a laughing stock. If Sophie had just come to me and explained I would have understood. I'm not such an ogre. *Hell*.'

He turned away in disgust, to look out of the window. Sylvie felt immediately chastened. She knew that he wouldn't have taken it out on Sophie...all of Arkim's anger was only ever for *her*.

She pushed down the sense of futility. 'You're right,' she said in a quiet voice. 'I should have come to you myself and said something... If we'd been able to stop the wedding a week before it would have avoided the messy scandal it became. But I knew how unlikely it was that you'd believe anything I said...'

Some of the tension seemed to leave his shoulders. He turned back, those black eyes like pools of obsidian. To Sylvie's surprise, his mouth quirked ever so slightly on one side.

'I guess I have to give you that... I would have seen it as just another jealous attempt to make me notice you.' His expression became shuttered. 'I believed you were *jealous*...you let me believe that, like a fool.'

She knew she owed him total honesty now—especially

after Sophie's bravery—albeit belated. She forced herself to look at him. 'The truth is…as much as I was doing it for Sophie I *was* jealous. I wanted you…for myself.'

She hadn't even properly admitted that to herself until this moment. Her head felt light.

Arkim's eyes gleamed. He breathed out. 'I *knew* it…'

For a second she thought he was about to reach for her, and her whole body tingled, but then a discreet tap came from nearby. It took a minute for her to figure out that the driver was knocking on the partition, alerting them to the fact that they'd pulled up outside a building on a quiet street.

Sylvie felt a little dizzy. She looked out of the window and didn't immediately recognise much, except for the fact that they were in a very expensive part of Paris. Her voice was husky. 'Where are we?'

'My apartment building on the Île Saint-Louis.'

She looked back to Arkim. She felt confused, she wasn't sure where they stood any more.

He said, 'I have something for you upstairs.'

She joked weakly, 'That's not a very original chat-up line.'

He was serious. 'It's not a chat-up line. I really *do* have something for you.'

'Oh.' She instantly felt silly. The driver—as if knowing just the perfect moment to capitalise on her doubts—appeared at her door and opened it. By the time she was standing, clutching her bag, Arkim was waiting for her, darkly handsome and very vital-looking against the grey stone of the old building.

How was it that he could look so devastating, no matter what milieu he was in? she grumbled to herself as she let him lead her into the building. She felt very dishevelled when she saw the marble floor and discreetly exquisite furnishings. And the uniformed concierge who treated Arkim like royalty.

There was a lift attendant, and Sylvie almost felt like giggling. It was so far removed from the constantly out of use elevator in her rickety building in Montmartre.

The lift came to a smooth stop and Arkim led her into a luxuriously carpeted hall, with one door at the end. He opened it and she walked in cautiously, her eyes widening as she took in the parquet floors and quietly sumptuous decor.

The reception rooms were spacious, with floor-to-ceiling French doors looking out over Paris and the Seine. The furniture was antique, but not fussy. Comfortable, inviting.

Drawn by something she'd spotted, she walked over to the opposite side of the room and stood before a black and white photo.

'It's Al-Hibiz.'

Arkim's voice was close enough to set Sylvie's nerve endings alight. 'Yes,' she said, remembering her first view of the majestic castle. A terrible sense of longing for that wide open landscape washed over her. *The oasis.*

This was torture, being so close to Arkim again and yet not really knowing what he wanted from her. She whirled around and he was a lot closer than she'd expected, within touching distance.

'Arkim?' Her voice croaked humiliatingly.

He was staring at her mouth. 'Yes...'

So she looked at his...at the strong sensual lines. And his jaw, so resolute. From the moment she'd first seen him she'd had that instinct to smooth the stark lines of his face.

She didn't know who moved first, but it was as if attracting ions finally overcame the tension between them, and then she was in his arms, her whole body straining against his, her arms tight around his neck. Their mouths were fused, tongues tangled in a desperate hungry kiss, the breath being sucked out of each other's bodies to mix and mingle and go on fire. Arkim's hands shaped and cupped Sylvie's buttocks, lifting her up, encouraging her legs to wrap around him.

She wasn't even aware that Arkim had collapsed onto a couch behind them until she pulled back from the kiss to gasp in air and realised that her thighs were wedged open, tight against his, and she could feel the potent thrust of his arousal against where she ached.

She felt shaky. The fire had blasted up around them so quickly. 'Arkim...what are we—?'

He put a finger to her lips. He looked fierce. 'Don't say anything—please. I need this. I need *you*. Now.'

There was something raw in his tone...something that resonated deep inside her. Who was she kidding? She needed this too. Desperately.

She levered herself against him, pushing back. Infused with a sense of confidence borne out of what this man had given her at that oasis, Sylvie stood up and slowly and methodically took off her clothes until she was naked.

He looked...stunned. Hypnotised. In shock. In awe.

Sylvie came back and straddled him again, every inch of her skin sensitised just from his look. His hands came to her waist and she felt a slight tremor in them. She reached down between them and undid his trousers, pulled him free, smoothing her hand up and down the silken length of his erection, her whole body flushing red with lust.

The fact that she was naked and he was still almost fully dressed was erotic in the extreme. But when Arkim's mouth latched on to her nipple, Sylvie's fleeting sense of being in control quickly evaporated, and he skilfully showed her who was the real master here. She was rubbing against him, thick and hard between her legs, feeling her juices anointing his shaft.

Arkim groaned and dropped his head against her and said, 'I need to be inside you...*now*.'

Sylvie raised herself up in wordless acquiescence while Arkim extricated protection from his pocket, smoothing the thin latex sheath onto his penis.

His hands were back on her waist—tight, urgent. He positioned her so that her slick body rested just over his tip and with exquisite care, as if savouring the moment, he brought Sylvie down onto his erection. She inhaled as he filled her, almost to the point of pain but still on the side of pleasure. When he was as deep as he could go he held her there for a moment, before it got too much and he had to move again...

There was nothing but the sound of their laboured breathing in the quiet apartment as the frenzy overtook them. Her knees were pressed to his thighs, her hands gripping his shoulders. Her whole body tightened and quickened as Arkim thrust hard and deep up into her, hips welded to hers. He was so deep...deeper than ever before. She could feel her heart beating out of time. And when the explosion hit there was nowhere to hide.

Sylvie's head was thrown back, her eyes shut, every muscle and sinew taut, as waves and waves of release flowed through her body, wrenching her soul apart. And Arkim was with her every step of the way, his own body as taut as a whip under hers.

It was so excruciatingly exquisite that it almost felt like a punishment. As if Arkim was doing this on purpose, just to torture her. It was shattering.

And when the waves subsided Sylvie subsided too, unable to keep herself upright, collapsing against Arkim's chest, her head buried in his neck.

She felt like a car crash victim. As if some kind of explosion had really just happened, knocking her out of orbit. The fact that his heart was thundering under hers was no consolation. Her skin was hot, sticky, but she was too wiped out to care.

She whispered into his damp neck, 'What are we doing?'

She felt Arkim's chest swell underneath hers, making her sensitive breasts ache. His voice rumbled around her.

'We're doing that again...as soon as I can move...'

Much later, when it was dark outside, Sylvie woke alone in a massive bed. She was disorientated for a moment, and then the pleasurable aches and tingles in her body and the tenderness between her legs helped her to remember the last few cataclysmic hours.

Arkim had been true to his word. As soon as he'd been able to move he'd carried Sylvie into the bedroom, stripped, and proceeded to make love to her all over again. Then they'd taken a shower...and barely made it back to the bed before making love again.

Sylvie groaned and rolled over, mashing her face into a soft pillow. What was she *doing*?

She flipped back again and looked up at the exquisitely corniced ceiling, her mind racing with the implications of what it all meant. Arkim knew now. He knew everything. Everything she hadn't been able to tell him out of loyalty to her sister.

Feeling curious, and wondering where he was, Sylvie sat up, wincing as tender muscles protested. She saw a robe at the end of the bed and reached for it, sitting up to pull it on. It dwarfed her slim frame but she belted it tightly around her, blushing when she thought of her clothes, which must still be strewn in that elegant reception room.

She padded barefoot out of the bedroom and back towards the main part of the apartment. As she was passing a door that was slightly ajar she noticed a dim golden light and heard a suspicious-sounding *yap*.

She pushed open the door to find a study, three walls

lined with bookshelves and books. A huge desk was in front of the window, its surface covered with a computer, laptop and papers… But her eyes nearly popped out of her head when she saw Arkim sitting on the ground, his back against the only bare wall in the room, wearing only a pair of sweats and cradling a familiar-looking puppy in his arms.

They both looked up at the same time, and it would have been comical if Sylvie hadn't been so shocked. The little dog shot out of Arkim's arms and raced over to Sylvie, yapping excitedly, its stubby little tail waggling furiously. She crouched down and was almost bowled over by his enthusiasm, his tongue licking wherever he could reach.

When she was over her shock she looked at Arkim, who was still sitting there, looking for all the world as if nothing untoward was going on. 'What on earth…? How did you get him here?'

And why? Sylvie wanted to ask, but was afraid.

Arkim shrugged one shoulder negligently. 'I brought him back to the castle with me that day…and then I just ended up bringing him to Europe.'

Sylvie's breath felt choppy all of a sudden, and her heart was thumping hard. In a flight of fancy in her head she was imagining all sorts of reasons that were all very, *very* dangerous.

She buried her nose in his fur. When she looked up again she said, 'He's all cleaned up…what is he?'

Arkim's mouth quirked. 'A Highland Westie mixed with something indeterminate.'

'Have you got a name for him yet?'

He shook his head. 'I couldn't think of one. But I want to give him to you…so you choose a name.'

Sylvie's mouth fell open and the dog squirmed to be free, so she let him out of her arms to go sniffing at something exciting nearby. 'But...but I can't take him. My apartment is tiny, and Giselle is allergic to animal hair.'

Arkim frowned. 'Giselle?'

Sylvie waved a hand. 'My flatmate. Arkim...why are you doing this?'

He rose lithely from his seat on the floor, his chest dark under its smattering of hair in the golden light. He came over to her and held out a hand. Sylvie took it and he pulled her up. He led her over to a seat and sat down, pulling her into his lap. He smoothed her trailing hair over one shoulder.

She felt extremely unsure of her footing, and vulnerable. 'Arkim—'

'That day...' he interjected.

She nodded.

'I regretted sending you away like that.'

Sylvie's heart palpitations were back. 'You did?'

He nodded, his black eyes on hers, not letting her look away. 'I was a coward. You were getting too close... I asked you if you'd thought we were going to stay there for ever, but the truth is I think that's exactly what *I* wanted. Never to leave. And it just hit me: I had a life to get back to and I'd almost forgotten it existed. That *I* existed outside of that place. I honestly haven't been able to stop thinking about you. We're not done, Sylvie... I need more time with you.'

'What exactly are you saying, Arkim?' Sylvie didn't like the unpalatable questions being thrown up by his choice of words. *'I need more time with you...'* It sounded finite. Definitely finite.

'I want you to move in with me. Stay with me for as long as...'

'For as long as what?' she asked sharply, tensing all over. Because she very badly wanted him to say, *For as long as you want. For ever.*

'For as long as this lasts…this crazy, insatiable desire.'
Finite. Definitely finite.

She pulled away from Arkim and stood up before he could see how raw she felt. The puppy sniffed around her feet and she picked him up and held him against her, almost like a shield. How could Arkim manipulate her like this? Give her a reminder of the exquisite pleasure he could wring from her body…tell her he regretted the way he'd behaved…the puppy…and now this. When her defences were down.

Because this is the man who all but kidnapped you and held you in his castle at his pleasure when he wanted revenge.

She pushed aside the memories crowding her head. She needed to lay it out baldly for herself. 'So you're asking me to become your mistress? Is that it? And the dog is meant to sweeten the deal?' She made a sound of disgust and turned round to face the window. How could she have been so stupid…so—?

She was whirled around again to face Arkim, looming tall and intimidating.

'*No*…it's not like that. I mean…yes, I want you to stay—but as my lover…not as a mistress.' He sounded almost bitter. 'Believe me, I know by now that you would never languish idly at someone's beck and call. And the dog… I hadn't even consciously realised I wanted him for you, but I got your address from Sophie and I brought him with me. I don't take mistresses,' he said. 'I thought you'd know me well enough by now to know that I don't indulge women like that. I don't do frills or niceties.'

No. He didn't. He could tear a woman's heart and soul to shreds just by being him. Raw. Male. Uncompromising. Tortured, but with a deep core of emotion that made her heart break.

'You were right, you know,' he said heavily.

Sylvie finally found her voice. 'About what?'

Arkim grimaced. 'About my motivations for agreeing to marry Sophie. She represented something to me—something I'd always craved. A respectable family unit.'

And that just confirmed for Sylvie what she'd already guessed. Some day Arkim would find a woman worthy of being his perfectly respectable wife, and then he *would* do frills and niceties. She didn't doubt it.

The hatred she felt for that future woman shocked her. But it also made her see her own weakness. She wanted more too. She wanted to take every atom of what Arkim was offering and gorge herself before he cast her aside again. Or—if she had the strength—gorge herself so that she could walk away before he could do it for her.

She lifted her chin. 'If I stay with you and we...we do this, I won't give up my job.'

Arkim was very still. 'I wouldn't expect you to.'

Sylvie felt a spurt of relief mixed with pain. As long as she stayed in her 'job of ill repute' she'd remember who she was—and so would he. There would be no dangerous illusions or dreams, no fantasies that things could be different. Because they never could be. She was *not* the woman who would share Arkim's life and mother his children. And she needed to remember that.

She forced a lightness to her voice that she wasn't feeling and said, 'Well, then, if this dog is really mine I'd better think of a name.'

'That's a *good* boy, Omar...'

Arkim stood at the door and watched Sylvie hand the puppy a treat from her pocket as she lavished him with praise, rubbing him behind his floppy ears. As far as he could tell the dog wasn't doing anything that vaguely resembled obeying commands, but Sylvie was too besotted to care.

He recalled the spontaneous urge he'd felt to take the dog with him when he'd been leaving the oasis, obeying some irrational impulse because it had been the last thing Sylvie had touched. And then he'd spent a month tripping over the damn thing in London, talking to it as if it could understand him.

An alien lightness vied with a familiar surge of arousal just to see her sitting on the floor, her hair in a plait down her back. She was obviously just back from work, still dressed in leggings and a loose top. Arkim was used to women in couture creations and the latest ready-to-wear casuals. Yet Sylvie would blow them all out of the water with her inherent grace and elegance, dressed just like this.

She insisted on taking the Métro every day, refusing his offer of a driver and car. And he hadn't even realised that his kitchen functioned until he'd come in one evening and found Sylvie taking a Boeuf Bourguignon out of the oven. Far from making him break out in a cold sweat at the domesticity, he'd found it surprisingly appealing. He'd never known what it was to come home to a cooked meal, and he'd found himself laughing out loud at Sylvie's wry tales of learning to cook when she'd first arrived in Paris.

When she'd told him that she regularly baked for the members of the revue, he'd found his conscience smarting at the thought of how badly he'd misjudged her from that first moment he'd laid eyes on her. Because at first glance she'd epitomised everything he'd grown up to despise in a lewd, over-sexualised world.

In fact she was anything but. He'd been wrong about her. *So* wrong.

It had been two weeks now since she'd moved in…and just like before, the more Arkim had of her, the more he wanted her. It made him nervous. This…this lust he felt was too urgent. Desperate, even. He couldn't let her go. *Yet.*

She looked up then and saw him standing there. Her

eyes widened, brightened, and she smiled. But then the smile slipped slightly and a guarded look came over her beautiful face. It made Arkim want to haul her up and demand that she... *What?* asked a small voice. *Stop shutting you out?*

Ever since that night when she'd agreed to stay Sylvie had locked a piece of herself away from him. She was careful around him—there was some spark he'd come to expect in her missing.

Except for when they made love... Then she could hold nothing back, in spite of herself.

But when they were finished she would curl up on her side, away from him. And Arkim would lie there and clench his hands into fists to stop himself from reaching for her—because he didn't do that, did he? That would send the wrong message...that this was something more than a transitory slaking of mutual lust.

Except it wasn't being slaked. It was being stoked.

'A function?' Sylvie felt a flicker of trepidation. So far she and Arkim had spent their time confined to his stunning apartment. They met here after work and indulged in satisfying their mutual lust until they couldn't move. Then they got up, went to work and repeated the process.

Every morning Sylvie woke up praying that this would be the morning when he didn't affect her so much...to no avail. And when they'd had dinner the other night... dinner she'd made...it had felt far too easy...seductive. She couldn't do that again.

Arkim was leaning against the doorframe, looking edible in a dark three-piece suit, his jaw stubbled after the day.

'It's a charity benefit thing...to raise money for cancer awareness. I thought you'd have an interest.'

Sylvie was shocked that Arkim obviously remembered her telling him that her mother had died of cancer.

'Well, of course I do... But... I mean, I didn't think you'd want to be seen with me. In public.'

Some fleeting expression passed over his face and then he came over and pulled her up from the floor, his hands resting under her arms. 'The reason we haven't gone out together is because the minute I see you I need you. And I need you now.'

Everything in Sylvie exulted. She felt exactly the same. The insatiable desire to cleave herself to this man.

She was barely aware of Omar—she'd named him after Al-Omar—pawing her calf, looking for attention.

'What about the function?' The thought of going out in public with Arkim was alternately terrifying and exciting.

'We're still going... But first...a shower?'

Sylvie hid her reaction to the fact that he was prepared to be seen in public with her and said, mock seriously, 'I think your dedication to water conservation is to be commended.'

Arkim snorted and tugged her to the bedroom, shutting the door firmly on Omar, who skidded to a stop outside the closed door and proceeded to whine pitifully and unnoticed for the next half an hour.

'Are you sure I look okay?'

Arkim was the epitome of civilised style in a black tuxedo. Sylvie hated feeling so insecure, but the full magnitude of what this public outing meant was sinking in—and not in a good way. She was nervous of people recognising him, recognising *her*, and the inevitable scrutiny.

He reached for her hand, lacing his fingers through hers. 'You look amazing. Just think of this as one of your father's events...you looked pretty confident to me in that milieu.'

She fought back a blush to think of how forward she'd been and plucked at the silky emerald-green material of her dress. The dress was gorgeous—a slinky column of pure silk—it covered her from throat to wrist to ankle but, perversely, it felt more revealing than anything she'd ever worn before, skimming close to her curves and cut on the bias.

It had been waiting for her in a silver embossed box when she'd emerged from her shower with Arkim, barely able to walk after his *very* careful ministrations. Every feminist principle in her had risen up to refuse it...but she'd taken one look and fallen in love. It reminded her poignantly of a dress her mother had owned—which Catherine had inevitably thrown out—and so, like a traitor, she'd accepted it.

She'd styled her hair into movie star waves and hoped that it wasn't too much. She knew how snobbish these events were, and if anyone recognised her... She gulped.

'Relax... I know how you feel—believe me.'

Sylvie was jolted out of her introspection and she looked at the wry expression on Arkim's face. Of course he knew. He was the son of one of the most infamous men in the world. When she thought of how proud he was... Her heart felt ominously achy at the thought of people looking at him and judging him.

As he did you, she reminded herself. And even though she could understand his motives now the hurt still lingered.

The car was drawing to a smooth stop outside one of Paris's most iconic and glamorous hotels. Arkim got out, and Sylvie drew in a deep breath as he opened the door and held out a hand for her. They joined a very glitzy throng of beautiful people entering the foyer with lots of expensive perfume and air-kissing. Arkim held Sylvie's hand, and she found she was clinging to him.

She reminded herself that she needed to be vigilant around him. She didn't want to lose herself again so easily. So she forced herself to relax and took her hand out of his, ignoring his look as she squared her shoulders and entered the massive ballroom where the function was being held.

His hand stayed on the small of her back, though, as waiters offered them drinks and they navigated their way around the room, constantly stopping when Arkim was recognised by various people.

Sylvie found, much to her relief, that she was usually given a quick once-over and then summarily dismissed. She didn't mind. She preferred that to scrutiny or recognition any day of the week.

When they were momentarily alone again Sylvie asked curiously, 'When do they announce dinner?' She was beginning to feel hunger pangs after their earlier activity.

Arkim grimaced slightly and gestured with his head to where a waiter was passing, with some teeny-tiny hors d'oeuvres that looked more like art installations than food. 'That's dinner, I'm afraid, I think most people here haven't eaten in about ten years.'

Sylvie grinned at his humour—and then her stomach growled in earnest and she blushed, ducking her head with embarrassment.

Arkim slid an arm around her waist and pulled her into his tall, hard body, creating a wave of heat that slowly engulfed her. When she looked at him again he said, 'Isn't there some leftover Boeuf Bourguignon at home?'

His use of the word *home* caused butterflies. She fought to stay cool. 'I believe there is...'

Arkim's gaze moved down to her mouth and now *he* looked hungry. 'Then let's get out of here. I've had enough.'

The thought of leaving now, getting out of the evening intact, without any awkward public meetings, was very appealing. Apart from what the explicit hunger in his eyes promised... Well, she *had* made a promise to herself to gorge, hadn't she?

Sylvie looked up at him and felt as if she was drowning. As if she was fighting a losing battle. 'Okay, then—let's go.'

They were walking out through the vast marbled lobby—hand in hand because Arkim refused to let her tug free—and Sylvie was floating on a cloud of dangerous contentment at the thought of being alone with him again, when a group of men stopped in front of them. Arkim stopped, making her jerk to a halt beside him.

She looked up, expecting it to be someone he knew. But the men were looking at *her*. At her body. At her breasts. Before Sylvie had even assessed the situation properly, icy-cold humiliation was crawling up her spine.

'Well, well, well...it's your favourite L'Amour revue artist, James.'

CHAPTER TEN

SYLVIE RECOGNISED THEM—sickeningly. They were regulars at the show—English ex-pats, working in Paris—and one of them had had a brief fling with Giselle, her flatmate. She remembered the guy blearily hopping around their tiny apartment the morning after, looking for his clothes.

Arkim snarled from beside her, 'She doesn't know who you are—now, get out of our way.'

Now all the men's attention was on Arkim. Sylvie wanted to curl up and die. He looked livid. A muscle throbbed in his jaw.

'And who are *you*, mate? Are you paying her well for the night? Cos if you've lost interest we'd be more than happy to stump up some cash for a good time.'

One of the others interjected then. 'She doesn't put out, remember?'

Sylvie felt as if she was in some kind of nightmare. She tried to speak. 'I'm sorry... I really don't think we've met...' But her voice came out all thready and weak, and now the tallest of the men—still a good few inches shorter than Arkim—was standing toe to toe with him.

'Think you're some hotshot, eh? Well, it happens that I recognise you too—*you're* the guy that got stood up at the altar.'

'Oh, God!' Sylvie hadn't even realised she'd spoken out loud. She felt nauseous.

Arkim let her hand go and pushed her away from him, saying in a voice edged with steel, 'Get into the car and wait for me—*now*.'

Sylvie started to back away, horror filling her at the murderous look on Arkim's face, but as she turned around one of the men who so far hadn't said anything blocked her.

'And where do you think *you're* going?'

Sylvie clenched her jaw. 'Get out of my way.'

He came closer and she could smell the reek of alcohol on his breath. 'Now, now…that's not nice, is it? I've *seen* you, you know…'

He stroked a finger up her arm and Sylvie fought not to flinch in disgust.

'You're my favourite of them all…but I'd like to see a lot more of you…'

Sylvie had just positioned her knee for maximum damage, in case he touched her again, and heard an almighty *crack* behind her. She whirled round to see Arkim staggering back, holding a hand up to his eye.

She flew to his side just as the hotel security officers rushed forward. Arkim, still holding a hand to his face, spoke to someone who looked like a manager. The eight or so English guys were rounded up within seconds, and it was only then that Sylvie realised just how drunk they all were, as they were led away with belligerent faces.

Her hand was in Arkim's again, and he was taking her out to the car so fast she had to trot to keep up, holding her dress up. Her stomach was churning painfully, and she breathed out as the car pulled away from the front of the hotel.

She looked at Arkim and winced when she saw his eye, shut tight. She knelt on the seat beside him, swatting aside his hand when he tried to stop her. 'What happened? How did you get hit?'

He looked at her with his one good eye. 'I recognised one of the men.'

Sylvie felt shaky. She reached for a bottle of water and unscrewed it, lifting some of the material at the bottom of her dress and wetting it to dab at his eye ineffectually.

'And?' she prompted, feeling sick all over again.

'He said something about you that I know isn't true.'

Her insides cramped.

'I told him that if he didn't take it back I'd spread the word about his out-of-control recreational drug use. So he hit me.'

Sylvie sat back on her heels, anguished. 'I'm so sorry, Arkim.'

His one good eye glared at her. 'What are you apologising for? *They* were at fault.'

'Yes, but if they hadn't recognised me…'

Arkim didn't say anything, and his silence spoke volumes.

With relief Sylvie saw that they were drawing close to the apartment. The traffic at this time of evening was light, and Arkim didn't live far away. The car pulled to a stop and Arkim got out, his movements jerky. Sylvie didn't wait. She clambered out, still holding her dress up in one hand. The feeling of contentment she'd had earlier had been well and truly shattered by a rude awakening.

In the apartment she could hear Arkim moving restlessly around the drawing room, the clatter of the drinks tray. He was angry. She wrapped some ice in a towel and brought it in, saying as authoritatively as she could, 'Sit down—let me look at you.'

He scowled at her. His jacket was off, his bow tie undone. His eye was closed and swelling. He looked thoroughly disreputable, and it only added to his appeal.

He sat down, legs spread, stretching an arm across the back of the couch. Approaching him, Sylvie felt as if she was approaching a bad-tempered lion. But she did it, and then observed, 'Your eye isn't bleeding—that's good.'

'You're a nurse now?'

Sylvie pushed down a flare of irritation at Arkim's

snappy mood. 'No, but I do tend to be the one people come to with minor injuries at work.'

Arkim made a *harumph* sound. Of *course* everyone went to her for treatment at work. He could just imagine her: compassionate, kind, soothing. Yet another unwelcome reminder of how badly he'd misjudged her all along.

He knew he was being a boor, but his gut was still too churned up after the confrontation for him to be sanguine. Sylvie pressed the ice near his eye, and he was aware of her wincing when he sucked in a pained breath.

The words that man had said came back to him: *'She tastes as sweet as she looks, doesn't she?'*

Arkim had had to call on a level of control he'd never used before. And what scared him even now was the instant volcanic jealousy that had swamped him. The tiniest implication that the man had been intimate with Sylvie had been enough to send him into orbit.

He still felt edgy, volatile. Sylvie was kneeling on the couch beside him, the silk of her dress straining across her breasts, outlining their luscious shape. Adrenalin still lingered in Arkim's blood. He needed to channel it...dilute it somehow. Sylvie shifted and her body swayed closer. His arousal spiked, mixing with the adrenalin, making him crave an antidote to this churning in his gut.

He put down his glass of alcohol and reached out and put his hands around Sylvie's waist. She took the ice away and looked at him. Her hair was tumbling over her shoulders, a glossy wave of bright red. She looked concerned. Eyes huge with worry. Remorse.

'Arkim—'

He took the ice pack out of her hands and threw it aside, then pulled her into him, his intent unmistakable.

Sylvie protested, even though he could feel her breath coming faster, moving her chest against his. 'You're hurt. We can't—'

He put a finger on her mouth, then cupped the back of her head. In spite of his need to devour, consume, he found that something happened as he touched her mouth with his. The tension in his body was fading away...and he was touching her as reverently as if she was made of china.

She braced herself with her hands on his chest. Desire rose up, fast and urgent, replacing the need to be reverent, and Arkim fumbled clumsily with his clothes and body, sheathing himself with protection. Sylvie rose above him, pulling her dress up, eyes glazed with lust, cheeks flushed.

Arkim tore Sylvie's delicate lace panties off and drew the head of his erection up and down her slick folds, tantalising her, torturing himself, until she was slick and hot. Too impatient to wait, she rose up and took him in her hand, then slowly slid down, taking all of him inside her body. It was so exquisite Arkim had to grit his jaw tightly.

They moved with a kind of slow but languorous intent...rocking, sliding...and when the need became too great Arkim held Sylvie's hips in place and lost himself inside her, burying his head in her breast, feeling her hands on his head, as his soul flew apart and finally he found the oblivion he was looking for.

A couple of hours later Sylvie was lying on her side, naked, her hands under her face, watching Arkim's chest rise and fall. He'd taken her to bed and made love to her again, and the after-shocks of pleasure still pulsed through her body at intermittent intervals. The intensity of the way he'd taken her on the couch still took her breath away. It was as if he'd been consumed with a kind of fury.

His face was in profile to her, showing the proud line of his nose. From here she couldn't see his injured eye. Sylvie couldn't help but feel that in spite of the passion with which Arkim had taken her just now something had altered since that confrontation at the hotel.

A cold weight settled in her belly as an ugly reminder reared its head. She'd been meaning to discuss something with Arkim for the past couple of days and had been avoiding it like a coward. Because she was afraid that it would prove to be some kind of a test. A test of where she really fitted into his life.

As his chest rose and fell evenly she envied him his peace, when *her* body and brain felt as if they were tying themselves into a million knots. Knowing she wouldn't rest, Sylvie slipped out of bed and got dressed, going into the living room.

She sat cross-legged on the couch and Omar jumped up into her lap. As she petted him absently and looked into the muted darkness she knew that she had no choice but to talk to Arkim. And after what had happened this evening she knew that he would have no hesitation in letting her go. For good, this time.

Dawn was breaking outside when Arkim woke. His head was throbbing and he wondered why—until he lifted a hand and winced when it came into contact with his black eye.

Sylvie. Anger jerked him fully awake in an instant. The memory of those men…eating her up with their eyes. And one of them had touched her. He'd seen it. His hands curled into fists just from thinking about it, remembering, his blood pressure increasing.

No woman had ever roused Arkim to the point of wanting to do violence on her behalf. But he'd been ready to take on all those men. His anger had been volcanic. It was something he hadn't felt in a long time…since the day that woman had controlled him for her own amusement and his father had thrown him out like unwanted baggage.

Sylvie. Arkim looked around. He was alone in the room…no sounds were coming from the bathroom. He wanted her even now, even after making love to her like some kind of feral youth on the couch earlier. Damn her. Would he *ever* not want her?

Not wanting to investigate the way his gut clenched at that prospect, Arkim got out of bed and pulled on a pair of sweats, feeling as if he'd done about ten rounds in a boxing ring. He frowned as he padded through the apartment, hearing nothing but silence. Not even Omar.

He checked all the rooms and came to the living room last—and finally he saw her. She was standing with her back to the door, looking out of the window. He noticed that she was dressed in jeans and a shirt. There was something tense about the lines of her body that made him stay where he was.

'You're dressed.'

The lines of Sylvie's body got tenser. She turned around slowly. Her hair was pulled into a low bun at the back of her head. She confounded him—she could go from looking like the sexiest movie star goddess to something like this, much more simple and plain, and yet his body reacted the same way every time.

He leaned against the door and crossed his arms, grateful for the fact that his sweats were loose. His susceptibility to this woman was something that still made him feel uncomfortable. Exposed.

Sylvie's arms were crossed too. 'There was something I wanted to tell you earlier, but I never got a chance.'

Feeling a flutter of panic, and not liking it, Arkim said, 'Is it so important it can't wait till later?' He stood up straight and held out a hand. 'Come back to bed…it's too early for talk.'

Sylvie smiled, but it was touched with something Arkim hadn't seen in some time. Cynicism.

'No, it can't wait…'

Arkim went over to the drinks cabinet and helped himself to a shot of brandy. He saluted Sylvie. 'Medicinal purposes.'

She paled at that, and Arkim paused with the glass halfway to his mouth. 'What is it?'

She looked at him, that blue-green gaze unnervingly direct. 'Pierre has offered me a bigger role in the show.'

The tight ball in Arkim's gut seemed to ease. *That was it?* 'That sounds good.' So why did she look so serious?

'It is good... But if I accept it I'll have to take off my clothes for the first time...like the other girls. Pierre has never pressured me about this before... I told you, he's been like a father to me. But he says now that if I want to stay I have to start delivering a fuller performance.'

For a second Arkim just heard a roaring in his ears. Images rushed through his head: Sylvie's pale breasts bared for thousands of people to see... Her perfect body... No wonder her boss wanted to exploit her.

And those men last night...they would look at her—every night if they wished. And taunt Arkim with the knowledge that they'd seen as much of his lover as he had.

He realised his hand had tightened so much around the glass that he risked breaking it. He forced himself to relax, to focus.

Sylvie continued. 'The truth is that I don't know if I should do it or not. I've been thinking...about doing something else.'

Relief vied with something much darker inside Arkim. Sylvie was looking at him far too carefully. As if his response mattered. As if she wanted him to tell her what to do.

The sheer volatility of his emotions was like acid in his stomach, inhibiting his response. If he told Sylvie he cared what she did she would have control over him...she would know his vulnerability. It would make a statement about what was happening here, would demonstrate a possessiveness of her that had already earned him a black eye. In public. In front of his peers.

He went cold—because he hadn't even contemplated that side of it yet.

He'd just weathered one public scandal...was he now in danger of being dragged into another one?

It was too much. Too reminiscent of that day when he'd lost his innocence and his self-respect. When he'd been found, literally, with his pants down and that woman's mouth around his— He blanked the poisonous memory. He wasn't going back there for anyone.

Carefully, he took a sip of his drink. He didn't even feel the burn. His voice when he spoke was cool. Calm. Belying the tumult underneath. 'I don't really know what you want me to say. It's your life, Sylvie. You should do whatever you think is best for you.'

She looked at him for a long moment, but it was a kind of dead-eyed stare. She was so pale that Arkim almost made a move towards her, but then she seemed to break out of her trance-like state and uncrossed her arms, her gaze narrowed.

'Yes, it *is* my life, and I *do* know what's best for me. Which is why I'm going to leave now.'

Arkim frowned. 'Leave...?'

Sylvie glanced down to where Omar was sitting at her feet, looking up at her adoringly, his tongue hanging out. But she didn't bend down to pick him up. Arkim saw her hands form fists, as if to stop herself.

She looked back at him, her jaw tight. 'Yes, leave. The new show opens in a week and there's a huge PR campaign starting tomorrow. In light of what happened last night I think it's best if we call it quits now.' Her chin lifted. 'I would prefer not to be responsible for any further public incidents, and when the new show takes off... Well, it's only more likely to happen.'

Something hard and dark and cold settled into Arkim's belly. 'So you're going to do it, then? Take Pierre up on his offer?'

Her face was like a pale smooth mask. She shrugged lightly. 'It's all I've ever known. They're my family... I'd be a fool not to want to progress in one of the most famous shows in the world.'

'By taking off your clothes?' Arkim almost spat the words.

Sylvie's gaze sparked. 'What's it to you? I have to worry about my career, Arkim. If I don't take this opportunity now there's a million girls coming up behind me who'll do the job.'

Arkim had to grit his jaw. He wanted to say, *What about the way you were dancing that day when I found you again?*

She had been so passionate and beautiful. But that wasn't really her, was it? If she was prepared to do this? Take the last step over the line...? Something within Arkim snapped and the words spilled out before he could stop them. 'What if I asked you to stay?'

A flare of colour came into Sylvie's cheeks. 'How long for? Another week? A month? Two months? We both know what this is...impermanent. Unless...'

Unless it's more.

The implication of her unfinished sentence made Arkim say harshly, 'Unless it's nothing.'

'It's nothing, then,' said Sylvie faintly.

She walked over and picked up her bag and a jacket, shrugging into it in jerky movements. She was avoiding Arkim's eye as she walked to the other side of the room, where he saw that a larger bag was waiting. So she'd packed already. Because she'd known how he would react? The knowledge sent a sharp pain through his chest.

She turned around to face him, looking very petite and

young. Delicate. He thought of her just a couple of hours ago, astride him, rocking her body against his. She'd been like a fearsome warrior, claiming her pleasure with a ferocity matched only by Arkim's desire to give it to her.

The image was so vivid that it took him a second to realise she'd gone.

No.

He put down the glass, uncaring that it fell to the floor, spilling dark golden liquid. When he got to the hall, he saw her holding Omar close, burying her face in his body before putting him down carefully. Something was constricting Arkim, like a band around his chest.

She didn't face him. She put her hand on the knob of the door and said tautly, 'I can't take him with me—it's not practical... But you will take care of him, won't you?'

Arkim was cold. All over. He hated his father. He'd never known his mother. He'd never known love. What he felt for Sylvie was just too...*overwhelming*.

'Of course.'

He wasn't even aware that he'd spoken. Cold was good. This was what he wanted. He didn't want volatility. Messy passion. *Emotions*.

'Thank you. Goodbye, Arkim.' She opened the door, and just before she stepped through she said huskily, 'Take care of yourself.'

After she'd gone Arkim was dimly aware of something warm on his toes, and he looked down stupidly to see Omar, tail wagging, making a small pitiful sound. He bent down and scooped him up against his chest, then went into the living room and sat on the couch, where the puppy settled trustingly into his lap.

He could smell Sylvie's delicate scent on the air. And something else. *Sex*. He realised that this was where he'd had her...only hours before. Every time he'd lost himself inside her it had felt as if another part of his soul was being altered.

He clenched his jaw so hard it hurt. Pain was good. The pain reminded him that he craved order and respectability above all. He didn't *need* his soul to be altered.

Sylvie Devereux had been a brief and torrid interlude in his life and now he was moving on. For good.

CHAPTER ELEVEN

A week later—L'Amour revue, final dress rehearsal...

'*Sylvie!* Hurry up! You're next.'

Sylvie took a deep breath, grabbed her prop sword, and made her way to the spotlit stage. The mood was controlled chaos. The new show was opening in a few hours and they still had lots to prepare. She was in a more elaborate version of the belly dance outfit that she'd worn for Arkim in Al-Hibiz, and the reminder was jarring.

When she got on stage the music started almost at once, so she had to jump straight into the routine. She wasn't overly worried about how precise her movements were because this rehearsal was really for the technical team, to make sure that all the timings for cues and lights and so on were lined up properly.

She had taken off her veil and head-covering and pushed her sword away, ready to move into the second part of the dance, when a loud *'Stop!'* sounded in the dark theatre.

Sylvie's heart stuttered, but she told herself she was imagining that she knew the voice. She was on her feet now and she kept going. It was probably just one of the stage hands.

Suddenly the music stopped.

She whirled around to hear some kind of a scuffle going on in the darkness backstage, and then a man walked out onto the stage from behind the curtains. Even though he was in the shadow of the lights she knew it was Arkim, taller and broader than everyone else.

He was holding something that looked like a vital piece

of audio equipment. Sure enough, he was quickly followed by an irate sound engineer, spluttering and gesticulating furiously, grabbing back his piece of equipment and disappearing again.

Sylvie wasn't sure she wasn't dreaming. 'Arkim...?'

He stepped forward into the spotlight. He wasn't a mirage. And then she became aware of the fact that they had an audience of crew and other dancers.

'What the hell are you doing? We're in the middle of rehearsals—you can't be here,' she hissed at him. But her mind leapt to the million and one possibilities of why he might be there anyway.

She noticed that the swelling on his eye had gone down, to be replaced by a dark bruise. He looked as if he'd just come from a brawl in an alley.

Her fault.

And, adding to her sense of everything being unreal, he was wearing faded worn denims and a close-fitting T-shirt, more casual than she'd ever seen him. It was almost as shocking as the time when she'd seen him naked in the pool at the oasis. His hair was messy and his overall demeanour was edgy and dangerous. He looked a million miles removed from the man she'd first seen in her father's house in his three-piece suit, so controlled. So disdainful.

'Arkim—'

But he cut her off, saying baldly, 'I don't want you to strip. I don't want anyone else to see you.'

Shock reverberated through her. And something scarily like euphoria. But just as quickly she feared that she was reading this all wrong.

She put her hands on her hips, anger flaring. 'It's okay for *you* to see me, but you're so controlling and possessive that you can't bear the thought that your *ex*-property might become a little more public?'

He stepped closer, the inevitable electricity sparking

between them. 'No,' he growled. 'I don't want anyone to see you because you're *mine*.'

Sylvie glared up at him. 'Do I need to remind you that you've let me go—*twice*?' The knowledge of her own weakness around him and the realisation that he'd never choose her to be a permanent part of his life made her say frigidly, 'What is it, Arkim? You're so concerned with your precious reputation that you're afraid my debauched lifestyle will come back to haunt you?'

A muscle in his jaw pulsed. 'No, dammit. I don't want anyone else to see what's *mine*.'

Emotion made Sylvie's chest ache. This man had started out rejecting her before he'd even known her, and even after getting to know her—intimately—he'd still ultimately rejected her. He was just here beating his chest because he couldn't bear the thought of sharing her.

'But I'm not *yours*. You let me go.'

They were so close now they were almost touching. Sylvie was unaware of anything but the man in front of her and those deep, dark eyes. Eyes that could look so cold and dead, but which she knew could turn her heart upside down and inside out.

'I don't want you to go. I want you to stay.'

Hating the little tremor of emotion that made her heart jump with irrational hope, Sylvie threw out a hand. 'We've *had* this conversation. For how long? Another two weeks? A month? And then you'll move on with your perfect respectable life and you'll meet some perfect respectable woman and you'll marry her—like you wanted to marry Sophie because she was so perfect for you.'

'*You* are perfect for me.'

Sylvie's mouth was still open. She shut it abruptly, aghast at everything that had tumbled out. And had he just said...?

'What did you say?'

'I said that you are perfect for me. I don't want anyone else.'

His words impacted like a sledgehammer, knocking her to pieces. And even though she'd registered them she shook her head, took a step back. It wasn't hard to envisage being rejected again, when Arkim woke up one morning and realised she wasn't perfect for him, wasn't really suitable for the life he wanted, and this time his rejection would be comprehensive and fatal. She wouldn't recover. And the worst of it was she *knew* why it was so important to him...she wanted him to be happy.

'This is just lust talking,' she said.

Before Sylvie could react Arkim had closed the distance between them and cupped her face in his hands. He blotted out the world when he lowered his mouth to hers. Sylvie might have expected devastation, bruising passion...but his kiss was like a kind of benediction. A kiss that was gentle and restrained, but with the unmistakable promise of *more*.

And, damn him, she couldn't help but respond. A sob of reaction was working its way up her throat, making her grab his T-shirt in order to stay standing. She just wasn't able to defend herself. The last week had been torture.

Eventually Arkim pulled back, his eyes glittering down into hers. Sylvie felt exposed...vulnerable.

'I know what I want and I want you.'

I want. Not *I love.* And Sylvie needed love. After feeling so bruised all her life from her father's rejection, she couldn't go through that with someone else. Better to be the rejecter. Arkim didn't want her. Not really. No matter what he said or how he kissed her.

She pulled free. 'It wasn't enough of a wake-up call that you got punched in the face? Are you so blinded that you've forgotten what I do? What I am? Wherever we go there's always going to be a risk that someone will recognise me...' She crossed her fingers behind her back at the white lie she was about to tell. 'And especially when I become famous for taking my clothes off completely. I won't be one of the less risqué acts any more, Arkim. Everyone will know what I look like naked.'

Sylvie could see him pale slightly under the olive tones of his skin. His face was starker, leaner than she'd ever seen it. As if he'd lost weight in the space of a week.

'If that's what you really want to do I won't pretend that I'll like it, but I'll support you.'

Sylvie reeled. Her jaw dropped. Eventually she got out, 'You're saying you'd *accept* me, no matter what?' She couldn't believe it for a second. Because if she did... Her heart contracted painfully.

She shook her head. 'This is not you talking... This is lust...desire. And once it's gone, Arkim—' Her voice broke traitorously. 'I won't let you send me away again when you realise that I'm not perfect after all...because I'm a constant reminder of some weakness you feel, of your life with your father.'

She'd moved to turn away, her vision blurring, when Arkim's hand shot out and caught her shoulder. She saw Pierre standing and watching, his gnarled old face incredulous. They had an avid audience. Everyone had gathered to watch the show.

Sylvie let Arkim turn her back towards him, saying in a choked voice, 'Arkim, you have to—'

'Stop talking, Sylvie.'

Her mouth closed. He had to know they were being observed. Why wasn't he leaving? Why wasn't he preserving what was left intact of his reputation?

Maybe because he means what he says? said a small seductive voice.

But before she could do or say anything more Arkim was reaching for the bottom of his T-shirt, pulling it up over his head and off, revealing his very taut and perfect musculature.

There was a collective intake of appreciative breath and a low whistle, which sounded as if it was quickly stifled by an elbow in the ribs.

Sylvie barely noticed, she was so shocked. 'What are you *doing*?'

His hands were on his jeans now. He looked grim. 'I'm trying to prove to you that I'll do whatever it takes to make you trust in me.'

He was starting to undo his top button, and Sylvie realised that he fully intended to strip completely. She put out a shaking hand. 'Stop.' And then she shook her head. 'Why...?'

Arkim dropped his hands, and now he looked bleak. 'Because I need to show you that I'm willing to bare myself totally for you. And that if you wanted me to stand in front of Notre Dame and do it, I would. I need you to know that I won't ever judge you again. I'm proud of you, and of everything you've achieved with such innate dignity and pride. You shame me. Everything I've been aiming for my whole life is empty. Meaningless. Without you.'

Sylvie was struck dumb.

He seared her alive with the intensity in his dark gaze. 'Don't you get it yet? I love you... But it took me a really long time to understand it because I've never loved anyone, so I didn't know what it felt like...and I'm sorry.'

To her absolute shock Arkim proceeded to get down on one knee in front of her. He took something out of his pocket. A small velvet box. He opened it up and took something out, held it up between his fingers. She could see that his hand was trembling.

He took her hand in his and said, 'Sylvie Devereux, I know I've given you every reason in the world to hate me...but will you please consent to be my wife? Because

I love you, and without you I'm just an arrogant, uptight prat.' He squeezed her hand. 'Whatever it is you want to do in this life I will support you, and I will take a thousand blows for you if that's what comes my way. Because you're mine to protect and cherish and love, and I pledge to do this for as long as I have breath in my body.'

Sylvie felt dizzy, anchored to the earth only by Arkim's hand wrapped around hers. She wasn't even looking at the ring, glinting with a green flash of colour in her peripheral vision. She wanted to believe...*so* badly. And then she realised that she was just as guilty as he of wanting to protect herself. She had to trust or she'd never move on from her old hurts.

She spoke with a rush. 'I'm not really taking Pierre's offer... I just said that to try and make you see how inappropriate I was for you. I'm only performing tonight as a favour, because we're stuck for an act. My modern dance teacher is putting together a company, here in Paris, and he wants me to be a part of it—as one of their lead dancers. I won't be taking my clothes off, but I still won't be perfect.'

He smiled a crooked smile. 'You *are* perfect. If you want to ride naked on a horse through the streets of Paris then I'll take off all my clothes too and join you.'

Another voluble sigh came from someone nearby. Sylvie ignored it.

Arkim's hand gripped hers. 'I just want you to be happy...'

And finally it sank in, and spread through her whole body like a warm glow, lighting up the dark corners that had been filled with pain and uncertainty for a long time.

Sylvie realised that Arkim was looking a little strained... He was still waiting for her answer. Unsure.

'Yes,' she said softly, her heart swelling. 'Yes, I'll marry you.' She got down on her knees and faced him, touching his face, tracing his mouth. She looked at him and said shakily, 'I love you so much... I think I've loved you for ever. And I knew it the moment I saw you, even though I couldn't understand how...'

For a second Arkim looked stunned, as if he truly hadn't known what she would say. Then she felt him push the ring on her finger, and glanced down to see a huge emerald flanked by smaller blue sapphires and diamonds. Like her eyes.

She reached for him just as he reached for her, their mouths fusing, bodies pressed close enough to hurt.

And then a very loud and obvious cough from nearby made Sylvie jerk in Arkim's arms. The theatre and their surroundings filtered back into her consciousness as if she were coming out of a particularly delicious dream.

She looked around to see a sea of faces and a lot of suspiciously shiny eyes. Pierre, however, looked familiarly stern. But she could see the glint of affection in his expression.

He eyeballed Arkim. 'If you've quite finished with my dancer, Mr Al-Sahid, I have a theatre to run and a show to put on in less than an hour...'

Arkim had a tight grip on Sylvie's hips and he was still unashamedly half naked. Something Sylvie was becoming more and more burningly aware of. The ring he'd put on her finger felt heavy and solid. A happy weight.

Arkim, totally unfazed by Pierre, looked at Sylvie. 'There's nothing I want more than to take you home right now...but do you want to do the show?'

The Arkim she'd first met might have carried her out of here over his shoulder. Or paid Pierre to release her.

Sylvie looked between the men and then back to Arkim. Her voice was husky when she said, 'Yes, I'd like to do it. It's to be my last performance, and it's thanks to Pierre I got a place with the modern dance company.' Sylvie grinned. 'He only offered me the bigger role because he knew I'd say no and that it was the push I needed to move on...'

Arkim looked at the older man, his eyes suspiciously bright. He stood up and, bringing Sylvie with him, reached out to shake the man's hand. 'Thank you for taking care of her—and for seeing her potential.'

Now Pierre looked suspiciously emotional. Sylvie fought back her own tears and pulled away from Arkim. She had to finish getting ready. He let her go with a look that told her he'd be in the front row, waiting for her. For ever.

Just before Sylvie went out of earshot, though, she thought she heard Pierre say hopefully, 'Mr Al-Sahid, are you *sure* you don't have any dance experience...?'

EPILOGUE

THE PRIEST'S EYES widened as he took in the spectacle approaching down the aisle. There was the slim figure of the bride, dressed from head to toe in white satin and lace, her face obscured by a gauzy veil. Her arm was tucked into the arm of the young woman who was giving her away. She was blonde and very pretty, dressed in dusky pink, and—the priest frowned—very familiar. Because, he realised, he'd watched *her* come down the aisle dressed as a bride only a few short months before. To stand with the same groom.

The groom now turned to look and the priest could sense his nervous tension. He hadn't been half as jumpy the last time.

The woman in pink handed the bride over to the groom with a smile and a look that said, *Take care of her or I'll kill you.* But the priest could tell that the groom needed no such warning. He looked as if he'd kill anyone who dared to come between him and this woman, who was now stepping up to the altar, her hand firmly in his.

But then, before the priest could open his mouth to start the proceedings, the groom lifted the veil from his bride's radiant face and pushed it over her head, before pulling her close to lower his head and press a kiss to her mouth.

Eventually, after realising that this was the same woman who had so sensationally interrupted the last wedding, the priest coughed loudly. They separated, the bride's face flushed, her eyes shining.

The priest was feeling rather hot under the collar by now himself, and said testily, 'If you're quite ready, shall we proceed?'

They both looked at him and the groom smiled. 'We're ready.'

And thankfully, when the moment came for anyone to object, there was nothing but happy silence…

* * * * *

COMING SOON!

We really hope you enjoyed reading this book.
If you're looking for more romance
be sure to head to the shops when
new books are available on

Thursday 28th August

To see which titles are coming soon, please visit
millsandboon.co.uk/nextmonth

MILLS & BOON

afterglow BOOKS

Afterglow Books is a trend-led, trope-filled list of books with diverse, authentic and relatable characters, a wide array of voices and representations, plus real world trials and tribulations. Featuring all the tropes you could possibly want (think small-town settings, fake relationships, grumpy vs sunshine, enemies to lovers) and all with a generous dose of spice in every story.

♪ @millsandboonuk
◉ @millsandboonuk
afterglowbooks.co.uk
#AfterglowBooks

For all the latest book news, exclusive content and giveaways scan the QR code below to sign up to the Afterglow newsletter:

SCAN ME

afterglow BOOKS

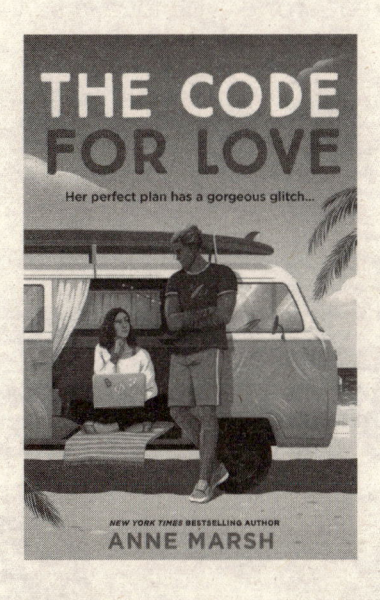

THE CODE FOR LOVE

Her perfect plan has a gorgeous glitch...

NEW YORK TIMES BESTSELLING AUTHOR
ANNE MARSH

✈ International

⛅ Grumpy/sunshine

🤝 Fake dating

OUT NOW

To discover more visit:
Afterglowbooks.co.uk

FOUR BRAND NEW BOOKS FROM
MILLS & BOON MODERN

The same great stories you love, a stylish new look!

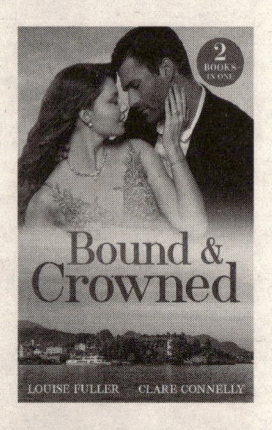

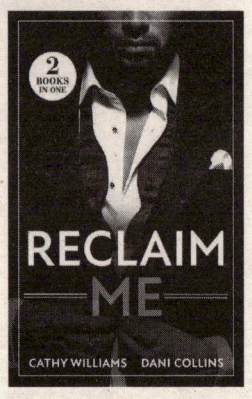

WED IN A HURRY
KIM LAWRENCE   LORRAINE HALL

Bound & Crowned
LOUISE FULLER   CLARE CONNELLY

Love to HATE HIM
JULIA JAMES   MILLIE ADAMS

RECLAIM ME
CATHY WILLIAMS   DANI COLLINS

OUT NOW

Eight Modern stories published every month, find them all at:

millsandboon.co.uk

OUT NOW!

Thorns of Revenge

A DARK ROMANCE SERIES

TARYN LEIGH TAYLOR · ABBY GREEN · JACKIE ASHENDEN

Available at
millsandboon.co.uk

MILLS & BOON

OUT NOW!

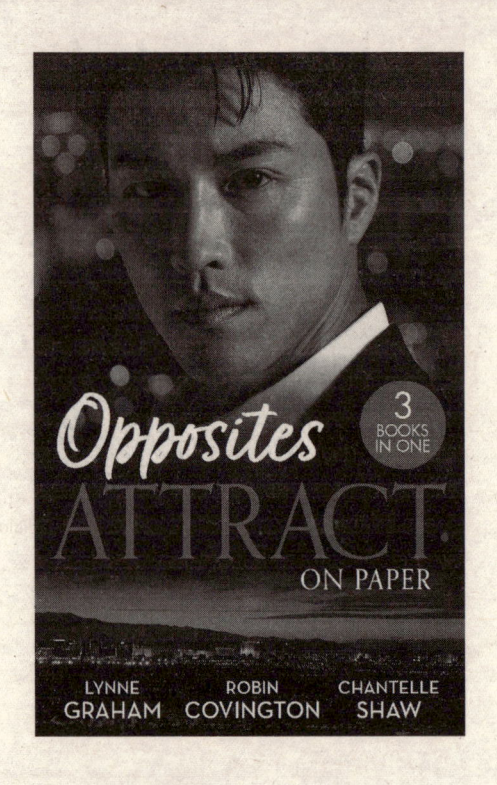

Opposites Attract On Paper

3 BOOKS IN ONE

LYNNE GRAHAM · ROBIN COVINGTON · CHANTELLE SHAW

Available at
millsandboon.co.uk

MILLS & BOON

MILLS & BOON

THE HEART OF ROMANCE

A ROMANCE FOR EVERY READER

MODERN — Prepare to be swept off your feet by sophisticated, sexy and seductive heroes, in some of the world's most glamourous and romantic locations, where power and passion collide.

HISTORICAL — Escape with historical heroes from time gone by. Whether your passion is for wicked Regency Rakes, muscled Vikings or rugged Highlanders, awaken the romance of the past.

MEDICAL — Set your pulse racing with dedicated, delectable doctors in the high-pressure world of medicine, where emotions run high and passion, comfort and love are the best medicine.

True Love — Celebrate true love with tender stories of heartfelt romance, from the rush of falling in love to the joy a new baby can bring, and a focus on the emotional heart of a relationship.

HEROES — The excitement of a gripping thriller, with intense romance at its heart. Resourceful, true-to-life women and strong, fearless men face danger and desire - a killer combination!

afterglow BOOKS — From showing up to glowing up, these characters are on the path to leading their best lives and finding romance along the way – with plenty of sizzling spice!

To see which titles are coming soon, please visit

millsandboon.co.uk/nextmonth

LET'S TALK
Romance

For exclusive extracts, competitions and special offers, find us online:

- **f** MillsandBoon
- **X** @MillsandBoon
- **◉** @MillsandBoonUK
- **♪** @MillsandBoonUK

Get in touch on 01413 063 232

For all the latest titles coming soon, visit
millsandboon.co.uk/nextmonth